INTERSECTING LIVES

A NOVEL OF MYSTERY, ROMANCE, AND REVELATION

Enjoy the journey!
Linda Edmister

LINDA EDMISTER

ISBN 978-1-64468-615-7 (Paperback)
ISBN 978-1-64468-616-4 (Digital)

Covenant Books, Inc.
11661 Hwy 707
Murrells Inlet, SC 29576
www.covenantbooks.com

This book is dedicated to my husband Brent

for his love, patience, and encouragement.

CHAPTER 1

*Trust in the Lord with all your heart and lean
not on your own understanding.
In all your ways acknowledge Him and He
will make your paths straight.*

—Proverbs 3:5–6 (NIV)

Rose Thompson heaved a deep sigh of relief after safely navigating an asphalt maze of intersections comprising the junction of three interstates in Louisville, Kentucky. A cautious driver, she lacked the steely determination necessary to maneuver a vehicle with confidence in city traffic so she very nearly sideswiped a big panel van in an effort to avoid exiting the freeway inadvertently (the van driver signaling his displeasure with a *very* rude gesture). A few minutes later, still gripping the wheel like grim death and totally oblivious to the big eighteen-wheeler in the neighboring lane, she caught sight of the sign for what she *thought* was the right interchange and promptly cut sharply in front of the huge truck, earning a decidedly lengthy and hostile toot from the horn by the irate operator. After almost accidentally heading north on I-65 instead of west on I-64, Rose finally made it successfully across the Ohio River, her nerves and confidence a little rattled. She continued her drive through the built-up area around Clarksville, watched the last of the metropolis fade away in her rearview mirror, and welcomed the sight of gently rolling hills as she made her way across Southern Indiana. Gradually loosening her tight hold on the wheel and allowing blood to flow through her white knuckles again, she resolved to see this journey in the light of an adventure. She gave herself a mental shake and challenged the fates to send her what obstacles they dared. Though had she been honest with herself, she had had little experience in facing or dealing with any great hurdles in life.

Growing up in a small town in Central Kentucky, Rose had been blessed with a haven of safety and love from her family and a grounding in Christian moral and ethical values—an appreciation of simple pleasures and lifestyle. Even the college she had attended was in a small town, and vacations, no matter how far from home, were always in the company of her parents and sisters. She had never been *un*happy and had, until recently, been content with her lot in life. Perhaps it was her very ordinary childhood, unalloyed by emotional trauma or upheaval but definitely lacking in anything *out* of the ordinary, that had imbued in her a well-developed imagination.

From her earliest years, she had found herself drawn to the stories of adventure and excitement found between the covers of novels or portrayed on film. Rose was a dreamer, much like one of her favorite literary characters, Anne Shirley, the imaginative heroine of *Anne of Green Gables*. In moments of boredom or quiet solace (such as a cross-country drive), she unconsciously suspended any tiresome tethers to reality, allowing her mind its full scope of creativity. And like most dreamers, she longed for her own adventure and the opportunity to own the role of leading lady in such a story.

In her fertile mind, any self-respecting adventuress would begin a great journey on the spur of the moment with little or no preparation. The tantalizing prospect of a vague unknown with any number of unforeseen challenges and perils would only appeal to her sense of adventure and fearless spirit. She would, no doubt, be as lovely and sophisticated as she was free-spirited and would either be traveling with a boon companion of kindred mind or would, in the course of events, have a chance encounter with a mysterious handsome stranger who would somehow turn out to be her one true love. Unless, of course, he eventually revealed himself to be an evil adversary from whom some other equally handsome mysterious stranger would rescue her and go on to fill the role of romantic suitor.

Another sigh, this time wistful, signaled the self-realization that she was never likely to experience anything even close to that idealized fantasy. No streamlined luxury car for Rose (an absolute necessity for fashionable heroines), rather a beat-up Chevy hatchback, christened Betsy, that was more serviceable than stylish. Rose had to own that nothing about her situation was in keeping with what an adventure should be. She was, in fact, on a journey but it had been weeks in the making with every conceivable mishap or problem anticipated by her (she thought) overly protective family.

All had agreed that this trip might be good for her, and she was fairly certain that they would have been happy to see her on the road to *anywhere* if it might help her find some direction in her life. For Rose was anything but the assured cosmopolitan young woman she longed to be.

Ironically the only aspect of the journey that bore any resemblance to her dreams was found in the presence of a companion of kindred spirit, though a far cry from what she had imagined. Rose laughed out loud at the thought, waking her fellow traveler who had been softly snoring in the passenger seat. She woke with a snort and a dazed expression until her eyes focused on the smiling girl beside her.

"I guess I dozed off," she said, smiling in response.

"Granny Gert, you fell asleep almost before we got to the end of your driveway!"

No eager young female had been destined as co-conspirator on this adventure. Instead Rose found herself chauffeuring her eighty-two-year-old grandmother, Gertrude Schmidt Gunn, to visit an old school chum in Kansas. The widow of the late Ernst Heinrich Gunn, also a descendant of German immigrants, Gertie to her friends and Granny Gert to her grandchildren, the elderly lady shared a latent free-spirited streak with her granddaughter and was fiercely independent. Almost as broad as she was tall, with thinning white hair and a beak-like nose, Granny Gert's brusque manner and unfiltered speech instilled most of her family with respectful awe, but Rose knew that under that tough intimidating exterior beat a heart of gold. Rose adored her.

After a lifetime in Winchester, Kentucky, Granny Gert now resided in Versailles with her eldest daughter, Patty, a single woman who had spent her adult life chasing the inner workings of the

Kentucky political machine. Gertie would have driven herself to Kansas but for the irritating fact that her license had been pulled two years earlier for one too many minor fender benders. So she had announced to her daughters that she would fly to Kansas, but as she tended to get disoriented in her own grocery store, let alone an airport, Patty and her sister, Beth, put their heads together to come up with a solution. Patty was the more pragmatic of the two, taking a straightforward no-nonsense approach to problem-solving, reflecting both Gert's personality and demeanor. Beth, on the other hand, was the antithesis of her mother. She was more prone to worry than action and her delicate sense of propriety often caused her to err on the side of indecision. But in this instance, they both immediately thought of Rose.

Beth Thompson had been worried about her daughter's future for some time. Rose, born the third daughter of Ralph and Beth Thompson, had always lived in the shadow of her successful older sisters, Violet and Lily. Like her sisters, Rose had been educated at a state university with numerous courses of study to choose from; but unlike her sisters, she had struggled in discerning a path to follow. Violet had found her calling in caring for women's health as a nurse practitioner midwife, and Lily had been destined for the courtroom since third grade when she had won an argument with the principal over playground equipment; but Rose had floundered. After changing her major three times over the course of a five-year college career, she barely scraped together enough credit hours to earn a BS in sociology.

A series of failed employment efforts had followed during the ensuing three years. Blessed with a sunny personality and a willingness to try her hand at just about anything, Rose appeared to be an ideal employee but her chronic habit of daydreaming and lack of attention to detail tried the patience of even the most understanding of supervisors. It was on the eve of a third job termination that Granny Gert's travel needs dropped into their lives like a gift from heaven. Knowing her mother would appreciate her interference as little as Violet, Lily, and Rose appreciated her well-meant intervention in their lives, Beth Thompson thought she might persuade the determined old lady to allow Rose to *accompany* (drive) her, if convinced that she was actually offering Rose an unlooked-for vacation. Whether it was Beth's persuasion or Granny Gert's secret relief (which she would have admitted to *no* one) that she would not have to find her own way to Kansas but would instead be traveling with her favorite granddaughter, the plan was a success. And as Granny Gert insisted on leaving by mid-June, the whole Thompson clan jumped in to help Rose prepare for the road trip.

Finally underway, Rose couldn't resist teasing her grandmother over her habit of falling asleep when traveling more than a mile in a car.

Choosing to ignore her granddaughter's impertinence, Granny Gert merely replied, "I know you're a good driver," (good thing she'd slept through the numerous near mishaps in Louisville) "so I didn't think you needed me to stay awake and tell you where to go. If I had, we'd probably have ended up going in the wrong direction." Kindred spirits indeed!

"I'm just glad you asked me to drive you out to Kansas. I was kind of at loose ends so your invitation came at just the right time. I wouldn't have wanted to travel with anyone else. You're my *favorite* grandmother," Rose added coyly.

"Don't try to sweet talk me, young lady. I'm your only *living* grandmother and well I know it!" she said, causing Rose to chuckle again. After a thoughtful pause, her grandmother added, "I love all three of my granddaughters but you're the best of the lot, as far as I'm concerned, so I'm just as pleased as you are that it's you taking me."

Somewhat taken aback, Rose started to respond, "But, Granny, Violet and Lily are so much smarter than I am. And more successful and attractive and—"

"They've both got brains and impressive careers, I'll grant you, but you're not a bad-looking gal yourself. And I know you don't think so but your name suits you. I will say this for your parents, they hit the mark when they named you girls."

There was much truth in the old woman's words. Violet was an exact description of their firstborn's dazzling eyes, Lily was the living image of an ethereally fair beauty, and Rose bore the blooming cheeks and soft complexion implied in her name. As a trio, they were quite striking—Violet's brunette beauty, Lily's fair poised grace, and Rose's petite frame crowned with soft auburn ringlets.

It wasn't so much that Rose didn't think her named suited her from a descriptive standpoint, she just thought it was old-fashioned and it's hard to be a sophisticated adventuress with an old-fashioned name. She was the only one of the three who would so much rather have had *any* other name—preferably a boy's name, like Taylor or Cameron or Jesse, that somehow, when attached to girls, irrationally made them immediately more feminine. But Rose it was with the inevitable nicknames Rosie, Rosebud, or even Buddie.

"I always said, if they'd had a shred of business sense, your parents could have gotten an early start on your college savings by hiring you out as the Thompson flower girls for those big fancy weddings I'm always reading about. I know I'm a bit biased but I swear the three of you were as pretty as a picture when you were little—could've been on a magazine cover."

Looking into the past, Granny Gert was quiet for so long Rose thought she might have dozed off, but she continued speaking again as if no pause had occurred at all.

"Yes, you've all got looks enough but I think you've got something more. You've got spunk. You may have had a few setbacks since you finished college but you always get back up on your feet and try again."

Setbacks. Memories flooded in and Rose cringed inwardly, thinking to herself, *I was about to be fired for the third time.* Aloud she said, "Granny, Mother can't possibly have told you all the details of my employment disasters. I couldn't even blend coffee properly or take care of a few dogs without making a mess of it!"

"Well, if you're talking about that business at the coffee shop, I say that could have happened to anyone, Rosie. Names are tricky things, I get them confused all the time."

Yes, but you're eighty-two years old. You have an excuse, Rose thought to herself then tried to explain the situation to her grandmother. "I suppose it's because I'm always daydreaming, imagining some unknown exciting future which is much more fun than trying to keep straight the details of all those designer coffee and tea blends. Steamed, steeped, whipped…they all just sort of got mixed up." With a resigned sigh, she went on, "And I could always make up more interesting names than the ones the customers gave but I was careless enough to write one of them on a cup for the worst possible customer," she recalled with embarrassment.

"So you wrote the wrong name on an order and called that old scrooge Phoenix instead of Felix. I'd call that inspired. Anything to do with ashes suits that dried-up prune-faced skinflint better than a name that means *joy*! I can't imagine what his parents were thinking when they named him."

Giggling, Rose pointed out. "I don't suppose he was *born* a dried-up prune-faced skinflint."

"Well, maybe not but I had the unpleasant task of babysitting Felix Lipton when he was a little boy and I never saw a more selfish, spoiled little hoodlum. He wouldn't share his books or toys or even snacks!"

"You mean with his brothers and sisters?" asked Rose, trying to keep Granny's memories straight in her own mind.

"Brothers and sisters? No, thank goodness his parents only had the one child. I meant with me!" Rose tried to imagine her grandmother as an outraged teenager—even her imagination couldn't conjure up that vision! "Why, I remember the last time I had to watch him like it was yesterday. I locked him in his room and didn't let him out till I saw his parents pull into the driveway."

Rose gasped at such at such dire tactics. "Weren't you afraid of getting in trouble for that?"

Granny Gert grinned at Rose's reaction. "We weren't so thin-skinned in the old days. Besides I told him if he said anything to his folks, I might have to mention that I'd seen him steal some money out of his mother's purse."

"You actually saw him do that?"

"No, but it's just the sort thing he *would* have done. Must've hit a nerve in what passed for his conscience because I never heard a word about it." Her granddaughter laughed in appreciation of her grandmother's audacity.

"Too bad you weren't in the coffee shop that fatal day," said Rose with a rueful grin.

"It probably wouldn't have made a lick of difference. But if Felix Lipton's bank hadn't held the mortgage on that precious coffee shop, your boss might've laughed right along with you instead of showing you the door!"

Realizing the old lady's severe tones were more a reflection of the resentment she felt on behalf of her granddaughter than any real hostility she felt toward her former employer, Rose gave Granny Gert's hand a squeeze.

"If ever I get into a real fix, I want you in my corner. I'll bet you could even have taken on Miss Ferguson and come out a winner."

Slewing around in her seat to set her piercing gaze on Rose, Granny Gert demanded, "You mean that mix-up with the basset hound? Why, that gave me the best laugh I've had in a long time. I can't say I was sorry to see that woman get her comeuppance," she said, smiling at the thought.

Comeuppance—hardly. Rose recalled the incident with considerably less humor. After her first job failure she had followed her mother's suggestion (not her usual course of action) and offered her services as a dog sitter/caregiver on Facepage, Neighbors.com, and any other website she could find to get her name and service out there. Word had quickly spread among family friends, neighbors, and acquaintances and her little fledgling business was born. Her mother urged her to cap her clientele at ten.

"You don't want to take on more than you can handle," she had cautioned.

How can Mother say she knows what's best for me in one breath and then tell me I can't handle it in the next? an exasperated Rose had thought to herself. *Animals live in the wild without any supervision at all. How hard can it be to take care of a few dogs?* More determined than ever to succeed in her new venture, Rose had squared her shoulders and opened her door for business.

Like all the Thompsons, she had an affinity for animals and was, therefore, immediately at home in her new occupation, finding favor with pet parents because of her obvious rapport with their precious four-legged children. With only one daughter now living at home, Rose's parents had given her the use of a large area of unused basement with outside access to a fenced yard—an ideal setting for Rose's doggie daycare.

She and the dogs became a little family and, being a warm-hearted girl, Rose grew quite fond of them all. What she hadn't counted on was any of them becoming quite fond of each other.

Growing up in a family that always responsibly spayed or neutered their pets, it never occurred to Rose that some pet owners intentionally chose not to follow this practice because they planned to breed their animals. One day, when dropping off her darling Gazelle (a singularly unsuitable name for a sixty-five-pound basset hound), the very proper Miss Estelle Ferguson, who had been the town's middle school principal practically since the founding fathers had been students, pulled Rose aside and murmured in arch undertones as if she didn't want the other dogs to overhear,

"You'll need to keep an extra eye on Baby today. She's not quite herself. You understand, of course. We have plans to visit a nice young man this weekend," she added with a knowing look.

Missing the veiled meaning in the euphemism entirely but not wanting to appear ignorant, Rose had assured the anxious owner that she would give Gazelle her special attention that day. And she might have succeeded but for the chaos that ensued when all the dogs rushed outside after lunch to run off their fidgets. During the joyful frenzy, Rose missed the absence of Gazelle and a cute Shar-Pei named Ruffles who was still struggling to immerge from all his wrinkles. Nine weeks later, the results of that truancy were born.

The arrival of Gazelle's first litter of puppies had been quickly followed by the arrival of an outraged Miss Ferguson at Rose's door. Thrusting a picture into Rose's face, quivering with outrage, she had unleashed her wrath on the unsuspecting girl.

"How dare you! You promised me you would look after my precious girl, now look what your neglect has brought about."

Confused and reeling from the infuriated woman's accusations, Rose had glanced at the picture, seeing only a basket full of sweet little puppies.

"Are these Gazelle's babies? Oh, I think they're adorable!"

"*Adorable?* They're mongrels! Don't think I don't recognize the Shar-Pei in them." It seemed that the "nice young man" Gazelle visited was another basset hound who was meant to have been the sire of her pups. When she presented Miss Ferguson with a litter of Ba-Shars instead, Miss F's golden plan for a bright retirement, adorned with blue ribbons from every dog show within 200 miles, came crashing in; and with her not-inconsiderable influence, she made sure that Rose's business went with it.

As had been her custom since she was a little girl, Rose had sought solace from that latest failure in the comforting chaos of her father's workshop. Initially more of a tinkerer than a carpenter, patient determination and hours spent in the little shed behind the family home had turned Ralph Thompson into an accomplished woodworker, his tool collection threatening to overrun the shop's limited space and his frugal wife's patience and understanding. Rose had always felt at home there, sharing her concerns with him as she learned to use simple tools to create her own projects. They might have been less polished than her father's but working with her hands seemed to soothe her churning thoughts. As she grew older, she began to suspect that this place was a haven for her father also, an occasional place of escape from the drama inherent in a house full of women—a place of quiet for a man who loved his family dearly but needed time for himself too. Rose was the most like him in temperament and the only one who showed any interest in his hobby so she had always known herself to be welcome there.

On that particular visit, Ralph, a pleasant, middle-aged man with graying hair and deep grooves around his mouth and eyes, had looked up from the bookcase he was sanding to see Rose standing in the doorway, her face full of woe. He turned off the palm sander, placing it carefully on a shelf, and moved to his daughter, arms open wide. As she walked into the circle of his sheltering arms, he admonished her, "Now, Buddie, you can't let that old biddy get you down. You were doing a great job with those dogs. Everyone said so, even old Miss Ferguson, until she realized that that oversized beast of hers had upset her plans. She had no business to leave a dog she suspected of being in heat with other dogs and then give you only a cryptic hint as to what might happen." He gently took Rose's face in his calloused hands and looked into her tear-filled eyes. "She is the irresponsible party in this business—not you." Dropping his hands to her shoulders, he gave her a gentle shake and added, "Now dry those eyes and help me with this bookcase."

The brisk, matter-of-fact tone of his last statement had helped to steady her as did the rhythmic movement of sandpaper over corners and edges of the wood.

"I saw the vet the other day," her father continued, "and he told me as soon as the pups are weaned, Miss High and Mighty means to give them to him so he can either find homes for them—or...not," he added, and shot Rose a meaningful look. Anticipating her dismay, he added quickly, "Your mother and I have kind of missed having an animal around the house since old Trooper died so we thought we might take one in. And you were right, they are awfully cute."

"Oh, Daddy, thank you. I know it will be happy here with you and Mother." She hesitated. "And it kind of makes me feel like God has somehow redeemed my mistake."

"He always does, sweet pea." They continued their sanding in companionable silence until the wood felt smooth and silky. "And with the house so empty now, she'll keep us company."

"She'll?"

"The pup. We've asked Doc to keep a female for us. We mean to name her Fergie," he added with a grin.

As the miles to Kansas sped away under her wheels so did the pain of those memories.

"Well, maybe you're right. Even fiascos can have a silver lining," she remarked to her grandmother presently.

"Fiasco—fiddle! Because of you, your parents have a dog in the house again. And they named her Fergie. I couldn't have come up with a more fitting name myself." Rose had to laugh in agreement.

"Now as to that nonsense about you being let go from the Golden Years Retirement Home, well, I just can't believe it. Remember, I lived in Winchester my whole life before my Ernst died so I know a lot of folks who live at that hoity-toity place and we've stayed in touch using that newfangled computer e-mail. I don't pretend to understand how it works but it does, and what I can tell you is this—the residents all love you, can't say enough nice things about you. A few even tried using you working there as an excuse for me to move in with them but I'm not ready to be put out to pasture just yet. Why that darned fool director couldn't see that you're a people person and not to be shut away in some office, I'll never understand.

"But, Granny, I was hired as the administrative assistant. Everyone in my generation has computer skills and I honestly thought it would work out. But whenever I saw someone sitting alone in the hall or a group of residents waiting for an activity to start, I just felt they needed me to spend time with them rather than produce another stack of calendars or schedules for them at my desk. Clearly I was wrong."

"Hogwash! If you have a good employee that's not suited to one job, you change the job to what they are good at. Makes sense to me."

Her smile a little awry, Rose responded, "Unfortunately that's not how the job market works, Granny Gert. I just wish I could figure out what I *am* good at. Like my sisters. Mother and Daddy sound so proud when they tell their friends about Violet and Lily's accomplishments." Sensing her grandmother was about to interrupt, she hurried on. "And not just about their professional achievements either. Violet's married to a pediatrician and she and Steve are about to produce the first grandchild—which practically makes them royalty. And Lily and Charles are the perfect power couple—two attorneys loaded with ambition." After a little pause, she added shakily, "And then there's me."

Contemplating her dejected granddaughter, Granny Gert hesitated before responding with uncharacteristic gentleness, "And then there's you—a beautiful young woman who is kind to animals and people in need, always has a song in her heart and a smile on her face and who will take the time and patience to put up with an old woman and make her feel like spending time together is a special treat." A watery sniff was the only response. "So what if you haven't found the ideal job yet—you keep looking. Rosie, the world is full of ambitious young women trying to climb up some invisible ladder.

Just have faith in the woman God made you to be and He'll show you where you belong."

Glancing doubtfully at her grandmother, she asked, "Do you really believe that?"

"Of course I do. I've known a lot of people in my eighty-two years and my money's on you, kiddo! Now show me that famous smile and tell me what you've got this limo stocked with!"

Her rallying tone and ridiculous reference to the old Chevy cheered Rose immeasurably. She responded in kind, "It would be easier to tell you what we don't have!" She then regaled Granny Gert with an account of the Thompson road trip preparation circus.

Ralph had had everything from the engine and tires and brakes to the windshield wipers checked out on old Betsy. He also insisted on giving Rose a crash course on how to change a tire, check the oil, and add water to the radiator. Beth gathered every scrap of information she could find on car insurance, health insurance, AAA, and maps and booked a hotel room outside St. Louis, insisting on a rest stop along the 650-mile route. Violet had located an urgent treatment clinic and pharmacy at their Kansas destination should Granny Gert need any medication refills and contributed a first aid kit for the trip. She reminded Rose at least three times that Granny needed to drink plenty of fluids, followed by Beth needlessly reminding Rose to make frequent stops. Lily contributed her bit by instructing Rose on every step to be taken in the event of an accident and how to contact the state police in each state the pair would be passing through.

"In addition to our luggage, we are fully stocked with a cooler full of water bottles, juice, diet soda, and snacks. We have a gas can—the fuel gauge is a little iffy—extra *gallon* water jugs because I guess the bottled drinking water wasn't enough?" Rose paused, laughing as Granny Gert rolled her eyes. "Daddy wasn't completely confident about the old radiator," she added by way of explanation. "And lastly, a backpack full of enough documents for both of us to apply for security clearances in any country on the continent."

Shaking her head in wonder, Gert remarked, "Good Lord! Were they preparing for a two-day road trip or an invasion?"

Rose suddenly felt herself filled with lighthearted joy and she responded impulsively, "Oh, Granny Gert, I'm *so* glad we're sharing this adventure together. I knew you would appreciate, more than anybody, how good it feels to just get away, make a fresh start."

Her grandmother, at that moment choosing to avail herself of some of the excessive stash in the back, was struggling to emerge from between the seats after her effort to wrestle a water bottle out of the cooler. Finally regaining her copilot perch, she fastened her seat belt and lifted the bottle in a toast.

"To the open road and kindred spirits. Tinkers Well, here we come!" Immediately followed by, "Start looking for a rest stop in about fifteen minutes…"

CHAPTER 2

For where your treasure is, there your heart will be also.

—Matthew 6:21 (NIV)

A determined beam of sunshine broke through heavy cloud cover to be caught and refracted by a sea of windows, creating a thousand points of light. Their brilliance momentarily blinded a man pacing to-and-fro in the penthouse of his gleaming office tower overlooking a labyrinth of steel and glass. His restless movement suggested the prowl of a sleek predatory animal on the alert for vulnerable prey. The black silk suit he wore fit him with the perfection of a second skin, moving effortlessly over well-defined muscle. His lean square jawline was broken only by a deep cleft in the chin. A thick mane of dark hair feathered with gray at the temples furthered the resemblance to a wild untamed hunter. At fifty-seven, Miles Hawthorne was as fit as most men twenty years his junior with the mental and physical discipline of elite athletes. Less could be said for his control of temperament. He was a man accustomed to respect, obedience, and unquestioned loyalty from those he favored with his business and employment. And while he enjoyed affable-enough relationships with those he deemed worthy of his time or astute enough to garner his approbation as fellow businessmen and entrepreneurs, he had less than no tolerance for human folly and ineptitude—in business or in life.

At the opening of his office door, he turned slowly from his unseeing contemplation of the teeming streets below to face the two men he had been expecting for some time.

"Good day, gentlemen," Hawthorne said, making no move toward them. "I trust my demands on your time have not proven to be too inconvenient," he added with a grim smile that left his eyes hard and cold. His less than welcoming greeting and penetrating stare seemed to unsettle one of the newcomers, a nervous youth with outsized ears, a receding chin, and thinning scraggly hair who more closely resembled a mouse than a man.

"Mr. Hawthorne...um...sir," he began haltingly as he warily approached his hostile host. "I know this meeting was supposed to be at 10:00 a.m., that is, it *was* at 10:00 a.m." A quick glance at Hawthorne's face and he dropped his gaze, hurrying on, talking as much with his hands as with his tongue. "But Ms. Simmons—that's my secretary, well, actually her official title"—here he gestured with quotes—"'Office assistant...' Anyway she forgot to remind me to pick up Mr. Atherton at JFK instead of LaGuardia just because I forgot to remind *her* to remind me, and then with the traffic, and road construction, and of course, I don't usually escort our operatives so I got a little lost and...parking! Oh, brother! I wish we'd taken a cab instead of driving because then we could've just hopped out at the door instead of hiking three blocks, and we had to wait *forever* for the elevator because, well, I forgot about the *other* direct elevator I was supposed to ask the doorman about, and gosh, I'm really sorry, sir... But you know how New York can be and..." The young man faltered as he became hopelessly lost in a morass of useless explanations.

"Enough!" Hawthorne spoke contemptuously. "Jenkins, you must tell me sometime, if ever I can rally the interest and effort to ask you, why a man as astute and competent as your employer sees fit to keep on his payroll a dolt with the seeming IQ of an amoeba."

Not a possessor of great mental acuity, Jenkins missed the verbal barb. And had he been looking at Hawthorne instead of studying his own nervously twisting hands, he might not have mistaken the comment as an invitation; but with his easily distracted gaze now turning to the spectacular view, he began an ill-advised response. "Oh, well, you see, the boss's wife is my big sister, and since she's always kind of looked after me since our folks passed on, well, she got him to give me a start with the agency. Burt's a pretty decent guy and all—"

"Silence, you idiot!" Jenkins jumped at the interruption this time, turning back so quickly that he swung his arm and knocked over a (presumably) priceless vase displayed on a beautiful ornamental table. Fortunately the third man in the room, until then merely an amused spectator, quickly reached for the vase before it could meet a crashing end on the floor and deftly replaced it to its place of honor. He deemed it time to enter the fray if for no other reason than to spare poor Jenkins the wrath awaiting him if left to continue speaking unabated.

Stepping forward and extending his hand to Hawthorne, he introduced himself with a cultured British accent that might have been at home in the House of Lords. "As young Jenkins mentioned, my name is Atherton, Simon Atherton. It's a pleasure to finally meet you, sir."

In an effort to bring the proceedings back to a professional level, and in response to innate good breeding, Hawthorne clasped Atherton's hand with as much warmth as his sorely tried patience could muster. "I trust your journey from San Francisco was unexceptionable. You come highly recommended by Burt Landrum or I wouldn't squander a small fortune to bring you in for what must seem a fairly routine *inquiry*"—placing a slight emphasis on the final word—"if I didn't believe the situation required your unique talents."

Meanwhile Jenkins, literally backing to the door to make good his escape before any other untoward incidents could occur, managed to knock over a lamp. In his gallant attempt to retrieve it, he accidentally stepped into a trash can. While Jenkins was still trying to extricate his foot, Hawthorne sprang forward, grasped the hapless courier by his collar and belt, and neatly tossed him out of the office, slamming the door to. After taking two deep steadying breaths, he managed to regain a grip on his composure and turned toward Atherton, who had contrived to hide a smile while setting the lamp aright, and gestured to the younger man to be seated on a sumptuous leather couch. As the two settled themselves comfortably, the door opened again just far enough for an arm to reach in with trash can in hand.

"Out!" Hawthorne bellowed. The second slamming of the door signaled the last of Jenkins.

"I can only guess at the inanity you've been forced to endure from the lips of that fool for the past hour. You have my sympathy," Miles Hawthorne offered by way of apology. "Perhaps we would both benefit from a restorative. I realize it's still before noon but surely close to teatime in England so perhaps a sherry or something…stronger?"

"Scotch, please. Neat."

"Scotch it is then." As the two men sipped their respective drinks in silence, Miles took stock of the sophisticated young gentleman seated next to him. Early thirties, elegant tailoring, fit, with a handsome lean countenance that would surely find favor with susceptible women. *If his reputed talent for subtle infiltration and emotional manipulation matches his looks, he will do nicely*, Miles thought to himself. While most men would have been unnerved by such obvious scrutiny, Simon found it diverting. He sat in comfortable silence as he patiently endured the other's obvious inspection without flinching, even allowing a wry smile to appear. At the smile, Miles gave a short bark of laughter, sat his empty glass down on an end table, and rose to resume his earlier pacing.

"I respect a man who is sure of himself," he remarked, briefly glancing at his guest. "I've found that one doesn't get far in life if easily rattled. I salute you." After a few more turns, he continued, "I don't know how much Burt told you about this mission but it is delicate at best."

"I understand it involves a land deed, an elderly woman, and a potentially enormous real estate deal, though I'm not entirely sure where I fit into the picture."

Hawthorne continued to move about the office without answering for a few minutes. When he did speak, he did so as if weighing his words carefully.

"In 1918, a wealthy philanthropist named Joshua Strong reacted to the return of troops from the first World War with what one might call an overdeveloped sense of altruism. A true American success story himself, he felt responsible for giving those men a leg up in life after their years on the battlefield."

As an aside, he spoke more to himself than to Simon Atherton, "Though why, when the United States had a perfectly good Veterans Administration established by then, he felt the need to squander even a portion of his considerable wealth on the wretched souls, I've never understood."

Focusing again on his narrative, Hawthorne continued, "Anyway the story goes that as a poor British immigrant from Liverpool, he worked his way up in the shipping business until he owned his own successful fleet of vessels. Having acquired a small fortune, he invested wisely in a variety of manufacturing enterprises which all seemed to prosper. In short, by the age of sixty, he had amassed so much wealth that he then spent the rest of his life working to give much of it away." He stopped to speak directly to his guest. "Which may go some way in explaining his strange bequest that is, at present, causing me such grief and necessitating the need for your assistance."

"I must say, I'm intrigued," responded Atherton, his curiosity piqued, "though I'm still not sure..."

Seating himself on a wingback chair opposite Atherton, Hawthorne went on with the story. "Joshua Strong not only possessed a tireless work ethic and a shrewd head for business, he was devoutly religious, crediting his many successes to Almighty God." Miles Hawthorne spoke the last two words with thinly veiled contempt. "This maudlin sentiment led him to purchase, in an act of generosity bordering on mania, four corners of 22nd and 23rd Streets in Brooklyn and two entire city blocks in the middle."

This drew a low whistle from Atherton.

"I see you can appreciate the enormity of the gesture but I've not shared the heart of it yet. Strong was able to purchase these properties for a song. He chose them specifically for their proximity to manufacturing districts and because the existing buildings were in such disrepair that they were virtually worthless. He then systematically began razing each one and, in place of the derelict structures, he built on each respective corner a church, a school, a hospital, and a village hall containing temporary living quarters for workers' families. Any buildings left on the two center blocks were also demolished. But there the cleared land became dedicated green space—a park area large enough to boast a baseball field, walking trails, and small garden plots for lease to nearby residents. Other developers were quick to see the benefits of snapping up adjacent properties where so much community infrastructure already existed."

Here Atherton interrupted. "I must be missing something. You're a real estate developer. I can't imagine the principles of the business have changed much over the last one hundred years. Such suddenly prime real estate would never be wasted on housing or shops for the working class. Surely the creation of upscale residences would undo any plans for a blue collar haven."

"Ah, you have been listening," Miles responded appreciatively. "You've hit on the cream of the jest. Old Joshua Strong truly had thought of everything. Unbeknownst to the other landowners, he had made an arrangement with the borough's planning council. In return for zoning the adjacent blocks for small community shops and apartment buildings for the working middle class, he agreed to set up a trust to cover building upgrades, city transportation, and road maintenance on the four corner properties he owned—" Leaning forward, Miles disclosed the critical part of the arrangement. "—for *fifty years,* after which time the real estate and developed property, excluding the church, would revert to ownership by the city."

Another low whistle from Atherton. "That sly old boots. Well, that explains how Strong controlled growth of the area for half a century, but that ended over fifty years ago. Surely those properties have changed hands since then, especially with zoning limitations removed. It's not like there's ever been a surfeit of land just sitting about in New York City."

"Very astute, my friend. They have changed hands—several times. And the resulting development has grown more lavish with each successive owner. Even three of the original four corners have evolved into a high-priced private school, a sanitarium and drug rehab facility for the wealthy elite, and an off-Broadway theater. The only thing that hasn't changed appreciably in over one hundred years is the church. A few years ago, I believe someone"—here Miles gave Simon a significant look—"was able to gain a foothold there through the financial difficulties of the congregation. They were committed to keeping their doors open for the community but couldn't afford to continue maintenance of the old building without taking out a sizeable mortgage on it. The mortgage holder could call in the loan at any time, payments, apparently, having been somewhat sporadic, but it suits him to leave the property as is…for now. It lends the neighborhood an air of old-world respectability."

"I see. And has the 'mortgage holder' had any other success in acquiring land in the area?" asked Simon, watching his host closely.

"Do you know, I am increasingly assured that we will deal splendidly together. In point of fact, over the past twenty years, the purchase of the entire area can be traced back, through various holding companies and investment firms, to…a single owner. Which brings me to the specific reason I have retained your services. I'm sure, as astute a listener as you appear to be, you noticed my omission about the disposition of the large green space in the middle. That property alone remained in the hands of the Strong family or, I should say, a direct heir. At the time old Joshua purchased that particular parcel, he stipulated in the deed that the land would pass to the eldest descendant in each successive generation and with it" here Miles paused to read from a photostat of an old newspaper clipping he picked up from the coffee table—"'The grave responsibility of maintaining a place of beauty and serenity in the maelstrom of a mighty city so that future generations can find solace in the peace of God's creation.'" The smirk of disgust on Hawthorne's face was enhanced as he continued, "Only the descendant possessing the deed has the authority to sell the land, and all have, lamentably, chosen to honor old Joshua's request."

"The old boy did have a flare for the dramatic, didn't he?" Simon remarked rhetorically. "But I have two questions. One, how is it possible that there was any of the original fortune left to maintain the property for even fifteen years, let alone fifty? I'm no Rhodes scholar but I seem to recall, in the dim recesses of school-day memory, that there was a great economic depression in the 1930s when even the very rich lost all their money. How did he or, maybe I should say, one of his descendants manage to keep up the properties, let alone hold onto the family fortune? And two, am I correct in assuming that you know who the current owner is?"

"Well-observed," responded Miles, appreciating the quick intellect of the other man. "In answer to your first question, old Joshua was not only shrewd and lucky but possessed an uncanny sense of timing. In retirement, while he was busy with all his philanthropic efforts, he turned the reins of his various enterprises over to his oldest son, Jeremiah, who had an eye on the future. During the Roaring '20s, as the economy was expanding at a terrific rate, Jeremiah was selling shares or entire businesses and investing in gold so that by the time businesses everywhere were failing and fortunes were lost overnight, he was one of only a handful of visionaries holding onto a negotiable currency. The one manufacturing concern he had continued was a cannery for processing tinned foods. As the economy had grown during the boom years so had the population in cities and, with it, the demand for food. Without easy access to fresh produce and meat, more city dwellers turned to tinned fruits and vegetables and meats like ham and fish. They had a long shelf life so they could be processed and stored compactly against requisite demand. When the Depression came, people still had to eat, and because Jeremiah had stockpiled a sizeable inventory, he landed a government contract to supply the food lines that fed the city for a number of years. He turned much of the profits into research and development and revolutionized the food packaging and storage industry.

"The answer to your second question is a bit more complicated. Ownership of the property is a matter of public record, of course. It happens to be an elderly woman currently living in a tiny outpost called Tinkers Well, somewhere west of Kansas City. And yes, I have tried to approach her through shadow companies but she refuses to sell. She is leaving disposition of the property to her son who will, presumably, receive the deed upon her death."

"Seems you have something of a dilemma" Simon said.

"I have been unsuccessful with the old woman but I have made a point of finding her heir, and *he is willing to sell*, provided I can procure the deed for him. He and his parent are at loggerheads on this issue—she being committed to honoring the family trust and he wanting to sell such a plum piece of real estate. So he eagerly welcomed my offer of assistance. And that, my young friend, is where you come in."

Without responding but continuing to look attentively at the older man, Simon waited patiently for his marching orders.

On the move again, Hawthorne explained as he resumed his pacing, "You are to head for Tinkers Well immediately. There, under whatever guise you choose to adopt, you will scrape an acquaintance with Aletha Mason, the elderly woman I mentioned earlier." Here he stopped briefly to glance at Simon. "Burt Landrum assured me that your aptitude for clever cover stories is rivaled only by your charming manner." Simon merely nodded his recognition of this professional tribute. "Insinuate yourself into her good graces. I understand, from my sources, that she appreciates the company of amiable people but she is shrewd and won't be easily taken in. Use whatever means necessary, within the limits of reasonable taste and general legality, to find that deed. I will contact you periodically to check on your progress." At this, he sat down across from Simon and bent a piercing look on the young PI. "And I do expect progress. Is that quite clear?"

"I understand two things. One, you need the property deed—rather badly, I believe—and two, my fee may need to be... renegotiated." He was looking down at his perfectly manicured nails as he spoke. After the last point, he raised his head and looked calmly into Hawthorne's face, now set in harsh lines. Without losing any of his polite demeanor, Simon's voice took on a steely edge as he continued softly. "I'm afraid I failed earlier to appreciate the critical role I am to play in this little game."

"Make no mistake, Atherton. I am not a man to be threatened. Find me that deed and I will make it worth your while but don't try to cross me." An uncomfortable silence ensued as the two men squared off.

After a short pause, Simon laughed as he rose from the couch. "It would seem we have reached an impasse." His practiced smile momentarily lost its mirth. "I too resent threats. Burt replaced me with one of my mates on what promised to be a very lucrative industrial espionage case in Silicon Valley so that I could take on this assignment. I trust it *will* be worth my while."

The harsh lines relaxed on Miles's face. He stood, as had Simon, and now extended his hand in a truce, again the composed urbane businessman addressing a skittish client. "It will, I assure you. Now let me see you out. My secretary will supply you with the address and any pertinent facts you'll need to know about your subject. You will also receive a prepaid credit card in the amount of $5,000 to cover expenses. For which I will expect a detailed account," he added with the hint of a smile. "I'll call you in a few days to see how things are shaping up."

He walked back into his office and was about to close the door when he was arrested by the usually frigid tones of Miss Limstock speaking to Simon with something approaching warmth in her voice. Even the iron maiden was apparently melting under Simon's expert handling. Miles smiled to himself in appreciation, closed the door, and began to recalculate the future with more optimism.

CHAPTER 3

The Lord keeps you from all harm and watches over your life.
The Lord keeps watch over you as you come
and go, both now and forever.

—Psalm 121:7–8 (NLT)

As gas station followed rest area in an alternating chain across Indiana and Illinois, the challenges of traveling with an elderly woman quickly became apparent to Rose. But she bore each stop with patient attendance on Granny Gert, declaring each break in the journey a good time for both of them to stretch their legs. She was determined that her grandmother would never suspect herself of being a burden. An early picnic lunch at one rest area, followed quickly by another brief pit stop for what Gert called "unfueling" and Rose was left to contemplate the scenery by herself as her passenger took a postprandial nap in the neighboring seat.

Rose was one of those people who possessed no real artistic ability of their own but could appreciate the simple beauty found in what other more discriminating observers might call the monotonous or mundane. Mile upon mile of cornfields lined the interstate on both sides, but rather than finding them boring, Rose marveled at the artistry of perfectly laid out rows topped with delicate tassels. Line after line of glossy emerald-green leaves clung to rigid stalks reaching to the sky as if paying homage to the Creator for the provision of his creation. Occasionally she spotted a giant combine making its way across a ripened field, moving through the rows like some great devouring beast, leaving flattened trails in its wake. Something about bearing witness to the age-old pattern of seedtime and harvest filled her with a sense of peace and contentment which lasted until Granny Gert woke up and asked when they could stop again.

By the time the pair reached the outskirts of St. Louis, Rose was lifting silent blessings for her mother's foresight in reserving a hotel room for the night. It was only 3:30 but they still had to make their way across the Mississippi River and around the city. The most recent gas station attendant had advised Rose to avoid going through the city at any time—especially close to rush hour. She set her sights on their interim destination and kept up a light flow of conversation to distract Granny Gert who grew more silent and restless as the day's journey drew out. A little hesitant to leave the directional safety of the long, straight road she had driven on for the past six hours, Rose had turned on her phone GPS at the last stop and enlisted Granny Gert's assistance in watching for the correct turnings. Since Rose had a nickname for almost *everything*, she had christened the faceless voice of the GPS Eloise—Siri and Alexa were *so* overused and unimaginative. Feeling a little cocky after safely negotiating the first interchange with I-255 North, she relaxed a little and nearly missed the interchange with I-270 West as both Gert and Eloise competed with conflicting instructions.

"In one mile stay in the right lane and take exit 1 onto I-270 West."

"That darned fool thing can't be right. She told us to get onto this road at exit 20. Why would we get off at the beginning—doesn't that mean we're going backward?"

"The exit numbers have to do with where different parts of the loop start, I think…"

"Get into the right lane."

"I don't think you should listen to her—just doesn't make sense."

"Take the exit and continue west on I-270."

"Wait! Rosie, are you sure about this?"

Not sure about anything, Rose clung to the word *west*, got into the exit lane at the last minute, causing a flurry of indignation in other drivers of which she was blissfully unaware, and followed the GPS directions without further mishap onto I-270. Realizing that too much information might not be a good thing, she breathed a silent prayer for traveling mercies and turned off Eloise. Recalling the simple instruction of the gas station attendant to just keep looking for signs to Kansas City, Rose finally made it onto I-70 with her shaky driving confidence mostly restored. She then started looking for the hotel exit number which she had scribbled on a sticky note attached to the dashboard.

She was sorely tempted to just check into the hotel when they exited the highway because she knew her grandmother to be reaching her limit of passable good humor but she remembered Violet's admonition to make sure that Granny Gert had a good meal before retiring so that she would rest more soundly and allow Rose a little time to herself for unwinding and relaxation. So she pulled into the adjacent restaurant, The Pickle Barrel, without telling her traveling companion that their hotel was a hundred yards away.

"What are we stopping here for? Why, it's not even five o'clock yet—too early to be eating. It's a waste of money to eat when you're not hungry," complained Granny Gert, leaning on Rose's arm, her legs a little shaky after getting out of the car.

"Well, I'm not that hungry either," Rose said, hoping Gert couldn't hear her stomach rumbling, "so maybe we could split a meal. Okay?" Gert brightened at the prospect of saving a little money so the two made their way inside where the origin of the restaurant's name became readily apparent. Shelves lined each wall of the entry and waiting area. Every pickle variety imaginable was presented for purchase—dill slices, sweet gherkins, bread-and-butter pickles, chowchow, and pickle relish. Granny Gert, momentarily recalled to distant childhood, pointed out the large crockery containers painted with the image of an American Indian surrounded by circles over the number 5.

"Where in the world did they get so many nickel pickle jars?"

"What are you talking about, Gran?"

"Those big crocks. I don't think I've seen one of those since I was a little girl," she mused. "I just barely remember going to the corner store with my older brothers. We'd each get a huge dill pickle that we'd gnaw on all the way home." She smiled at the remote memory.

"But why nickel?"

"Because that's how much they cost, silly." Gert laughed at the look of skepticism on Rose's face. "Yes, money went a lot further back then. That picture on the barrel is of an Indian Head nickel and the 5 is for five cents. Hmm, never thought I'd see one of those again…"

Taking advantage of her mellowed mood, Rose steered her grandmother to a table by the window. She knew that Granny Gert enjoyed people-watching, and here, she could check out both those in the parking lot and those at neighboring tables. After ordering something she knew her grandmother would enjoy, Rose herself began looking at new arrivals. She too found it a diverting way to pass the time. Her grandmother simply observed the superficial— age, adults, children, clothing styles—but Rose found it much more satisfying to weave outlandish histories around each one by guessing at the reason they came to this location, at this precise moment, and speculate about highly improbable occupations or future glories that she would somehow be linked to, just for having shared a random intersection of paths in a restaurant on a cross-country journey. She sighed, thinking to herself, *Wouldn't it be exciting, if just once, reality would imitate fiction and some tall handsome stranger with a storied past would step into my world…*

*****

Miles Hawthorne urgently needed results from Simon Atherton's Kansas investigation but decided to first utilize the young agent on a short case-related research trip to Chicago. By the time Simon had completed the short flight from New York to the Windy City, he had already developed a plausible cover story and, upon landing, contacted the Landrum Agency to create the required web-based background necessary to sell the story should anyone in Tinkers Well feel the need to verify his credentials. For many years a lone wolf in the private investigation game, Simon had come to appreciate being part of a large organization that could provide the technical skills he lacked and access to clientele it would have taken decades to reach on his own.

While driving to the lawyer's office that Hawthorne had insisted he visit, in the hopes of finding some elusive information other inquiry agents had failed to obtain, Simon mused on the irony of a poor kid from the east side of London being driven in luxury through the city of Chicago at the behest of a New York millionaire business tycoon. He laughed out loud at the thought, causing the chauffeur of the limousine to glance in his rearview mirror and shake his head. Some of Simon's childhood friends might have laughed too—if they had recognized him at all.

Simon Giles Atherton, born Simon Jones, had spent a lifetime remolding himself into whatever image he could sell, steal, or impersonate in order to climb out of the relative poverty and stagnant lifestyle of his birth. The only child of a marginally interested mother and a chronically absent father, he decided early in life that just having enough to eat, a roof over his head—albeit a leaky one—and something akin to proper clothes to cover his scrawny frame was not enough for him. He wanted more. He studied the swells on the telly, their mannerisms, accents, and cadence of speech. He found that he possessed a gift for mimicry, entertaining his classmates and irritating his teachers by trying it out at the most inappropriate times. His quick mind also grasped the importance of compiling knowledge on any and everything so he became a voracious reader, causing his sorely tried teachers to think that there might be more hope for him than for his less-motivated companions.

As a teen, Simon found that he could attract more customers for whatever bobble or shoeshine he might be trying to sell in the theater district by loudly proclaiming that he could recite all the kings and queens of England back to the Norman Conquest or his product was free. But if he could successfully recite the hierarchy, he expected double for his services. Such a challenge rarely went unanswered, especially by young aristocrats who enjoyed putting such impertinence in its place. Unfortunately for them, they underestimated the wit and determination of the young entrepreneur who quickly shifted from his Cockney whine into such cultured tones that he was accused of having them on. But they paid up and he began to receive repeat business. This trick might have lost its novelty over time but he varied his performance of knowledge, from history to Shakespearean soliloquies to rules of etiquette, and stumped his challengers almost every time. Some among his then-considerable audience suggested he go on the stage and he might have considered that career field if he hadn't received his first gig as a discreet investigator at about the same time just as he was completing high school.

One evening, as most of the crowd had made its way into a nearby theater, the young Marquess of Wellingford pulled Simon aside and offered him an intriguing proposition. He asked Simon to pose as his long-lost second cousin (because no one in his social circle would recognize him) and gain entrance into a certain society lady's house by whatever cajolery necessary to recover a set of cuff links left there after a clandestine rendezvous. Upon further inquiry, Simon learned that the cuff links had been a gift from the marquess's fiancée who would take a dim view of their absence during an impending visit. The marquess promised to provide Simon with some posh togs for the venture and a sum upon successful completion that made Simon's head spin. He had no idea how to go about the business, but when dressed in the secondhand Savile Row suit, he suddenly felt like somebody! Surely he could fool the woman long enough to discover the jewelry and be gone.

And he had. Not only was the mission a success, he learned something else about himself—he could charm even the most wellborn woman. He had always been a favorite of giddy school girls, but at just seventeen, he could wield his burgeoning charm without really even understanding what he was doing. With his windfall earnings weighing in his pocket, he packed his bags, waved off the prospect of additional schooling in college, and spent the next two years studying the private investigator business. His indifferent parents saw him off with a modest show of support to hide their relief at having one less mouth to feed.

Simon's education was not the route of formal training, rather odd jobs offered through word-of-mouth recommendations from those for whom he had provided services. It was enough to live on but he suspected he was being taken advantage of in terms of fees and was never likely to attain the success he craved without earning a license from the Security Industry Authority (SIA) as a private inquiry agent. With help from that first client who had successfully married his fabulously wealthy fiancée at a time when be badly needed money, Simon secured the needed references, got a license, and improved his prospects somewhat but hadn't been able to break into the big money available mostly from the well-connected.

He also soon discovered that there were plenty of agents in England with charming British accents and was weighing other options when he had an unexpected but fortuitous meeting with Burt Landrum, in London for a convention. Recognizing some of Simon's unique abilities, Burt offered him a trial assignment in the States and a subsequent job offer with his agency. Without any emotional ties to his homeland and a strongly held belief that America really was the land of opportunity, Simon had readily accepted. A successful career had followed—partly because of his innate skills, partly because of his ruthless determination to succeed, and partly because of his willful ignorance of legal procedures. Now here he was, on his way to learn what he could from a certain lawyer before heading further west on what might prove to be his most profitable mission yet.

His business in Chicago completed, though with an ill-received negative report for Hawthorne, Simon might then have flown to Kansas City and rented a car for the rest of his journey but he'd spent more than enough time in a plane over the past two days. He chose instead to rent a modest vehicle (or so he thought—a Cadillac Escalade) rather than the luxurious Mercedes or BMW he was accustomed to driving as he thought it best not to present too ostentatious an appearance in a small town or create speculation about his cover as a blogger who, presumably, would not work with an unlimited expense account.

He had decided to pose as a blogger researching small towns on the radar of midsized Midwestern cities looking for expansion locations to fill an ever-growing need for commuter-bedroom communities. After studying the information provided by the accommodating Miss Limstock, Simon discovered that Tinkers Well was a small but growing town about twenty-five miles from Kansas City. And like many cities who had attracted the attention of businesses and manufacturing concerns no longer able to operate in a cost-prohibitive larger metropolis, Kansas City had expanded to meet the influx of new industry. But room for affordable housing needed by the working class who manned the industries was rapidly being exhausted. With so many of those people willing to take a thirty to forty-five-minute commute in stride, outlying communities had become the target of developers. Those towns, twenty to thirty miles outside the city, usually offered a considerable drop in cost of living, the lure of a small-town atmosphere and the promise of better public schools. If Tinkers Well was not already in the sights of Kansas City developers, Simon would convince its inhabitants that it should be, and he could be very persuasive.

Cutting across the state on I-55, he reached the greater St. Louis metro area in the late afternoon and opted to make it through the city before stopping for fuel and an early dinner. He left the city behind quickly, so quickly that his choice of eateries became quite limited. Like most men of a fastidious nature (though in Simon's case, it was more an acquired pretense than an inherent quality), he abhorred dining in fast-food places, feeling them unworthy of the restaurant designation. His need for fuel becoming pressing, however, he left the interstate, filled the seemingly bottomless fuel tank, and looked around for a food source that didn't involve entrées served in paper wrappers. Not seeing anything resembling a four-star restaurant or even a good old English-style pub, he pulled into the parking lot of an establishment touted as The Pickle Barrel. The name left him with some misgivings but he'd missed lunch so his stomach overruled his head. He entered what appeared to be a dining mecca for the local population.

*****

After a few moments of indulging in flights of fancy, Rose suddenly took a deep breath and held it without thinking. For stepping out of a huge Escalade, she beheld the most handsome elegant man she had ever seen outside of a magazine cover or movie screen. Time seemed to slow down. He moved with effortless grace in tailored slacks and button-down shirt with sleeves rolled up just above his wrists, exposing tanned arms and a (surely) expensive gold watch. A wisp of breeze lifted a lock of his straight brown hair, only to let it fall back, perfectly in place. Leaving his four-wheeled black steed behind, he walked toward the entrance. Rose forgot to breathe until he passed out of her range of sight and then gulped for air as if she'd been running.

"What on earth is wrong with you, child? You look like you've seen a ghost," Gert asked with genuine concern.

"Did you see him?"

"See who?"

"That guy who looks like a model or maybe a movie star..."

"What are you talking about? I think you've been driving too long—you're seeing things!"

"Oh my gosh! Don't look but he's coming this way!"

Thus admonished, Gert promptly turned around in her seat to watch a man walking across the dining room. With the volume of the somewhat hearing impaired, she said, "Well, what is the big deal? He's good looking enough, I suppose, but a little too polished for my tastes. Seems he'll be sitting right behind us. Now don't let me see you staring at him all through dinner or you'll pass out from lack of oxygen."

The mortified Rose, whose flaming cheeks had abruptly turned ashen white, whispered, "Shush! He'll hear you!"

"Well, what if he does? You know I always speak my mind. No point in tap dancing around the facts."

Trying another approach, Rose reminded her outrageous grandmother, "Now haven't you always told me to be polite to strangers so they won't feel ill at ease? *Please,* Granny," she added softly with a pleading look that Gert couldn't ignore.

"Well, all right," Gert answered more quietly. "But you've got to stop falling for every attractive man you see. He's only a traveler stopping to eat at a restaurant, just like you and me. Now you forget about him and pass me some of those rolls. I told you I was hungry."

*****

Despite a conspicuous lack of cloth table coverings and obvious nonexistence of a respectable dress code, Simon agreed to be led to a small table near the window. He studied the other occupants of the room while waiting for his waitress, the cheery Lola, to reappear with something called chicken fried steak which she assured Simon would be a real treat. He was so hungry he would have eaten almost anything—as long as it wasn't some cheap cut of beef smothered in breading. Surely the food would be more tolerable than those who frequented the establishment. He had been a little disconcerted by an elderly woman sitting in front of him who had declared her opinion of him to the room at large as he crossed the space *en route* to his table. Fortunately she sat with her back to him so he could avoid any further exposure to her hawk-like gaze, allowing him, instead, to study at leisure the rather pretty girl sitting opposite her. He found her obvious efforts to avoid looking in his direction quite entertaining and kept an amused watch on her face, waiting for her surrender to curiosity and the unveiled admiration that must surely follow. She did not disappoint. A gentle blush bloomed on her cheeks as she shyly returned his smile. In the act of reaching for her water glass, however, the visual distraction caused her to sideswipe the glass rather than pick it up, resulting in a mess on the table that spilled onto the floor. As she reached for a pile of napkins to mop up the pool, she turned back too quickly, misjudging the close proximity of her salad plate to the edge of the table and sent lettuce, plate, and all to join the water on the floor.

"Rosie, what has gotten into you?" the old crone demanded of the flustered girl who was trying valiantly to clean up the mess while avoiding the handsome stranger's stare.

"I told you to stop looking at that fellow. Now look what's come of your daydreaming."

Not usually one to consider anyone's comfort other than his own, Simon uncharacteristically took pity on the mortified girl being chastised by the old ogre and knelt beside her.

"You must let me offer my assistance. I feel somewhat responsible for your present distress. It was rude of me to stare at you so but it's not often I encounter such a pretty face on my travels."

She whispered a barely audible thank you as she looked briefly into his warm brown eyes, framed with impossibly long lashes, and allowed him to replace the now-empty plate and glass on the table as the waitress appeared to mop up the remaining spillage. He then reached his hand to gently clasp hers, helping her to her feet, not realizing the very real service he performed by steadying the girl's stance on legs that had turned into Jell-O ™.

"Please do forgive me for being at fault in causing your present *contretemps.*" Turning to the waitress, he said, "Lola, be a dear and bring this young lady another salad and water." Happy to comply with a request so charmingly made, Lola hurried back to the kitchen as Simon smiled and nodded to each of the ladies at the table, though the old woman only returned his smile with a calculating look, before resuming his seat.

I wouldn't mind whiling away a few hours with the local lasses of Tinkers Well, if this girl is any representation of the Midwestern sisterhood but not—no, most definitely not—if accompanied by an old gorgon like the one attached to her, lovely though she may be. Food and fellow diners thus evaluated and summarily dismissed, he thought to himself, *Hope on, hope ever.*

*****

How Rose got through that meal, she couldn't later recall. It was a nightmare of worrying whether Granny Gert would say anything else about the man behind them. She tried to divert her grandmother by asking her about Grandpa Ernie, though she'd heard the old stories many times, all the while trying to catch the sound of the stranger's rich cultured British voice as he spoke to the waitress who was obviously as putty in his disarming hands.

Stop it, Rose! She told herself. *Granny Gert is right. You are hopeless—you don't even know his name!* She managed to keep Gert distracted until the stranger left. It took every ounce of determination she possessed not to watch him as he left the restaurant. *Phew!* she thought. *At least I won't see him or any of these people ever again.*

Embarrassment is easier to bear if one can leave all the witnesses behind.

Not happy about getting back into the car, Gert was pleasantly surprised when Rose drove into the hotel parking lot next-door. "You mean we're going to stop for the day?" She looked hopefully at her granddaughter. Unloading everything her grandmother was certain she would need for the night wasn't quite as big a fuss as packing the little car for their two-day trip but it ran a close second. Safely settled in their room, Granny Gert had only to criticize the firmness of the bed, the lamentable supply of towels in the bathroom (two apiece), and the lack of options for TV viewing before she fell asleep, leaving Rose to enjoy a few hours of mental rest. A good night's sleep and warm shower restored her completely, and Granny Gert's approval of the free breakfast that came with the lodging sealed the positive start to day 2 on the trip to Tinkers Well.

As they continued their journey west to Kansas City and beyond, Rose asked her grandmother about their destination and their hostess whom Rose had never met.

"Well, I don't know anything about Tinkers Well other than it's the original home of her second husband, Matthew Mason. I never actually met her first husband because after we left school, I married my Ernst and we were so busy raising our family and working on the farm there was no time, or money, for travel. And back then, I'd have had to go to New York City to see her."

"So she didn't stay in Kentucky after you both graduated from Antioch College?"

"No, because she wasn't from Kentucky in the first place. We, that is our little circle of friends—" Gert screwed up her face in an effort of memory and counted them off on her fingers as she spoke their names. "—Letha…Philly…Gracie, Toots…and Dorie. That's only five, isn't it? Oh, and me of course! Well, anyway we—none of us—found out until the end of the first term when a flashy Cadillac, complete with chauffeur, pulled up in front of our dormitory that Letha was from a very well-to-do family in Cincinnati. You'd never have known it by the way she acted. She was just as down-to-earth as the rest of us and her last name was Strong—not Mansfield or

Rockefeller or Vanderbilt or anything like that. I remember wondering why she didn't study education or nursing like the rest of us—there weren't many choices for women back then. But business made sense when we found out her family had some big manufacturing empire."

"Wow. I've never met a millionaire before. What did her family make—luxury furnishings, cars...*yachts*? Can't you just imagine sailing along the coastline in a sleek yacht with the wind blowing your hair out behind you?" Rose said, momentarily lost in a beautiful daydream.

"Yachts! How did you get from manufacturing to yachts so fast? No, it was *not* yachts—they canned food. Or stored food... or shipped food..." said Gert, trying to order her distant memories. "Well, whatever they did, it had something to do with food. I do remember that. Now how's that for glamour, you silly minx?"

"*Food?* You're right, that's not glamourous at all—it's positively *ordinary.*"

"Well, ordinary or not, there are a sight more folks who spend money on food than on yachts. Just think about that, missy!"

"I suppose you're right," Rose answered reluctantly. After a moment, she added with a perplexed look on her face, "But how did a wealthy Cincinnati heiress end up at a little college in rural Kentucky? Surely she could have gone to some expensive finishing school in Switzerland or France or somewhere equally romantic?"

"Because her parents, despite all their wealth, possessed a healthy dose of good common sense. They didn't want her to become a spoiled miss who put on airs and looked down her nose at people. They may have had a lot of money but they gave a lot of it away too. The Strong family from way back, Letha told me, had a deep faith in the Almighty, and all the generations were raised to respect and honor others and help those in need. I've never forgotten a Bible verse she had taped to the mirror in our room. I can't recall the exact chapter or verse but I think it's from somewhere in Philippians, chapter 2 maybe. '*Do nothing through faction or through vainglory, but in lowliness of mind each counting other better than himself (ASV).*' And I can tell you, she did too. I think that's why they wanted Letha to go to a small Christian college instead of one of those snobby highfalutin schools or a big university. Antioch's always had a commitment to community service so it was a good fit for her to their way of thinking.

"I'm sure they thought she'd head right back to the family business when she graduated but her parents reckoned without Letha's independent streak." Granny Gert chuckled softly as she continued her narrative. "You see, during the last semester of classes, the college tried to help students find jobs for after graduation. I knew I'd be getting married. My parents had said I was too young to get married when Ernie came home from the Korean War in 1953, and they were determined I was going to be the first generation of Schmidts to go to college, so after six years of waiting, Ernie put his foot down and we were married the week after graduation!"

Rose smiled to herself. She had heard this part of the story the evening before when Granny Gert was recounting her romance with the long-suffering Ernie. The smile faded as she remembered her distraction tactics to avoid comments about her handsome table neighbor. *Best not to dwell on that humiliating hour*, she thought and focused her attention on her grandmother again, now in full spate.

"—was born a year later and your mother two years after that, so my career was a short one but I wouldn't have traded raising my girls and taking care of Ernie for all the careers in the world." With that, she smiled, folded her arms, and contemplated the scenery.

"And Aletha?" Rose prompted her.

"What about Aletha?"

"You were telling me how her independent streak affected her post-graduation plans?"

"Now how did you know she had an independent streak?" Looking at Rose, as if discovering she was clairvoyant.

"You just told me."

"Did I?"

Rose patiently helped direct Gert's erratic reminiscences.

"Oh, that's right. I was telling you about what happened to Letha after college. What a clever girl you are to remember that. Now where was I…"

"Her parents thought she'd go back to Cincinnati but she—"

"Wanted to go to New York City, of course, to see where the Strong family got started in America. And it just so happened that some Antioch alumnus from decades earlier had gone to New York and 'made good,' as the saying goes. Every year, he offered a job to a business graduate. Letha's parents didn't know it but she applied for the job that year and got it. And that's how she met her first husband." Smiling at Rose as if that explained everything.

"She married the man who hired her?" Rose asked, trying to unravel the threads of Gert's tangled story.

"Of course not, you goose, he'd have been much too old for her. She married a young man that she worked with and they set out to start a business of their own, though I can't, for the life of me, remember what it was. I never met him but I think his name was James. Or was it John? Something biblical anyway."

"Did they have any children?"

"They did—but just the one. I haven't heard anything about him for years. I seem to recall that he had some sort of dustup with his parents right after he finished college—he *did* go to a fancy business school   and just sort of walked out of their lives. It nearly broke Letha's heart, especially since…whatever his name was died shortly after that."

"Oh, how sad! I can't imagine how crushing that would be. How does someone go on after that much tragedy?"

"Well, I hope you never have to find out. I've been very blessed with my family, but when you get to my age, you'll find that you can't have love without pain. Some just have more of one than the other. And poor Letha's had more pain than most." Gert was silent for a few moments, looking into the past. "I got real worried about her when I didn't get a Christmas card from her for two or three years…" Suddenly she became more animated and looked at Rose. "But then out of the blue, I got a letter, from Chicago of all places, saying that she had remarried."

"I'm so glad for her! Was he a good man?"

"Well, I gathered from her letter that she was as happy as sunshine. And when Ernie and I finally decided to take a real vacation after you and your sisters were born and out of diapers and we didn't feel so needed anymore, we decided to accept an invitation to visit Letha and Matthew in Chicago. We had a real good time, and Ernie and I both took a liking to Matthew. They showed us all the sights, and I'll tell you what, they aren't kidding when they call it the Windy City. I don't know why I bothered to fix my hair at all while we were there!" She was silent for a few minutes and turned to Rose as if for inspiration. "Now what was I going to tell you?" she mumbled softly. Suddenly she snapped her fingers and continued the story. "The sights. We could just about have seen most of them from their apartment. It was *mammoth* and perched way up near the top of one of those high-rise buildings. Did I mention that Matthew was a millionaire too?"

"*Too?*"

"Didn't I tell you that Letha and her first husband—"

"What's his name," Rose interjected helpfully.

Granny Gert grinned in appreciation. "Saucebox! Now where was I…Oh yes, they started a business. I told you that."

"Yes, but you couldn't remember what it was."

"I may not remember what it *was* but I *do* remember that they made a barrel full of money. And Matthew's wealth came from working his way up the ladder too, just like—"

"What's his name," they said in unison, both laughing.

"Rosie, you do my heart good. Now as I was *saying*—" looking pointedly at Rose—"I like to think that Letha was their good luck charm."

"I'd be happy to be a good luck charm for just *one* millionaire!"

"Be careful what you wish for, young lady. She may have a lot of money but she's also had a lot of grief in her life. And now that I think about it, a while back, she mentioned in a letter that she'd started having some pretty serious health problems and that's why she and Matthew moved back to Kansas. Don't envy someone until you know their whole story. Remember, money can't buy happiness."

"You're right, of course, though it *pains* me to admit it," Rose said with a wink.

"You may not marry a millionaire, young lady, but I don't think you'll have any trouble finding a husband if you'd just turn that beguiling look on some passable male instead of wasting it on your old granny!" she said, causing Rose to laugh and blush.

"I haven't talked this much in years. Feel like my mouth's just about turned to cotton. What have we got in the way of soft drinks back here?" Gert asked as she dug through the contents of the cooler. Emerging with some difficulty from the recess behind the front seats, she settled back into her seat, took two whole sips from a soda bottle, and insisted Rose drink the rest of it. Rose knew that her grandmother abhorred waste even more than her daughter Beth did so she told her to drink a little more and then pour the rest of it into her YETI ™, still empty, in the cupholder.

Refreshed yet tired from her animated conversation and efforts at memory, Gert's head slowly fell forward as she began to snore softly.

Rose accepted her momentary solitude and turned her attention to the endless fields along the highway. Corn was succeeded by ripening wheat, its golden leaves moving in ever-changing waves at the whim of the arbitrary winds. She was so engrossed in following the patterns that she nearly woke Gert when the car strayed over a rumble strip. A mishap averted, Rose fixed her mind on the task at hand and was thankful that her grandmother slept until they reached Kansas City.

CHAPTER 4

In my Father's house are many rooms; if it were not so,
I would have told you. I am going there to prepare a place for you.

—John 14:2 (NIV)

After traveling more miles than she cared to count and feeling almost as road weary as Granny Gert, Rose finally turned off of the narrow country road onto a dubious-looking private drive shrouded by overgrown trees. Surely Eloise, the disembodied voice, had made a mistake. The directions appeared so improbable that Rose double checked the address in her phone contacts list. Still hesitant to leave the larger road, and seemingly all ties to humanity, she tentatively made a left turn onto the rutted surface and, in doing so, spied a sign leaning toward the roadside ditch with the barely discernable single word, "Mason," just visible on its worn surface. Feeling a little more assured that they were tracking in the right direction, Rose carefully negotiated the potholes on the rough surface while Granny Gert mentally chided her friend Aletha's lack of attention to obvious landscaping needs. Any light from above was nearly shut out completely by the canopy of interlocking branches that met over the center of the little lane (it could hardly be called a road), almost tempting Rose to turn on her headlights. But that would have destroyed the illusion—springing effortlessly from her fertile imagination—of driving through a lovely enchanted forest with heavily veiled sunshine poking intermittently through the thick cover of foliage. Emerging from the winding drive that must have been a quarter of a mile long, Rose would have greeted with alacrity the sight of a ruined castle but was literally stopped in her tracks by the very real sight that met her astonished gaze. Lost in wonder, she forgot all about depressing the clutch and abruptly stalled the car in an open clearing. She tumbled out of the old Chevy, took a few wobbly steps forward—her legs stiff from the long drive—and fell instantly head over ears in love.

She beheld the house of her dreams. No streamlined modern dwelling with clean lines and sharp angles for her—no. It was this unexpected structural gem, brilliantly combining whimsy and dignity, personifying all she felt a house should be. The towering three-story mansion before her stood as a glorious testament to the craftsmanship, architectural detail, and grandeur of the Victorian era.

Rose, rooted to the spot, tried in vain to take in every detail of this old beauty, from the balconied turret nestled into the third-floor roofline to the tiny corner balcony and double porches on the second floor to the huge wraparound veranda, beckoning visitors to the gracious front door. The exterior was a perfect combination of stone, wood, and shingle and every covered outdoor space was fringed with what she could only think of as wooden lace. She knew these lovely details must surely have magical names and she vowed then and there to devote her stay in Kansas to learning each one of them.

Her visual senses were overwhelmed by all they sought to capture in those first few moments of discovery. So caught up was Rose in admiration of the grand old home, standing proudly before her amid carefully laid out formal gardens, that she completely forgot about the grand old lady she had left in the car. She was dragged out of her reverie and recalled to her chauffeur duties by the sound of Granny Gert huffing and puffing as she struggled to extricate herself from her seat belt, jacket, and pillow in an effort to try and pull herself out of the low-slung vehicle.

"Rosie, could you stop gawking at that big heap long enough to help your old gran out of this contraption?"

"I'm *so* sorry, Granny," cried Rose as she hurried to her grandmother's side. "I just can't believe it—I've never seen a more beautiful house! Why didn't you tell me we had such a treat to look forward to at the end of our journey?" As she spoke, she gently pulled the old woman to her feet and kept a bracing arm around her until she was sure that Granny Gert had her sea legs under her. After driving for so long, there was an odd sense of movement, even on the solid ground.

Gert turned her head to look at the house Rose was again admiring, then looked at her granddaughter with an expression of disbelief.

"Are you *kidding* me? You can look at this old pile and call it *beautiful?* It's falling into the ground! Don't you see the sagging porch roofs and water stains on the siding? And it looks like that chimney's about to crumble in place. Honey, you need to take off those rose-colored glasses you're always looking through and see this place for what it is—a dump!"

Forcing herself to make an honest assessment of the house, even Rose had to admit, grudgingly, that it had seen better days. But surely a little paint and minor repairs would set it to rights. Now that she looked more closely, evidence of repair work was visible in multiple places which cheered her immeasurably. But the formal gardens were that in name only, overgrown and untamed. A huge weeping willow in the far corner of the garden beckoned visitors with gracefully swaying tendrils as if pointing to a neighboring archway, now covered in unruly clematis vines. A walled area beyond suggested a spot for formal seating, though the surrounding low brick wall lay in partial ruin from the invasion of tree roots and effects of neglect. Yet her hands itched for a shovel and wheelbarrow to try and dig out the original plantings that must be there somewhere, lining the weed-infested walkways. She continued her appraisal, only half-listening to Granny's ongoing comments.

"I'll tell you, I'm frankly amazed that Aletha, with all her money and finicky ways, would ever live in a place like this. Either she's changed a lot in the last twenty-plus years or she's demented," she said, shaking her head. "I just can't understand it. Why don't you toddle on up those rickety stairs and see if anybody's home. But you be careful—I'm not sure it's safe."

Just catching the end of Gert's comments, Rose willingly complied with the suggestion while Gert pondered hopefully, "Maybe Aletha sent me the wrong address…"

Reaching the porch at the top of a short flight of broad but warped steps, Rose walked around a ladder, barely missed stepping in a sizeable hole in the porch floor, and made her way to the massive front door which, at closer inspection, was more rough and gray than gracious. But she gave the old rusted knocker, shaped like a lion's head (which she found delightful), a few good raps and waited. In seconds, she heard footsteps approaching but they were clearly not from inside the house. She realized they were coming rapidly from the other side of the wraparound veranda, just as a young man rounded the corner with anything but a welcoming expression on his face.

"What in God's name are you doing? Can't you see this is a construction area? Hell, this old roof could fall in on you any minute!"

"Well, I-I w-was just—"

"This is not a photo op for tourists. It's a private residence and you're trespassing!"

"B-but I only—" Backing instinctively from the verbal onslaught, Rose might have fallen into the hole she had missed a few minutes earlier but for the timely intervention of the furious stranger. He grabbed her arms just as her foot felt nothingness and pulled her close to him—rather too close in her opinion, even if the alternative was a black hole. At such close proximity, Rose couldn't help noticing that the exasperated face before her might have been a pleasant one without its continued scowl. The lean angular features were framed by thick sandy colored hair and a short well-trimmed beard, now both liberally sprinkled with sawdust. His grip on her arms was firm but not ungentle. She sensed rather than felt the strength of his arm muscles barely concealed by a filthy work shirt. She found herself curiously short of breath and was thankful when he moved carefully toward the front steps, pulling her with him.

"If you will *kindly* get back in your car and head back to wherever you came from, it would be much appreciated," he said civilly but with a note of finality.

Rose felt momentarily ashamed and humiliated. After all, she wasn't sure she *was* in the right place—but this sullen young man had hardly given her the opportunity to find out. She was physically and emotionally shaken by the unexpected encounter. Then she began to feel a twinge of annoyance. She yanked her arm out of her host's compelling clasp and stood her ground at the top of the porch steps. She saw that he was taken aback by her gesture and the small twinge of annoyance grew into full-blown glorious anger. It was an unfamiliar feeling for her. She had such a naturally sunny disposition that few things really rattled her, and when they did, she lacked the self-confidence to do anything about it. But here in this unfamiliar place, in the shadow of this wonderful house that once represented strength and pride, Rose finally found some for herself. She was not going to be pushed around anymore—at least not by an angry oversized dust bunny.

"Look, I don't know what passes for hospitality in Kansas but I hope this isn't par for the course. Since you were too busy being rude and unwelcoming to introduce yourself or to find out who I was, I'll help you out. We are not tourists or interlopers. My name is Rose Thompson. I've driven my eighty-two-year-old grandmother, Gertrude Gunn, all the way from Kentucky at the invitation of her friend, Aletha Mason. This is the address Mrs. Mason sent us, but if we're in the wrong place, perhaps you would *kindly* point us in the right direction or have the goodness to let Mrs. Mason know we've arrived. Either way, I'm not moving until you give me some answers."

Rose then folded her arms as much to steady herself after such a fiery speech as to add credence to her words. While she was speaking, the young man's jaw dropped. *He is clearly not used to having someone stand up to him*, Rose noted with great satisfaction. Little did he know that she would ordinarily be the *last* person to do so. She thought it best not to enlighten him.

Just as she was feeling very pleased with herself and totally in control of the situation, the slack jaw slowly changed into a grudging smile (she had been right about how attractive he might look without a perpetual scowl) that caught her completely off guard. She suddenly felt awkward and a little out of her depth but she kept up a brave, if somewhat cowed, front.

"I guess I owe you ladies"—glancing from Rose to the obviously impatient elderly lady leaning on the car—"an apology. You're absolutely right, I was inexcusably rude."

How dare he take all *the wind out of my sails…*

"It's just that since Aletha moved back here and opened up the new driveway, we've been inundated with nosy locals trying to get a glimpse of the old place." Looking up at the house, he continued, "You wouldn't know it to look at her now but this grand old lady used to be the showplace of the county."

"Oh, but I think she's beautiful *still,*" seconded Rose with genuine enthusiasm. The stranger shot her a surprised look of reappraisal. Focused on avoiding rotten treads as she descended the steps, Rose missed the look of grudging approval on the man's face.

"Here I go blabbing on and I still haven't introduced myself," he said. "My name is Ludlow, Timothy Ludlow, but everyone calls me Tim. And I really *am* sorry about earlier. Forgive me?" As he spoke, Tim extended his hand and Rose shyly placed hers in his, now thoroughly regretting her earlier outburst.

"Are you two going to start dancing or are you going to find Letha?" Gert shouted from the car. "I'm not getting any younger while you're figuring it out."

"Now it's my turn to apologize. I'm afraid my grandmother is exhausted from the drive and needs somewhere to rest. *Is* this Aletha's house?"

"Technically yes, but she's not living here presently. The truth is, it's not fit for occupancy. The caretakers, by the name of Johnson, really let the place go. They were left in charge when Matthew moved to Chicago in the mid-'80s to build up his business. An old house like this needs constant attention and I'm afraid Aletha and Matthew were more trusting than the Johnsons were trustworthy. When the Masons returned here a few years ago, they found a mess so they had the gatekeeper's cottage refurbished to live in while they waited for the work here to be done. Unfortunately Matthew died the year before last, and Aletha hasn't really been herself since then so forward momentum on the house kind of stalled. You and your grandmother will be staying with Aletha in the cottage. I'll give you an escort if you'll follow my truck."

"Cottage?" Rose sounded confused. "We didn't see a cottage, or a building of any kind for that matter, when we came down the lane from the main road."

"You must have come in the back way—probably the way your GPS routed you. Maybe the new driveway from the bypass hasn't made it into their memory banks yet, though that wouldn't have done you much good since there are gates across the new entrance now. I guess it's a good thing I never got around to putting up a gate across that old lane. I kind of wondered how you'd gotten in." He glanced at the little Chevy and added with a laugh, "Your tires apparently survived the pothole landmines."

They had slowly been walking back to Rose's car as they talked. Gert was ready from the peanut gallery.

"It's about time you got something sorted out. You have got something sorted out, haven't you, sonny? And I hope it doesn't mean we're staying in this decrepit old dungeon." Rose noticed that Granny Gert was getting more cantankerous than usual, signaling an urgent need for rest. She glanced anxiously at Tim, lest he answer the old lady as rudely as he had spoken to her earlier. But she needn't have worried. He was as kind now as he had been brusque before.

"Mrs. Gunn, I'm sorry to have kept you waiting. Unfortunately I mistook your granddaughter for an intruder but we've cleared up the confusion, and I'll be happy to take you to Aletha if you'll get back in the car and be patient just a bit longer. I know you must be tired but I promise it will only be a few more minutes," he said with a rueful grin.

"Well, you're a scruffy-looking fellow but at least you're respectful. Let's saddle up this wagon and hit the trail. If I know Aletha—and I have for sixty-plus years—she'll have the welcome mat out and everything as fine as can be. Lead the way, Horatio!"

*****

The cottage may not have displayed the grandeur of the main house but it had a charm all its own. This Victorian beauty was much smaller—only one story—but boasted many shared details, including a deep wraparound porch that led to an attached gazebo on the back corner of the house facing west—an ideal spot for breakfast or morning tea. The entire length of the porch roof was hung with fern baskets, and the carefully tended flower beds below boasted a mix of colorful annuals and leafy variegated perennials. Lace curtains in windows crowned by stained glass transoms added to the welcoming exterior.

"Now this is more like," commented Granny Gert as they drove up the short driveway and parked in the shade of one of a ring of mature oak trees surrounding the house.

Even given its well-maintained structure and freshly mown lawn, this little gem was only a shadow of its sister structure down the lane. But Rose kept these reflections to herself as she helped her grandmother out of old Betsy for the final time on their westward journey. Tim had pulled up next to them and gone ahead to alert Aletha about the arrivals. "It really is very pretty," Rose had to admit to herself as she and Granny Gert walked slowly up the flagstone path to the porch where Tim stood waiting with the door held open for the ladies. Then, as if by magic, they stepped over the low threshold and into the past.

Rose caught her breath at the old-world elegance inside and had to admit that she might have underestimated the little house. Near the door, an antique coatrack and umbrella holder in glowing mahogany looked almost short reclining against wallpaper-clad walls leading up to ten-foot high ceilings. A bronze chandelier hung from an ornate plaster medallion and a marble top antique mahogany table, with elegantly scrolled legs, claimed ownership of the longer foyer wall. An oval mirror above the table reflected a large vase of fresh flowers sitting atop a delicate lace doily. The foyer lacked only a sumptuous oriental carpet to complete the impression of a time warp and Rose wondered at its absence. The gleaming wood floor seemed lonely without it.

As her eyes adjusted from bright sunshine to the dimmer interior, Rose saw a petite woman with a halo of soft white hair approaching them. She was short and a little stooped like Granny Gert but there the similarity ended. She was slender where Gert was stout and her delicate facial features looked as if they had been fashioned out of porcelain. Gert's square Teutonic jaw and prominent nose could only be compared to something chiseled out of stone. Rose also noticed that their hostess was leaning on a cane.

"Is that you at last, Trudy?" she asked with a smile. "Welcome to Fern Cottage!"

At the name Trudy, Rose half-turned to see if someone else had come in behind them, then realized with a smile that it must be a nickname for a much younger Gertrude. The old friends embraced as if no time at all had elapsed since their last visit.

"Letha, I can't tell you how glad I am to be out of that car and on solid ground! Now before I do anything else, I want to thank you for inviting Rosie and me. I can't tell you how pleased I was to receive your invitation to come and see you after all these years. Especially since you included Rose."

At that, she grabbed her granddaughter's hand and pulled her closer to Aletha. "Here she is, Letha, the sweetest little gal you'll ever want to meet. Rosie, say hello to my old friend, Letha."

Feeling as if she'd been reduced to about the age of six, Rose blushed and placed her hand into the one held out to her. "I'm very happy to be here, Mrs. Mason. Thank you so much for having me."

"What a lovely voice. May I look at you, child?"

Rose thought it an odd request since she was standing directly in front of her hostess but responded politely, "Of course."

She was completely taken by surprise when, after asking Trudy to hold her cane, Aletha reached both hands to Rose's face and gently traced the line of her jaw, her eyebrows, nose, and lips. *Why didn't Granny Gert prepare me for this?* The china-blue eyes in the face turned toward hers were unseeing. Aletha Mason was profoundly blind.

"A lovely face too. Thank you, child. Now I'll be able to see you in my mind's eye. Trudy." Aletha reached out her hand as she spoke. The bewildered Gert took her friend's fragile hand in both her sturdy ones. "I'm sorry I didn't warn you about my blindness. I didn't want you to take some foolish notion into your head that you would be a burden to me and turn down my invitation."

"All the same, you should have told me." The angry bluntness of Gert's statement failed to hide the deep pity she felt for her old friend. "You did tell me that you and Matthew moved to Kansas for your health but I never imagined it was anything like this. I'm truly sorry, Letha," she added with real emotion in her voice.

"Now don't you feel sorry for me, Trudy. I get along just fine. Matthew set up everything in the house so that I could function as safely and independently as possible which is why there are no rugs on the floor," she said, answering Rose's unasked question. Aletha laughed softly, a lilting musical laugh. "He would never admit it but I think he was happy to sell his business and retire to his boyhood home. At first, he felt so badly about failing to pay as much attention to the old property as he had his business. But all things really do work together for good because this cottage suits me much better than the main house ever would have."

She stopped suddenly, somewhat conscience-stricken. "Here I am, going on and on about myself instead of inviting you in. Trudy, I'll need my cane. Come, Prince." As she moved ahead of them into the living room (Rose mentally labeled it "the parlor"), a large black German shepherd moved out of the shadows and sat submissively by her chair. Rose, accustomed to far more rowdy dogs, marveled at his quiet obedience. She realized he must be a trained helper dog but noticed that he wore no harness. Her curiosity roused, she was about to ask about him when Aletha, almost as if reading Rose's thoughts, introduced her companion.

"This handsome gentleman is Prince. He's been my constant companion since my eyesight started failing." She laid her hand on the shepherd's head and gently stroked his brow. "I told Matthew I didn't need a helper dog because I never went out alone but he insisted and I've never been so thankful. I don't really need his guidance to get around but he has been my truest friend and support since I lost Matthew."

Catching the last phrase, a deep voice interjected from the foyer, "I'll remember that when you need your faucet fixed or railing repaired," causing Aletha to laugh. Rose had all but forgotten Tim. "I won't track any dirt into the parlor, and I need to get back to work, but I wanted you ladies to know that I've put your luggage in the guest room at the end of the hall. I'll leave Aletha to give you the nickel tour." Looking directly at Rose, he added contritely, "I really do apologize for my earlier behavior." Seeing the easy blush rise in her cheeks, he smiled, nodded, and was gone.

"Now what was all that about?" Aletha asked.

Before Granny Gert could give away more than Rose cared to share about their arrival at the big house, she explained that he simply mistook them for tourists.

"You mean he was rude, overbearing, and dictatorial?" Aletha asked with a smile.

Feeling the description completely apposite, Rose immediately contradicted her own thoughts by quickly disagreeing with her hostess. "Of course not. He was just being protective of you and the house. He very kindly brought us to the cottage."

"After first assuming you were interlopers rather than asking who you were?" Rose found Aletha's uncanny ability to read her thoughts a little unsettling.

Laughing, she admitted, "Well, he did make a few false assumptions, but honestly, he couldn't have been more helpful when he knew who we were."

"He is a dear boy but can be a little fierce. I suppose that is a character trait that has carried over from his time in the army. I've known him since he was a baby and look on him as a grandson. He and his mother have been so good to me but I can't help teasing him about his ferocious disposition. He sometimes reminds me of Matthew—the strong protector. I don't want Tim to know this—it's never good to overinflate a man's ego—but I wouldn't have him any other way." Having disposed of introductions, she asked, "Would you ladies like some refreshments after your long journey?"

Gert just needed to refresh herself. This initiated the nickel tour hinted at earlier by Tim. As Aletha and Rose waited for Gert in the wide hallway, Rose looked into neighboring rooms and marveled, as she had in the parlor, that every inch of the cottage was beautifully almost-lovingly decorated. There were sturdy dressing tables made whimsical with decorative carved accents, huge headboards giving substance to delicate linen-covered mattresses, and walls covered in everything from fine oil paintings to sepia-toned photos of long-dead ancestors. Everything was perfection of line and color. Pondering over such attention to detail in a house whose mistress was blind, she was again amazed by Aletha's next prescient remark.

"I imagine you're wondering about the décor. No, I can't see it but I picked out every piece of furniture and each wall hanging. You see, when we were first married, Matthew brought me here to visit his old home, the mansion you saw earlier. I loved it on sight but it was in much better repair back then. Looking forward to the day we would retire here, I spent years collecting furnishings that would be worthy of such a house. It's quite large, and when I saw it that first time, many of the rooms were empty because a lot of the furniture had been sold off during lean years to keep the property going. I wanted it to be a showplace again." Laughing, she said, "You can imagine how out of place these pieces looked in a modern Chicago apartment! But I had such plans to make that lovely old Victorian monument a showplace again that Matthew let me bring the old world into our modern surroundings while we waited for retirement. We stored much of the furniture, and because the old house wasn't fit to live in when we finally got back here, most of it is still stored locally. My favorite pieces are here, and though I can't actually see them anymore, I can touch them and remember." She sighed as the deep blue unseeing eyes clouded over. "I sometimes wonder if God is punishing me for my vanity," she said as if to herself.

"Oh, that can't be!" Rose responded quickly. She continued a little uncertainly, "I...I don't understand why God allows people to go through...trials. And I know I'm young and haven't experienced a lot in life but I'm sure He doesn't work like that. I mean, there must be a reason because I know He loves us and...oh, I'm not very good at expressing myself. I'm sorry, I didn't mean for you to think I know...why..." She stopped, at a loss.

"Dear child, you are absolutely right. Don't ever apologize for believing in God's goodness. You mustn't listen to the ramblings of an old woman who grows maudlin from spending too much time by herself." She reached out her hand toward the girl and Rose laid hers in it, not sure of what she should do. "That's why I am *so* happy to have you and Trudy as guests. I hope you'll feel you are welcome to stay as long as you like."

"I promise to do that if you will tell me why you call Granny Gert Trudy?" she asked, a smile in her voice.

Aletha laughed responsively. "When we were young college coeds, we all changed our names a little so that each of us in our little clique had a nickname. I'm sure you've noticed that Trudy calls me Letha, dropping the A? Well, your grandmother became Trudy. I do see that Granny Gert suits her now but she will always be Trudy to me."

As if on cue, Trudy joined them in the hallway, shaking her head. "Letha, I never, in all my born days, saw such a bathroom—you ought to charge admission! Nickel tour indeed. You could bring folks in by the busload to see this little 'cottage' of yours. I can't imagine what you'd do with that big pile we stopped at first. I will say this for you, you've always had a good eye for anything artsy." Realizing her reference to sight, she gruffly added, "I'm sorry, Letha. Didn't mean anything by it—the eye thing, you know."

"I knew exactly what you meant. Trudy, do you know what I've always admired about you? You always say exactly what's on your mind."

"Well, I find it saves time and neither of us has much of that left," she said with a wink that Aletha couldn't see but nevertheless sensed.

"Ladies, shall we continue the tour?" After an exhaustive round of the house, filled with details about the littlest things, almost as if Aletha described them from sight, she and Gert left Rose in the guest room to unpack while the two old chums adjourned again to the parlor for a good long chat.

Packing completed and suitcases stowed in the closet, Rose was sorely tempted to stretch out on one of the twin beds for a short rest. But she knew she would probably be seven leagues under in a matter of minutes if she lay down on what promised to be a cloud of blissful comfort so she opted for a stroll instead. Poking her head in the parlor, the scene of two old friends slipping effortlessly into a shared young womanhood warmed her heart. She almost interrupted to ask Aletha if the dog, Prince, would enjoy a walk but assumed he wouldn't leave his mistress's side. She had the door half-opened when she heard Aletha calling her back.

"Rose, dear, is that you? Are you going for a walk? Would you mind taking Prince with you? He doesn't get the exercise he needs since Matthew died, unless Tim or one of the boys stops by."

How does she do *it?* Rose wondered. *Maybe she's telepathic…*

"I'd be happy to but will he go with me?"

"Just come and introduce yourself. Once he knows you're a friend, he'll be quite content to go with you."

Rose squatted down in front of the big dog, stretching out her hand that he might smell and lick it as a form of certification. Approval being granted, she scratched the precise spot behind his ear that brought his tongue lolling out of his mouth (she *had* picked up a few tricks during her tenure as custodian of a doggie daycare!). Stroking the thick dark fur, she spoke softly to him. The bond was secured. Prince trotted happily after her when she bade him follow her outdoors.

As if by homing beacon, she was drawn in the direction of the big house. Walking in the shade provided by the waning sun, she caught her breath as they rounded a corner and saw the looming structure, this time from a different angle than her initial view of the house. The spacious Fern Cottage seemed dainty by comparison. The new perspective showed the other side of the wrapped porch which ended in a second entrance to the house, perhaps into a study or dining room. The roof gable encased a tiny window surrounded by cedar shingles and underscored by a ledge artistically supported by carved braces. Scaffolding held up the porch roof on this side, and more of the stone foundation was visible where the stumps of dead shrubs or trees stuck out just above ground level. Rose stood and stared at it for a full five minutes until Prince barked, reminding her to stay in motion. She took a wide berth around the front of the house, lest she draw fire from Tim if he was still on the premises. The far side featured a three-story bump out with double windows on the first two floors and yet another balcony covering what must be the kitchen entrance. The covered porch beneath led directly into a glass-covered greenhouse which, sadly, showed some cracked and even missing panes.

Determined to see the entire exterior (since presumably, she would *not* be invited to see the interior in the foreseeable future), Rose and Prince walked all the way around to the back of the house, keeping to the edge of the formal garden. Here she could see more clearly what must have been a conservatory. She had noticed it protruding off the back of the house as she had approached from the other side but couldn't see the full height and protrusion of vaulted windows surrounding the large add-on. Behind the house, they found a triple detached garage, doubtless originally used as a carriage house, displaying familiar architectural details. A large stone and timber barn some distance beyond was the only indication that horses had ever made a home there.

Careful not to step inside, Rose got close enough to the opened doors to see Tim's crew cab pickup truck parked inside the large structure. Flustered by their initial encounter, she had failed to notice the placard on the front driver side door that read "Three Brothers Construction, Inc."

Oh no, Rose thought, *Tim must still be here!* She was making good her escape to avoid being caught snooping where she had been warned off earlier, when she heard a door close on the house and an unfamiliar voice hailing her.

"Is that Rose? Hey, wait up. Don't leave on my account."

She turned to see a young African American man walking quickly toward her, wearing a hard hat and carrying a bag of tools. Politeness compelled her to stay put, though she really wanted to avoid a second confrontation that day. However, the greeting this time had sounded a lot friendlier so she waited for the man to catch up with her. Smiling, he tipped his hat in recognition as he walked past her, slung the bag of tools into the bed of the pickup truck, threw the hat in after it, and then walked back toward her with his hand held out in welcome.

"You must be Rose. The cap'n said you were awful pretty and you blush a lot," he said in a manner calculated to set the rising color in motion. Watching the flame bloom in her cheeks, he laughed and said, "Yep, he was right about that blush."

"Warner, pipe down. Rose, don't listen to him. He's an idiot." She recognized Tim's voice. He must have walked up behind her as she had turned her back to the house in order to face the other man. Certain that he had overheard the interchange, she wasn't sure whether she was glad to see him or not.

"Let me introduce my business partner before he embarrasses anyone else." Ignoring the other's grin, he said, "Rose Thompson, meet Derek Warner." She laughed at the formality of the introduction and at the exaggerated bow executed by Mr. Warner.

"At your service, ma'am. You can call me Derek. If you can't tell us apart, just remember that the cap'n is the boss, I'm the brawn," he said, pausing to flex his muscles accordingly, "and Abe here is the brains of the operation." Rose had seen a third man approaching more slowly from the house with a golden retriever at his heels. As he drew closer, she could see that he was of Middle Eastern descent and protruding from one leg opening of his dirty cargo shorts was a prosthetic leg. "We are Three Brothers Construction, Inc.," said Derek. "Don't you see the family resemblance?" he added with a grin nearly wide enough to split his face in two.

It would have been difficult to find a more mixed trio. Standing between Tim and Abe, Derek appeared quite short, his torso that of a bodybuilder. He opted to dispense with facial hair altogether and sweat clung to his clean-shaven head. Abe, the tallest of the three, bore the olive skin of his race and a head of thick curly black hair framing a face with deep-set hooded eyes. A prominent nose and full lips overshadowed a scruffy soul patch.

"You must forgive, or possibly just ignore, the LT," said Abe in a rich cultured voice and with a smile almost as big as Derek's. "My name is Abraham Yousef. Unfortunately my simple friend here can only handle names of one syllable so I have become Abe." He said, adroitly dodging a slap on the head from Derek.

"Okay, knock it off you two or she'll think we're *all* idiots!" After chiding his friends, Tim bent slightly and tapped his shoulders. Prince reared up on his hind legs and put his front paws on the spots indicated. "How's my buddy?" Tim asked, scratching behind the dog's ears. "Are you having a nice walk with Rose?" Prince promptly responded with a sharp bark, followed by a howl. "Hey, Warner, this dog's got to have an IQ at least as high as yours."

"Probably higher." Amazing how quickly a man with a false leg can move when motivated!

"Abe, you haven't introduced your companion," said Rose as she got acquainted with a second four-legged charmer that afternoon.

"Scout is, by far, the most well-mannered of us all. It seems he approves of you." Scout seconded this observation by enthusiastically licking the face of the laughing girl.

Now completely at ease, Rose asked, "I gather the three of you are in business together. Please tell me you're restoring this grand old house."

"We're trying to when we can find a few free hours not spent on refurbishing houses or commercial properties in town. Unfortunately those hours are few and far between," Tim responded with a wry smile, having bid Prince sit beside him.

"But I don't quite get the 'Three Brothers' or the—what was it? Cap'n or LT…"

"I am the former Captain Ludlow, the amiable lunatic here"—Derek grinned even wider (if that was possible)—"was First Lieutenant Warner, and Abraham was Staff Sergeant Yousef. We all served together at different times when we worked for Uncle Sam."

"Oh, so the Three Brothers means brothers in arms? Is that the right term?"

"Well…" Shooting a look at the other men, he said, "Yes. *Formerly* brothers in arms. We're civilians now, just trying to make a living."

"You might say we are brothers from different mothers," Derek added by way of explanation that only left Rose confused. She had only heard that term used in describing brothers of the same faith and surely someone with the name Yousef was Muslim, not Christian.

It was none of her business so she kept any questions to herself and responded to such open friendliness by offering impulsively. "Well, maybe I can be your sister?" She caught a strange expression on

Tim's face and hurried on. "I don't mean being part of your business or anything like that, just a friend, you know?"

Derek had seen the look on Tim's face too, but he assured her, "I believe I speak for all of us when I say we would be honored to have you as a sister *and* a friend. And maybe if you bring Miss Aletha and your grandmother, is it?" Rose nodded. "We'll see you at church tomorrow."

Was the "we" he referred to him and Tim? For no reason she would admit to, she hoped so.

"I'd like that. Well, I guess Prince and I should head back or Granny Gert'll send a search party out after me." She smiled and waved to the three men as she turned to walk away, still perplexed by the look on Tim's face. It was almost one of disappointment or maybe resignation yet they seemed to be getting on better since their initial meeting. "Men are mysteries, Prince," she remarked to her partner. He barked in agreement, eliciting an answering chuckle. The pair continued in companionable silence until they reached the cottage.

CHAPTER 5

Suppose one of you has a hundred sheep and loses one of them—
what do you do? You leave the other ninety-nine sheep in the
pasture and go looking for the one that got lost until you find it.

—Luke 15:4 (GNT)

"I hope you'll forgive the simplicity of breakfast this morning. I usually eat light on Sundays because I dine at the Ludlow's afterward and Marilyn always puts on a feast. I know you'll enjoy meeting her. She's a dear, just like her son."

"Oh, but we don't want to impose on anyone. She doesn't even *know* us." The agitation Rose felt was rooted more in a reluctance to see Tim again than it was to meet his mother. She wasn't sure if he even liked her—he sent such mixed messages. She could only imagine what he must have told his mom about her—if he had mentioned her at all.

"Nonsense. She specifically asked me to include you in her standing invitation so no more about that. Would you prefer tea, Rose, or orange juice?"

Objections dismissed, Aletha resumed the role of hostess. Her deftness in retrieving dishes and assembling them, along with cereal, milk, and spoons, on a tray could rival that of any sighted person.

"Would you mind carrying the tray, dear? I'll just get the teapot." Rose followed her outside to the gazebo, impressed by Aletha's ease of movement by using the handrail and posts as guides. "I like to eat my breakfast out here as often as I can. The sound of the birds and rustling of leaves in the morning breeze helps me to feel alive. I can't see them anymore but it's nice to know they're there."

Rose was fascinated as she watched Aletha serve tea. Using the sound of the spout hitting the rim of a delicate china teacup and her finger as a fill gauge, Aletha never spilled a drop. As she handed the cup to Rose, she urged her to go ahead with her meal. "Trudy popped into the kitchen just before you did and said she would be ready... now how did she phrase it... 'just as soon as her highness is finished monopolizing the bathroom!'" Rose, in the act of sipping her tea, choked as she was caught between laughing and swallowing and went into a coughing fit. Assuring herself that Rose was all right, Aletha went on. "I can't tell you what an endless delight your grandmother is to me. She is a real gem."

"Piffle!" Gert commented on hearing Aletha's tribute as she approached the table. Seating herself, she said, "If I'm a gem, it's a pearl irritating an oyster!"

Later as she was helping the two older women into her old beat-up Chevy for the trip to church, Rose felt a little embarrassed, especially after spending just one night in Aletha's immaculate beautifully furnished cottage. Aletha had explained that Tim usually came to fetch her on Sunday mornings but was sure Rose wouldn't mind driving this morning. "I do so appreciate it, Rose. I wish I could see your Betsy (Rose was thankful she could *not*) but I can hear her engine chattering merrily." Rose was sure the "chatter" was apt to be the portent of some automotive disaster but kept her mechanical evaluation to herself.

They left the property by way of the long perfectly level drive they missed the day before. Rose smiled in approval at the fresh stretch of concrete, lined on either side by fledgling redbud trees, also native to Kentucky. Rose recognized their flat rounded leaves and tried to imagine how beautiful the drive would look in five to ten years when the trees were covered in reddish-purple blooms during the spring. The drive ended in an intricately worked wrought iron gate giving access to the bypass into town. To her mind, it was the appropriate entrance for the grand Victorian house standing to receive guests on the other end of the long approach.

On the short journey into town, while providing flawless directions, Aletha recounted the history of Tinkers Well. "Early travelers west stopped here, drawn by a grove of trees in an otherwise barren plane, much like an oasis in the desert. You see, during the dry season, the smaller streams and rivers can dry up or become murky and unpalatable. But folks found a clear clean watering hole in the midst of the trees and built a well to better draw the water in buckets. Because the spring-fed well provided an endless source of fresh water, the spot became a regular stop on the trail west. There was even a Pony Express office here at one time."

"Seriously?" Rose interjected.

"Oh, yes. And because of the constant stream of people passing through, enterprising businessmen built shops, offering dry goods and sundries. People began settling here, creating the need for carpenters, smithies, and other craftsmen who serviced not only the town but wagon trains passing through and, later, railroad passengers. You wouldn't know to look at it now, but in its day, it was a hub of commerce."

"But where does the Tinker come from?" asked Rose, easily envisioning covered wagons, locomotives pulling cars full of hopeful settlers, and horses grazing under giant shade trees.

"People came here to have items, legal matters, even health issues fixed. Those who fixed them—craftsmen, lawyers, doctors—were said to 'tinker' with whatever the problem might be, and because this was the only place for miles, west of Kansas City, to find those needed skills, it became Tinkerers Well. But that didn't really roll off the tongue so it was shortened to Tinkers Well. It's not a storied town, filled with a history of famous battles, or any significant role in the Civil War—like Leavenworth or Lawrence or Mine Creek. Nor do we boast any notable residents, just a place where folks came together."

"I think it's a *wonderful* history. But you said 'in its day.' Does that mean that all those craftsmen and 'tinkerers' left or closed their businesses?"

"No, they never really closed but never expanded either. There are still small stores and services here to cater to the needs of people in the area, mostly farmers, but when the major highway systems were built, Tinkers Well was too far from the direct route between

Kansas City and Topeka to figure as a cross-country way station any more. People could travel farther in a day so they began driving from city to city on interstates instead of town to town on smaller state roads. I personally am thankful that we have avoided the building boom thus far and so have maintained a sense of community. But I fear more and more people are moving out of the big cities to small towns." Then with a resigned sigh, she added, "I suppose we must have progress but I count on young people like Tim and his friends to build new homes or, better yet, refurbish the existing ones in a way that honors the town's character."

"Aletha, you rattled that off just like a tour guide. I think you missed your calling!" commented Gert in admiration.

"I just hope I haven't missed our turning! Rose, have you seen a sign yet for Tinkers Well?"

"It's just coming up, I think…Yes, I need to turn right in half a mile."

"Precisely. Now that will take you directly to the town square. Even though this is a county seat, you won't find the courthouse in the middle of the square. The early settlers didn't want to lose the green space around the well so they created a park and built the main roads along its perimeter. We'll come in on the side by the courthouse…"

"I see it…"

"But you'll just keep going straight and turn left onto Church Street at the end of the park…"

"It's so pretty and peaceful—"

"And turn right beside Community Church. Parking is in the rear."

Rose had tried in vain to take in every detail of the town center as they drove by; first, the courthouse and government buildings on State Street, then the quaint shops lining the perpendicular street, aptly titled Commerce, and finally the buildings fronting onto Church Street. They passed an imposing brick Catholic Church and turned in by a pristinely white clapboard-sided building crowned with a steeple and cross.

Rose had no sooner parked the car than the passenger door was opened and someone was helping Aletha out. Rose could only see a hairy muscular arm but heard Aletha say, "Thank you, Tim. You see, Rose got us here just fine." As Rose alighted from the vehicle, she quickly looked to her right in time to see Tim raise his head to smile and nod in welcome. She returned the smile, noting that he cleaned up rather well. No sawdust this time, just neatly pressed khakis and a button-down shirt.

"Rose! Do you mean to forget about me every time you see that fellow?" Granny Gert bellowed in a voice that could be heard clearly in a ten-foot radius.

Wishing momentarily that the ground would open up and swallow her whole, Rose quickly turned her attention to her grandmother. She sometimes wondered if Granny Gert took a secret delight in saying outrageous things at the most inopportune moments.

Rose felt at home as soon as she walked in the church door where she was greeted by Derek, looking anything but the sweat-stained construction worker of the previous day. The dog Scout was also in attendance, sitting quietly at his feet. If she had given it any thought, Rose might have wondered at Scout's presence there instead of keeping company with his master but the notion never occurred to her. After introductions by Rose, the gregarious Derek made much of Granny Gert, paying her fulsome compliments to which she replied severely, "Save that for someone who believes it!" mitigating her severity with a wink that elicited a shout of laughter in acknowledgment.

The service was simple but meaningful. It fit neither the mold of a contemporary service—though they sang some newer songs— nor the more sober mood of a traditional service despite the inclusion of hymns and formal liturgy. It was just church and Rose found it refreshing. She couldn't quite put her finger on its uniqueness until she realized that she could actually hear the sound of her own voice— and Granny Gert's monotone—during congregational singing. No overpowering lead voice drowned out the some two-hundred others present, and none of the instruments, including the guitar, flute, and violin accompanying the piano, were amplified. It was just pure sound created by the worshippers present. Rose found the experience both novel and moving. The only magnified sound came from the pulpit mic where Tim, who was apparently the lay leader that day, led the responsive reading and read the daily scripture passages in his clear baritone voice. Pastor Lindeman preached from 2 Timothy for the first installment of a sermon series entitled "Sharing the Faith through Generations." While convicting, the short message was really only an introduction. The theme was driven home by the unexpected illuminating personal testimony that followed.

"This morning, I'd like to welcome Abraham Yousef forward to share his story of God's work in his life and how the faithfulness of a fellow believer opened the door for a miracle. Abe…"

Rose, feeling ashamed at having made the stereotypical assumption that Abraham was Muslim, glanced over at Derek and Tim who smiled encouragingly at Abe as he awkwardly mounted the steps to the platform one at a time with his right leg while dragging his artificial limb up behind. He made his way to the pulpit and, looking a bit nervous, fidgeted for a few moments with the paper he had drawn from his shirt pocket before hesitantly addressing the congregation.

"Good morning," he began in that educated voice, with a hint of accent, that seemed so at odds with his profession. "I have met many of you, but for those who don't know me, my name is Ahmad Yousef. Yes, I know the pastor called me Abraham, which is the name I go by now, but I'll explain all of that in a few minutes." He then turned to his notes, cleared his throat, and began reading.

"Imagine, if you will, utter darkness. The only sound is made by your booted feet walking across rocky ground. You feel as if you are moving toward the end of the earth. The brilliance of the stars in the night sky is sporadically blocked by drifting clouds so you rely on your night-vision goggles to illuminate the shadows. Instead they cast everything into a monochromatic green-gray scale like a scene in an old movie. You know your squad mates are nearby, moving in predetermined intervals, but there is an implicit loneliness in the silence necessary to detect any movement other than your own.

Suddenly the darkness and silence are shattered by incoming mortar rounds. You scramble for cover as you try to determine what direction the rounds are coming from. Someone calls for a fire mission. After a bombardment of the nearby high ground, the shelling stops and darkness and silence once again prevail. You make a hasty retreat to the rally point where a quick head count is made to determine if there are any casualties. Though hearts are racing and limbs are shaking from the sudden adrenaline rush, everyone is safe. As dawn creeps over the mountaintops into the valley of your area of operations, you return, weary but alive, to the observation post as another platoon prepares to head out on patrol. The cycle repeats itself *over* and *over* again until your platoon is rotated back to the company outpost."

The congregation sat mesmerized by Abe's narration. He had taken everyone to a place that most had never been. Of all those present, Aletha, in her blindness, probably had the clearest picture besides Tim and Derek and other veterans present who had inhabited that world themselves.

"Fear is a constant companion. The only respite is sleep and the occasional package from home, bringing reminders of the life and loved ones left behind. But fear is not an end in itself. It sharpens our senses and has the ability to drive us to extremes, whether that be into a pursuit of excellence at our jobs—which can be *very* helpful in a combat situation," he added on a lighthearted note, momentarily relieving the tension in the sanctuary and drawing a few appreciative chuckles, "or into emotional immobility or, in my case, into an intense awareness of my faith as it related to a very possible death.

"You see, I was a devout Muslim. I was raised in a Muslim home and, unlike the Christian faith that a believer *chooses* to follow, my faith in the Allah of Islam was considered a birthright. I was the eldest of five children, having immigrated to the United States from Lebanon when I was ten, just a year before 9-11. And though my parents were peace-loving Muslims who abhorred and renounced the attacks, the backlash of mistrust against the Muslim community in general, which was understandable given the circumstances of the event, drove them further into their faith. I studied the Qur'an with the imam of our mosque while, at the same time, attending public schools so I grew up with this juxtaposition of two cultures. After I finished university, I was expected to follow my father into a professional field. He was an engineer. My degree was in computer science and technology.

"But while at university, I met some fellow students planning to enter the military. They wanted to serve their country, they said. By this time, the United States *was* my country, all of my family having received their citizenship of which they were very proud. I decided I would show *everyone* that a Muslim could be a good American too. So without discussing it with my parents, I enlisted in the army. They were *not* happy. 'This is *not* for you,' they said. 'You are wasting your education. You are not setting a good example for your younger brothers and sisters. You will be fighting against other Muslims. This cannot please Allah.'"

Looking up from his notes, Abe added as an aside, "Never mind that Muslims have been fighting other Muslims for *centuries*." Then he looked back at his notes. "And worst of all, 'How will you have the opportunity to do all that Allah demands of you to enter heaven?' You see, in Islam the good deeds of the faithful must outweigh the bad to have a chance of going to heaven. The most important of these deeds are the Five Pillars of Faith that include witness, the giving of alms to the poor and the mosque—what you might call tithing—daily prayers—five times a day, every day—fasting, and a pilgrimage to Mecca. These are not optional—they are *mandatory* to even be *considered* worthy of the rewards of heaven. Christians pray, speak openly of their faith, and help those in need out of love for all that God has done for them. Muslims do it out of fear.

"I tell you all of this so you will understand my mindset when I was deployed to Afghanistan a few years ago. I had never lived with the very real possibility of death on a daily basis before. I watched the other men in my squad and platoon. When I had time to process it, I thought about the way they reacted in firefights, how they behaved in our downtime, and their demeanor under prolonged stress.

"And one man stood out. He was as loud and profane— unfortunately profanity often surfaces when confronted with heart-stopping terror—as anyone else and as intense and watchful while

73

on patrol, but when we returned to the OP or the COP, he had a peace that enveloped him like a cloud. He laughed and joked with the others but something about him was different. I saw him reading a Bible one day so I asked him if he was a man of faith. He said he was a Christian, and I explained that I was a Muslim. Then he did something totally unexpected. He asked me about *my* faith. I immediately felt defensive, suspecting a theological trap, but he just listened intently and told me he would like to learn more about Islam. Aha! I thought. A possible convert—*big* points on the credit side of my deeds ledger! So I would speak to him at every opportunity, sharing my concern of dying without an assured place in heaven. He continued to ask more about my personal faith and relationship with Allah until I felt compelled, by common courtesy, to ask about his.

"Did he not fear death as I did? 'Oh, I fear death, all right,' he said, 'because I'd really like to make it home to see my mama again and maybe find a cute girl, get married, have kids. I know you do too but the difference is that whether all those things happen or God decides to call me home tomorrow, I *know* where I'm going because the price for all my mistakes has already been paid. There isn't anything I can *do* that will change that. So I could live another sixty years on this earth or leave it right now. Either way, I *will* spend eternity with Jesus.'" He looked up again, this time with a big smile. "Then *I* started asking all the questions!" This drew responsive smiles from the captivated audience.

"I fought hard against giving any credence to this Christianity. I had been taught that Jesus was a real person in history, a prophet, but the Qur'an teaches that it is wrong to believe that God has begotten a son. You can see how difficult it is for a Muslim to accept the idea that Jesus is the Son of God. But what I did *not* know was that this man had started praying for my salvation. Talk about stacking the deck! He gave me *his* Bible to read. We discussed many passages. I was especially interested in the stories of Abraham, a common figure in the history of Judaism, Christianity, *and* Islam where he is called Ibrahim."

He paused for a few moments, took a deep breath, and spoke quietly with evident emotion. "Finally I ran out of arguments, and one night, this man helped me to pray and ask Jesus to be my Lord and Savior." Abe paused again, trying to master control of his voice. There were few dry eyes in the church. "I can't *tell* you what peace I felt. It was as if a weight had been lifted from my heart. I don't mean to make light of any of your own decisions to follow Christ but I tell you that for someone who has lived his *whole* life believing in a tragic lie—a lie laden with guilt and fear—the freedom of forgiveness and grace I experienced..." His voice was momentarily suspended. After a few moments, he began again. "The life of Abraham was an early distortion of God's story by the prophet Muhammad. Muslims believe Abraham and his son, Ishmael, the father of the Arab race, built the Kaaba, the holiest of Muslim worship sites, under the direction of Allah centuries before the birth of Muhammad. The sacred black stone was actually the site of ancient pagan worship. When he conquered Mecca, Muhammad simply destroyed the pagan idols and rededicated it to the worship of Allah, then attributed its history to a recognized historical figure[1]. You must understand that *Allah* is simply the Arabic word for God, but make no mistake, the god Allah, lower case g is not *the* God Yahweh. The truth is that through Abraham's son, *Isaac*, God established the earthly ancestry of Jesus, the Messiah, my Savior. I chose to be called Abraham so that if people ask me about my name, I can set them straight. And I would change it *officially* if I could just get Tim Ludlow to *pay* me enough for the legal fees." Rose snuck a peep at Tim to see him grinning even as he brushed tears from his eyes. "Before I go on, I would humbly ask that you pray for the millions of Muslims all over the world that they might know the truth and, as Jesus said, 'Be set free.'

"Now you need to know the rest of the story," Abe continued more evenly. "The *next day*, we were on patrol in an area affected by the drawdown of US troops in country. We were providing security for departing units, covering too much territory with too few men. We received incoming fire. But our luck had run out. One of our men was killed. I took a hit that shattered my knee. By the time we

---

[1]. "The Call of Muhammad," *The Dispatch from Jerusalem* (reprinted from Second Quarter 1990 issue) a publication of Bridges for Peace, Tulsa OK.

could get covering fire and draw back to safety—we both had to be carried out—I was unconscious from pain and loss of blood. I was airlifted to Germany, then spent several months at Walter Reed for multiple surgeries and rehab. I had lost my left leg from midthigh down."

"My family met me at the hospital in Virginia. It was there I told them of my faith in Christ. Nothing prepared me for their reaction. I expected disappointment, even anger, but I never expected their *total* rejection." Abe paused once again. "I learned very early in my faith walk what it means to leave Father and Mother, take up my cross, and follow Jesus." Abe stopped to wipe his eyes before continuing. "First my parents told me it was surely Allah's will that I received punishment, in the form of a lost limb, for my wicked heresy. Then they told me that I was no longer a member of their family. I would only be welcomed home when I came to my senses and returned to the faith of my birth." The whole congregation was with him now, willing Abe to complete his story through the emotion that threatened to overwhelm him.

"I tell you now, as God is my witness, that the pain, the alienation, the loss of my personal faith history is *nothing* compared to the incomparable peace and assurance I have found in Jesus Christ." The church burst into applause. They stood as one to honor the courage and faith of young Abraham. He motioned for their silence with one hand as he took the wireless mic out of the mic stand and moved over to the center of the platform.

"Please, please, there is a little more." As everyone resumed their seats, he finished with a bombshell. "Because of the compassion, patience, and perseverance of one faithful man, I now have a new home and family and a future here on earth *and* in eternity. He shared his faith…his heart…and, most importantly, his Savior with me. He was my platoon leader. His name…is First Lieutenant… Derek Warner." The stunned congregation watched Derek join Abe on the platform. As the two friends shared a bear hug, the room erupted in cheers. Even Granny Gert was beaming and she was not one easily swayed by sentiment.

Pastor Lindeman looked dumbfounded. He was apparently as surprised as everyone else. He knew that Abe and Derek had both served in the army but had never put all the pieces together before. After embracing Abraham and Derek in turn, he managed to regain control of the congregation. "Wow! Thank you, Abraham, for sharing that incredible story. And thank *you*, Derek, for your obedient witness." Turning to the congregation, he said, "Wow! If that didn't inspire you, you weren't listening! Now let me hear you sing the closing song like you *mean* it."

Those gathered for worship that day sang with more passion, more volume, and more joy than they had in some time. Rose, accompanied by the musicians who continued to play, was softly singing the last verse of the song again as they made their way to the vestibule after the benediction.

No guilt in life, no fear in death. This is the power of Christ in me.
From life's first cry to final breath Jesus commands my destiny.
No power of hell, no scheme of man can ever pluck me from His hand.
Till He returns or calls me home, here in the power of Christ I'll stand.

"Well, Pastor. If the service is like this every Sunday, you can count me in!" said Gert as they filed out of the building.

Retaining a clasp on her hand, he smiled, looked her directly in the eyes, and said, "I'll hold you to it." Rose committed to ensuring they both kept that promise.

*****

Dinner at the Ludlow home was a somewhat-bewildering parade of faces and names but everyone was very friendly. Their hostess, Marilyn, kindly led Aletha and Granny Gert to the dining room where Aletha was greeted by several other elderly friends who instantly included Gert in their social circle.

[2.] Keith Getty, Stuart Townend, "In Christ Alone" (Thankyou Music [administered at CapitolCMGPublishing.com], 2002). Used by permission.

"Gertie, is it? Have a seat, Gertie. We won't expect you to remember our names all at once…"

Marilyn then introduced Rose to the musicians and their families and the pastor's wife and children who only slowed down long enough to grin at Rose before running outside where the youngest generation was holding court around a large picnic table. Marilyn, noticing that Rose was looking a little overwhelmed, invited the younger woman to sit next to her on a soft cream-colored sofa. Rose had been a little shy of meeting Tim's mother but she needn't have worried. In less than no time, the two were chatting like old friends.

"Tim told me that you two met at the big house yesterday. You mustn't mind him when he puts on his lord-of-the-manor act," she said, eerily echoing Aletha's comments. "But from what he said, you held your own. Good for you!" She smiled at the blush rising in Rose's cheeks. Tim had told her about that too. "He really is concerned about someone snooping around and getting hurt before he can stabilize the dated structure."

"Oh, I know. And I probably shouldn't have walked up to the door, but honestly, I was so blown away by the…*grandeur* of that gorgeous old place that I didn't really notice the condition it was in." By way of explanation, she added, "Granny Gert says that I always look at life through rose-colored glasses."

"Well, *I say* the world needs more people like you and fewer that insist on filling every silver lining with a cloud! Now I've managed to put a smile on your face and a bloom in your cheeks just in time to greet the guests of honor."

Rose turned to see Abraham and Derek enter the house with Tim a distant third and Scout bringing up the rear. It was nice to see some familiar faces, and after Abe's testimony, she felt that she knew them a little better than she had from the brief introduction on the previous day. She certainly respected them and appreciated the sacrifice they had all made in military service. But Abe's faith story had really touched her heart.

Derek yelled out, "Okay, we can start the party now!" On impulse, Rose stood as the room at large greeted them and surprised everyone, herself included, by hugging first Abraham and then

Derek. Looking from one to the other, she said with tears in her eyes, "I didn't know yesterday, when you said I could be your sister and your friend, just what you meant or what a privilege it would be."

"That's got to be one of the nicest things anyone has said to me for a long time," Derek said at his gallant best. Then with characteristic attitude, he added, "But if you're going to make folks cry every time you open your mouth, we're going to have to ask you to leave!" A watery chuckle greeted this sally. "All right then, let's eat."

"Your halo's so tight you forgot something, Warner." This from Tim who had watched the exchange with a strange warmth in his heart. It was Rose's impulsive gesture and genuine sincerity that had put it there.

"Sweetheart, will you do the honors," called Marilyn from across the room. She had gathered the kids in from the backyard and Tim stood in the doorway to the dining room so everyone could hear.

"Father God, thank you for food that smells fabulous, for the loving hands that prepared it, and for fellow believers who share the faith and their lives." A collective "Amen" signaled a sprint by the young and nimble to the kitchen to get first dibs on the chicken legs.

After filling her plate with fried chicken, mashed potatoes, beans, carrots, and a deviled egg, Rose checked in on Granny Gert. She found Marilyn Ludlow placing brimming serving dishes on the table in the dining room, enabling the older members of the party to simply pass food around the table and serve each other home-style rather than trying to maneuver through a buffet line.

"What a great idea," Rose commented as Marilyn passed her on the way back to the kitchen.

"I wish I could take credit for inspired genius," Marilyn responded with a smile. "But it was suggested by a dear friend who, unfortunately, couldn't be here today. The process has proven to be simpler for both the seniors and for me. Now, why don't you join the heroes of the hour." She indicated the three young men sitting around the coffee table.

As if sensing eyes on him, Derek looked up from a heaping plate and spoke across the room to Rose. "I told you your granny was in good hands so come on over and join us for lunch." Abe, in the act of stuffing a ham roll in his mouth, waved enthusiastically, and Tim rose to come take her plate, politely gesturing her to go before him to the couch. Everything neatly settled, Rose felt at leisure to accept the invitation.

During the meal, the three friends kept her laughing so much with their constant competition for floor time and trying to one-up each other or provide caustic comments about whatever story another was telling that she found it a challenge to actually consume any of the delicious food. She contributed little to the conversation, other than acting as arbiter over a disputed point, but enjoyed herself immensely.

As she shared the moment with the three men, Rose compared it to relationships with others of the male population. She had had lots of male friends growing up. She had felt the inevitable crush on one boy or another during early adolescence, only to discover that her chosen idol had feet of clay in the form of stupid jokes, disgusting habits that only other boys found impressive, or, more probably, a lamentable lack of interest in her.

By the time she was old enough to date in high school, the awkward, self-conscious, immature boys that comprised here dating pool were cast into relative obscurity by her favorite heroes of fiction. A young teenaged swain with acne and braces, however personable, was no match for a literary leading man like Mr. Knightly or Heathcliff or even Gilbert Blythe. So she unwittingly left many disappointed suitors in her wake. For though she failed to recognize the dating potential of her male peers, she was universally admired for her unpretentious prettiness and easygoing personality. And because she met the same callous youths in her college classes, she was content to simply fill the role of friend to her male contemporaries, unwilling to settle for less than her romantic ideal. Her mother and older sisters cautioned her that heroes of fiction rarely exist in reality. But Rose, ever the optimist, refused to believe that the man of her dreams wasn't waiting around some, as yet, undiscovered corner. She had never felt anxious about meeting Mr. Right but, unconsciously or not, held every man she met to the unrealistic exacting standard she had set.

It wasn't until she and Granny Gert broke their journey west that first night that the acme of male perfection had strolled into her orbit in the unlikeliest of places—the dining room of The Pickle Barrel. He had checked off nearly every requirement on her list: handsome, sophisticated, charming, and well-mannered despite Granny Gert's remarks. However, even as she recognized his manifold attributes, Rose knew he was just passing through her life like any chance-met stranger. At least he had given her hope that such men actually existed.

Fresh from that encounter, she had been greeted by a hostile filthy antagonist in a moment when her heart, like warm putty, was smitten by the old Victorian mansion and all the romance it evoked. He had verbally assaulted her and stomped on her dreams, and although he had apologized with apparent sincerity and humility, Rose couldn't help comparing the two men. Had it not been for the stranger, Tim might have figured more prominently in her esteem. He really was quite attractive, having shed a perpetual layer of dirt and sawdust, but his appeal went deeper than superficial appearance. He wore the hallmarks of life experience in the rough callouses on his hands, the defined lines at the edges of his deep-set blue eyes, and in the sturdy breadth of his shoulders that had born the mantle of leadership. Unfortunately Tim lacked the charm that flowed so effortlessly from the man who had set the gold standard for Rose, making him appear either incapable or unwilling to converse with her when Derek and Abe left them to refill their plates. Little did Rose know that while she wondered at his mute attitude, Tim sat in an agony of insecurity trying to think of some clever remark to jumpstart a one-on-one conversation with her. While Derek and Abe were present to keep the verbal ball rolling, talking freely had been almost effortless; but at their departure (*Those sorry losers*, Tim thought), he became suddenly tongue-tied and shy.

After a few moments of awkward silence, Rose ventured a comment on the inspired novelty of the house's interior. It truly was food for her whimsical soul. Marilyn Ludlow possessed a natural flair for decorating. But unlike the planned perfection and coordinated furnishings of Fern Cottage, the totally *un*coordinated furniture pieces, artwork, and hangings mixed so brilliantly by Marilyn displayed a genius for making the ordinary exceptional. A rustic coffee table covered with minimal bric-a-brac and an oil lamp sat atop a plush oriental rug. Two stuffed coarse burlap bags leaned against the wall in one corner under a ficus tree adorned with colorful nonseasonal ornaments. Thrift store lamps and old pottery on the fireplace mantle blended effortlessly with a central crystal chandelier. The Jacobean floral window treatments (that Rose later learned had been made by Marilyn) shared the living space with large checked sofa pillows and their smaller paisley neighbors. Rose felt like she had walked into a cover spread for *Southern Home* or at least a collection of the best of IdeaTag.com. It struck her that, in comparison, Aletha's carefully crafted Victorian showplace—though exquisitely decorated—was somehow less homelike than this eclectic decor of harmonious chaos.

"I really admire your mom's ability to put all these dissimilar things together and make them feel so cohesive. I just love it," Rose said with simple honesty.

That finally drew a reaction from Tim. Grinning, he said, "My mom could never pass up a discarded piece of furniture or scrap of fabric. It drove my dad nuts when we had to drag home some piece of junk every time we traveled anywhere. He would just shake his head and find somewhere to stuff it in the back of the car. But I have to admit, she usually turned it into something special."

"I'll say! I think it's great. I wish I had an eye for discovering beauty in the broken," Rose said with a wistful sigh.

At that, Time cocked his head to one side, as if assessing some quality, and said to her, "But I think you do."

Somewhat taken aback, she looked at him, a question in her eyes.

"I saw the way you responded to Abe's story. Talk about someone who was broken."

"Yes, but I think pretty much everyone felt the way I did about that."

"Maybe but I've also seen the way you look after your grandmother," Tim said, glancing toward the dining room. "It can't have been easy driving her out here."

Rose opened her mouth to speak but was forestalled by his lifted brow, demanding an honest response. She smiled ruefully. "No, it wasn't exactly *easy* but she's only difficult when she's tired or unsure in unfamiliar situations. Besides I love her dearly and really do enjoy spending time with her."

"You know, I believe you. But there aren't many people in our generation that can appreciate the intrinsic worth and societal contributions of the elderly."

"Well, I don't know about that, but if it wasn't for Granny Gert, I wouldn't be here in Tinkers Well."

"If that's the case, then God bless Granny Gert." As Tim spoke, he reached out and gently squeezed her fingers, gazing directly into her eyes with a look that was at once intense and diffident.

Rose, momentarily bereft of speech, was spared the necessity of answering him when he stood and looked across the room, saying, "I see Mrs. Gunn headed this way. I'd better hit the road before she accuses me of monopolizing your time."

Too late.

"I figured as much," Gert said, fixing Tim with a pointed stare. "Sonny, you'll excuse an old woman's rudeness if I reclaim my granddaughter now," thus rendering silent the young man towering over her. "It's time to go, Rosie. Come say your thank-yous to our kind hostess."

Mortified with embarrassment, Rose followed in Gert's forceful wake, glancing quickly at Tim in apology, only to see him grin and shoot her a conspiratorial wink.

Duly bidding Marilyn farewell, Rose was a bit surprised to receive a kiss on the cheek and a friendly hug. "You are both welcome here any time, and I insist you accept my standing invitation to Sunday dinner."

Driving Granny Gert and Aletha back to Fern Cottage, Rose mused over the events, people, and places of the past few days. The sum of them all might not add up to a great adventure, but collectively, they promised a pleasant way to pass the summer, allowing her to postpone, at least for a little while, the dreaded question of "What comes next in my life?."

Had she known the answer, she might have loaded Granny Gert into the old Chevy and headed straight back to Kentucky, her heart and delusions still intact.

But life is a lesson that must be learned one day at a time.

CHAPTER 6

I was a stranger and you invited me in.

—Matthew 25:35b (NIV)

Rose flipped her pillow to the cool side, fluffed it, and snuggled her head back into its downy softness, hoping to recapture the last elusive moments of sleep. But the insistent sunshine and her own internal clock, still running on eastern time, won the day. Accepting defeat in the sleep stakes, she focused instead on the enticing aroma of fresh coffee and cinnamon rolls (she fervently hoped) wafting down the hall from the kitchen. She didnt know *how* a blind woman managed so well on her own but nothing about Aletha surprised her now.

An unexpected stranger in the kitchen, however, did.

Rose stopped in the arched doorway, unsure of whether to enter. A woman of indeterminate age—anywhere from forty-five to fifty-five—her head wrapped in a floral scarf, stood before the big farmhouse sink perpendicular to the hallway. She swayed rhythmically while humming a syncopated tune, her smooth mocha-colored arms and hands moving with dance-like grace even in the prosaic act of breaking eggs into a bowl. Like a hibiscus bloom thrust into a bowl of field daisies, this woman, in her brightly patterned dress, feet clad in worn espadrilles, was an anachronism in the carefully recreated period kitchen. But an intriguing one. Unaware of the girl's presence, she glanced toward the doorway after retrieving some spices from a rack to the left of the sink. Surprised out of her solitary preoccupation by the sight of a newcomer, she threw up her hands, almost dropping the spices.

"Lawks, child, you nearly scared me to death!" Then recovering, she laughed and said, "You must be Rose," and flashed a brilliant smile that reminded Rose of someone.

"Um…*yes*. Do I *know* you?"

"I'm sorry, child," the other said, still smiling. "It's just that we've been expectin' you for a few months now, but you probably only expected to meet Aletha so we have the advantage."

"We?"

"I *am* doing a sad job of introducin' myself. Please forgive a foolish woman. My name is Angelica Warner and I too would like to welcome you to Fern Cottage. I believe you met my son, Derek, on Saturday."

Rose was so captivated by the lilting almost-melodic accent, with its broadly flattened vowels and clipped *R*s, that she nearly missed the names. Warner. Derek. The coin dropped. "*Oh*. That's why you looked familiar. It's your smile, and I think"—Rose paused in consideration—"your facial features too, maybe." The nose was finely drawn with rounded rather than flared nostrils and the lips full without being protuberant.

Laughing, the older woman said, "Well, don't tell Derek that. He's more interested in the size of his muscles!" She continued breakfast preparations as she spoke.

Rose had been right about the cinnamon rolls but their heavenly spicy scent was almost eclipsed by the bacon sizzling on the stove. The gastronomic sights and smells of the room would have adorned any kitchen but even a TV chef might feel right at home here. The space was deceptively large but made smaller by the cozy trappings. During the house tour on their arrival day, Rose had noted with delight the perfect mix of gingham café curtains—now lit with morning sun—natural stone floor, and a gaily patterned wallpaper border just above the top of the custom cabinets, cleverly making the ceiling appear lower. She was most enchanted by the reproduction black enamel gas range in a brick alcove. It looked like an antique but Rose knew (from hours spent in home improvement stores with her father) that it was both state of the art and cost the earth. The final touch that gave the room its warmth, and a little authenticity, was an old wooden table placed in the center, topped with worn butcher block.

Looking around with supreme satisfaction, Rose murmured under her breath, "This really *is* the heart of the home."

Angelica, smiling in agreeable appreciation, motioned the girl to a seat at the table and sat a piping hot mug of coffee in front of her. "Let me guess. A little sugar and some creamer. Vanilla or hazelnut?"

"Mmm, this is good," Rose said, sipping the hazelnut-infused liquid. "And I can't tell you how amazing everything smells. Do you cook like this for Aletha *every* day?"

"Well, yes, I come in most mornin's to help Aletha with breakfast and household chores but she won't hear of me comin' in on Sundays—says 'that's the mornin' you should spend with your boys.'"

"Oh, I didn't realize. You have *another* son. Derek didn't mention any brothers other than the brothers he works with, Tim and Abraham, and I didn't notice anyone else sitting with him at church yesterday. I didn't see you either, for that matter." It was a statement and a question.

"Well, the reason you didn't see me in church was that I was volunteerin' in the nursery—I just love holdin' those babies. But I *was* standin' in the back of the sanctuary durin' Abraham's talk," Angelica explained. "I wouldn't have missed that for the world!" Smiling a little mistily, she added, "I don't know when I've been more proud of those fine young men. And as for my other son, that's Abraham. You see, Abraham lives with Derek and me so I think of him as my son too. And he has been such a blessing."

"So when he spoke about a new home and family, he meant Derek and you, not Derek and Tim…"

"No, it was Derek and *Tim* that invited him to make his home in Tinkers Well and join them in their business, God love 'em both, but Marilyn—I believe you met her yesterday—was still a recent widow. I thought it best to give her some time with Tim to grieve her husband, Peter, so Derek and I took Abraham in. And, of course, the three boys all work together." Laughing as Rose raised her eyebrows and shook her head, Angelica went on, "I know it must be a little confusin' to sort out all o' these new names and faces but I reckon it'll all fall into place when you get to know us a bit better."

"I look forward to that." Rose sipped her coffee and watched in appreciation as the older woman's beautiful hands turned chopping, flipping, and stirring into a waltz of flowing movement. "I'm surprised Aletha isn't shaped more like Granny Gert if she eats all of this *almost* every day."

"Well, I wish she *would* but she eats like a bird so I only have the privilege of fixin' a proper breakfast for special occasions, and believe me, your visit is very special. She has been lookin' forward to your arrival for weeks."

"I know Gran's been excited about it too. It's so funny to listen to them talk about the days they were at school together. I haven't heard my grandmother laugh so much in a long time."

"Well, I think as folks grow older, they have fewer people to share their memories with, you know, especially those memories from long ago. She won't let on but I know Aletha gets awful lonely sometimes since Matthew's death last year. I've offered many a time to stay and sit with her after insistin' she eat a good hot lunch but she's a proud woman and still wants her independence, bless her," she said.

Rose asked hesitantly, "I know it's none of my business but I'm just curious…because of your, well…unusual accent. Where are you from? Surely not Tinkers Well…"

"Heavens, no! And I don't mind you askin' at all. I'm originally from Jamaica but my family immigrated to Chicago when I was a young woman. That's where I met Derek's father, you know. He was the love of my life—and full of life too! Why that man could fill a room just by walkin' in the door. That's where Derek got his personality," she said, again flashing that wonderful smile. More quietly, she added, "Derek also got his strength and integrity from my Isaiah." Her face lost its light for a few moments and her hands stilled in the act of whisking eggs. Rose waited quietly for her to continue.

"I'm afraid we lost him when Derek was a teenager, but I still miss him every day…" She spoke softly, looking into the past. An ill-concealed sneeze from Rose brought Angelica back to the present and the task at hand. "My goodness, I didn't mean to burden you with all o' that. Rose, you must have the gift of listenin', I think. But don't you mind me. I have a good life here with Derek and Aletha and all the kind folks who've made me feel welcome. Now I'm about ready to get this feast together. Why don't you get your granny and join us in the gazebo. I woke Aletha just before you came in so let's start the day with a party. Okay?"

And a party it was. Great food, good friends, and the leisure to enjoy them. When Angelica quietly started clearing the table, Rose jumped up to help her. As they gathered dishes and serving plates, Gert was in full spate, recounting yet another incident highlighting Aletha's hopelessness as a cook.

"You nearly burned down the dormitory and you were just trying to make *toast*."

With feigned indignation, Aletha responded, "Now, Trudy, you know you're exaggerating—"

"Exaggerating! Why, there was so much smoke, the whole volunteer fire department showed up!"

"Yes, but weren't the firemen *handsome* in their uniforms?" Aletha answered innocently with a twinkle in those beautiful sightless eyes.

Rose was still laughing as she and Angelica entered the kitchen. "I think those two could go on talking forever and never run out of stories!" Then glancing at the clock, she was surprised to see that it was after ten o'clock. "Good grief! I never stay in my pajamas this late," she said to Angelica, a little embarrassed.

"Do you have anywhere you need to be?"

"No…but I feel like I should be doing…*something* useful."

"*Useful?* Child, you are giving two old dears a priceless gift. Not many of us have that privilege in a lifetime."

"Oh, I know, and I really am happy that they have this time together, but I can see that I'm going to have to find something to occupy *my* time or I'll become completely *useless*."

"I'll tell you what, after lunch, Aletha usually takes a nap, and I fancy your gran will too, so why don't you and I put our heads together over a nice pot o' tea and see what we can come up with. Now why don't you go and get dressed while I finish the washin' up."

Rose started to argue and insist on staying to help when the doorbell intervened.

"Now who can that be? We aren't expectin' anyone and the boys would just come right on in…"

"I'll get it, Angelica. At least let me do that for you." She hurried off before the other woman could protest. Rose assumed the "boys" Angelica referred to were Derek, Abe, and Tim. She conceded, grudgingly, to a slight sense of disappointment that it wouldn't be Tim. When she opened the door, however, the disappointment was relegated abruptly to ancient history.

*****

Three Brothers Construction, Inc. always made an early start, allowing them to beat some of the Kansas heat and squeeze a few more working hours out of a day.

"We should be able to finish the Bennett place today," Tim said to Derek as they loaded the truck in their garage/storage building cum office. The rented building, formerly a gas station on the edge of town, was filled to overflowing on one end with salvaged building supplies and shelves of tools lined the back wall. The small office space in front had been opened up by removing the wall separating it from the maintenance bays. It was a functional space and afforded them a place to hang their business sign so folks could find them. "Then I guess we need to get started on that reno for the diner. I promised Milly we'd have it finished by the time school starts. Hey, Abe, the skiff dumpster's being delivered today, right?" A silent thumbs-up was the only answer from his friend perched in front of a computer in the front corner.

"Tim, why don't you let me get started at Milly's—you know I love demo—and you can finish the floor of the porch at the big house. That way, we'll have a solid covered place to stack materials while we're working our way in."

"Look, Aletha basically told me to give priority to projects in town. Besides Abe's still got to order everything from the inventory we did Saturday."

"Working on it now, Cap'n," Abe interjected.

"Yeah, yeah, but if you spend a little more time at the big house, you *might* just run into that sweet Rose we met." Derek argued, careful not to catch Tim's eye.

"Dude, I just met the girl a few days ago and I didn't exactly overwhelm her with my charm," Tim replied with heavy sarcasm. "Besides she's here to visit Aletha, not hang out with a guy covered in sawdust and sweat. And you know how…awkward I am around women. I always seem to say the wrong thing and…well…oh, forget it." He ended in frustrated self-doubt.

"Man, you never give yourself a *chance*. It looked like you were getting along just fine at lunch yesterday."

"Yeah, but that was in a group of people. That was until you two traitors deserted me and I suddenly became the town mute."

"Don't blame me, boss, it was *his* idea," yelled Abe who had been straining to follow the conversation from his desk."

"That's it. Just throw your old buddy under the bus," Derek yelled back, hands on hips. "You might as well just wipe that grin off your face because I didn't hear you saying (in a perfect imitation of Abe's rich cultured accent), 'No, I don't believe I desire any thirds, thank you.'"

Laughing in spite of himself, Tim shook his head and said, "I don't know how we get *anything* done around here!"

Fixing his attention on Tim again, Derek replied, "Because your partners know what's best for you, even if you don't."

"Are we back to that again? Look, I know you're just *trying* to be helpful but I'm sure Rose has plenty of men in Kentucky interested in her already. Men who aren't so…rough around the edges.

"So you spent six years in the army, living with a bunch of dirty stinking guys with hardly any social graces—"

"*Hardly any*? Those guys had never even *heard* of social graces!"

"Well, maybe not but you're not necessarily those guys." Derek's engaging grin appeared. "Statistically you're quite a catch." Then speaking in his best radio announcer voice, he said, "Former army captain, combat vet, business owner." He reverted to the natural Derek at Tim's smirk. "Heck, I don't know why women aren't lined up around the block to go out with you." Shouting toward the corner, "Hey, back me up, Abe."

"Ordinarily I make it a point *never* to agree with the LT but I'll make an exception this time." Abraham's grin reflected his friend's. He had joined the other two at the truck, now adding more sincerely, "Derek's right, you know. You should have a little faith in yourself. Look, if you can lead a company of soldiers in battle, start your own business, and take care of your widowed mother, you can surely muster the courage to ask out a nice girl like Rose."

Still filled with insecurity, Tim looked from one encouraging face to another, laughed, and threw up his hands in mock surrender. "Okay, okay, I give up! Though I don't know *why* I should take advice from two other hopeless bachelors. I'll go by the old house this afternoon *after* I help you start the demo at Milly's," he said to Derek who rendered a mock salute, "and I'll invite Rose out for coffee or something and try to convince her that I'm Prince Charming, Superman, and St. Peter all rolled into one."

Abraham suggested Tim throw a clean shirt in the truck, then saw his buddies off to their first scheduled stop at the Bennett's. Still holding onto the lead of the ever-present Scout, who had a tendency to run after the truck, he bowed his head and prayed softly, "Dear Lord, bless my brother Tim. Please fill his heart with courage and kindness and guide his path. Amen." He and Scout turned deliberately and went back to work.

*****

Rose opened the door and froze into sudden immobility. It was him. The man from The Pickle Barrel. The gorgeous, elegant, well-dressed, charming man from The Pickle Barrel. She tried to say something but her lips refused to move. Fortunately the newcomer was not likewise afflicted. He smiled, trying to conceal his amusement, and said in pleasant, well-modulated tones, "Good morning. My name is Simon Applegate and I'm here to see Aletha Mason, if she is available."

He looked inquiringly at Rose, whose knees felt like warm butter, but she was too moonstruck for rational speech. He tried another tack. "Do I have the pleasure of addressing Mrs. Mason?" Rose's only response was a snort of laughter. She continued to look at the man, smiling like a dumb simpleton.

"I apologize for not making an appointment. Should I call again at some other time?"

The threat of his imminent departure finally kicked her brain into gear and she managed to utter, in a voice she hardly recognized, "Oh, n-no...I-I...th-that is..." She was suddenly overcome by a fit of giggles that she quickly stifled. Gathering her scattered wits, she assumed a poised stance and said calmly, "It's you. I mean, you're him." She looked at him as if she had spoken words of supreme significance and expected him to respond accordingly.

He thought for a moment that he had strayed into Bedlam. Had Miles Hawthorne sent him on some kind of sadistic wild goose chase? Yet something about this disheveled young woman adorned in worn flannel pajamas, with her ponytail wildly askew, tickled a shadowy memory. A recent memory. But try as he might, he could not recall any interaction with a village idiot of late. In fact, the only eccentric that had crossed his path in the past few weeks was the ancient gorgon he had encountered at that deplorable eatery outside St. Louis, and though sadly simple, this girl was no ancient. She was young and might even be quite pretty if properly attired. Quite pretty. The shadowy memory was pushing its way to the fore. He was about to put it all together when Gert walked up behind Rose and he realized with horror that the gorgon had reappeared and the half-witted girl standing before him must be the old woman's traveling companion.

Oh god, he thought to himself, *Can* this *be Aletha Mason?*

"May I help you, young man?" Gert asked in her booming voice. Her hostile hawk-like appraisal unnerved him as Hawthorne's had not. The telltale blush rushed into Rose's cheeks as she perceived her grandmother's presence with dismay.

Turning a smile on the old lady that was calculated to penetrate the strongest armor, Atherton replied with all the charisma at his disposal. "Good morning, madame. Simon *Applegate* at your service," he said, bowing slightly. "You must be Mrs. Aletha Mason. I hope I—"

"Well, you're out there, mister. *I'm* Gertrude Gunn and I don't *need* your service. Now state your business."

"Granny Gert," Rose spoke softly out of the side of her mouth, moving her eyes significantly in Simon's direction. "Mr. Applegate is here to see Aletha. Don't you remember his kindness to us at the restaurant on Friday? *Shouldn't we invite him in?*"

Realizing his talents were wasted on the old woman, he addressed the granddaughter who had proven herself again to be both verbal and ridiculously susceptible. "Thank you for your kindness, Ms.... er...Gunn?"

Blushing even more furiously, Rose managed to stutter, "N-n-no. It's Th-Thompson." She gulped and continued, trying to ignore his direct gaze. "B-but you can c-call me R-r-rose," she added, darting a shy glance at his dreamy eyes.

"Rosie!" A swift smack between her shoulder blades brought Rose cruelly but effectively out of her daydream. She glowered at Granny Gert who chose to ignore her. "You can come in, young fellow, but you sit right here"—motioning to the most uncomfortable chair in the living room—"while I get Aletha. You come with me, young lady." Rose continued smiling at Simon as she was dragged out of the room.

Thrust purposely into their shared guest room, Gert admonished Rose to think twice about entertaining strange men looking like a dowdy and went in search of Aletha. Rose had to admit the wisdom of Granny Gert's words. She felt sick when she looked in the mirror and realized how frumpy she had appeared when greeting the most attractive man she had ever met. And because she had little faith in his continued presence at Fern Cottage, she threw herself into a whirlwind of primping, determined to show him an entirely different girl—one that was both well-groomed and sophisticated. Well, at least one with her hair brushed and wearing decent clothes.

Left alone in the living room, Simon critically surveyed his surroundings, mentally noting possible hiding places for documents. He also noted with appreciation the expensive furnishings, recognizing a designer unfettered by monetary considerations. He fervently hoped that Aletha Mason in no way resembled her coarse friend and, considering the elegant surroundings, was fairly certain that she would be a woman of grace and refinement. He was not disappointed. With Gert following behind like some kind of stunted security guard, Aletha joined him, apologizing for not receiving him herself. "You see, Mr. Applegate, is it? My guests and I were breaking our fast outside this morning so I failed to hear your car drive up or the bell ring." She motioned him to be seated. "I must say, it's a wonder you were able to get through the gate at the end of the drive. I don't believe the call monitor has been installed yet." Was it a question or an accusation?

"I was fortunate enough to catch the mailman who kindly opened the gate for me when I explained my mission." He then launched into his prepared story, carefully dropping verifiable bits of information and offering his business card which, oddly, she failed to take.

"I'm afraid your card won't be of much use to me, and I have not yet developed the needed skills to use the Internet. I content myself with reading braille but I'm sure your research will be very useful for those desiring to learn more about the area and Tinkers Well in particular. Forgive me but I really don't see how I can be of any help to you."

She had moved so assuredly into the room and, he swore, spoke directly to him that Simon was taken aback by Aletha's unexpected revelation. He quickly recalculated his search options. It would have been a stroll in the park if he'd only had to work around one elderly blind woman but he noticed that a dog, now sitting quietly next to her chair, never left her side. He felt a nerve start to throb in his left forearm and realized his breathing was coming faster. Mastering his own irrational aversion to the attentive animal, now sitting quietly at his post, Simon continued his situational appraisal. The gorgon might prove a hindrance but he was certain he could enlist the aid of the unwitting Rose to further his cause. As she entered the room at that moment, now turned out in an attractive sundress, subtle but flattering makeup, and her soft curls brushed into submission, his expectations climbed. He stood as she approached the couch and politely remained standing until she was seated.

Simon knew instinctively that Rose would be his greatest ally so he cunningly steered the conversation to include her. "I was just telling Mrs. Mason and Mrs. Gunn"—best not look at that suspicious stare—"that I'm researching information about Tinkers Well for my blog. Of course, I went to city hall and then the library to research historical archives but I was told that the Mason family, being both influential and involved in local and state government, kept much of that information. They suggested that I appeal to you, Mrs. Mason, to gather what history I could from your family records."

Rose, for no logical reason, felt inordinately proud of Simon's knowledge and resourcefulness. What a combination—a handsome face and brains! She continued to sit there with a look of fatuous adoration on her face.

"Letha, where would you put a lot of old dry documents in this place? You barely have room for all this ornate furniture."

Smiling, Aletha said, "I know I'm a silly old woman, Trudy, to want my things around me but they give me pleasure. Matthew understood that. The boxes of historical documents you alluded to, Mr. Applegate, were kept in the attic of the main house for years but Matthew had them moved to a storage unit in preparation for all the remodeling work that needed to be done there. I believe all of those boxes are contained in a single unit in town. I can't imagine you would find anything of interest there but you're welcome to sort through them." She hesitated then continued diffidently, "I'm sure you'll understand that I'll need to confirm your antecedents before allowing you access, and I know it may be an inconvenience, but I must insist that you leave all the document containers at the storage facility. I'm sure you have a means of photographing any pertinent information?"

Bother! he thought to himself. *The old bird does appear to have a little native shrewdness under that guileless demeanor, just as Hawthorne had suggested.* But he answered her with grave respect, "Of course. I would expect nothing less." Now it was his turn to hesitate before adding in a cajoling tone, "I do apologize for being a nuisance but do you think that might be possible in the next few days. You see, I'm rather on a deadline…"

"Well, I suppose I could have my young friend, Tim, verify your background and possibly find a few hours to escort you to the facility, but it may not be for several days."

Simon cast Rose a rueful glance. She rose beautifully to the bait. He couldn't have scripted her reaction better.

"Aletha," Rose spoke enthusiastically, "let me take care of that for you. I'm sure Tim is much too busy and I'm a wiz on the Internet. I can look up the blog site. Besides I have plenty of time on my hands." Then shyly, she said, "Would that be all right with you, Mr. Applegate?"

"I hate to impose on you, but yes, that would be quite satisfactory." Rewarding her with his most appealing smile, he added, "And you must call me Simon. I insist." She felt a little dizzy and supremely happy. It must be fate that had brought them together in such an improbable way. Her summer in Kansas might turn out to be an adventure after all.

*****

The Bennett job went more smoothly than planned so Tim and Derek found themselves a little ahead of schedule. They made it to Milly's Diner by 10:30 a.m. and Derek basically let Tim help him unload the truck before shoving him out the door. "Get on over to Miss Aletha's. I can handle this. You need to go handle that." He stood in the doorway, powerful arms crossed, barring admittance.

"For Pete's sake, Warner! Give me a break. I can go over there this afternoon. Now let's get to work."

"Uh-uh. I'm not moving and don't try to pull rank on me." Knowing belligerence would only go so far with Tim, he then tried coaxing his friend. "I know you, brother. You'll just keep making up excuses until the summer's gone and Rose right along with it. Man,

I've seen the way you look at her. Do you really want to take a chance on not giving *her* a chance?"

After a short personal struggle, Tim acquiesced. "Damn it! I hate it when you're right! Okay, but you'd better have that dumpster full when I get back."

Derek grinned as his friend drove off and did a little spin dance move as he retreated into the diner.

Derek did know Tim well. He knew that despite Tim's moral and physical courage, he was totally insecure when interacting with women of his generation. That's why army life had suited Tim. He understood the concept of setting goals and completing a mission. He felt comfortable operating within set protocols and obtaining quantifiable results. And even though he had had to face the unexpected in training and in combat, he knew his men and how they worked together as a team. He had earned respect as a leader because of his measured approach to problem-solving and the honorable way he treated both subordinates and peers. But those organizational parameters went out the window when it came to relationships outside of his family and close personal friends. He had seen long happy marriages modeled by his parents and by the Masons. He wanted that for himself but the whole dating process felt like going into battle without any defensive weapons. He was completely vulnerable. It was not something he could train for. It was rather a leap of faith. He sometimes wondered if there might be something to the concept of arranged marriages.

Tim ran through all the old arguments and pitfalls again in his head despite reaching Fern Cottage in record time. Pulling up to the house, he recognized Rose's old Chevy and Angelica's car but he had no idea who owned the gleaming Escalade parked next to them. As he approached the door, he heard voices, including an unfamiliar male voice, coming through the open windows on the front of the house. Letting himself in, as was his custom, he walked into the living room and immediately noticed several things. Aletha was entertaining a man, a very sophisticated good-looking man about his own age. The kind of man most other men distrust on sight—too good-looking, too polished. The ladies all seemed captivated by him and his conversation with the exception of Mrs. Gunn who appeared skeptical. Rose looked adorable. And adoring. He imagined just such devotion on the face of a nymph worshiping at the feet of a god.

No one even noticed his entrance until Prince came forward to greet him.

"Is that you, Tim? You must come and meet our new acquaintance. Mr. Simon Applegate, this is Tim Ludlow. Our families have been friends for years."

"It's a pleasure," Simon spoke easily as he stood and held out his long thin hand to the other man. Tim merely nodded his head and clasped the hand offered to him in a vise-like grip. He noted with grim satisfaction the barely discernable wince on Simon's face.

"Simon is doing research for a, what do you call it?"

"A blog, though if I can gather enough information and graphic input, I might make it a video blog or *vlog*," he kindly explained to Tim.

"Thank you for the clarification but I am well-aware of what a vlog is." The smile never really reached Tim's eyes. His expression was more wary than welcoming.

Sensing but not really understanding the palpable tension between the two men, Rose hurried into speech. "Tim, I'm going to be helping Simon gather information about Tinkers Well and other towns nearby from Aletha's historical records so I'll get to know about the area too. Isn't that great?"

Seeing the patent enthusiasm on her sweet innocent face, he answered flatly, "Great. What did you say the name of your blog/vlog was?" Tim asked, addressing Simon again.

"*The Fastest Growing Small Towns in America*. Satellite communities of larger cities…that sort of thing."

"Sounds fascinating." Tim looked anything but fascinated. "May I have one of your cards? Thanks." He took the slick artistically rendered card held out to him. "Here, you can have one of mine too. You might want to find out about local housing availability, building restoration…that sort of thing," Tim said, echoing Simon's flippant description.

Staring unflinchingly at Simon for a few moments before addressing the room at large, Tim apologized for the interruption. "I just stopped by to see if you ladies needed help with anything since I'm working at the main house today but it looks like you're in good hands so I'll be off." He kissed Aletha and Angelica on the cheek and shook Gert's hand in parting.

He was a little surprised when the latter said under her breath, "I'm with you, sonny," eyeing Simon fixedly. Tim bade Rose farewell without really looking at her. His eager first glance had shown him how lovely and beguiling she looked today but Tim had quickly realized that the extra effort had not been made on his behalf.

He effected his exit with what dignity he could rally, but when he got to the main drive he laid a strip of rubber all the way to the gate. No work was done on the big house that day.

CHAPTER 7

Be sober-minded; be watchful. Your adversary the
devil prowls around like a roaring lion,
seeking someone to devour.

—1 Peter 5:8 (ESV)

Simon drove away from the cottage supremely secure in his operational camouflage. The Landrum Agency always created the most thorough covers. All the photos, information, and locations on "his" website were plucked directly from other blogs, edited for any personal comments, dated recently, and given the final touch of authenticity by inserting his byline and latest portrait. He knew the blind woman could not access the information by her own admission. The old crone, though suspicious, had proudly proclaimed that she had "nothing to do with all that nonsense on the 'interweb' or whatever it was called. E-mail was all anyone really needed to use a computer for!" And Rose would find exactly what he wanted her to find. The full website address was printed on his business cards alone and could only be accessed with those characters. An encryption device had been inserted into the site, making it impossible to find on a random search unless the searcher was extremely tech savvy. Simon had been reluctant to give his card to the unforeseen jealous boyfriend but was confident in the belief that anyone who worked with their hands (recalling the limited mental capacity of his own father—a common laborer) lacked the necessary intelligence and technical skills to penetrate the blogger disguise. It was equally unlikely that anyone would make the effort to look up similar blogs and happen on to the coincidence of shared content during what he planned to be a stay of no longer than a week, two at the most.

After Simon's departure, Rose wasted no time in checking out his website. She went directly to the small library, formerly a third bedroom prior to its conversion when the Masons took up residence in the house. Rose had quickly learned that here was the only point of Internet access in the house. Aletha hadn't felt the need for Wi-Fi after Matthew's death but kept the computer, connected directly to DSL, for use by guests. Like all the rooms at Fern Cottage, the library was a period piece. Sturdy oak bookcases with scrollwork across the tops and bottoms covered one wall and a relatively simple walnut desk with turned legs—really more a table with drawers—held the place of prominence in front of the window facing the door. The only other furniture in the room was a distinctly non-Victorian overstuffed chair and ottoman that Matthew had insisted on. This room had been his sanctuary, a more refined version of a man cave. There was even a small flat-screen TV tucked in the middle of leather-bound classics on a tall shelf. Most of the volumes on the shelves were Matthew's favorites but the remaining space was occupied by a few books in braille belonging to Aletha and a good many audiobooks on CDs. Rose had been drawn to the snug restful feeling of this little space during the initial house tour and looked forward to whiling away some pleasant hours here between the covers of a well-worn book.

Sitting at the desk, Rose turned on the computer and eagerly looked up the blog from the information on Simon's card. Navigating through the site, she was impressed by the striking photography and descriptive accounts of all the locations he had researched. They were quite prolific, covering locales from Columbus, Ohio, to Lafayette, Louisiana, to Spokane, Washington. She felt an unaccountable sense of pride in his professionalism and accomplishments.

Even though Granny Gert had granted a grudging approval for Rose to accompany Simon on his research into the Masons' document repository, he had insisted that Rose meet him there rather than being picked up at the cottage. If Rose was disappointed at missing out on driving off with him in the Escalade, she kept it to herself and mentally congratulated Simon on his expert handling of her two well-meaning but careful guardian angels. She set off the following day in her rusty little car with high hopes and expectations of—she couldn't say exactly what—but was sure anything that happened would be out of the ordinary. She was doomed to further disappointment.

Meeting Simon at the storage facility, she punched in the entry code provided by Aletha while Simon stepped discreetly aside to check something on his phone. Upon opening the storage unit, they found boxes packed in the space seemingly from front to back and top to bottom. Simon looked at Rose with comical dismay. She responded with her infectious laughter to which Simon made a show of rolling up his sleeves and diving into the wall of boxes before them. After little more than an hour, Rose began to find the task of going through old dusty documents a bit tedious despite Simon's ongoing light banter and entertaining anecdotes of other such grim research efforts. Though casting a knowing eye over the contents of the boxes they had managed to get through in that relatively short time, he had also kept a knowing eye on his companion. As he noticed her verbal responses growing curt, he judged her to have reached the optimal level of boredom.

"This really is a bit more than I had anticipated and it *is* rather warm in here," Simon commented, watching Rose out of the corner of his eye. "Do you know? I rather fancy a chai tea latte right now. What do say to that?" He said, looking directly at her with a coaxing smile.

She brightened up immediately. The thought of leaving these dusty old papers and enjoying a cool drink with Simon held great appeal. In addition to the tedium of their present task, she had also been feeling physically uncomfortable for some time in her tight skirt and high heels that were infinitely more suited to spending a few pleasant hours in some cozy coffee shop rather than grubbing through a warehouse. Accordingly Rose jumped to her feet, eager to help Simon replace the boxes in the storage unit. But she noticed that he had returned to his search. "Yes, I think a large chai tea latte in a jolly great cup of ice." He glanced up at Rose's bewildered expression, and then as if realizing his oversight, he hastened to his feet as he reached for his wallet.

"How rude of me! Of course, I don't expect you to pay for it. Here," he said, thrusting two twenty-dollar bills into her hand. "Feel free to get yourself anything you like. I noticed a promising little coffee bar somewhere behind the courthouse as I was driving round town, getting acquainted with the area last night." Aware of her continued hesitation, Simon looked at Rose with open contrition. "I have made a muck of everything, haven't I? You promised Mrs. Mason that you would accompany me while I went through all this," he said, moving his arms in a big sweeping gesture at the towers of boxes. "And here I am, asking you to leave me alone with her precious family history. I am *so* sorry!" As he bent to pick up a box and replace it in the container, he continued, "I just thought it would save time and you a great deal of discomfort," Simon offered solicitously while glancing appraisingly at the now conscience-stricken girl, "if we could divide our forces, so to speak. But I can see that would really be inappropriate under the circumstances."

Embarrassed that he might think she suspected him of anything dishonorable, Rose hurried into a disjointed denial of such a notion. "Oh, no! I m-mean no, that wouldn't be a problem. That is, of *course* you can stay here. I'm sure Mrs. Mason would understand, and I would be happy to get you anything." She smiled willingly at Simon. He returned the smile with a raised eyebrow and the corner of his mouth turned up in a quizzical smile, causing her to add quickly, "That you'd like—to drink, that is." In her embarrassment, she stepped backward and almost fell over the box she had been sitting on. Simon's action in reaching out to rescue her was reminiscent of Tim snatching her roughly from a misstep a few days earlier. But all she remembered about close proximity to Tim, at their first meeting, was the smell of sweat and sawdust and a desire to move away. As Simon caught Rose and pulled her gently toward him, she felt a little lightheaded and keenly aware of his touch and the hint of some tantalizing cologne.

As he stepped back, he still held her hand lightly, looking into her eyes. "You do still have the combination for the outside keypad, yes?"

Rose just nodded her head mutely. "Well, be off with you then. Hopefully I'll have made it through a fair number of these by the time you get back. There's a good girl." And softly touching his knuckle under her chin in a playful gesture, he turned back to perusal of yet another box.

As soon as Rose disappeared around the corner, Simon stealthily followed her. Counting to ten, he stepped out to see her driving away in the little Chevy. "All right then, lad, you've got about twenty minutes." He ran back to the storage unit, shoved in the open boxes willy-nilly, and slammed the door. Checking once more that Rose was out of sight, he sprinted to his car, hopping into the back seat, and began a practiced transformation. A few minutes later, a rough-looking character with a blond ponytail and walrus mustache stepped out of the Escalade and headed to a beat-up truck, rented the day before from a small town in a neighboring county. Now clad in dirty blue jeans and a flannel shirt, Simon drove quickly to a nearby hardware store where he had a duplicate key made for the storage unit. He could have just made a mold of the key and gotten the copy later, but this way, he could ensure its fit, saving some time. Fairly certain that his own mother would have failed to recognize him, he added to his anonymity by speaking to the store clerk in flat Midwestern tones.

Learning to change his sharp Cockney into the refined tones of the socially elite had come with some practice, but because he possessed a quick mind and a keen ear, Simon had also added to his repertoire the voices of a merchant from Mumbai, a professor from Berlin, a Chinese sea captain, and various others. He could adopt both their vocal patterns and mannerisms on a whim, making himself virtually invisible.

The chatty clerk had cost him precious time that he could ill afford so he called Rose (whose cell phone number he had thoughtfully acquired the day before) to add another delaying tactic.

"Hello, darling. Have you already gotten the tea? Ah, well, never mind. I'll just do without then…what's that? Oh, I hate to ask you to go back. You've already been such a good sport…Well, if you insist, I'd really love a scone or English muffin or something. You see, I was in such a hurry to see you this morning that I forgot to eat any breakfast, silly of me really, but there it is…No, I *mean* it, and I'm afraid I'm getting a bit peckish…Oh, you are rather a dear. Thanks so much, love. Ta!"

He hurried back into the Escalade and a return to Simon Applegate, a.k.a. Atherton. He had carefully videoed Rose punching in the code on the keypad earlier so he could let himself into the compound. Since he had given himself a few minutes to spare, he strolled into the office, a glorified title for a dingy cubicle on the street side of the building, to ask where he might find the loo. Explaining the term referred to the restroom, he struck up a conversation with the unsuspecting attendant, an awkward youth with an oversized Adam's apple and spotty complexion.

Reaching out his hand in greeting, he said, "My name's Applegate, Simon Applegate."

"Um, Bud," returned the boy, taking the offered hand uncertainly.

"I'm a friend of Aletha Mason's. I'm here on an errand with one of her house guests." Simon had always found timely name-dropping very useful, especially when dealing with the undereducated. "I'm surprised to find a modern facility like this in such a small town. I don't suppose you have proper surveillance cameras though. I imagine that would be rather cost-prohibitive."

"Oh, well, I don't know about that, but yeah, we do actually have surveillance cameras," Bud replied, indicating a row of video screens adjacent to the desk. Noticing the skeptical look on Simon's face, the boy added, "But since hardly anyone ever comes here, I don't look at 'em much. Makes me sleepy."

"I can certainly understand that," Simon responded with an appreciative grin. "But I suppose you keep security tapes in case someone should slip in while you're on the nod, shall we say."

"Well, we used to but the machine is sort of broke." Leaning forward, Bud added conspiratorially, "I kinda knocked my drink over on it when I dozed off a few weeks ago and I haven't told the boss yet so if you could, you know, keep that to yourself…"

"Your secret is safe with me, my friend…er…Bud. Perhaps you might consider eating lunch out?"

"Oh, I usually do. The boss gives me an hour for lunch every day, but sometimes, I take a little longer if my girlfriend can get away from work."

"A girlfriend. I felicitate you," Simon said, making a gesture as if doffing his hat to the young man, drawing a grin and an ugly rush of color into the mottled cheeks. "I expect you look forward to noon every day, then?"

"Noon?" the boy asked, puzzled. Then as light dawned, he said, "*Oh*, because of lunch, you mean. Nah, I leave at eleven on account a how that's when Kitty has her lunch break."

"At any rate, I should imagine this place is only opened until 5:00 p.m. or so. Not a bad workday."

"Oh, you can get in after that. There's just nobody here to rent new units or do paperwork stuff. You just need to use the keypad. At least, you can get in until midnight, then the overnight alarm is activated. But who wants to go rummaging through a bunch of junk in the middle of the night?"

"Who indeed? Well, you mustn't let me take up any more of your time as I see the clock marching toward eleven now. Give my best to Kitty," Simon added in parting. Returning to the storage unit, he quickly set about recreating the scene Rose had left. He was just delving into another box as she rounded the corner bearing the spoils of her errand.

She was not in the sunniest of moods, and had it been anyone but Simon, she might have let her exasperation show. The coffee shop, little more than a shed, was *not* behind the courthouse; it was on the opposite side of the square behind Church Street, practically the farthest point from the storage facility. The server had never heard of chai tea but suggested a nice iced coffee or sweet tea instead. Though she was frustrated, Rose, remembering her days behind the counter, took pity on the apologetic girl and settled for one of each. Hopefully Simon would find one of them acceptable. She hated the thought of disappointing him. She had carried her precious cargo back to the car and made it halfway round the square when Simon called. Already a little disappointed at merely fetching refreshments rather than enjoying them publicly in Simon's company, she tried to sound happily accommodating at his added request, though she had to admit to feeling a little disgruntled. But when he had explained that his hunger sprang from his earlier impatience to see her, she turned the little car around on a dime. After waiting in line a second time and finding the only pastry available was a good old American banana nut muffin, she made her way back across town, getting slightly disoriented along the way, and ended up at the storage facility feeling a little frazzled.

Anticipating the strain on a temperament even as docile as Rose's, Simon hurried to meet the girl on her return. Adopting an attitude of humility and gratitude, he greeted her enthusiastically. "Oh, you clever girl. How could you possibly have known? I actually thought about asking for an iced coffee instead when I called about the scone but felt like such a cad for putting you to the extra trouble that I didn't bother, yet here it is. Rose, you are truly an endless delight," he said with the melting smile that never ceased to leave her speechless. Dropping a light kiss on her forehead, he invited her to sit and enjoy their "feast." Wondering if this was how the beggar maid felt in the presence of King Cophetua, Rose floated along in a happy dream, all annoyance forgotten.

Simon finished going through the few boxes left out and explained that he had seen quite enough. "I actually dug through three layers of boxes while you were away and found that beyond the first few rows are pieces of large furniture so this task wasn't as onerous as I had anticipated. I don't think there's much material here that I can use which *means* that we can close up shop." Pausing, he pulled the door down and locked it. As he placed the key in Rose's hand, he grabbed the other one and continued, "And take a spin around the countryside," as he impetuously spun Rose around in circles.

"Ooooh…" was her only breathless reply until they stopped turning. Clinging to his arm for a few moments until the dizziness passed, she happily agreed to the plan. They spent the next few hours exploring winding roads and hidden lanes, waiting to see if they ended in picturesque towns or local highways. They passed small white farmhouses overshadowed by towering grain silos, huge irrigation machinery watering large expanses of crops, and happy cows cooling themselves in a muddy pond. Freshly laundered sheets floated on the breeze, secured to straining clotheslines by even harder working clothes-pegs, and a would-be cowboy raced across a grassy pasture on horseback while, in the distance, the steeple of a quaint country church reached upward as if to touch the slowly drifting clouds. Witnessing the idyllic rural scenes with the almost impossibly perfect man of her dreams, Rose found the simplicity of everyday events instilled with an aura of magic. Simon noticed nothing but the road before him and the girl beside him. As he drove, he regaled Rose with tales of his travels all the while drawing her out, getting her to talk about Fern Cottage and its occupants without her realizing she was being skillfully interrogated.

"We've only been here since Saturday, so I'm not exactly an expert, but I did hear Aletha mention something about going to the senior citizen's center in town for dinner and Bingo on Thursdays, and then of course, there's church on Sunday. Granny Gert and Aletha both napped yesterday afternoon, just as Angelica said they would and that's probably going to be a pattern." She laughed, adding, "I think they wear themselves out just from talking for hours! Don't you think it's nice that they can enjoy sharing so many memories together?" she asked, looking at Simon expectantly.

He couldn't care less about the conversational habits of two human antiques but he obligingly agreed, adding, "That does rather leave you to your own devices though, doesn't it?"

"Well, Angelica was going to help me find something I could do to occupy myself while they're snoozing or talking endlessly of things I know nothing about, but when you showed up yesterday, I completely forgot to ask her…so…"

"So you are entirely available to help me with my research excursions." Before Rose could argue, though he suspected that would be unlikely, he went on, "I do believe I really would *enjoy* having a partner? I've never been fortunate enough to meet anyone quite like you in the other towns I've visited," he said, keeping his eyes on the road but stealing a glance at Rose who gratified his efforts by producing that adorable self-conscious blush. "We'll have such fun jaunting about the countryside like we've done today. But I'll pick you up at midday so that we can share lunch together tête-à-tête. Does that sound amenable to you, Miss Rose?" he asked.

Amenable, Rose thought, *It sounds perfect!* She turned to him impulsively. "Oh, I'd love to." She paused briefly before adding with a teasing smile, "*Mr.* Applegate."

Simon answered the demure use of his surname with a shout of laughter. "Definitely no one quite like you!"

Before she knew it, they had returned to the storage facility where Rose reluctantly bid Simon farewell, promising to be ready on time the next day. She then spent the entire drive back to Fern Cottage trying to figure out how to convince her grandmother to okay the outings she was sure to disapprove of. For reasons that Rose could not fathom, Granny Gert seemed to have taken an unaccountable dislike to Simon. She was clearly suspicious of his motives, though he had behaved with honor and politeness at each of their meetings. Maybe she needed a third party to convince her.

Rose hadn't talked to her mother, Beth, since their arrival in Kansas on Saturday afternoon. Beth, therefore, didn't yet know about the incredible coincidence that had brought the handsome stranger from The Pickle Barrel to the front door of Fern Cottage or that he had made such a powerful impression on her daughter. Rose was sure she would appreciate a glowing account of his sterling qualities and act as a coconspirator in her little romance. Conveniently forgetting all the times she and her mother had failed to see eye to eye on any number of things, Rose parked in the shade at Aletha's house and reached for her cell phone. There was no time like the present.

*****

Demolition at Milly's Diner was completed in record time. The last update of the hundred-year-old building fronting onto the town square had been done over fifty years ago so everything—from cabinetry, plumbing, wiring, drop ceiling, and cracked tile floors— had to go. Given the scope of the remodel, the initial clear out should have taken several days. Derek had spent much of the previous day in conference with the owner, making sure of what to rip out and what to leave. And since Milly enjoyed a nice gossip with a friendly soul, she had cut substantially into his workday. But he was a good sport and recognized that the best service you can offer some people is to just listen to them. Besides he did love to talk—almost as much as he loved to demo. It turned out though that Tim would take the honors on this project.

Derek showed up early at the work site the next day, expecting to have the place to himself and was, therefore, a little surprised at seeing Tim's truck parked outside the diner. Neither he nor Abe had seen any sign of Tim since sending him off to Aletha's the day before and had congratulated themselves on their success in shoving him in Rose's direction. One look at Tim's face though and he knew that success must have been replaced by a fail—apparently an epic fail. With only a cursory nod at Derek, Tim continued to work. And he worked like a man possessed.

With every swing of the sledgehammer and pull on the crowbar, Tim tore away at his frustration and disappointment. He hardly knew Rose. Why was he so upset about her interest in another man? Why did he see Simon Applegate's face on every light fixture he ripped out of the ceiling or every floor tile he smashed as he slammed it into a wheelbarrow? That he was being irrational he knew, but something was gnawing at his gut, telling him this was not the time to be rational. He had barely spent three or four hours with Rose but it was enough to tell him that she was a godly woman with a kind heart who deserved to be treated with dignity, respect, and honor. He couldn't say how he knew but he *knew* that those were the *last* character traits Simon Applegate would reveal to her.

During his tenure in the army, Tim had learned to sum up people—to distinguish those who were sincere in their attitude toward service and those who were just brown-nosing. He had had to know instinctively who he could trust and count on because lives depended on that trust. His men had looked up to him for guidance and it had been his responsibility to protect them—through rigorous training, discipline, and accountability. He had accepted that responsibility willingly. But now, when he felt an almost overmastering desire to guide and protect Rose, he had to recognize that he had absolutely no authority to do so.

Slam! Tim tore through a half-wall divider with the power of a jackhammer. Couldn't she see past Applegate's pretty boy good looks? Didn't she realize he was just using her for something? Tim didn't know what that was but he intended to find out. *Crash*! He sent large sections of the lunch counter mirror hurling into the waiting dumpster, obliterating them into tiny pieces. Tim had sensed a connection with Rose every time they had met, even after that first disastrous confrontation. She obviously had a forgiving spirit because she had greeted him in a friendly manner at each subsequent meeting. And after church on Sunday, she was so openly genuine in her conversation and praise of the house that he had actually felt secure enough to offer *her* praise, hoping she would see herself for the truly special person she was. And he had tried to express in that parting glance, as she was dragged away by her grandmother, all his assurance, understanding, and appreciation for the humor of the situation. He had fallen asleep that night thinking about her grateful answering smile.

And then Applegate had waltzed onto the scene. Tim knew he could never compete with a guy who oozed charm from every pore, wore designer clothes, and spoke glib continental pleasantries with the knowledge that he was the best-looking man in the room. Tim couldn't really blame Rose for her obvious admiration of Simon. He probably affected most women that way. But even though she only had eyes for someone else now, Tim was determined to make darned sure that she was safe, whether she wanted his help or not.

Derek, watching the emotions play across his friend's face, knew instinctively to give him space. This was not the time for talking it out with a buddy. He honestly hadn't realized that Tim's affection for Rose had gone so deep so quickly. Never having really been in love himself, he was a little surprised at Tim's reaction to what he assumed had been just a little setback. But then, he didn't know anything about Simon Applegate.

What he *did* know was that he was witnessing again a shadow of the pain and disappointment Tim had worn like a shroud after the death of his father over a year ago. That he suspected some of Tim's disappointment was in himself made it that much harder to observe. As he had before, Tim was throwing himself into work, keeping the body active so the mind couldn't dwell on the grief and, in this case, self-doubt and insecurity. He had only begun to pull out of that earlier valley of despair when they came together to help Abraham. *It's amazing*, Derek thought to himself, *how quickly our own troubles fade away when confronted with someone else whose burdens seem almost insurmountable. At any rate, he needs a distraction. Maybe Abe can help me come up with something…something that will bring Tim and Rose back together and give him some hope.* But for now, Derek was content to swing his sledgehammer alongside his friend's. He knew that the best support he could offer his buddy in the moment was the silence of companionship and a shared goal. The words would come later.

*****

Armed with the information he had gathered that morning, Simon waited a block away to watch Bud depart the storage facility a half-hour before the posted closing time. So much the better. Parking the borrowed pickup truck in the loading zone, he entered the now unmanned facility and opened the Mason's storage unit with the key copied earlier that day. He then spent the next five hours moving boxes from that unit to one in the truck's town of origin, some twenty miles away. Contrary to what he had told Rose, boxes filled the unit—what he wouldn't have given to have them displaced by the fictional furniture! He was able to move about half of the boxes that night. But by the time he locked the initial storage unit for the last time, Simon was cursing Miles Hawthorne with every expletive in his well-stocked arsenal. He knew it would take several days to get through the mountain of papers and honestly held out little hope of finding the document in any of them but knew he must be thorough. Meanwhile he would endeavor to gain a foothold in Fern Cottage and the legitimacy to spend an increasing amount of time there. Rose was the link he must exploit but there was no reason he couldn't enjoy the process. She was the sweet morsel on an otherwise dull plate of tedious routine and he meant to savor every delicious bite.

CHAPTER 8

*Likewise, teach the older women to be reverent in
the way they live...to teach what is good.
Then they can train the younger women...
to be self-controlled and pure...
So that no one will malign the Word of God.*

—Titus 2:3–5 (NIV)

The ladies of Fern Cottage settled quickly into a pleasant if uneventful routine. Breakfast in the gazebo, augmented substantially now (to Angelica's delight), luncheon in the chintz-hung dining room on a highly polished oval table, surrounded by ornately carved chairs, and quiet afternoon rest time when Rose began her vigil for Simon's arrival. Though the pair had discussed lunch on the road as an option on their outing the previous day, Rose felt it best to honor Aletha and Angelica's hospitality by eating the midday meal at the house before leaving with Simon. He had not been best pleased when he called for her on that first Wednesday, but as his idea of lunchtime was one o'clock or later, she had already eaten by the time he arrived.

"I believe we had settled on an intimate meal together during our travels today but I can see you thought better of my idea," he remarked as he opened the car door for Rose, an edge to his voice.

"Oh, no! I mean, no, I thought it was a lovely idea, but in all the excitement of talk about working with you as your assistant, I agreed to the plan without thinking. I'm sorry." She shot him a look of contrite apology. "You see, lunch is the main meal at the cottage and Angelica works so hard to prepare something special every day, and well, I don't want to offend Aletha since she's been so kind to Granny

Gert and me. I hope you'll understand." His immobile profile wasn't very encouraging but Rose added diffidently, "Besides you weren't here at noon so I thought that maybe you had changed *your* mind."

"I never change my mind," Simon stated on an unyielding note. Then catching the chagrin writ large on her face, he added with something approaching a thaw, "But you do raise several good points. I'm afraid I've never really adjusted to the early dining hours favored by you Yanks and you are quite right to show deference to your hostess's wishes." He certainly wanted to win favor with Aletha for his own ends. Best not put that in jeopardy at the outset. "I'm afraid I have a confession to make." Rose, relieved at his returning good humor, waited expectantly. "I was rude simply because of disappointment at not sharing the experience with you." Gauging her response correctly, he put the icing on her cake by offering, "I know. I'll introduce you to the lovely practice of afternoon tea. What do you say to that?" Her glowing face said it all.

Simon had done little homework on the local dining scene, if one could call it that. He presumed that tea shops would be few and far between (if not altogether nonexistent) in the Kansas outback; however, he had discovered that restaurants started serving dinner around 4:30 p.m., the only civilized time for tea, so he would plan their excursions accordingly.

But tea would keep for a few hours. First, to business. They drove into Tinkers Well by way of Commerce Street, just as Rose had on Sunday. Since he was ostensibly gathering information for potential incoming residents, and because he was sure Rose would enjoy it most, he decided to begin their "research" in the shops that lined Commerce Street, facing the park in the center of town. The unique layout of Tinkers Well had allowed for augmentation of limited parking along the two commercial streets in town by annexing a strip of land on opposite sides of the park (not without heated opposition from local residents) so that the growing population could better access the shops on Commerce Street and the eateries and service-related businesses on Main Street. Simon was fortunate enough to find a parking space just in front of The Unique Antique.

"Now if you *truly* want to be my assistant—you don't have to, you know. I would be completely happy just to enjoy your company..."

"Oh, but I *want* to help. Besides I'll learn more detail about the local area."

"In that case, I present your official assistant's notebook," Simon said, handing her a thick spiral-bound journal. "And camera," he added as he hung a large digital camera around her neck.

Rose was a little taken aback by the cumbersome load and ventured to suggest timidly, "Wouldn't it be easier to simply use an iPad? I could type notes directly into it *and* take pictures with it."

"Yes, I suppose that would be simpler, but you see, I'm rather a purist and the camera really does produce better-quality photographs. But if this is too much for you—"

"Of course not!" Rose hastened to assure him. She readily chose to sacrifice herself on the altar of inconvenience rather than admit she found any part of her assumed duties to be onerous. Bravely summoning an enthusiastic smile, she arranged her official equipment as she waited for Simon to open the car door for her.

Rose had had little opportunity to really take in the essence of Tinkers Well the previous Sunday as they had driven directly to church and then to the Ludlow home. And Tuesday had been wasted on trying to locate a stray coffee shop. Now she stood on the cobbled walkway that ran the length of the street and soaked up the timeless appeal of architectural individuality. The shop buildings were all connected like a row of town houses but each shop front's facade featured a variety of detail. As far as Rose could see, each store was two-storied, presumably originally built to house the store owner on the second floor. Some shop fronts featured a rounded central arch bracketed on both sides by a wide overhanging cornice. Others had a square-stepped front leading to a flat roof section in the middle where the business's name was prominently displayed on an artistic sign. Most, but not all, boasted large plate glass display sections flanking a recessed front door. Further variation came from a multitude of building finishes—different tones of brick, multiple colors of siding, and one building covered in stucco. Faux gas lampstands with hanging baskets full of trailing petunias lined the street, providing a unifying touch. Great care had been taken to maintain the old buildings and the sense of timelessness they evoked. Rose, the dreamer, soaked up the inviting quaint atmosphere with frank admiration. Someone whose occupation demanded attention to detail, and the desire to relay it in a positive light, should have noted every structural nuance. Simon merely glanced down the street and started up the shallow steps to the double door. As he opened the door to an irritating jangle overhead, he stepped back to allow Rose to enter and realized that she had unconsciously begun walking away down the cobblestones, gazing with pleasure at all she saw.

She really is alluring but her penchant for rustic charm may wear a little thin. I'll have to be more intentional about leading her attention in my direction if she is to be of any use to me. Making the mental note, Simon called laughingly after Rose, "Darling, if you're going to be enraptured by the local flavor everywhere we stop, I fear we won't make much progress."

She woke from her abstraction with a guilty start and turned hurriedly to join him. "I'm so sorry, Simon. It's just that everything is so quaint. I feel like I've stepped back in time."

A sign hanging from an oak hall tree, crowded into one of the front glass-enclosed displays, tempted visitors with hidden treasures and one-of-a-kind finds. Looking at the shelves, crammed to overflowing with every kind of dish, cooking utensil, book, artwork, and yes, even a kitchen sink, Simon gave an inward shudder and forced a smile. Momentarily distracted by the overwhelming display, he nearly forgot his rehearsed speech for the store owner, explaining his presence in town and asking permission to be included in his blog. He needn't have asked.

Dottie Patton was beside herself with excitement at being featured in a blog. All three of her chins quivered with delight setting the numerous strands of beads around her neck in motion. "I don't even know what a blog is but it sounds thrilling, just *thrilling*." She patted her bright-red-haired wig with chubby fingers boasting at least three glittering rings each. "Now I insist you take as many pictures as you like." She leaned suggestively against the worn wooden counter, an arm extended from the loose brightly patterned caftan she wore. "Fancy people all over the world looking at pictures of me and my little shop. And, Mr. Applegate…"

"Simon."

"Simon, if you or your girlfriend—what was your name, honey?"

Blushing, the "girlfriend" managed a confused "Rose," all the while secretly wondering how Simon felt about the title.

"Rose. What a pretty name for a pretty girl. You're a lucky man, Simon," she said, and winked outrageously. "I suppose you folks are staying at the Wayfarer Inn." The question was implicit.

"No. Rose is actually a guest of Aletha Mason. Are you acquainted with Mrs. Mason?" Rose didn't even notice the evasive response about himself.

Losing some of her posturing attitude, Dottie answered, "Everyone around here knows Aletha. Why I've been trying to sell her some of my furniture for years—you know, to fill that big house of hers." She looked speculatively at Rose, wondering if she might prove a helpful entrée into Aletha's circle.

Simon, far more adept at reading people than the naive Rose, drew Dottie's attention by commenting on the number of merchants in Tinkers Well. "You obviously have a thriving business here. I can't imagine anyone rivaling your merchandise." Surely no one else would gather so much junk under one roof! He could certainly imagine Aletha's reluctance to shop in Dottie's store.

Almost as if she followed his thoughts, Dottie sidled up to Simon, placing a chubby hand on his arm and saying archly, "My really good furniture is in the back."

"I'm sure it is."

"Now if you'd like me to give you a private showing"—again that deplorable wink—"I'd be happy to oblige."

Still smiling good-humoredly, Simon responded with a wink of his own. "I think Rose and I can find it on our own."

A little disappointed at being dismissed, even if it had been done very deftly, Dottie added, "Now if you or your Rose need help finding anything, just any little thing, you let me know." Simon placed his arm around Rose's waist and quickly propelled them away from the garrulous proprietor.

Having reached the nether regions of the cluttered store, Rose spoke anxiously to Simon. "I'm sorry if I gave her the wrong impression, you know, about…us."

"I'm not." The succinct response, coupled with the acute awareness of his arm still lightly encircling her waist, brought the color back into her cheeks.

Stepping away from him, Rose raised the camera to take a picture of what she thought was an appealing assortment of old dishes but she couldn't figure out how to turn on the high-speed camera. She had only ever taken pictures with the one on her cell phone. The complex workings of a Canon™ PowerShot were a little beyond her scope. Looking apologetically at Simon, she said ruefully, "I'm afraid I'm not going to make much of an assistant if I can't even figure out how to use the equipment."

"No, it's my fault. I shouldn't have put such expectations on you. It's really not complicated once you get the hang of it. Here, let me show you." Rose started to pull the camera strap over her head but Simon hung it round her neck again. "Now what is your focal point?"

"That table full of old dishes. I thought it would make an interesting grouping with all the different shapes and colors."

Grimacing inwardly at the pile of chipped china and earthenware, Simon moved to stand behind Rose and reached around her to take the camera in both hands. Heads close together, he spoke over her shoulder and pointed out the power button, shutter, zoom, and lighting effects then encouraged her to try a few shots. Rose was a little delirious at Simon's close proximity and the enticing scent of his cologne so her first attempts were a bit off but she persevered and managed a few creditable shots. She turned her head slightly as she held the camera up to show him the fruits of her labor. He smiled his approval into her anxious eyes just inches away. Rose thought for a moment she might actually find out what it felt like to swoon but her dignity was spared when Simon broke the spell by lightly touching the end of her nose, saying, "We may make a photographer out of you yet." Then he moved away to look at some old books.

Rose gathered her scattered wits and took a few more photos in between scribbling comments tossed to her by Simon as they moved through the store. Waiting until the talkative Dottie was engaged with other customers, they made their escape.

"Shall we see what—" Simon began, looking at the neighboring store, "—Pins and Needles has to offer?"

The pair spent the next few hours repeating the interview formula as they made their way down the street, and at each stop, Simon worked in a few questions about Aletha Mason. Rose was so busy taking pictures and recording his verbal asides in the journal that she hardly noticed the intentional direction of his conversation with each shopkeeper.

"No," answered the spare Mrs. Elder whose tired face was reflected in her weary demeanor. "Mrs. Mason wouldn't have any need for sewing fabric or notions, being blind and all. Though I suppose she could try taking up knitting since it's really more about counting stitches." She seemed to chew on the idea for a few moments, contemplating an untapped lucrative income stream, but was interrupted in her calculations by Simon bidding her farewell.

Not to be dismissed so easily, Mrs. Elder added hopefully, "Now Angelica, the woman that sits with Mrs. Mason is here most every week. I can't keep enough of that flowery tropical fabric in stock to suit her."

"Then I'm sure she'll be happy to provide a positive customer review when I see her tomorrow. Good day." Mrs. Elder's eager response (if one could so describe the utterings of an individual with the personality of Eeyore) was spoken to an empty shop.

"You really cannot laugh at all the local yokels, Rose. It simply isn't done." Simon's stern tones belied the laughter in his eyes. Finally free to release the giggles that had been building during the brief but agonizingly slow verbal exchange between Simon and the sluggish Elder woman, Rose gave vent to a peal of laughter. "I can't help it." She gasped, trying to catch her breath. "Her face reminded me of a worn-out old gray mare on Grandpa Ernie's farm." Simon, mimicking the face in question, set her off again. She was still chuckling as they entered Happy Soles shoe store. Shoes were followed quickly by a florist, a hardware store, a furniture emporium, and Freck's General Store—a sort of mini department store carrying household goods, sporting equipment, and pet supplies. The last shop they entered had clearly had a recent face-lift. Its extended glass display window was tastefully adorned with mannequins arrayed in the latest fashion trends. The elegant sign touted Miles of Styles Boutique. Rose started clicking away with the camera even before they entered the store.

Once inside, Simon gave Rose carte blanche to wander at will. As a cultivator of women's attentions, he had developed a keen eye for fashion and had recognized a conservative but classy ensemble on one of the mannequins as the same as that worn by Aletha Mason when they first met. Here, finally, he might elicit some helpful information. The store had several customers, but as he always managed to stand out as the exotic among the ordinary, especially as an attractive man among women, Simon soon had the eye of the owner, Gayle Harwood. Introductions made and a friendly rapport established, Simon set to work. Gayle, a handsome woman in her mid-forties with a pleasant nature and a well-shaped figure, was happy to answer his questions. She too saw the potential for increased commercial visibility through Internet coverage.

"Why yes, Aletha is one of our best clients. In fact, it was actually she that insisted on investing in the remodel we did last year. I'm paying her back, of course." Gayle hastened to point out. "And the reason I can do so is because the update has generated substantially more business. Matthew may have been the well-known entrepreneur but she has a pretty shrewd head on her shoulders."

"I must say, I find her a remarkable woman, even more so now after you allowed me knowledge of this added dimension to her character. The thing that impressed me at our first meeting though was the seemingly effortless way she functions in her blindness."

"Oh, I know what you mean," Gayle answered in conspiratorial tones. "We've just known her a lot longer so we've gotten used to it."

Continuing to expand on the topic, Simon mused, "I don't know that I've really ever given much thought to the practical everyday issues that the blind must deal with. For instance, how would one pay one's bills? Surely they aren't printed in braille, and then how can a check be written? She mentioned to me that she has not learned to use the computer but clearly she has a very well-run household. It's a mystery." Simon left the statement hanging, waiting for Gayle to respond to his look of curiosity mingled with respect.

"Well, I can tell you—and this is just between us—"

"I wouldn't last long in my profession without discretion..."

"—that she probably has accounts at stores all over town. That's how she does business with us."

"But she still has to make payment. I can't imagine that she carries a great wad of cash around with her. It simply wouldn't be safe—especially for a woman in her position."

Gayle explained, "No, she doesn't actually settle the account herself. You see, in his will, Matthew gave power of attorney to Mr. Thurston at the bank to manage her household accounts. I send my bill to him and he pays it. Lord knows, she doesn't have to worry about running out of money!"

"*The* bank? Surely I've seen more than one."

"Oh, didn't I say? It's the Midwest Union Bank—on exactly the opposite corner of the square, in fact." She nodded her head, indicating a diagonal direction. "It was founded decades ago by some Mason ancestor so, of course, it's the main bank in town. There are a few branches of Kansas City banks, you know, catering to newcomers, but it's the Midwest Union for us locals."

"I can't tell you how helpful you've been, Gayle. Not only do you have a first-rate establishment here, which I will make special mention of, but you've given me a lead on financial establishments in the area—must-have knowledge for potential newcomers." He was perfectly aware that most people under forty did all of their banking online now but that admission hardly furthered his cause.

"Now if you'll excuse me, I must find my assistant, who has undoubtedly unearthed some treasure on one of your racks, and continue on my quest." Gayle smiled appreciatively and nodded slightly in farewell. Simon wandered through racks of silky blouses, classic dresses, and seductive lingerie (his personal favorite) before he found Rose turning circles in front of a full-length mirror as she watched the skirt of a deceptively chic casual dress flare out with her movement. The neckline of the form-fitting bodice was cut decidedly lower than she would normally be comfortable in but the skirt, when hanging naturally, came almost to her knees. Rose knew it wasn't really her style but she just wanted to experience the feel of looking more sophisticated. She turned away from the mirror to see Simon standing there, a look of blatant approval on his face.

Feeling a little self-conscious, she said, "I…I'm sorry to keep you waiting. I was just…playing dress up. Give me a minute and I'll be ready to go."

"Take all the time you need. By the way, you do mean to buy that delightful frock, don't you?"

"Heavens, no! I could never wear something like this in public."

"You're *joking*, of course. I for one have never seen you look lovelier. I'll tell you what. I will purchase this for you if you promise to wear it whenever I am able to convince you to have dinner with me sometime. We'll call it payment in kind for all the help you've given me."

"Oh, Simon, I don't think that would be appropriate. Goodness, what would Granny Gert say?"

He walked over to her, taking both her hands in his. He stepped back, raising her arms, and surveyed her critically from head to toe. Her objections melted away in the glowing look from his eyes. He stepped forward, still holding her hands, and said in a compelling soft voice, "Granny Gert will say that *you* look stunning and that *I'm* not good enough for you. Now off you go." And he released her to change.

Still shaking a little from another close encounter with Simon, Rose walked beside him as if in a dream. He had generously taken the journal and camera from her so that she could carry her new "frock".

Wouldn't Violet and Lily be surprised to see me now? Little sister is growing up! she thought. Depositing everything in the car, they walked through the park to Main Street and the promised afternoon tea.

*****

"Knock, knock," said a woman's voice as the front door of the little bungalow was opened.

"Is that you, Marilyn? Just come right on in. I'm in the kitchen."

Marilyn Ludlow made her way past the snug little living room marked by its brightly covered draperies and wicker furniture upholstered in floral patterns. The whole space was filled with so many potted plants that it more closely resembled a tropical rain forest than a sitting area. Marilyn almost expected to see sand under the woven rattan rugs rather than sturdy oak. She found the Jamaica-meets-Kansas interior a little like taking a short vacation without ever leaving home. She'd even tried incorporating a few Caribbean touches in her own eclectic décor.

Following her nose, Marilyn identified the scent of cloves, ginger, and some strong pepper by the time she discovered Angelica Warner tossing first one exotic spice after another into a big pot on the stove.

"Smells fabulous! What is it this time, curry?"

Angelica just smiled as she shook her head and started stirring the concoction.

"Ackee?"

The smile broadened but the head kept shaking.

"Is it jerk—"

"Chicken. Very good! Your Jamaican palate really is comin' along."

"Looks like you're making enough for an army!"

"Two words—Derek and Abraham. They *are* an army when it comes to food. You know, if I didn't know better, I'd think Abraham *was* part Jamaican. And that boy can *eat!*"

"I'm afraid all I can manage for Tim is plain old American food."

"Well, if you ask me, it must suit him for he's a strong healthy young man if ever there was one."

Marilyn sat down at the little kitchen table where Angelica had placed a cup of tea. "He may be strong and healthy but he's not happy." She added some sugar to the teacup and stirred it absentmindedly. After a few moments, she looked at her friend in despair and asked, "What am I going to do about Tim and Rose? What can I do?"

Setting the big pot to simmer, Angelica sat down next to Marilyn and placed a comforting hand over the other woman's. "The first thing *we're* goin' to do is *not* give up." Giving the hand a squeeze, she let go and picked up her own teacup. "Derek told me about Tim's… disappointment over the way things have turned out with Rose. It seems he took quite a likin' to her—and who could blame him."

"I tell you, Angelica, I hadn't seen Tim as happy in years as he was after brunch on Sunday. He went on and on about Rose— her beauty, her kindness, her tender heart. I can't remember when he's been so taken with a girl. And watching them while they were together, I could have sworn that she was warming to him too. But I tried to caution him by reminding him that she was only here for the summer. Even if she returned his feelings, would she be willing to move her whole world and make Kansas her home? But he wouldn't listen to anything I said. I guess love hits people like that sometimes…"

"Mm-hmm," was Angelica's reply. "And sometimes it grows out of friendship."

Marilyn sighed. "I suppose it's a moot point now since this Applegate fellow showed up. Tim has hardly spoken a word since Monday. You've met Simon. What is he like—truthfully?"

Angelica didn't answer right away, then narrowed her eyes, and finally said cryptically, "Samuel Jamison."

Confused by the sudden introduction of an unknown person, Marilyn said, "I beg your pardon…"

"Samuel Jamison," Angelica repeated, nodding her head like a wise sage.

"I'm sorry, I don't follow…"

"When I was a young girl, maybe sixteen or so, I had a friend, my best friend, though she was a few years older than me. Her name was Sabryna. She was as pretty as a fresh summer mornin' but not in that flashy way that some girls go for so as to look older than they are. No, she was a good girl—went to church every Sunday, minded her parents, and worked hard. But she was a dreamer, always fancyin' herself in some glorious impossible future. She knew that wasn't ever goin' to happen but liked makin' up stories all the same. Besides she'd been walkin' out with a fine young man named Joseph for some time and they were plannin' to get married as soon as he could provide for a family. While he was workin' as a bellhop, he was takin' some hotel management course evenin's so he could qualify for a job on the other side of the counter. And Sabryna was perfectly happy with Joseph and their plans. That is until the day this fella, Samuel Jamison, took a room in the hotel where we worked."

Angelica paused for a moment, scrutinizing the past, before continuing her narrative. "Anyway Samuel Jamison was as handsome a man as I'd ever seen. Tall, muscular, and well-dressed with a voice as deep and hypnotic as the ocean and as smooth as waves washin' up on the beach."

"Excuse me for interrupting, Angelica, but surely you didn't often come into contact with the guests. Don't hotel employees usually clean the rooms during the day when they are more likely to be empty?"

"A very astute question, my friend. You're right. We did. But he always seemed to be in the room when we were cleanin'—like it was intentional. I remember the first time we knocked on his door to make sure the room was unoccupied, you know. No answer. So we let ourselves in, and there he was, standin' there, wearin' nothin' but a pair o' Bermuda shorts. I was that embarrassed, I can tell you! I grabbed Sabryna and told him we'd come back later but he insisted he would soon be out of our way and invited us to go about our business. Then he started talkin' to us. I guess he could tell I wasn't interested in what he had to say but Sabryna was. He *told* her he was actually from the islands but had moved to New York or Miami— you know, some big city—and done well for himself. I don't know if any o' that was true but Sabryna believed it. And he knew it. Knew just how to string her along too. He was one good-lookin' man and had a come-hither way about him that drew unsuspecting women like bees to honey. He frightened me a little so I was havin' none of it, but it surely did work on Sabryna. She was fairly swept away by his charm. Samuel Jamison made sure he was in the room whenever we were cleanin' and talked her up sweet. I found out later that he took her to fancy dinners in the local restaurants, convinced her that she was somethin' special, and even entertained her in his *room*."

"Mm-hmm," Angelica uttered in response to Marilyn's expression of shocked disapproval. "One day, about a week or so after he had checked in, we went to clean his room. I could tell by the way Sabryna was smilin' that she expected to find him there. And I noticed somethin' different about her that day—she was fairly glowin'! It was like she was huggin' some wonderful secret to herself, not even lettin' me in on it. But the smile died when we entered the room—it had been cleared out. All we found was a card on the table with Sabryna's name on it. Samuel Jamison thanked her for 'her help' and the 'delightful interludes' they had shared together—I can still remember that disgustin' phrase—and hoped they might meet again someday. I can tell you, she was crushed, almost distraught."

"What a jerk!"

"You don't know the half of it. We found out later that day that several rooms had been burglarized. All the staff were questioned by the police and since Sabryna and I worked together, they talked to us at the same time. Now I had known Sabryna all my life and I could tell she was really afraid to answer the questions so I spoke for both of us. Fortunately the police just chalked up her silence to the nervousness of a young girl and moved on. But on the way home, I made her tell me everything.

It seems that Samuel Jamison had told her he was an undercover agent from the security office of the hotel's corporate headquarters." As an aside, she said, "Our hotel didn't *have* a corporate headquarters. It was privately owned but Sabryna didn't know that.

"Now where was I? Oh, yes, that scoundrel told Sabryna he was there to check on the hotel's security measures and was under no circumstance to let anyone on the management team know of his mission. Instead he was to enlist the aid of someone 'above suspicion' on the hotel staff to help him gain access to guests' rooms for the purpose of ensurin' valuables were adequately secured and was sure that Sabryna was the perfect person to be trusted with such an important task. Of course she was flattered and so gullible that she was completely taken in by all his smooth talk. She told me he promised to see that she would get a pay raise and would even help her friend, Joseph, get a management position.

"And she fell for that? Poor foolish girl! Well, at least she escaped any implication in the robberies, right?"

"Yes, but he nearly ruined her anyway."

"But how? Surely she got over him in time."

"Unfortunately he left her more than just a card." At Marilyn's questioning look, Angelica added grimly, "He left her with a babe on the way."

"Oh *no*! What did she do?"

"I'll tell you what she did. She listened to me for the first time in weeks. I told her to go straight to Joseph and tell him everything. I knew he truly loved her, and though I know it cost him dearly to do it, he swallowed his pride and married her anyway. Then he raised that child and loved him like his own."

"Just like another Joseph. What an incredible story of redemption," Marilyn said with an appreciative smile. "It takes a rare man to act that generously." She then added softly, a faraway look in her eyes, "I knew a man like that once…

Ignoring Marilyn's last statement, though it might lead to something interesting, Angelica agreed. "And do you know, I think that whole experience helped Sabryna finally grow up and open her eyes. Not just to the recognition of cleverly disguised evil but also to what a blessing she had in Joseph." Smiling suddenly, she said, "Do you know, they had five more children and are happy as can be. Joseph is assistant manager at the hotel now and that proud of his family, you'd never know how it all started."

After a moment of pleasant reminiscence, she planted her hands firmly on the table and said, "Now back to the present. I'm sure you can see why I thought of Sabryna as soon as I met Rose. She's the same kind of sweet innocent girl that thinks too much with her imagination and not enough with common sense. A dreamer. Then when I saw the way she reacted to Simon Applegate when he came to the cottage that first day, I was afraid it was Sabryna and Samuel Jamison all over again."

"Oh dear. Well, if that's the case, maybe we should warn her or at least her grandmother."

"I'm afraid that wouldn't work. She is so smitten, she can't see past his charm."

"But Rose is a grown woman. Surely she'll be able to see through him."

"I wouldn't count on it. Men like that possess their own kind of armor. No, I think our best plan of attack is to get him to expose himself. Show his true ugly side in contrast to someone else—a man of integrity."

"But how? If you're thinking of enlisting Tim's aid, I'm afraid you'll be disappointed. He'll hardly talk to me, let alone anyone else—especially Rose."

"So we have to give them some common ground to focus on. That way, they aren't even aware of 'Tim and Rose' but of something greater."

"Well, that sounds good in *theory*," said Marilyn. Then added skeptically, "But how do you expect to pull it off?"

"By letting everyone but Tim and Rose in on the plan."

"Huh?"

Angelica rose and went to the stove. She grabbed the red enamel teapot with a well-worn pot holder and returned to the table. "Here, let me freshen your tea." After passing the cream and sugar around, the two friends put their heads together and worked out the details of Angelica's plan.

Two hours later, sitting in Angelica's driveway in her car, Marilyn Ludlow paused for a few minutes before driving home. "Dear Lord," she prayed. "I know you are holy and just and that you have a perfect plan for all of us. It's just hard to see your plan for Tim and Rose right now. If our schemes to help them are not pleasing to you, stop us now. But if we can honor you through our efforts, I pray for success. Please give us your wisdom and guidance and thank you for my precious sister, Angelica, who willingly shares my burdens. Bless you, Lord. Amen."

Marilyn drove home with a sense of purpose and renewed hope for Tim's future happiness.

CHAPTER 9

*Fools, because of their transgression, and because
of their iniquities, were afflicted.
Their soul abhorred all manner of food.*

—Psalm 107:17–18 (NKJV)

Settlers Park covered a generous three square acres in the heart of Tinkers Well. Dedicated by the citizens of the town in 1856, it boasted, besides the storied well, a covered bandstand on its northwest corner between Main and State Streets where many a politician had addressed crowds during whistle stop campaigns, signaling the town's relative importance in the region where speeches had typically been made from a railroad car momentarily stopping at a rural train station. The bandstand still served as the focal point for the annual Harvest Festival held in October.

On the opposite end of the park, facing Church Street, stood several memorials erected after each military conflict to honor the fallen of Tinkers Well and surrounding lesser communities in the county. The imposing granite stone, marking the War on Terror, showed clearly the names of young men called to duty after 9-11 who had never returned home. The earliest memorial, set in its sacred spot in December 1865, was hewn out of local stone where names had been rendered almost illegible after decades of exposure to turbulent Kansas weather. Those new Americans whose state had only entered the union in January 1861, just months before the Civil War began, were emblematic of the generations of Jayhawkers who had stood to defend freedom. The names of their descendants were scattered across the other memorials, marking all the international wars that followed.

As Rose and Simon wandered slowly through the park, she marveled at the spreading grandeur of the great old trees. Many of the hardwoods, particularly the bur oaks, still stood rooted to their points of origin after hundreds of years. Walking beneath their spreading branches, her fertile imagination conjured up visions of hopeful travelers resting under the same cool shade and she suddenly felt a poignant heartwarming connection to the past. Visions of pioneer women bringing their wooden buckets to the stone well to draw life-giving water sprang easily to mind despite the well having been capped some seventy-five years ago over safety concerns. The original structure was maintained for historical interest, though it was now lined with shade-loving hostas and impatiens instead of thirsty travelers. A winding cobblestone path, dotted here and there with wrought iron benches, meandered through the park where decades of courting couples must have strolled just as she was doing today. Rose tried to express her feelings to Simon. He listened politely but seemed a little bored by such sentimentality and instead drew attention to the dining possibilities on Main Street. Having been teased by her family for years about her fanciful ideas, she wasn't particularly pained by his lack of interest and excused him on the grounds of his obviously superior focus—gathering information about the present, not dwelling in the past.

As they stepped out of the pleasant relative coolness of the park into the full afternoon sun, Rose was instantly conscious of the desire for an icy cold soft drink. When she said as much to Simon, he chided her gently, saying, "Don't you remember, love? I am going to introduce you to the civilized practice of afternoon tea, and we certainly can't do that with a glass of carbonated artificially flavored soda water now, can we?" His teasing smile robbed the words of their sting. He took her hand and led her slowly toward the likeliest looking option on the street. In fact, it was the *only* option other than a tiny juice bar squeezed in between the town's doctor and Wally's Widget World, a sort of hybrid mechanical repair shop and computer store. The Early Bird Bakery was situated near the end of the street, next to a much larger establishment that was clearly undergoing extensive remodeling. A sign in the window informed passersby that Milly's Diner would reopen for business on or before August 10. As Rose and Simon strolled past the work site, they nearly collided with a workman walking purposely out of the doorway. He was just about to walk right into Rose when he raised his head from contemplation of the clipboard in his hands and stopped short, dropping his pen. As he bent to retrieve it, he began a hasty apology.

"I'm so sorry. I should have been paying attention. Are you all ri—" Finally focusing on the girl he'd almost run down, he said in surprise, "Rose!"

"Tim! It's so nice to see you again. I guess this is one of those places you talked about renovating in town."

Her genuine smile of greeting and obvious memory of an earlier conversation drew an answering smile from Tim. That is until he noticed Simon overtly intertwine his fingers with Rose's, obviously intending to add a note of intimacy to their companionship. Tim's face hardened into impassivity but he answered courteously enough, "It's good to see you too, Rose." He merely nodded recognition of Simon's presence. "If you'll excuse me, I need to pick up some supplies." Then he looked intently at Simon, a challenge in his eyes. "I look forward to seeing you both at church on Sunday."

Rose sensed the same peculiar tension between the two men that she had noticed at their first meeting but appreciated Tim's effort to include them both in the invitation to church. Watching his retreating form as he climbed into his truck and drove away, Rose turned impulsively to Simon and said, "You will join us at church on Sunday," looking hopefully into his suddenly rigid countenance.

Having followed the retreating truck with narrowed eyes, Simon glanced at the expectant expression on Rose's face before answering. "I *am* sorry but I'm afraid I'll be gone this weekend."

"Gone!" Rose responded in alarm. Was her dream to end so soon?

Reacting to her obvious dismay, he laughed. "Have no fear, my love. Did you think me so untouched by your loveliness that I could just walk out of your life forever after only a few short days of acquaintance?" He spoke with such tenderness that Rose felt gratified but a bit flustered while the betraying blush suffused her cheeks yet again.

He went on as they continued toward their destination, not looking directly at the girl. "I will be gone this weekend *only* because I need to make a trip to both Topeka and Lawrence. One is the state capital and the other is home to the state's largest university, both of which might hold interest for my blog readers. You do understand, darling?"

Relief made Rose feel a little giddy. "Of course! Maybe I'll plan a special surprise for you when you get back." She had no idea what that might be but she wanted to make sure he would want to return!

The Early Bird Bakery was intended to be just that—a haven for doughnut and muffin lovers with the only other breakfast offerings in the form of sausage and egg biscuits or ham and egg croissants. But with the temporary closing of the diner next-door, the original early bird herself, Maggie O'Donnell, offered to help her neighbor by hiring Milly's unoccupied staff to augment the bakery's store hours and provide simple lunch and dinner sandwiches for the populace until Milly was back in business. The little shop, not used to accommodating the extra clientele, tended to be a bit chaotic during peak dining hours; but fortunately for Simon and Rose, they entered the café during a lull. Adjured by a sign at the entrance inviting guests to seat themselves, Simon chose a snug nook by the front window and waited to place his order.

While they waited for what seemed an interminably long time to Simon, he reached his hands, adorned by a solitary ring, across the table, compelling Rose to place hers in his. As he held them gently, his thumbs softly rubbing the backs of hers, he asked, "You are enjoying yourself, my sweet, aren't you?"

Nervously avoiding his piercing gaze, Rose was almost hypnotized by the movement of his touch. "Y-yes. Of c-course." She hazarded a quick peek at his face to encounter an appealing look that could have melted the granite monument in the park. Rose felt an odd sense of relief when, at last, a waitress appeared and she could surreptitiously withdraw her hands from Simon's flirtatious clasp.

"What'll it be, folks?" asked a harassed-looking woman in her midthirties with hair escaping from a lopsided bun on top of her head. She shifted her weight form foot to foot as if they pained her, and her smile held about as much energy as a stagnant pond. Her nametag proclaimed her to be "Sunny."

"We're here for afternoon tea," explained Simon. "You do *serve* tea?"

"Oh, sure. Do you want that sweet or unsweet, honey?"

"No, you don't understand. We would like a pot of tea—preferably Lapsang souchong or Darjeeling."

"*Huh?*"

Rose intervened on behalf of the bewildered waitress. "We would just like two cups of hot tea, please. Er…what brands *do* you offer?"

"Well, basically America's Favorite, if you want it hot. Of course, if you'd like something cool—and I've gotta say, on a hot day like this, that's what *I'd* want—we've got several varieties of fruit tea."

Rose saw Simon grimace and hastened to assure the young woman that the hot tea would be fine. Then added hopefully, "Do you have any pastries left? I know it's a little late in the day—"

"I'm afraid all I can offer you is some no-sugar-added apple pie and some sugar-free wafers." Then after looking around the small space to see who might be able to overhear, she added softly with a meaningful look, "And just between you, me, and the gatepost, there's a reason they're still here."

In an effort to forestall any negative comments from Simon, Rose assured Sunny that the two cups of tea would be just fine.

"Well, milady," Simon drawled sarcastically after the waitress departed, "it would appear that we are definitely *not* at the Ritz."

Rose couldn't help laughing at the comical look of dismay on Simon's face. It grew even more pronounced when Sunny returned and plunked two cups of hot water on the table with a tea bag in each. But Rose's final downfall was the absolute outrage Simon displayed when Sunny generously added, "I thought you all might want some cream and sugar." And pulling some packets out of her apron she tossed them on the table, managed a half-hearted smile, and trudged to the next table. Rose was now doubled over with laughter.

Focusing only on the offerings before him, Simon said with utter disdain, "They can't *possibly* pass this off as afternoon tea. Cream is *not* a *powder and*—" Finally aware of Rose in dire straits, he started to laugh in spite of himself, her infectious giggle getting the better of him.

"Oh, it's all very well for you, you wretched girl, to sit there, laughing every time one of the bucolic natives strikes you funny but I have to *write* about this. How on *earth* am I to make *this* sound appealing?"

Struggling to regain her composure, Rose said between persistent giggles, "I wasn't...laughing at Sunny..." And off she went again as Simon rolled his eyes at the ridiculous misnomer. Valiantly trying again, Rose said with commendable control, "I was laughing...at you!" She mistook his expression of shock and looked away to keep from starting off on another bout of laughter so she missed seeing the smile harden on his face.

No one laughs at Simon Atherton—not even the delectable Miss Rose, he thought to himself as he watched the girl opposite him wipe her eyes, a smile still hovering on her lips. Fortunately for the harmony of the afternoon, Rose applied herself to dunking the tea bag in her cup and, with her eyes focused on her task, reproved him in good humor.

"Honestly, Simon, what did you expect in a small Midwestern town? After all, this isn't Meryton." Her allusion to the fictional English home of another favorite fictional character momentarily diverted him—long enough for her to add with genuine admiration, "Besides you add a touch of class to every room you enter so just add that touch of class to your description."

"You do me honor, madam. I shall endeavor to secure your approbation through my humble literary endeavors."

"That was perfect! You sounded just like Mr. Darcy!" Rose exclaimed in delight and her amusement at Simon's expense was forgiven. Tea was finished quickly as Simon found it virtually undrinkable and Rose because she drank it quickly to spare Sunny's feelings. After all, the waitress could only offer them what she had.

When the beleaguered server came to leave the check, Simon began his now customary search for local information.

"No, Mrs. Mason hardly ever comes in here but Angelica, the foreign one that takes care of her, will pop in and pick up some fresh croissants every now and again. I hear she's a pretty good cook herself, but of course, I don't suppose she knows how to make flaky pastry." That the croissants in question came already prepared in frozen form and only required baking in the shop was beside the point.

"She is a terrific cook," Rose affirmed.

"But surely Mrs. Mason must want to dine out from time to time. Is there nowhere in Tinkers Well for fine dining?" Simon asked suggestively.

"Oh, yeah! Now that you ask, there is that new place. It's only been open about three months. I think a retired couple runs it as kind of a hobby. They must have money because they bought the old train station behind Commerce Street and converted it into a restaurant. They even had an addition built on—I guess for the kitchen. But like I was saying, the owners don't keep it open all the time so it has kind of strange hours." Whether unconsciously, because her tired feet needed a rest or because her audience seemed open to a cozy chat, Sunny pulled out an extra chair at the table and sat down.

Knowing that people are more forthcoming when at their ease, Simon marked her action by standing in a gentlemanly way as she was seated and encouraged her further by simply saying, "Oh?"

"Yeah. I mean it's only open on Thursday, Friday, and Saturday nights and..." Sunny pursed her lips in an effort at recollection. "Saturday lunch...and...Monday breakfast. Yeah, that's right. I think it's called Louis's...Beast...Toe...no, that doesn't sound right..."

"Could it be bistro?" Simon offered helpfully.

"That's it! And they serve that fancy food. It sounds a lot like... hot...cousin. But that doesn't make sense either, does it?" she asked, looking at Simon for enlightenment.

"I believe it's called haute cuisine."

"Well, sugar, aren't you the knowing one?" Sunny said in blatant admiration and newfound animation. "Are you folks new to the area?"

"Yes and no," Simon answered and launched once again into his cover story. Sunny was as duly impressed as the others had been with the possible exception of the weary Mrs. Elder; and now that the knowledgeable and charming Simon had taken center stage, Rose was all but forgotten. She took no offence. It was entertaining to watch Simon drawing out all sorts of local gossip from the unsuspecting Sunny, using his wit and charismatic appeal. What Rose failed to realize was that he had been doing the same thing to her for days. Simon Atherton was a consummate professional.

*****

"Well, Aletha, what do you think of the idea? It's up to you, of course, since it's your home, but I think we can pull it off, and Angelica and I are both agreed that the sooner we give Rose some other interest the better."

Aletha had been listening intently to her friend's conversation on the other end of the phone. "I quite agree with you, Marilyn. Trudy and I have spent the past few days bemoaning the arrival on the scene of as smooth an operator as it has ever been my misfortune to meet. I know he's up to something but I can't, for the life of me, imagine what he wants in Tinkers Well or, quite frankly, with Rose. That type of man is usually in the company of a very different kind of woman…Yes, you're right about trying to warn dear Rose. Young women rarely heed the advice of their elders when it comes to affairs of the heart. Besides I need to move ahead with restoring the old house. I lost interest after Matthew died but I think he would approve wholeheartedly of the new plan so count me in…What's that? Oh good. I'm afraid organizing everything is quite beyond me these days, but if you and Angelica will see to all the details, I am happy to work on Tim from my end…That's right, dear. I'll call him tonight after dinner…Oh, and you'll call Pastor Lindeman. Wonderful… All right. We'll talk tomorrow morning and compare notes. Do you know, Marilyn, this is the most excited I've been about anything since I found out Trudy and Rose had accepted my invitation. I just had no idea their visit would prove to be so entertaining…Yes, I'll pass everything on to Trudy… Mm-hmm…Goodbye."

"Trudy," she called as she walked purposely toward the living room, cane gently tapping and Prince at her heels. "Trudy, we have something important to discuss."

"I'm here, Letha," said Gert, entering the house from the gazebo. "I was enjoying your peaceful garden. I find the quiet helps me think but I…" Then after a short struggle with herself, she blurted out, "Letha, I don't know what to do about Rose and it's worrying me half to death. I don't trust that Simon fellow as far as I can throw him, and I don't mind saying so, but Rose won't listen to me." The deep furrow between her brows grew more pronounced as she spoke.

"You just sit down here with me, old friend, "said Aletha, indicating the kitchen table, "and I'll tell you about the plan Angelica and Marilyn have hatched. Is there any coffee left?" Gert filled two cups and placed them on the table. "Now I'll try to outline everything for you before Rose gets back. But Angelica and Marilyn can fill us in on the details tomorrow morning."

Gert warmly approved of the plan Aletha had laid out. She slapped the table and said, "Now that's what I call taking care of business. Letha, I'm on board 100 percent."

"Do you know, I feel like a coconspirator in a suspense thriller," Aletha said with a laugh.

"I know what you mean. It kind of reminds me of the time we plotted to get Dorie away from that brainless football player… what was his name…something…Buckner. Rocky Buckner," Gert said with satisfaction as she snapped her fingers.

"Yes, he was quite the bad lot," Aletha agreed. "Do you remember how we…" And the two old friends were well away on another shared adventure from the past. They were still arguing over differing remembered details as they put the finishing touches on the simple dinner Angelica had left for them.

*****

"I can't say much for the Early Bird Bakery but that bistro sounds promising," Simon remarked as he drove Rose back to the cottage. "You know, if you wanted to make a gesture of appreciation to Mrs. Mason, you and your grandmother might consider taking her there for dinner on one of their few open days."

"Simon, that's a great idea. She's done so much for us and it might be nice for Granny Gert and Aletha to get out of the house more." Having planted the seed, Simon could only hope it would grow to fruition, affording him another opportunity to search the cottage unimpeded if his first two efforts resulted in failure.

"Perhaps you and I could try it first, just to make sure it would be suitable. What do you say to a romantic candlelight lunch or dinner?"

"I say *yes*!" Rose responded with enthusiasm.

"Then it's a date. Perhaps Saturday week after I've made my little side trip South. And I insist that you wear the alluring dress we bought today." Then he added, noting her self-conscious smile, "Do you know what it does to a man's ego when he walks through a door with the most beautiful woman in the room on his arm? I'm not sure you won't be my undoing, darling Rose." And reaching for her hand, he carried it to his lips, kissing it lightly and retaining it in his hold, his eyes on the road. Rose smiled happily and considered the promising prospect during the remainder of their drive.

Simon soon perceived an advantage to a later afternoon start as they approached the house. He had provided himself with a blameless excuse for taking Rose home just as Aletha and Granny Gert were preparing for dinner. Simon insisted on seeing Rose to the door and speaking to her grandmother and hostess, offering heartfelt apologies for their late return.

"Rose and I had such an enjoyable afternoon that we completely lost track of time. I hope I haven't caused you any inconvenience by getting her home late for dinner which, by the way, smells delicious. What do you call it?"

"Leftovers." Granny Gert had met them at the door, silently noting the dress over her granddaughter's arm. After receiving Rose's impetuous hug with good humor and admonishing the girl to "get washed up for dinner," she moved into the breach like a human barricade, making it impossible for Simon to encroach on the household any further without appearing boorish. "I'm afraid Angelica only left enough food for the three of us, but then, I'm sure you have better things to do than spend your evening with two old ladies," she said jovially but with a penetrating scrutiny that always left the suave sophisticate a little unnerved.

Never one to let an opportunity for graciousness go unexploited, however, Simon replied, "And I'm quite *certain* I should find your company enlivening. But perhaps we'll have that pleasure some other time."

Gert just smiled, nodded, and said, "Perhaps," then backed Simon to the door like a bulldozer in high gear. He had no option but to retreat. Driving back to the waiting piles of unopened storage boxes, he thought to himself, *I will definitely need to cultivate Rose to have any hope of penetrating that fortress. It's guarded better than Fort Knox! And the two ancients never seem to leave the place.* Then he remembered the information Rose had volunteered the day before and spoke out loud with grim relish, "Except, my boy, when they go to the old folks village hall on Thursday evenings. I believe I'll have myself a little look round then." After a brief pause, he added under his breath, "I trust the blind one will take that blasted dog."

Five hours later, his back aching and eyes strained, Simon was ready to hurl the stack of Mason historical archives into the nearest dumpster. As he sat in consideration of yet another of the endless repositories of useless information with outright loathing, wondering whether to ply its depths or just call it a night, his cell phone rang. The shrill sound broke the stillness of the Kansas night, offering the only audible competition for the never-ending chorus of crickets chirping outside. It was Miles Hawthorne.

"Damn!" Simon was in no mood to deal with Hawthorne's demands and probable criticisms but he achieved an attitude of calm complacence before answering.

"Good evening, Mr. Hawthorne. To what do I owe this pleasure?"

"You mistake my calling you, my friend. You owe me nothing but a positive report of progress. I trust you are able to meet such a request?" Hawthorne's tone did not brook disappointment.

"Things are proceeding quite as planned, despite an added obstacle in the form of guests visiting Mrs. Mason. An old school chum and her granddaughter have taken up residence at the Mason home and rarely leave the premises. I am presently cultivating the granddaughter, who has proven herself to be easily manipulated, with the intent of insinuating myself into the household as a regular guest. I've also gained access to Mrs. Mason's document storage unit which I am working through when not trying to gain entrance to the house."

"Well, damn it, man! Can't you just break in? I assume you possess those skills?"

Simon bit back an acid comment before answering, "Of course, sir. But I will have full unalloyed access to the house tomorrow evening while the ladies are scheduled to be out."

"Are you such a lout that you can't search the house while they're all home sleeping?"

"Now why didn't I think of that?" Simon replied caustically. "Could it be that I find watchdogs particularly troublesome even when one works with considerable stealth?"

"Seems to me you won't have any more luck when they're all gone if they keep a confounded animal to guard the place. You'll just have to leave something outside that it can ingest. Something laced with a tranquilizer."

"I can see I haven't made myself clear. The animal in question never leaves the blind woman's side.

There was a brief pause before Hawthorne asked sharply, "Blind woman? What blind woman?"

"Why, Mrs. Mason, of course. Didn't you know? I should have thought her son might have mentioned it during your negotiations with him."

Silence.

"Mr. Hawthorne? Miles…are you there?"

"Of course I'm here!" came the harsh reply. "I was…never mind."

"As I was saying, the dog goes with her wherever she goes so I should have the house to myself tomorrow evening, then again on

Sunday morning. I'm quite sure, if it's there, I will have located the document by then."

"I'll hold you to it. And, Atherton…"

"Yes, sir?"

"I need that document and I'm not averse to a little surreptitious burglary—provided you don't get caught—but I won't have anyone harmed. Is that clear?"

"Believe me, sir. I have no intention of harming anyone or anything. I abhor violence, so uncivilized."

"Then we understand each other. I'll contact you again on Sunday and I expect results."

As Simon stood holding the phone after Hawthorne abruptly rang off, his eyes narrowed and a calculating smile dawned. "So Hawthorne has a conscience. Surely I can use that to my advantage…" he murmured to himself. Turning his back on the pile of unopened boxes, Simon switched off the light and secured the unit. As he walked to his car, his fertile brain was working out a new plan of attack. He would have to make the most of his time with Rose tomorrow. Press her for details on Aletha's habits, choice pieces of furniture, and somehow employ her, unwittingly of course, to gather just the sort of information that would be most helpful to him.

Dear Rose, he thought to himself, *what delightful button shall I push this time?*

CHAPTER 10

Don't fool yourself. Don't think that you can be wise
merely by being up-to-date with the times.
What the world calls smart, God calls stupid.
He exposes the chicanery of the chic.
The Master sees through the smoke screens of the know-it-alls.

—1 Corinthians 3:19 (MSG)

"A picnic in the garden at the big house? I think that's an awesome idea!" Rose spoke with characteristic enthusiasm about Angelica's idea for a church fellowship event.

The Fern Cottage ladies had been joined by Marilyn Ludlow and all were gathered around the kitchen table, breakfast having been forced indoors by inclement weather. Soft under-cabinet lighting alleviated the gloom from overcast skies, and the gentle patter of rain on dripping windowpanes provided an asymmetrical rhythmic background for the animated discussion now in full swing.

"Well, it may be an awesome idea," replied Aletha, "but I'm not sure we can pull it off. I did speak to Tim last night, and though Three Brothers has several other commitments, he thought he would be able to repair the porch and have a functioning restroom ready in two weeks. No, the problem, really, is the garden itself. It was neglected for so long that it would almost take an army of gardeners to make it even passable." Feeling a warning pinch from Gert, she quickly added, "I'm afraid Tim told me that all the local landscaping crews are already spoken for," should Rose wonder that so wealthy a woman not simply hire a landscape architect to do the job.

Sprung from a long line of do-it-yourselfers, the thought never crossed Rose's mind. She did, however, question the short-term preparation period for the event. "But why does it all have to be done so soon? Couldn't we just push the picnic back a few weeks? Granny Gert and I will be here all summer..."

After an almost indiscernible pause, Angelica explained, "Well...we'd like to hold it before Pastor Lindeman and his family take their summer vacation."

Four heads nodded in relieved agreement until Rose suggested, "But surely he'll only be gone a week or so. Couldn't we hold the picnic after he gets back?"

"I thought of that too," said Marilyn, jumping into the breach. "but...then we'd be competing with...preseason sports practice, band camp, and all of us teachers prepping for the start of school. You know, we start the year so early now—the second week in August—and teachers have to be there the week before that so..."

"Well, I guess two weeks it is then," conceded Rose. "It looks like we'll need that army after all," she added doubtfully.

"I may not qualify as an army but I have a fair bit of free time on my hands during the summer. I will happily volunteer my unskilled labor for the project. I can at least clip and weed," Marilyn offered right on cue.

Appreciating the older woman's willingness, Rose said in a cooperative spirit, "Then we have an army of two. I wanted to start to work on that garden the first day I saw it but wasn't sure I wouldn't be in the way on the work site," she added. Looking at her grandmother, she said with a wry smile, "Grandpa Ernie *tried* teaching me about gardening. Maybe I'll remember some of his helpful hints once I get started."

"Rosie, whether you remember or not, he'd be right proud of you for even trying," Granny Gert said, giving the girl sitting next to her a quick hug.

"Now I can't have you two out there muckin' about in the mud by yourselves. It was my suggestion, after all. As soon as I finish the washin' up and laundry and such, I can join you," said Angelica from the sink.

"Seems that all you youngsters"—Marilyn nearly laughed out loud at Gert's comment—"have forgotten about Letha and me. We may be old and have our challenges but there's still a thing or two we can do for ourselves. Angelica, you just leave the housework to us. Letha is perfectly capable of helping me with the dishes and probably knows the surface of every piece of furniture in this house better than anyone."

"That's right, Trudy. I can take care of the dusting—"

"And I've been doing laundry since I helped my mother with an old wringer washing machine. These automated models make clothes washing a cakewalk—why, they practically fold the clothes *for* you. As for meals, we can fix sandwiches and whatever else you might want for your lunches."

"And we might even order out for pizza!" Aletha suggested, catching Gert's spirit.

The room fell suddenly silent. Everyone looked at the well-bred, precise, particular Aletha Mason as if she had just suggested drying her panties in public. Gert was the first to recover.

"And why not? I think pizza might be just the ticket!" she said with a chuckle. "What we need is a little something to shake things up around here."

"I agree, Trudy," declared the woman known for her strict adherence to routine.

"Good. Then let's get down to business," Gert spoke as one accustomed to command.

Marilyn and Angelica exchanged a look that spoke volumes. Each smiled to herself thinking, *We've made it past the first hurdle*, and waited for Aletha to take the reins.

"Might I suggest that we adjourn to the dining room where the table is bigger? We'll need some room to spread out the blueprints." Speaking in Rose's direction, Aletha asked, "Rose, dear, would you mind digging out the old plans for me? If you'll go to the escritoire in my room, you'll find a false back on the drawer when you pull it out. There's a little release in the back right corner. Push that and you'll find the cavity behind it. That's where I've always kept the plans for the house. I used to pull them out from time to time when we lived in Chicago, dreaming of the day we would return here. Tim has the blueprints for the house but the plans for the garden should still be there."

"Of course. I'll be right back." Rose was tickled to death about the prospect of seeing the old house come back to life, if only in small measure. That she could be a part of that effort was a gift she had not anticipated. And it exactly suited her idea of planning a great venture (though most people wouldn't see a church picnic in that light) by first recovering documents from a secret hiding place. Accordingly she hurried to Aletha's bedroom at the back of the house. The massive four-poster bed and matching armoire almost dwarfed the room but a delicate writing desk, now doing service as a dressing table, held its own in one corner.

After pulling out the solitary drawer of the elegant little piece, she located the precise location of the switch. Rose pressed it and was thrilled when the false back fell forward, revealing the space behind. She then carefully drew out the large roll of fragile paper, yellowed by the passage of time, and hurried back to the dining room with her treasure. She spread the tissue-thin sheets across the surface of the gleaming table, studying them as she waited for the other ladies to join her. She had been right about the sitting area beyond the great willow tree but the plans also showed several ornamental trees, planting beds, and a central fountain, none of which had been evident when she walked around the garden the day she had arrived. There was little hope of putting everything to rights in two weeks, but with everyone working together, they could at least clean it up and add some bright annuals, maybe have some sod delivered for the larger open area, and plant a few hardy shrubs that wouldn't shock so late in the season.

Aletha, when questioned, echoed the girl's suggestions. "Rose, I'm officially putting you in charge of the project." As Rose immediately balked at such a responsibility, Aletha reassured her, "Nonsense. The only expertise required for a project like this is a love for the old place and I believe you possess that, second only to me. The scope of the work is beyond me now but I trust you to make it beautiful again." Rose wasn't sure Aletha should trust her to dig a hole, let alone lay out and plant an entire garden, but she wanted to please her hostess so kept any more misgivings to herself.

Marilyn and Angelica stepped in to add their encouragement. "We'll be right there with you, honey. And it doesn't have to look just like this," Marilyn said, indicating the ornate layout. "It just needs to look welcoming, and I can't imagine that the three of us can't manage that."

"Marilyn is right, Miss Rose. Have a little faith and listen to Angelica. We'll make it a place to be proud of, and if I have anything to say about it, we'll get those young men to help us with the heavy liftin'. Mm-hmm," she said, nodding her head knowingly. "They won't eat until I finish workin' in the garden. That should be motivation enough."

Rose couldn't help laughing at such tactics. She spent the rest of the morning engrossed in the garden plans. At Marilyn's suggestion, she started a list of items they would need to purchase from the local nursery, Plants Aplenty, out on old Route 226. "Abe can probably take you out there tomorrow morning. I think the rain is supposed to stop by early afternoon today so the weather shouldn't be a problem." Rose just nodded, still deep in concentration over the blueprints. *Or maybe he'll be unavailable and someone else, Tim perhaps, will have to take you...* Marilyn thought to herself. She had a momentary twinge of conscience at such machinations but decided to wait until she had met the demigod, Simon Applegate, before committing to an accelerated strategic timeline.

She hadn't long to wait. He took all the ladies by surprise when he rang the bell just after 11:30. Rose, who had moved onto the library computer to do some research on garden equipment and paver suppliers, heard the bell but ignored it. *Probably a delivery or something*, she thought vaguely. Gert and Aletha were in the kitchen, arguing about the best way to season a pork tenderloin, while Angelica expertly completed the task and popped the double roasts in the oven. So it was left to Marilyn to answer the summons.

Though they had never met, as soon as she opened the door, Marilyn knew who the caller must be. Her heart sank. He was exactly as Angelica had described him—handsome, debonair, assured, with one corner of his mouth lifted in a quizzical smile that never failed to charm. "I'm sorry, madam, I don't believe I have the pleasure of your acquaintance. My name is Simon Applegate," he said, extending his hand in anticipation.

Even though she was on her guard, Marilyn couldn't ignore the distinct magnetism of the man. She took his proffered hand without thinking, then recalled her role as gatekeeper. After the briefest of handshakes, she introduced herself and invited him into the house. Knowing Rose was in the library, she steered him into the living room, indicating he take a seat on the tufted sofa. The rich brocade served as an ideal backdrop for the polished visitor. "I take it you are here to see Rose. I'm not sure she's expecting you quite so soon. I understood that you were to call for her after one o'clock."

Not the least bit put out by her direct statement, Simon merely looked amused and said, "I see you are well-informed."

So Rose has acquired another protector, he thought. *I wonder they don't collectively demand I cross a fire swamp to speak with her!*

Aloud he said, as if considering a puzzle, "Ludlow. It seems I met another Ludlow recently, a tall chap with an iron grip and a propensity for straight talk—your brother, I take it?"

Oh, you are good. I can almost see the shadow of Samuel Jamison looming up behind you, Marilyn thought grimly. Nothing but polite interest showed on her countenance, however, as she responded with her own amused smile, "Really, Mr. Applegate. You needn't waste your blandishments on me. I'm much too old for that. No, I am Tim's mother, Marilyn. And I'm happy to have met you but I'm sure you would rather speak with Rose than trade pleasantries with me. If you'll excuse me, I'll just see if I can find her."

Simon thanked her politely and, just as politely, stood when she rose from the cushioned occasional chair opposite him. Marilyn took her time leaving the room but moved quickly when out of view. She hurried into the library where Rose still sat, eyes glued to the computer screen, her hand slowly gliding over the mouse pad.

"Rose!" Marilyn said softly. No response.

"Rose!" A little louder.

"Hmm?" came the absentminded reply.

"Rose!" Marilyn was now shaking the shoulder of the preoccupied girl. That finally got her attention.

"I'm sorry, Marilyn. Did you need me to help with something?"

"No, no. Angelica is well-away on lunch prep despite 'help' from Aletha and your grandmother." The apt description of kitchen operations drew a responsive smile from Rose. "No, sweetie, I just wanted you to know that Mr. Applegate is here. I didn't think you were expecting him quite so soon…" She glanced significantly at the girl's attire.

Looking down, Rose exclaimed in dismay, "Oh, good grief! This is the second time he's caught me in my pajamas. He wasn't supposed to be here until later. That is…what time is it, anyway?"

"It's nearly noon. Can *I* help *you* with anything?"

"Oh, *would* you? I can't believe I've been in here so long! I hate to lose all these leads I've found for things we'll need. Would you mind saving them to the favorites bar?"

As Marilyn took her place at the desk, Rose said, "Thank you! And could you stall Simon for a few minutes? I need to get cleaned up, do my hair, put on my makeup…Aaagh! Why do men think they can just drop in on women and assume they'll be sitting there waiting for them?" Since that was precisely what had happened the day before, it seemed an irrational question, but Marilyn found the impatience with which it was uttered hopeful.

Hope, however, took a setback some twenty minutes later.

Marilyn returned to the living room just as Aletha and Gert emerged from the kitchen, having been kindly but firmly shooed away by Angelica.

"Oh, it's you," was all Gert said in acknowledgment of Simon's presence.

Aletha, a little more tactful, said, "Is that you, Mr. Applegate? I'm sorry, I didn't hear the bell. Rose must have answered it. Or perhaps…"

"No, I had the pleasure of meeting Mr. Applegate, Aletha," Marilyn explained. Turning to the guest, she said, "Rose will be with you shortly. I'm afraid she wasn't expecting you so soon and was caught up in the preparations for a church event we'll be holding at the main house in a few weeks. It will be quite an undertaking and Aletha has put Rose in charge of—"

"I thought you weren't going to pick up Rosie until she's had her lunch," Gert said, abruptly cutting in on Marilyn's explanation.

"I wouldn't dream of taking her away before she's had a chance to taste whatever that delectable smell represents. I suppose I just came early on a whim, hoping you might have room for one more at table," Simon said wistfully.

Before Aletha or Marilyn could fall into that trap, Gert said with relish, "Now aren't you one for bad luck! We only had enough leftovers for the three of us last night, and Angelica's only prepared enough for five today. You see, Marilyn will be joining us for lunch," she added, glaring meaningfully at the other women as she spoke. Marilyn struggled to keep her quivering lip under control.

"That is, unless you mean to treat Rosie to a proper meal. I believe all you managed yesterday was some tea and the day before that was coffee and a muffin. Aren't you the big spender!"

"You mistake me, Mrs. Gunn," Simon said with a glittering smile. "I would happily squander the riches of Croesus on Rose if only you would afford me the opportunity. Her time does seem to be, however, somewhat...er...regulated." He raised a challenging eyebrow at Gert.

I can keep this up all day, you old battle-ax, he thought to himself, enjoying a twisted kind of mirth in baiting the old woman.

Not as skilled at verbal fencing as the worldly young gentleman confronting her, Granny Gert was about to launch into a stinging reply when Rose, still fastening on earrings, entered the room a little out of breath. Marilyn, watching her covertly, thought she looked a little put out, and felt a resurgence of the hope she had experienced briefly as Rose had left the library. Then Marilyn witnessed a transformation so ludicrous it might have been amusing had it not involved the object of her son's affections.

Simon jumped up from the sofa at the sound of the girl's approach and stepped toward her, hands held out in welcome. "Darling Rose," he crooned at his honey-coated best. "How *do* you manage to look more ravishing each time I see you?" Any sign of annoyance was put to flight as Rose happily placed her hands in his and lifted a face both worshipful and self-conscious. She was a little embarrassed by his blatant display of affection in front of the older ladies she had come to respect and care for.

Marilyn felt disheartened. She glanced at Angelica who nodded her head meaningfully. Marilyn almost imagined an audible, "Mm-hmm."

That Rose was besotted was evident. Belief that a man found her ravishing in simple Capri pants, loose print top, and sandals she had scrambled into moments before required a total detachment from reality. It was almost as if Simon held some hypnotic power over the innocent girl.

Catching sight of Granny Gert's disapproving eye, Rose quickly pulled her hands out of Simon's clasp and took a step backward. "I...I...didn't realize you were...that is, you *are* here early today. Are...are you joining us for lunch?" She looked hopefully at the other women and found four blank faces.

"Why, no. Your clever grandmother has suggested that we dine out together instead of merely settling for afternoon tea. I think it's a splendid idea, don't you?" Rose, completely misunderstanding Simon's reference to Granny Gert, smiled and impulsively hugged the disgruntled old lady. "You all," she said, addressing the room at large, "are full of great ideas today!"

Not one to be bested without a fight, Gert threw down her final gauntlet. "Seems to me if you two are so set on spending so much time together, you should both join us for dinner and bingo with the town senior's group tonight."

Rose, eager to endorse any plan that included Simon, turned to him expectantly. "Can you? Join us this evening, I mean? Last Sunday, I met several of the people that will be there and I think it would be a lot of fun."

Even if Simon hadn't already made clandestine plans for an uninvited visit to the empty cottage that night, he would never, in his wildest imaginings, have accepted an invitation to a social event that combined the word *fun* with an interminable evening spent in a room full of octogenarians. Impossible! However, he managed to reply graciously, with almost believable regret, "I *am* sorry but I have allowed myself to get a trifle behind in my writing which is, of course, all *your* fault." He paused to gently touch Rose's glowing cheek. "I've been having such a marvelous time in your company, my love, that I have neglected my work."

Marilyn groaned inwardly. Gert snorted audibly. Angelica rolled her eyes, uttering her customary "Mm-hmm." Aletha's face reflected her growing concern while Prince watched over his domain with a suspicious eye.

"Shall we be on our way?" Simon said as he tucked Rose's hand under his arm and pulled her toward the door.

As they heard the Escalade drive away, Marilyn looked at Angelica and said, "You were so right. Samuel Jamison." Neither Aletha nor Gert understood the enigmatic remark but they were all as one in their resolve to separate Rose from Simon Applegate before it was too late.

*****

It took Rose a good fifteen minutes to realize that the big Escalade was making good time *away* from Tinkers Well. She had been content to sit in silence, relishing the feel of her hand being gently massaged by Simon's as it lay on his knee. She couldn't help being thankful for the slow tentative manner in which he conducted his courtship. Surely his determined pursuit could mean nothing less. Not given to considering the long-term implications, Rose was happy to live in the moment and experience more of Simon's enticing romantic overtures in the absolute belief that he looked upon her as a gift to be treasured. His actions spoke for themselves. A caressing touch here, a demure embrace there, a soft kiss dropped on her forehead. Was not this truly the hallmark of a gentleman? If his eyes conveyed a deeper longing, he obviously honored her shy response to his respectful physical advances in a way that assured her of his affection and her utter security in his company. She had said as much to her mother the night before.

"Of course he can be trusted, Mother. He's not like anyone else I've ever met before...he's so respectful and gallant. He makes me feel... special...and not just because I'm helping him in his work. Just ask Granny Gert. I'm sure she thinks as highly of him as I do..."

Beth Thompson *had* spoken with her mother, prompting the call to Rose.

"Yes, Mother. I promise to remember to act like a lady...oh, for heaven's sake! 'No touching between the neck and the knees.' Now are you happy? I think you can safely rest assured that he would never *impose himself on me like that..."*

Musing over that conversation, Rose glanced at Simon's profile and noted, once again, the well-defined jaw line, the fine soft brown hair left full but trimmed neatly over his ear. Then her eyes drifted to the sodden landscape beyond the car's window. As predicted, the rain was letting up and narrow rays of promising sunshine reflected brightly off of dripping trees and tin roofs. Following the undulating line of rolling hills, marked intermittently with farmhouses and barns, Rose finally realized that they were nowhere near Tinkers Well. She wasn't concerned at all, just curious about Simon's plan for the day and said as much.

"Well, my love, since your grandmother gave her blessing for us to spend more time together, I thought we'd take a holiday and drive into Kansas City where I'm *certain* we'll find more dining choices and perhaps a museum or two."

"But I thought you were behind in your writing," she reminded him. "At least, that's what you told Granny Gert."

"I did, didn't I?" he responded with a grin. "But what she doesn't know won't hurt her," he added with a wink. Noticing her conscious-stricken expression, he continued smoothly, "Come now, darling, I think we can play truant for a few hours without committing too many mortal sins. Besides I am *always* collecting information, and if I can manage that while enjoying the company of a beautiful woman, so much the better. And I faithfully promise to keep my nose to the proverbial grindstone tonight while you hobnob with the venerable aged of Tinkers Well. Okay?"

Rose seemed mollified but only nodded her head in agreement.

"Where is that winning smile that I have come to adore?" Simon said, coaxing her to let down her tiresome guard of small-town scruples. Hardly impervious to his expert emotional manipulation, Rose rewarded his efforts with a smile that lit up her whole face.

Knowing her to be fully on his side once more, Simon questioned her about the time and duration of the ladies' excursion that evening. Knowledge of his precise window of opportunity for searching the house was critical. After dropping off Rose the day before, he had found a disused dirt road about three hundred yards from the Mason driveway. Directly across the road in a bunch of overgrown bushes, he had cut through the wire fencing surrounding the property, thus providing himself with both an undetectable entrance and egress for the grounds and a hiding place for his second vehicle, though it was unlikely that the truck would be recognized by any of the inhabitants of Fern Cottage.

Complying with yet another inquiry into her life, she countered with, "Simon, you have asked so many questions about me and my family and Aletha but I know almost nothing about you."

"I was always taught not to talk too much about oneself when fostering new friendships but rather, out of respect, draw the others out and accord them the courtesy of speaking freely."

Anxious that he not think her critical of his conversation skills, Rose hurried on. "Oh, I know you were just being courteous and I respect that about you. I've noticed you do that with all the people in town that you've interviewed which not only shows your good manners but you've gotten a lot of helpful information too, "she commented naively.

"Indeed I have," he answered with an odd inflection in his voice that was lost on Rose. "Now what would you like to know? I can assure you that the life of a blogger is not very exciting."

"I can't believe that but what I'm trying to say is that *I'd* like to know about the *real* Simon. You know, your childhood, hobbies, favorite sports teams…" Nothing really personal had ever surfaced in the anecdotes he had shared with her about his work. They were all humorous indictments of the people he had encountered in his travels. For a brief moment, she recalled the lively conversation between Tim, Derek, and Abe on Sunday. During those short hours of listening to the three men swap stories, she felt like she'd learned more about any one of them than she knew about Simon.

"I'm afraid you won't find the account of my life the least bit compelling but here is Simon Applegate in a nutshell." He cleared his throat with great flare, went through a few comical vocal exercises until Rose was laughing, and launched into his "history." "I was born in London and attended a respectable though not well-known public school—"

"There, you see. I would have thought, by the educated way you speak and your knowledge of all things cultural, that you went to a private school."

"I *did* attend a private school—Broadmoor to be precise."

"But you just said you attended a *public* school..."

"Oh, I see the confusion. In England, a public school *is* a private school." Laughing at her baffled expression, he merely said, "Never mind. You'd have to be a Brit to understand. Now where was I? My father worked in civil engineering for the city." Which, strictly speaking, was true—a day laborer who sought irregular employment as a ditch-digger on road crews. "My mother worked in the food and beverage industry."

"Well, that explains your cr...er...appreciation for fine dining." Rose had almost said "criticism of everything you eat" but stopped herself in time.

No need to explain to Rose that his mother's employment had involved making a name for herself as the favorite barmaid at the corner pub. As a youth, Simon began to suspect that she favored choice clientele with special "service" in one of the rooms above the Rose and Thorn. How else could she explain the growing wardrobe and real jewels that had replaced the bobbles she had always adorned herself with? He had never felt a need to make it his business to know more as long as he had something to eat.

"I went to work for a travel agency straight out of college." Their relative educational systems had already proven confusing so he thought it best not to try and explain that college referred to Lower and Upper Sixth forms or eleventh and twelfth grades rather than university. No need to muddy international waters any further. Besides he'd chucked it all at the end of year ten. Let her think him as well-educated as she was. "One of the perks was earning points toward plane fares, tours, and the like so I saved up all my points for a once-in-a-lifetime trip to the States. I spent two weeks here and decided this was the country for me so I stayed. I worked at any job I could find in New York City to keep body and soul together until I hit on the idea of putting my travel knowledge to work for me as a travel blogger."

"Wow! That was a courageous leap. I mean, leaving your family and moving across the world. Don't you miss them?"

"Of course I miss them." Simon nearly choked on the words. "But they've made several trips across the pond to see me and I've been back to England a few times," he rattled off glibly. "And then there's e-mail, RealTime, and Facepage. This *is* the twenty-first century after all." He pointed out to the gullible girl with a hint of mockery.

As a story, it was masterful. Had Rose known that it was a complete fabrication by the man she believed to embody the noblest characteristics of a gentleman, she would have been horrified. She might have demanded that she be returned immediately to the bosom of her grandmother and a world of truth and honor. But Simon had no intention of allowing her to be disillusioned while he still had need of her.

"So I 'see' Mum and Dad, or at least talk to them, as often as I might have done living in the same city."

"I suppose you're right. After all, I'm only a few states away from my folks but we talk almost every day." That settled, Rose tried to wrap her brain around Simon's profession. "But I still don't understand how the whole blogger thing works. How is blogging a regular job?"

"Oh, there's nothing regular about it. That's why it suits me so well. I live by my wits." Truth at last. "The more compelling my posts, the more followers I have and the more I make from advertising. It's a little more complicated than, say, writing for a magazine or newspaper. I had to 'sell' my name through Facepage, Twidder, and so on to pique people's interests. Have you looked at it yet, the blog I mean?"

"I have and it's *very* impressive. Beautiful photography. Captivating descriptions. You almost had me ready to move to at least six different places at once!" said Rose with enthusiasm.

"And did you notice the links, pop-ups, and ads that appeared?" At her nod, he continued, "That's my income."

"I may not fully understand it but I do appreciate the work you do." After a short pause, she added shyly, "I'm just happy it brought you to Tinkers Well." Without looking at Rose, Simon reached for her hand, brought it to his lips, and kissed it tenderly, repeating a gesture she had come to know and anticipate with pleasure.

Reaching the outskirts of Kansas City, Simon had to concentrate more on maneuvering in traffic so Rose did a little research of her own. Pulling out her cell phone, she looked for places of interest in the area. Making a note of one promising venue in particular, she took in the sights of the metropolitan area that she had missed on her drive west. On that first pass through the city, her attention had been focused on making it through the center of town without a wayward shift in the wrong direction.

Taking a turn to the south, they crossed to the Missouri side of the city and finally stopped at a place called the Silo Market and Feed. The repurposed grain silo and feed store proved to be a top-notch restaurant boasting farm-to-table cuisine. The interior was chic farmhouse with clean lines and minimalist decor that hinted at rustic and homey without really achieving it. Rose would have felt more at home in The Pickle Barrel but Simon was clearly pleased.

"A far cry from the Early Bird Bakery, eh?" Rose mentally described the meal as designer food, though it was delicious, but she was shocked at the prices—and at the amount of wine Simon consumed. The waiter, Jeremy, an effeminate twenty-something in skinny jeans with a man bun and multiple nose rings, kept the wine flowing and offered unsolicited suggestions for their entertainment while in the city.

"You've simply *got* to see the Newsome-Allen Gallery," lisped Jeremy, filling Simon's glass once more, and gesturing in a coquettish way that almost made Rose nauseous.

"Simon, I was hoping we might go to the—"

"Any contemporary art, Jeremy? I've not much use for the stagnant precision of the masters."

"Of *course*. I *adore* contemporary art," gushed Jeremy. "So raw and *visceral*."

"I don't really care for modern art, Simon—" said Rose, trying vainly to squeeze in a word between exchanges in the unlikely bromance playing out before her.

"Raw and visceral. Do you know, that really is a very apt description, my friend."

"And there's a work in industrial steel called *Strangled Hope* that will simply make you *weep*—"

Rose persevered. "But the National Agriculture Center and Hall of Fame isn't far from here and—"

Simon and Jeremy both stopped in midsentence and stared at her as if she had two heads and had suggested watching paint dry on the far side of the moon.

"Rose, darling, you're not serious—"

"But it looks like a lot of fun. There are hands-on exhibits and tours—"

"Rose—"

"And milk practically fresh from the cow." Jeremy visibly shuddered.

"*Rose!* Darling. I'm trying to gather information that will interest educated cosmopolitan people, not a following of the hairy unwashed. Now be a good girl and say you'd rather go to the art museum."

Rose thought fleetingly of Grandpa Ernie who had toiled his whole life to support a family, contribute to the community, and honor God with his generosity to those in need. Simon's flippant description of the farming fraternity hurt. She realized that he spoke out of ignorance but the comment stung all the same. She also realized that she would not enjoy herself at the Agriculture Center with an unwilling companion so she showed a brave front and agreed to the art museum but with little enthusiasm.

"I'm sorry, my love. Have I said something to offend you?" asked Simon, her reserved manner finally filtering through his slightly fuzzy brain.

"No," she said, mustering a hopefully convincing smile. "I'm sure the art museum will be nice."

"I *promise* you'll find it illuminating, darling."

Jeremy was quick to second Simon's assertion. "He is *so* right."

He was *so* wrong.

Rose wandered through a stream of exhibits containing paintings and sculptures that resembled nothing even remotely recognizable. She feigned interest as Simon tried to explain the finer points of each work and its inner meaning, all the while thinking a hayride would have been so much more enjoyable.

Worry was added to disappointment as Simon helped himself to yet another glass of wine in a nearby café before heading back to Tinkers Well. Naturally Rose understood that in enlightened sophisticated circles, the consumption of fine wine figured as something akin to a hobby. But she had never moved in those circles. Instead she had been raised by two teetotalers who *might* imbibe a few sips of champagne at a wedding or New Year's Eve party. So she was understandably a little nervous around those who drank alcohol to what she considered excess. Simon's demeanor was as gracious and charming as ever, but for the first time in their acquaintance, Rose felt a tinge of uncertainty in his company. When they returned to the car she offered to drive.

"Afraid, little Rose?" Simon gently teased her. "I would never hurt a hair on your exquisite head," he assured her in soothing tones as he looked tenderly into her troubled eyes, stroking her soft curls. She wanted so badly to believe him, and when he relinquished the keys, her qualms temporarily abated. But he soon fell asleep, leaving Rose to continue the drive virtually alone, lost in her disquieting thoughts.

CHAPTER 11

You shall stand up before the gray head and
honor the face of an old man,
and you shall fear your God: I am the Lord.

—Leviticus 19:32 (ESV)

Harvest Hall, located on Maple Street just a block behind the courthouse, was already abuzz with activity when Rose escorted Granny Gert and Aletha through the large front door that was manned by a smartly dressed elderly gentleman in sport coat and tie. Rose recognized Mr. Taylor from Marilyn's Sunday brunch and was surprised and pleased when he greeted all three ladies by name.

"What a memory!" remarked Gert. "I can't even remember what I ate for breakfast this morning!"

"Well, I hope you remember what you have for dinner tonight, Gertie. I believe the ladies have outdone themselves. Oh, and I see you've brought a dessert." Peering inquisitively at the round pan carried by Gert, he added hopefully, "Please tell me it's Angelica's Jamaican apple pie. I find it irresistible."

"It's the rum," Gert remarked shrewdly as she set the pie on a table laden with other tempting desserts. "I watched Angelica make this pie. She was *very* liberal with her measurements, if you know what I mean."

She and Rose were greeted as old acquaintances by those they had met on Sunday and were welcomed to a seat at Aletha's regular table. A slightly overwhelming but friendly rapid-fire interrogation followed with one question asked before the former was answered.

"Now that you've been here a few days, what do you think of Tinkers Well? Have you been to the main house yet? Don't you think Aletha's cottage is just lovely? I know Angelica cooks divinely…"

"Gertie brought the Jamaican apple pie!" Mr. Taylor interjected, taking his place at the table.

"But have you been to Milly's Diner for breakfast? Her pancakes are as light as air…Martha, they can't have been to Milly's yet. Remember, it's closed for renovation…Why don't you plan to join our Sunday school class this week…" And on it went.

Still a little troubled by Simon's behavior earlier, Rose wasn't in a very talkative mood so she left Granny Gert to fend for herself while she listlessly gazed around the room. Red, white, and blue fabric swags festooned the length of the two longer paneled walls while lengths of similar striped material draped the corners of the shallow, slightly elevated platform at the front of the hall. An American flag stood prominently on one end of the platform and a Kansas State flag on the other. Patriotism was alive and well in mid-America and with Flag Day and the Fourth of July in such close proximity on the calendar, the town council determined years ago to decorate for the one and leave the hangings in place for the other. It made for a very festive atmosphere and cheered Rose's dampened spirits. Congeniality figured abundantly in the faces around her and at all the neighboring tables. The fellowship of friends and neighbors in community always served as a powerful elixir of encouragement, especially for those who spent most of their days alone. At twenty-six, everyone over fifty looked old, but Rose guessed that most of the people present were in their seventies or eighties. However, she had noticed a big birthday cake topped with a "93" among the other sweets on the dessert table and was idly speculating on who might have achieved such an impressive goal when the room suddenly erupted in cheers. She had to stand to see what the big fuss was all about.

Rose looked toward the door to see a man being wheeled into the room by someone in military dress uniform. The huddled form in the wheelchair was dressed in coat and tie, like most of the other men present, but he sported a hat decorated with several pins and some sort of insignia across the bill. She couldn't make out the details from where she stood but suddenly caught her breath as she recognized the uniformed man guiding the chair to a table in the front of the room. It wasn't so much the uniform that had thrown her, it was the facial hair or total lack thereof. A clean-shaven Tim Ludlow deposited his charge in the place of honor then rendered the old man a sharp salute which was returned with a shaking hand and a broad toothless grin. Tim shook the gentleman's hand and held it for a few moments, covering it with his other hand. After saying something that brought a shout of laughter from the guest of honor, Tim executed a precise about-face and walked toward the back of the room.

Everyone had returned to their seats by then so Tim nodded or waved to familiar faces as he passed them. That included those at Aletha's table. He stopped to greet Aletha and drop a kiss on her forehead. Then glancing a few chairs over as he started to move on, he saw Rose and halted in midstride. He uttered what had become his customary greeting—"Rose!"—and stood rooted to the spot. Tim had fully expected to see Aletha and Mrs. Gunn at the seniors' event but it never occurred to him that Rose would stay for the festivities after dropping off the older ladies. Now it was his turn to blush, and with a face unencumbered by a full beard, the red flooding his cheeks was obvious to all those seated at the table. Two thoughts flashed through his mind. *She looks like she's worried about something*, and, *There is no sign of Simon Applegate—interesting*.

Rose had the advantage in that she had prepared for his approach but was still taking in the full impact of his new look when he reached her table. "Hi, Tim. I didn't recognize you at first. The uniform is *very* impressive and so is your face." As she saw his eyebrows lift in surprise, she realized how that last comment must have sounded. "I...I don't mean your *face* is impressive..." His eyebrows drew together. "Th-that is, you look really nice...I mean, without the beard." She ended in confusion.

As Tim and Rose greeted each other, they might have been the only two in the room but a captive audience witnessed the amusing exchange with lively interest. Aletha felt an elbow in her ribs as Gert mumbled, "Letha, *do* something..."

"Uh, Tim, I wish I could offer you a place at our table but we're already full up with Gert and Rose swelling our numbers this evening." Then as if thinking of an important detail, she continued, "And I just remembered that Mildred Putnam will be joining us a little later." She then pulled out all the stops with the perfect rendition of a flustered old lady. "Oh dear, how will everyone fit? And poor Prince has almost no room under the table as it is…"

Like the waiting partner in a vaudeville act, Gert chimed in with perfect timing. "I've got just the ticket. Sonny, would you mind if Rosie sat with you tonight? I'm sure you young people would rather talk about the interweb or I, J, or K phones instead of listening to us old folks compare notes on the latest blood pressure medicine. What do you say?"

Rising swiftly to the challenge, Tim responded with commendable aplomb while mentally saluting the old woman's strategy. "Always happy to be of service, ma'am. Rose, will you do me the honor?" As he spoke, he stepped behind her, politely pulling out her chair. She glared briefly at Granny Gert who merely smiled and nodded her head.

"That's right. You children run along and enjoy yourselves."

Embarrassed but left with no options, Rose graciously took the arm offered her. Stealing a look at Tim's face, she encountered a friendly smile and returned it a little ruefully. "I'm afraid my grandmother can be a little…obvious at times. I hope you'll forgive her scheming."

"Are you kidding? I tip my hat to her. Mrs. Gunn would've made a heck of a military tactician." Rose couldn't help laughing, grateful for his casual handling of an awkward moment.

As he seated her at a table near the door, Rose said, "I really did mean it when I said that your uniform looks impressive. But I thought you weren't in the army anymore."

"I'm not on *active duty* anymore but I'm still in the army reserve." Anticipating her next question, he explained, "I'm assigned to an army unit that is activated as needed during wartime when regular army forces require augmentation." Still seeing a puzzled look on her face, he added, "I'm what's referred to as a weekend warrior. I train with my unit one weekend a month and two or so weeks during the summer. Make sense?"

"More or less. Sorry. I'm not very fluent in army speak."

"That's okay. I wasn't either until I got into ROTC in college."

"But I still don't understand why you're wearing the uniform tonight? Or why you saluted that man in the wheelchair."

"That 'man' is Corporal Henry James, the last living World War II veteran in Tinkers Well," Tim said with great respect in his voice and a hint of emotion. "His generation saw and did and endured things that would make most of our generation run for the hills. Do you know, old Henry was not quite eighteen years old when he took part in the D-Day invasion? There were thirty-odd thousand troops on Omaha Beach that day and he's one of the lucky few who lived to tell about it. His older brother, George, is one of the names on the memorial in the park. He wasn't so lucky." There was still an air of reverence in Tim's attitude, even after he finished speaking. He misunderstood Rose's respectful silence and added apologetically, "I'm so sorry. You asked a simple question and I gave you a lecture."

"Please don't apologize. I love to hear stories about every day heroes. Do you think I could meet old Henry?" Rose smiled as she said the name.

"Absolutely. But I think I should warn you—he's quite a character. He's also an incorrigible flirt and you are clearly the prettiest girl in the room."

"I'll be on my guard," she said, laughing. How odd that Tim's last comment was virtually identical to one made by Simon the day before but Tim's sounded more like an honest compliment than grandiloquent flattery. She wasn't sure which she appreciated more. "And you're wearing your uniform because..."

"In honor of Henry's birthday. It gives him a kick to hang out with the captain. And that's why I had to shave off my beard. It's against regulation when in uniform. Besides it's getting a little hot to have that extra layer of insulation on my face *and* I have annual training at Fort Riley next month so it was good timing."

"Well, for what it's worth, I think the look becomes you, especially since you're not hiding that attractive dimple in your chin anymore." Immediately conscience-stricken for verbalizing such unsolicited praise, Rose thought, *Oh, golly! Why did I say that? It's not as if he could compete with Simon in the good-looks stakes. All the same, Tim does look awfully handsome in that uniform. That's it—it's probably just the uniform.*

Her reason partially assuaged, Rose just caught Tim's response. He had been caught off guard by her unexpected compliment and decided there and then to swear off beards forever. However, he simply replied, "Why, thank you." Fortunately the emcee for the evening intervened, sparing both any further embarrassment by calling their table and the two adjacent ones to line up for the buffet.

A rousing chorus of "Happy Birthday" after dinner signaled the cutting of Henry's birthday cake and preparation for bingo. Cards were handed around and Rose waited in pleased anticipation as Tim took several cards and handed her two of them.

"You mean, we're actually going to play?" asked Rose. "I thought this was meant to be an innocent entertainment for the seniors."

"Innocent my foot. Don't let the silver hair and soft pink cheeks fool you—these people are cutthroat competitors, especially Aletha."

Laughing at Tim's description of the hardened gamblers around them, she asked, "But how does Aletha play? Surely she doesn't have braille bingo cards?"

"You bet she does and she doesn't miss a trick," he said with a grin. "If it wasn't for the letters and numbers printed underneath the raised braille symbols, she might be accused of cheating. I'm telling you, she *always* wins. And I think it only fair to warn you that I'm usually pretty lucky too," he added with a cocky look that brought a challenging expression to Rose's face.

"Is that so?" she said with narrowed eyes. "Then bring it, Ludlow."

"You're on, Thompson," replied Tim, hugely entertained by her sporting banter.

The ensuing battle brought as much—if not more—delight to the two young people in the back of the room as it did to their seniors engaged in intense rivalry all around them.

"Ah, I saw that. I'm pretty sure he did *not* call I-18. Boy, I'll have to watch you every minute," Tim said in mock censure.

"He most certainly did and—hey, you marked it on *your* card. You turkey!" Rose countered.

"Did I? Wait…hush, I can't hear…did you catch that last one?" Tim looked at Rose, her face a study of innocence.

"I'm not sure. *Someone* was *talking*," Rose added pointedly.

Tim grinned and said under his breath, avoiding eye contact, "Works *every* time…"

He felt her response in the form of a playful punch on his arm.

By the end of the evening, Aletha was a big winner, as Tim had predicted, but Rose won too. Tim did not. "Well, I guess we know who the superior player is," she said with an arch smile and no humility whatsoever.

"Care for a rematch next week…punk?" Tim asked with such a bad impression of a Hollywood legend that Rose burst out laughing.

"Do you come every week then?" she asked, a little surprised.

"No, but I try to be available to help Henry when he feels up to getting out. And my mom and I take turns picking up Aletha if one of her other church friends aren't able to so I'm usually here once a month or so. But I would be willing to make an exception if it means bringing you down…"

"You're on." Hesitating a little, Rose added sincerely, "Thanks for a really fun evening. I didn't expect to enjoy myself so much." It had certainly been more enjoyable than the art gallery but she wasn't ready to examine that comparison quite yet.

"You bet," was Tim's succinct reply. "Well, I'd better get old Henry home. He's probably already asleep in his chair."

"Oh, shoot. Then I guess I'll have to meet him another time."

"I promise I'll take you to visit him one of these days. Oh, I almost forgot. I guess I'll see you at the old house this weekend. Mom told me you had agreed to head up the garden restoration project. I know that means a lot to Aletha. Thank you," Tim said with genuine sincerity.

"I'm just excited to see the old place come to life. I'll see you there then."

Tim nodded and made his way to old Henry. Rose, looking after him, thought, *You know, he really is a nice guy.*

*****

"Damn! Damn! And blast!" Simon said under his breath as he went through one oversized piece of furniture after another. "Did these people have a penchant for hiding things or just an overzealous inclination for the ornate and devious," referring irreverently to the Victorians.

Entry to the cottage had been as simple as opening the backdoor, thanks to the information Rose had kindly provided, explaining that Aletha left it unlocked so that neither the Ludlows nor Warners ever need worry about a key. Rose had also talked at length about the secret cavity in Aletha's desk, inspiring Simon to check every nook and cranny of the furniture in each room. But he found nothing. Either they contained no hidden compartments or he had been unable to locate the switch to access them. That simply meant more dreary research about antique furniture construction before his return to the cottage on Sunday morning.

A search of the bedrooms produced no results but the need to leave everything as he had found it slowed his progress considerably. Looking into the library, he had discovered with dismay the numerous literary volumes lining the shelves. Feeling a trifle overheated, both physically and mentally, he allowed himself a brief recess in the comfortable overstuffed chair in the corner, all the while cursing Miles Hawthorne and his document to the pit of hell. In the kitchen, he observed a ridiculous number of cookbooks, not to mention cabinets crammed with every form of crockery imaginable. He also noted the door leading to the cellar. There was still much ground to cover but, he assured himself, plenty of opportunity for success. Glancing at his watch, he noticed that it was nearly time for the ladies to return from a titillating evening of baked chicken and bingo. Cringing at the thought of such banal recreation, he was just letting himself out of the house when he saw headlights approaching down the long drive. He sprinted for cover in the long grass beyond the encircling trees and followed the trail he had left earlier, making his way back to the opening in the fence wire and his waiting truck.

As he drove back to his lodging, a modest hostelry along the main highway, Simon considered the events of the day. Not one given much to reflection, he had to admit that he had perpetrated a misstep with Rose that afternoon. He had *abundant* experience in dealing with women but none with a girl quite as inexperienced or unworldly as Rose. He found her unique blend of refreshing beauty and intellectual simplicity both exasperating and enticing. She wasn't stupid, merely naive and untried. He would enjoy the schooling of her but realized he must regain her trust and allegiance first. *Now what do women always respond to as a symbol of humble contrition?* he thought to himself. He smiled smugly as he planned their outing on the morrow.

*****

Granny Gert noticed, with gratifying amusement, that the withdrawn, unusually reticent girl who had driven them all to Harvest Hall a few hours earlier had been replaced by a lively, chatty young woman, full of smiles and laughter on their return. Gert noticed but wisely said nothing other than to express her enjoyment of the evening. She was still teasing Aletha over her winnings when the two older women bade each other good night. She also congratulated her quick-witted friend on her adroit handling of an unforeseen opportunity.

"It was all I could think of," Aletha replied. "I felt such a fool playing the flighty old woman but thank heavens you jumped right in on cue. I was running out of ideas."

"Did you see how cheery Rose was on the way home? Not the long face I saw after that Applegate fellow dropped her off this afternoon. I think if we could just get her and Tim together more often, she might open her eyes and recognize a real man when she sees one!"

Rose's brain was too animated for sleep (and it was only nine o'clock) so she donned her pajamas, fixed herself a cup of chamomile tea, and curled up in the overstuffed library chair to continue work on preparations for the garden project. She tried to concentrate on lists of plants, pavers, and landscaping equipment but her mind kept drifting to thoughts of winning bingo cards and uniforms. Rose took another sip of tea and drew out a timeline for each stage of the overall gardening scheme, idly wondering what days Tim might be on site to work on the building. He had mentioned this weekend. She also reflected fleetingly on the afternoon in Kansas City. After the entertaining evening spent with Tim, her worry over Simon's behavior had been diluted to mere passing disappointment. Any lingering annoyance gradually gave way to pleasant memories of his winning smile and irresistible appeal. She could almost smell his provocative cologne.

Rose nearly dropped her teacup when she woke with a start. "Wow, I guess I was more tired than I thought." She gathered her notes and laid them on the desk before turning for the door. As she passed the big chair, she swore she caught a whiff of Simon's scent. "But that's impossible," she told herself. "He's never been in this room. Maybe it's my subconscious willing him into my conscious." She was happy to oblige and fell asleep picturing his handsome face, melting brown eyes, and soft brown hair. *No...wait...when did his hair turn blond...and why did his eyes appear to be deep-set blue?*

*****

With an enormous yawn, Rose stretched from head to toe like a cat awakening from an afternoon nap. She followed her nose to the kitchen where she was greeted with a smile and a hug by Angelica and a nod by the unexpected Abraham making his way methodically through a plate of scrambled eggs and bacon. Rose shuffled to the table, feeling a little groggier than usual, and glanced at the kitchen clock.

"No wonder I still feel sleepy. It's only 6:30!"

"I'm sorry if we woke you, child," apologized Angelica as she handed Rose the sure-fire cure for sleepiness. "We were tryin' to be quiet so your granny and Aletha could get their beauty sleep. You don't need it." She spoke the sweet compliment as a point of fact.

"Oh, I'm sure I look pretty fabulous right now," Rose said with self-effacing mockery.

"You look like you need to dress for dirty work." Abe pointed out between mouthfuls.

"Dirty work?" The coffee hadn't quite cleared all the mists from her brain yet.

"You know. The plant nursery. The garden," Abe explained, watching her expectantly for realization to dawn.

"Wait…the plant nursery…" Rose was slowly putting the pieces together. She smiled suddenly and exclaimed, "The garden! We're going to start work on the garden today. How could I have forgotten? Angelica, I think I need a refill. My brain's a little slow this morning."

"What you need is a good hearty breakfast," Angelica replied, placing a basket of hot biscuits on the table between the two and setting a loaded plate of eggs, bacon, and hash brown potatoes in front of Rose.

"Icy, I didn't get any hash—" A plate of crisp potatoes appeared at Abe's elbow, ending his grievance. He just grinned in thanks and went to work buttering some biscuits to fill an empty corner of the plate.

Forty-five minutes later, Abe and Rose, lists and plans in hand, set out for Plants Aplenty. Not having packed for any dirty work, as Abe called it, Rose only had one pair of jeans. Her wardrobe consisted mainly of shorts and summer tops and skirts and dresses for church. Angelica, who consistently thought of all things practical, had brought some of Derek's old T-shirts that morning for her to make use of.

"They're not pretty but they're clean, and I don't want you ruinin' any of your nice things. You might consider pickin' up some cheap cargo shorts at Freck's—the general store, you know. I would offer to loan you my muck boots but your feet are so tiny, you could get both o' them into one o' my boots, so you should probably get a pair o' those too. Abe will help you with what you need." It was an imperative.

"Because *I'm* an expert on women's clothes?" the young man responded, his voice heavy with comical sarcasm.

Angelica answered in severe tones but with a betraying twinkle in her eyes, "Now don't you sass me, young man, or you may not get any o' that chocolate cake I promised to make."

"As I was saying," Abe continued smoothly, "I read an article in *Vogue* last month detailing the *haute couture* trends for the fashionable gardener." Carrying on in the same vein, he kept Rose giggling all the way down the driveway.

It was nearly noon before the industrious pair had finished all their preparatory errands but they returned to the big house with the truck full to overflowing with work clothes, tools, some bedding plants and bags of soil amender, and an ancient rototiller. Abe had dug it out of the dark recesses of the old garage and taken it to George Wilson's small engine repair shop in hopes of resuscitating the old machine. George had worked his magic with a little fresh oil and a thorough service and the much-used earth grinder came roaring back to life. Truckloads of topsoil, sand, and gravel and the larger plants and shrubs would be delivered later that day.

Though Rose would dearly have loved to dive into the project as soon they had unloaded everything, making sure the plants were moved into shade, she realized Simon would be arriving soon and she needed to get cleaned up for their date. Abe was ready for lunch so Rose reluctantly agreed to join him when he suggested walking toward the cottage but not before adjuring him to faithfully follow her endless instructions on where to locate the dirt, gravel, and sandpiles, where to place the order of plants upon their delivery, and how to prep the planting beds for tomorrow. He rolled his eyes a time or two when she wasn't looking but placed his hand over his heart and swore a solemn vow to complete her orders as instructed.

"I guess I get a little carried away sometimes," Rose admitted sheepishly.

"Not at all. It is important to speak passionately about that which you are passionate."

"Is that an ancient Middle-Eastern proverb?" she asked curiously as they began walking toward the cottage.

"No," Abe said. "It is a modern Abeism. I've considered publishing a collection of them. What do you think?"

"I think you should be a philosopher," she responded with a smile.

"Derek thinks I should keep them to myself. Ah, well, there are those who simply cannot appreciate genius," he mused with a sigh.

When they reached the cottage, they found that Granny Gert and Aletha had been true to their word. Sandwiches, fruit, and chips had been laid out on the kitchen table, buffet-style, under Angelica's patient supervision.

Rose had barely finished lunch and changed clothes when she heard the summons of the doorbell. The bright sunlight of day brought a clearer memory of yesterday's discordant parting and left her suddenly hesitant to open the door to Simon. But Rose believed him to be an honorable man and, as such, deserved the opportunity to make amends; so she schooled her expression to one of guarded welcome, took a deep breath, and turned the knob.

She opened the door to an enormous bouquet of pink roses that completely hid their bearer but his voice carried over the mountain of flowers, crooning a classic ballad of apology. When he reached the lyric "*Why can't we talk it over,*" he lowered the roses and looked beseechingly at Rose, the personification of guilt and remorse. True to form, Simon's calculated romantic assault melted any lingering doubts in her heart.

"Oh, Simon, they're *beautiful!* You didn't have to do that—but I'm glad you did."

"Then you forgive me for being a selfish, thoughtless, ill-behaved fool?" Contrition dripped from every word.

In the face of such evident emotion, Rose began to wonder if perhaps she had overreacted a bit. Hadn't he merely comported himself in a way considered normal behavior by sophisticated persons? Simon's subtle ability to make her call her own reason into question caused Rose to overcompensate in accepting his apology.

"Please don't say that. It's I that should be apologizing to you for being so unfairly judgmental. Could we just agree to be friends again and forget yesterday ever happened?" she suggested.

Simon had gently pulled Rose out onto the porch where they might enjoy a little privacy. "I will happily comply with the second request but I'm afraid I can't agree to the first one."

He managed to maintain his serious countenance, though he had all he could do to refrain from laughing at her ludicrously crestfallen expression of woe. Placing the bouquet in one of the rocking chairs, he gently took her face between his hands, his own so close she could feel his breath on her skin. Simon drew her eyes to his like a snake hypnotizing its victim and whispered, "Darling Rose, I do not wish to be your friend because I desire to call you something infinitely more dear." Then he barely brushed her lips with his. The gesture, coupled with the Austen literary quote, could not fail. They hadn't yet. He felt her responsive shiver and stepped away just as he sensed she was ready for more. The hook was set. Now he could carry on as planned, though more wary, lest he stumble again.

"Why don't you find a suitable vase for my humble offering and we'll be on our way." Simon had resumed such a casual attitude that Rose thought she must have dreamt that magical moment. But as she picked up the flowers and moved past him toward the door, he stopped her, his hand on her arm. Fleetingly caressing her cheek with the back of his fingers—a butterfly's touch, no more—he released her and nodded toward the door.

Simon, waiting impatiently for Rose on the front porch, turned quickly when he heard the front door open. The persona of adoring suitor, which he had conjured up in the act of turning, froze into immobility and the proposed flowery speech died on his lips when he beheld not Rose but Aletha Mason stepping carefully onto the porch. It took him less than a split second to realize that she could not possibly detect anything amiss in his expression—she couldn't see it. A cloud of relief and cunning enveloped him.

People—self-absorbed, supercilious people—never failed to underestimate Aletha Mason. She saw nothing but missed little. That Simon had been expecting Rose was evident in the suspended breath, held for the briefest of moments, but detectable nonetheless, likewise the interruption of energy in motion. Aletha chose to say nothing because it suited her purposes. She too was on a fishing expedition.

"Good morning, Mrs. Mason. I don't often have the opportunity to see you on my visits to your charming home." He hadn't missed a beat—even found an opportunity to censure and praise in the same greeting.

"Why, Mr. Applegate, I didn't realize you were out here." Two could play at this game. "I thought you and Rose had already left. I'm happy to have a few moments to talk to you privately. Won't you join me on the porch swing? It helps me, you know, to have people nearby when I'm speaking to them."

Simon would have preferred a seat in his comfortable New York office, pumping her for information over the phone, so tedious had this job become, but he snatched at opportunity wherever it presented itself. He slipped his phone out of his pocket, setting it to record the conversation. Aletha, sensing the rustling of his fingers as he manipulated the device, reached her hand out in the direction of the movement, resting it over the phone. If possible, she became an even more dithery and addlepated old woman than she had the night before. Her performance would have done Miss Jane Marple proud.

"Oh, dear. I know your generation practically have their phones surgically implanted but you see..." She paused to take the offending device and wrap it in a fluffy shawl she had worn wrapped around her shoulders, then tucked the whole under a large pillow. "We old people treasure conversation so much that we really can't abide any kind of distraction. I'm afraid we have very few diversions anymore," she said, adding a forlorn sigh for color, "so that we are especially jealous of our social time. Now if you were engaged in checking e-mails or text messages while we were talking, I would feel... snubbed. Absolutely snubbed."

Simon, completely unprepared for Aletha's clever maneuvering, was rendered mentally impotent when his phone disappeared. His first-rate wit produced the brilliant reply, "Wha..."

"I know you must think it rude of me but please say you understand, *dear* Mr. Applegate." Now Aletha's hand rested on his arm. She squeezed it in appeal (and to keep him from reaching around to the pillow).

"W-why, o-of course. I can only hope that you will forgive *me*." Simon felt quite at sea with the shoe on the other foot. How had the master of manipulation lost control to a flustered old blind woman?

"Not at all," Aletha said, patting his arm in a friendly (but most unwelcome) way and retaining her hold. "We've had so little time to get acquainted. You've probably found my old friend, Trudy, a little… difficult." She giggled as if they were sharing a joke. "She really is a good sport but perhaps a bit overprotective of her granddaughter." Aletha gave Simon an obvious wink that he found a bit off-putting. "*But*…Trudy has asked Angelica to run her into town to have a tooth looked at Monday morning and, of course, Rose will be busy with the garden *so*…why don't you plan to come by for a comfortable coze? Say about nine o'clock?"

Not sure what the dotty old woman was up to, Simon, nonetheless, accepted the invitation.

"Wonderful! And we won't have any interruptions as I'll be sure to leave Prince in another room. He's usually quite friendly, but for some silly reason, he seems to have taken an unaccountable dislike to you." As if on cue, Simon could hear the dog growling through the window.

Just then, Rose practically ran out the door, yelling behind her, "I promise to be home in time for dinner." Simon, gratefully taking the phone now held out to him by Aletha, bade her a hasty farewell before driving off with Rose.

Gert, peeking around the doorframe to make sure the Escalade was gone, joined Aletha on the swing. "Well, what did you find out?"

"I'm not sure but you'll have to get Prince to do that again when young Simon returns on Monday. I could actually feel him flinch when my furry friend growled. An unaccountable dislike indeed…"

CHAPTER 12

And the Lord God planted a garden in Eden, in the east.
Out of the ground the Lord God made to grow every tree
that is pleasant to the sight and good for food.

—Genesis 2:8–9 (NRSV)

Rose felt unsettled and found it difficult to compose her churning thoughts brought about by the events of the day, so she and Prince took a walk to the big house after dinner. She had made the walk many times and each time had found solace in the journey and the destination; but on that evening, the crickets seemed to chirp in sweeter harmony, the birds sang their evening songs with symphonic gusto and the very breeze, stirring to cool the earth after the heat of the day, whispered sighs of promise and hope. As she and Prince rounded the corner where the old asphalt-covered road to the cottage joined the new cement surface leading to the house, the setting sun behind her cast a spotlight on the west facade of the grand old building, causing the glass to sparkle, the weather vane on the turret's roof to shine and covering the whole in roseate hues as the light filtered through a translucent veil of cloud vapor. Rose felt a lump rising in her throat. She knew it was nonsense to feel personal attachment for an inanimate object but she sensed an inexplicable connection to the stately house. She realized that their association would be short-lived—only the duration of her summer stay in Kansas—but she wanted it to be significant. Rose would be soon forgotten but she determined that her efforts on behalf of…Rose stopped and looked at Prince, momentarily perplexed, unable to complete her thought.

They had been walking around the perimeter of the garden, avoiding the mountains of dirt, gravel, and sand that had been delivered in her absence. She stopped on the near side of the gravel pile as enlightenment dawned. Prince regarded her expectantly, his head cocked to one side. Rose had realized for the first time that, unlike Fern Cottage, this imposing structure had no name. A home this grand *must* have a name. But she had only ever heard Aletha and Tim and his friends refer to it as the main house. She now had an additional mission—find the perfect name for her stone, wood, and shingle-clad friend. "Don't you worry, my lady, it will be worthy of your grandeur!" Rose said out loud and bowed in tribute to the silent matriarch before her.

She nearly jumped out of her skin when an answering voice said, "I'm not sure that I like being called my lady, and I've never been credited with grandeur before, but I *am* interested to know what worthy 'it' you're referring to." A man's voice. Tim Ludlow's voice. Rose looked around quickly but saw no one. Then she noticed Prince eagerly swishing his tail, looking pointedly toward the other side of the gravel pile as Tim stepped out with a sheepish grin on his face.

"You just about scared me to death!" Rose tried to sound stern but couldn't help laughing a little as Tim walked toward her, the sheepish grin now a pleasant smile of welcome. He gripped her hand firmly in a friendly greeting before tapping his shoulders, inviting Prince to jump up for a scratch behind his ears and a pat on his shiny coat. While Tim was otherwise engaged, Rose marveled again at the change wrought by the simple removal of a beard. He looked more himself now in cargo shorts and T-shirt, though both were unusually clean.

"I gather you haven't been working here today."

"No sawdust in my hair or holes in my shirt?" he remarked as if he had read her thoughts.

Could it be that he and Aletha are distantly related? Rose wondered. *Maybe it's just a well-developed power of reasoning.*

"Exactly," she responded with a smile. "You don't miss much."

"It's my army training—attention to detail. Though there's a lot of that in the building trade too, especially on a project like this," he said, nodding his head toward the house. "I'm actually here just because I wanted to stop by and see that you had everything you needed to get started tomorrow. Excited?" He asked, glancing down at her profile as she stood gazing at the project site.

Without looking at him, she nodded her head and said simply, "You have no idea."

"Oh, I think I do." Rose looked up at Tim's earnest face as he continued, "I've been itching to really get going on this project since I came here—over a year ago now."

"But I thought you told Aletha you had too much work in town to have time for the old house?"

"You don't miss much either, do you?" he answered. "I thought if I convinced her that my time was limited, she might be concerned and ask me to make this a priority. But I underestimated her thoughtfulness. She didn't want to be a burden to me as I was trying to launch my business—and there really is a lot of work to be done in town—so she kindly let me off the hook. She's also quite comfortable at the cottage so I wasn't sure how I was going to motivate her to focus on *this* wonderful old beauty, even though I know she's always had a real affinity for the place." They had been walking through the garden area as they talked and had reached the corner of the porch. With his last statement, he reached out and touched the wood railing, looking up at the house with respect bordering on reverence.

"Oh my gosh! You love her too!" Rose exclaimed unexpectedly.

"Aletha?" Tim asked, a little confused.

"No…well, yes…Aletha, of course. But I meant the house. You love her too."

"Too?"

"I think you may be the one person who doesn't think I'm just a fanciful dreamer. When I first laid eyes on this grand old home, it was love at first sight. I think that's why I was so defensive when you met me that first time. I'm really sorry I was so antagonistic. That was *so* not me."

"Well, you had every right to be. I acted like a jerk. And you own *no* responsibility for my bad behavior. Now let's leave that all behind us and agree to be…friends, okay?"

It had happened again. Essentially the same conversation but with the roles reversed this time. She was truly grateful that Tim really seemed to expect nothing more than friendship. Simon's earlier declaration had left her deeply moved and a little uncertain, especially since he had virtually ignored her the rest of the afternoon in favor of talking up service shop owners on Main Street—the computer repair geek, the dry cleaner, and the dentist, or rather his bouncy young assistant who happily chatted with Simon while Rose was left to study wall charts warning of the dire consequences of gingivitis.

Tim offered her genuine uncomplicated friendship and she accepted it with relief. Finding a common passion cemented the pact, and they talked easily for some time about restoration plans.

"You're no crazier than I am," Tim was saying. "You see, this is more than just another renovation project for me. It's a real test of my knowledge and training. Unlike Derek and Abe who went to regular colleges and got normal degrees in—"

"Oh, let me guess. Derek…communications? No, wait… *physical* education?" At Tim's nod, she added, smiling, "That makes perfect sense—he's *all* about the muscles."

"Bingo!" Tim answered, laughing. "And of course, Abe is the techno genius with a degree in computer science and technology. But I've always been interested in building things. Creating something substantial out of a lot of sticks and nails was a challenge I could get behind. But I wanted to learn the science and the art behind it too so I attended the American College of the Building Arts and got a BA in architectural carpentry. You won't hear about ACBA on any sportscasts but it *was* featured on *Old House, New Home*."

"I *loved* watching that show with my dad. He's kind of a self-taught DIY carpenter, and I spent hours in his little workshop growing up…Wait a minute, you know, I *do* remember those episodes, fairly recently too—Charleston, right? It looked like an amazing place. But surely they didn't offer ROTC there? Or at least, I don't remember seeing anybody in uniform on any of those episodes."

"Right on both counts. Wow, you really don't miss much at *all*." Tim was impressed and touched by her interest. "I had to drive into old town to take military science classes at another school but we spent a lot of time in the old part of the city my last two years anyway, getting hands-on training in historical restoration, so it wasn't a big deal."

They were sitting on the porch steps, watching the gathering dusk twinkle with the advent of evening fireflies.

"What an incredible education. I can see how important it was in preparing you for your job now but were you able to use any of that in the army?"

"Oddly enough, I was. I think *because* of my unique training, I was able to get branched into combat engineers, though most army engineer officers have engineering degrees. My job was to oversee building structures and bridges *and* I got to work with demolitions. I don't use much of *that* experience anymore," he remarked with a grin, "but it was all great training for the management end of running a construction business. You know, estimating materials, man-hours, evaluating structures. Yeah, it was a good life but I've moved on to something a *little* different—I've never had anyone *shooting* at me on a jobsite—"

"Well, I sure *hope* not!" Rose said, half-serious, half-laughing.

"But I think this will be a good life too. Especially if I can really get my hands on this old place," he said, looking behind him at the house, little more than a looming bulk in the quickly encroaching darkness.

"Good Lord, it's almost dark!" Tim had been so lost in the happiness and tranquility of sharing time with Rose that he'd lost all *track* of time. "I'd better see you home before your grandmother comes after me with a broom...or worse!" Rose could barely see his grin from the light of a waning moon.

"She didn't know you'd be here so I think you're safe," Rose assured him, laughing. "I didn't know you'd be here either, for that matter, but I'm glad you were."

The sincerity in her voice moved Tim. He stood and reached his hand down to pull her to her feet. "Well, whether she knows or not, I'll see you home."

"Oh, that's not necessary. I'm perfectly capable of walking back to the cottage by myself. And I have Prince to keep me company. Right, boy?" Prince thumped his tail on the ground in agreement and let his tongue loll out the side of his mouth in a lopsided grin.

"Prince or no Prince, you're not wearing night-vision goggles and I'd hate for you to twist an ankle in the dark." Rose started to protest. "No more arguments. I want you in good working shape for tomorrow."

"And here I was, thinking you were just being chivalrous," she answered in shocked tones, belied by underlying laughter in her voice.

As they walked toward his white truck, still reasonably visible in the failing light, Tim asked as an afterthought, "Hey, you never told me what the 'it' was that would be so worthy."

"Oh, gosh. I'd almost forgotten that. A name."

"A name…"

"For the house. You know, like Fern Cottage. The grand old place ought to have a proper name so I intend to come up with one befitting her stature."

"Well, I suggest you wait until you can *see* her again." Tim held the door of the truck for Rose while Prince jumped into the back seat.

"Good idea." The short drive to the cottage accomplished, Rose waved goodbye and Tim drove home slowly, anticipating the morrow.

*****

Rose awakened almost before first light, filled with the excitement and anticipation inherent in a visionary embarking on a quest. Today she would begin work on the garden in earnest.

Granny Gert and Aletha quickly shooed Angelica and Rose out the door and on to the front porch as soon as the breakfast dishes were carried into the kitchen from the gazebo.

"Off with the both of you and no arguing—either of you. Now get." Gert first planted a kiss on Rose's cheek then swatted her behind with the porch broom as an additional motivator. Angelica laughed all the way to the end of the driveway.

"I do love your Granny Gert, Miss Rose. She reminds me a lot of my own grandmother—all prickles and vinegar on the outside and sweet marshmallow fluff on the inside."

As they approached the garden area of the big house, Rose stopped in her tracks. There were people everywhere. She recognized Pastor Lindeman and his family, the dapper Mr. Taylor—now attired in well-worn coveralls and toting a wheelbarrow full of dirt—the violinist marking time with a leaf rake, and scores of others she did not yet know. Angelica registered no surprise at all.

"Well, o' course folks have turned out to help. Marilyn and I made a few calls and here they all are. I think they're as excited about fixin' up the old place for the picnic as we are. Besides Aletha has done so much for the church over the years that members see this as an opportunity to do something for her. Come, I'll introduce you."

The morning flew by as weeds and weary old plants were uprooted and thrown on the compost pile down by the old barn. Scraggly shrubs lining the house's foundation were dug up, not without great effort and the use of pickaxes and even a chain saw. Walkways were surveyed and lined out just wide enough to allow a small front loader to dig out any remaining broken stones or bricks, making way for loads of fresh gravel.

Rose looked up from winding a piece of twine around a peg to mark one of the pathways and saw Derek and Abe engaged in heated battle over who would operate the front loader.

"Dude, I've *got* this. Look at these guns," Derek said as he flexed his triceps. "This baby is *not* going to get away from *me*."

"Derek, operation of this machine requires manual dexterity, not brute strength. You know, *mental* prowess," Abe argued.

"Say *what?*"

"*Brain* muscles. Try *flexing* those for a change," Abe challenged his friend, grinning as he deftly avoided a ringing slap on the head.

While the two were still fighting for control, Tim showed up out of nowhere, nimbly hopped in the little machine, cranked it up, and followed Pastor Lindeman's waving arms to a path already marked for excavation.

As they watched the machine driven literally out from under their noses, Derek and Abe looked at each other in amazed perplexity.

"How does he *do* that?" Abe asked.

"I didn't even know he was here. I guess he finished whatever he had to do at Milly's sooner than he expected. Figures," said Derek, shaking his head. "So, mental prowess, want to help me fire up the tracked trencher? We've got to get the PVC pipe laid for the fountain."

"Absolutely! And don't forget the electrical conduit for power to the pump. Of course, *you'll* have to do all the groundwork. Remember," said Abe, pointing to his prosthetic leg, "no knee."

"No problem. *You* can man the shovel." Giving him a slap on the back, he reminded Abe, "Two good arms." Abe just shook his head, raised his hands, and looked toward heaven in a playful gesture of supplication for sympathy.

An hour later, Rose stopped in the middle of her chores, paralyzed by panic. She saw her car weaving haphazardly up the drive from the cottage with Granny Gert at the wheel and Aletha in the passenger seat, gesticulating wildly as she hung out the window, adjuring everyone to "Stay out of the way! Stay out of the way!" Rose watched in horror as she heard Granny Gert trying to (hopefully) downshift. But the rusty driver had her eyes set on the gearshift rather than the road and failed to see she was headed directly for the back of Tim's truck. Fortunately Gert stalled the engine instead and, deciding she had reached the precise parking spot she wanted all along, tooted the horn to let all and sundry know she and Aletha had arrived without mishap *and* without anyone's help.

Marilyn was the first to reach the car, helping first Gert then Aletha out of the vehicle. Both were a bit shaken but would never admit it except to each other. "Why, Mrs. Gunn, I didn't realize you were such an…accomplished driver," she said, offering an arm to each of the older women.

"Well, of course I am. Been driving for years. Nothing to it."

Just then, Tim bolted past them at full tilt with Rose a close second.

"Now where in thunder are those two off to just when lunch has arrived?" Gert demanded, trying to look behind her. Marilyn thought it best to propel them all forward so as not to witness Tim brace himself on the bed of his pickup, lifting his legs to push against the bumper of the little Chevy that was still determined to run into, or rather under, the big truck. While he held old Betsy at bay, Rose jumped into the driver's seat and hit the brakes. Gert, a little rustier than she realized, had forgotten to leave the car in gear or pull up the emergency brake. Rose took care of both oversights and heaved a sigh of relief. She pulled the keys left in the ignition and deposited them in her pocket. Granny Gert would *not* be driving back to the cottage.

"Hey, we make a pretty good team." Tim observed as Rose joined him, slapping his hand in a raised high five.

"Thank you *so* much," Rose said. "I don't think I could have managed by myself."

"That's what friends are for." Then to draw her thoughts away from worry about her grandmother, he pointed out. "If I'm not mistaken, that's the Little Italy delivery van unloading enough pizza for a whole battalion. Race you to the front porch." And before she knew it, Rose was running after him again, though headed for a more welcome destination.

*****

Simon spent several tiresome hours compiling, he hoped, an exhaustive list of possible hiding places in Aletha Mason's gallery of Victorian antiques. Drawer filets (long pieces of thin wooden planks) attached to hidden end compartments. Secret cavities accessed by a lever revealing yet another subcompartment behind. False facades manipulated by built-in books that revealed a hidden safe, a stepladder, or even a fully stocked bar. Now *that* Simon wouldn't mind finding—though unlikely in Aletha's home. By the time he had reached his fill of research, he was ready to hurl his laptop through the window of his dingy motel room—its only real amenity being decent Wi-Fi service.

The afternoon held no alleviation from boredom. Once again donning his rough-neck disguise, he drove the pickup truck to the storage facility in Tinkers Well to finish perusal of the last of the

Mason document containers. No sign of the trusting dim-witted Bud or anyone else. But in disguise, Simon took no unnecessary chances. As he slammed the door on the unit and locked it for the last time (he had no intention of returning the ridiculous number of boxes he had transferred off-site), he felt some sense of accomplishment, even if essentially negative. If the document could not be located in one place, it was simply in another; and having ruled out the mountain of historical archives, he could focus his sights more intently on the cottage. One other option had yet to be explored but he required the Mason woman's unwitting assistance to pursue that avenue. Her unexpected invitation for a social call played right into his hands, and having witnessed her irrational anathema of digital devices, he planned to utilize a far more sophisticated stealth means of accomplishing his ends.

Fed up with the almost nonexistent social scene of rural Kansas and needing to maintain a low profile in case any of the locals saw him when he was allegedly in Topeka, Simon opted to spend the evening in Kansas City. He discovered a passable nightclub with the help of the obliging Jeremy, his waiter friend at the Silo Market and Feed, and spent an agreeable evening—and morning—with a young woman whose appetites rivaled his own. Sober again, and with the edge taken off his more pressing needs, Simon once more turned toward the west, trying in vain to remember the girl's name.

*****

The afternoon passed in a blur, but by five o'clock, Rose stood surveying the site in wonder and delight. The team from Community Church had made enormous inroads on the garden restoration project. All the pathways had been filled with a layer of gravel, prepped for sand and pavers; an extensive irrigation system had been laid out, awaiting connection to the control box; the large green space had been cleared, leveled, and covered in fresh sod; and the foundation for the fountain poured. The piles of paving materials still had to be moved, and though all the planting areas had been tilled and the soil amended, crates of plants still waited in the shade of the willow tree for a permanent home. But Rose could see the vision now. As she contemplated the work yet to be done, it no longer presented an insurmountable task, rather a glorious purpose, and she was resolute in her intent to fulfill it.

Feeling like the novice D'Artagnan in the seasoned presence of the three musketeers, a weary but deeply contented Rose walked back to the cottage with Tim, Derek, and Abe who had collectively insisted she call it quits for the day. The three men were beat but convinced Rose they would happily have continued working were it not for their concern that she not overexert herself.

"A rose that blooms too soon loses its petals," Abe uttered profoundly.

"*What?*" Tim and Derek spoke in unison.

Laughing, Rose asked, "Is that another Abeism?"

"God, give me strength," Derek said under his breath.

"Of course," Abe said, ignoring his friend. "Very fitting, don't you think?"

"Very *funny,* maybe," Derek muttered.

Rose merely smiled and fell in step with Tim as Derek and Abe, a few yards behind, argued over the merits, or even the existence, of Abe's sagacity.

"Tim…"

"Mmm?"

"I wanted to thank you for driving Granny Gert and Aletha back to the cottage after lunch. I wasn't sure how to do it without embarrassing my grandmother or hurting her feelings. You must be some kind of wizard with elderly ladies."

"Hardly," he said, laughing. "I have simply learned to tell them only what they are willing to hear and then wait for them to decide that my plan was their idea all along."

"So what was Granny's idea?"

"I asked her if she had noticed a knocking in the engine when she drove your car and told her that *you* had mentioned it to *me* and asked me to test-drive it sometime to see if I might be able to diagnose the problem."

"So…"

"She *offered* to let me drive her home so I could listen for the engine trouble. Simple."

"And you managed that without a fight?"

"Without a single argument."

Rose stared at him in awe. "You *are* a wizard."

"You should have seen Aletha. She *jumped* on the idea. Wouldn't take no for an answer." After a brief pause, he added in a more serious tone, "You know, I think your grandmother's company has done wonders for Aletha. I haven't seen her this animated and… alive since Matthew died. It's almost as if she has a new lease on life." Then looking at Rose, he said earnestly, "I may have done you a small service by driving Aletha and Mrs. Gunn home today but you performed the real act of service when you drove your grandmother to Kansas. You have both been a real blessing to Aletha." Then looking away, he continued, a little unsure of himself, "You've been a blessing to *all* of us."

They had stopped on the covered porch before entering the cottage. Tim turned and took Rose's hand uncertainly but spoke with heartfelt sincerity, "Thank you."

The simple honesty of the gesture and words touched her in a way that Simon's polished dialogue and calculated caresses could not. She replied with equal candor, "What a nice thing to say. You are entirely welcome." The two stood thus for several moments without any sense of awkwardness.

Derek and Abe, who had caught up with them, witnessed the interchange with interest but decided Tim might have worked himself into a corner and probably needed a little timely intervention.

"Hey, you two. What are you hanging around out here for? I can smell my mama's curry from here and it has *my* name on it. Rose, after you," said Derek as he held the door for Rose—and *only* Rose. Tim and Abe were left to fend for themselves.

Tim was actually relieved when Derek and Abe showed up. Rose's open acceptance of his gratitude encouraged him. But a minute more and he might have felt like an idiot standing there, holding her hand with no idea of how to move on. The success of the gesture, however, bolstered his confidence and gave him an increased feeling of ease in her company. If she welcomed friendship, he would be the truest friend she had ever had and maybe, just maybe, as he spoke words to her that she was willing to hear, Rose—like Granny Gert— might recognize the deeper affection he offered and eventually claim it as her own.

*****

Despite every intention of rising early enough to get Granny Gert and Aletha to church in time for Sunday school, the effects of hours of hard manual labor under a hot Kansas sun had taken their toll. When Rose finally rolled over to look at the clock on the nightstand, she let out a howl that would have woken the other inhabitants of Fern Cottage—and the rest of the county at large—if they hadn't been up for hours already. Gert came running as fast as her little sausage legs could carry her.

"Rosie? Rosie, are you all right?"

"I hurt," said Rose plaintively, trying to lay perfectly still, lest she move her aching muscles and they start screaming at her again.

"You hurt? Where?"

"It would be easier to tell you where I don't hurt…which is, maybe, the end of my nose—maybe."

"Muscles talking to you, are they?"

"*Talking*? They're singing a rousing chorus of 'What Were You *Thinking*?' at full volume!"

"I *told* you last night to take some anti-inflammatories but you must have forgotten by the time you made it to bed after falling asleep at the kitchen table. I know it'll hurt but you have to get up and start moving." Gert helped Rose out of bed, aiding her to suit actions to words. Aletha arrived to add her encouragement and the two older women got Rose to walk around the room and sit and stand a few times to force the frozen aching muscles into mobility again. Eventually they made it down the hall to the bathroom where Gert shoved Rose through the door, closing it behind her.

"Now don't come out until you've had a long hot shower."

"But I need coffee—"

"Shower. Now."

"Aaargh!"

Gert left Rose to the miracle effects of hot water on sore muscles and gathered her Bible and purse, ready for church. She handed Rose an apple as her towel-clad granddaughter emerged from the shower and told her she had exactly ten minutes to finish the only breakfast she could expect, get dressed, and put on her makeup before they needed to leave for church.

"Ten minutes! Couldn't we skip Sunday school this week and just go to the service?"

"Honey, Sunday school is nearly over. Church starts in twenty-five minutes. Now scoot."

The need for haste coupled with a determination *not* to leave the house looking like she had just rolled out of bed, Rose met the impossible deadline and found the muscle pain slightly less pronounced, possibly because it had taken backstage to more pressing activities or because the hot shower and ibuprofen had done their job.

Later, sitting between Tim and Granny Gert in a packed church pew, Rose found herself wincing every time she had to stand or sit. Tim, watching her out of the corner of his eye, whispered in her ear during an announcement, "Are you grinning or grimacing?"

Turning her head slowly because that was the only speed she could move anything, she replied with feeling, "*Guess.*"

"I'm sorry." He was trying hard to hide a smile. "Have you taken any muscle relaxants?" Rose winced as she nodded her head. "I think I have a suggestion that might help...wait, let Tom explain." He nodded at a gray-haired man Rose judged to be about the age of her father. He was making an announcement at the podium.

"—Are hosting a pool party/barbecue at our place at five o'clock this evening for the Crossroads Connect Group. For those who may be unfamiliar with our small groups, Crossroads is comprised primarily of our twenty and thirty somethings, married or single, with or without kids. It's going to be a scorcher today so you won't want to miss it."

"But I don't have a swimsuit. I didn't think to pack one," she whispered back a little wistfully.

"Yes, you do." It was hardly a whisper, though Gert probably thought it was. "Letha told me you might need one so she called her friend at that dress shop in town and ordered one for you. Gayle, I think her name was. Anyway she met you when you were in the store buying that…dress so she knew your size. Angelica picked it up for you on Friday so no more arguing!"

Because the last words were spoken in the relative silence between announcements and the opening hymn, all eyes turned to see who was arguing and about what. The unflappable Granny Gert merely smiled and nodded to everyone, wondering what the holdup was for the music.

On her first visit to Community Church, Rose had had so much to take in; new faces, new format, and a heartrending testimony. Today, when she forced herself to think about anything but the pain that seemed to have returned in full on the short drive from Aletha's, she noticed details that she had missed before. The light shining through the stained glass windows, the scent of fresh flowers wafting across the sanctuary from a simple ceramic vase in front of the altar, and the mix of ages represented in the congregation, especially kids. Lots of kids. Angelica had mentioned a nursery for infants and toddlers but Rose counted at least fifteen preschoolers corralled by determined young mothers or doting grandparents. Elementary-aged children sat with their parents, some snuggled on their daddy's laps. Teens congregated in several rows at the front. This was a real church family, not the demographically segregated congregations she had experienced at other churches where families arrived together then split up, going in three different directions, only coming together again for the ride home. Like the mix of traditional and contemporary music, Rose found this integrated model of church attendance refreshing and more in keeping with what she imagined early churches of Tinkers Well might have looked like.

The pastor invited them to stand and have their favorite hymn number ready for the quarterly hymn sing, reminding everyone that the next worship song Sunday would be in August. Rose found it inspiring when a young boy, not more than seven, stood with confidence to make the first hymn request, the song leader recognizing him by name. If he could do it so could she. As they concluded the chorus of "The Old Rugged Cross," Rose already had her hand up. She couldn't see Tim's long arm waving behind her to attract the song leader's attention so she was pleasantly surprised when the man called on her rather than the other twenty-odd people equally eager to sing their favorites. As they sang three verses of "Be Thou My Vision," Rose forgot all about her muscles, thoughts about the garden project, or any romantic dreams. She was lost in the beautiful combination of music and words.

> *Be Thou my Vision, O Lord of my heart*
> *Naught be all else to me, save that Thou art*
> *Thou my best Thought, by day or by night*
> *Waking or sleeping, Thy presence my light*
>
> *Riches I heed not, nor man's empty praise*
> *Thou mine Inheritance, now and always*
> *Thou and Thou only, first in my heart*
> *High King of Heaven, my Treasure Thou art*

Before the final verse, the pianist changed keys, elevating the haunting Celtic melody, while the flutist and violinist played a soaring obbligato duet.

> *High King of Heaven, my victory won*
> *May I reach Heaven's joys, O bright Heav'n's Sun*
> *Heart of my own heart, whate'er befall*
> *Still be my Vision, O Ruler of all*[3]

Little did Rose know how she would cling to those words in the weeks to come.

---

[3]. 8th Century Irish hymn, "Be Thou My Vision". Translation by Elinor Hull, (1912).

CHAPTER 13

My command is this: Love each other as I have loved you.

—John 15:12 (NIV)

Simon reached the entrance to Aletha's driveway just before noon. His preoccupation with his companion of the night before had lingered longer into the morning hours than he had planned. Not to worry. He believed to still have at least two hours of undisturbed time at Fern Cottage which he considered ample time to finish his search. But to avoid being caught out early, he opted to park in the hidden drive used the previous Thursday. He set to work, methodically working his way through every room, save the library. Hoping the blasted document would come to light long before he would be compelled to inspect every book and dust jacket on the well-stocked shelves, Simon decided that room would keep till bingo night if necessary.

Duly following the meticulous notes he had made on hidden furniture compartments, he began in Aletha's bedroom. Bureau followed armoire, dressing table and nightstand followed bureau. Turning up nothing in the back of the cottage, he made an exhaustive search of the dining room sideboard and hutch, the hall table, and every other piece of furniture in the house containing any conceivable kind of drawer or cabinet door. Looking at the "treasure" he had unearthed, he swore in disgust and frustration. A recipe for suet pudding (how could that *ever* have been considered fit for consumption) and a badly written poem from a long gone suitor to his beloved. Either Aletha had nothing to hide or she had secreted it somewhere in the library. Simon was weighing the rival merits of tackling that hateful task immediately or waiting until Thursday when he heard a car door slam. Glancing at his watch in surprise, he found that it was already 2:30. Looking around quickly to ensure no sign of his presence could be detected, he started for the kitchen door but was arrested in midstride when he heard Angelica's voice admonishing Prince to "finish your business, your highness" as she opened the door. Simon ran on cat's feet to Rose's room where he would have to let himself out the window as soon as the front of the house was clear. Always careful to check for alternate points of exit, he had already loosened the screws holding the screen in place. He had just dropped over the window ledge and replaced the screen as Rose entered the room followed by the ancient one.

"Now you just slip this bathing suit on and get ready to go. If Tim is going to pick you up at three o'clock, you don't have a lot of time to get gussied up. Though why you need to fix your hair when you're just going to get it wet is bey..." Gert's voice trailed off as she closed the door. Simon was sorely tempted to stay and surreptitiously watch Rose exchange her virginal Sunday draping for that of a water nymph but knew he needed to make good his escape as soon as Prince entered the cottage. He peered carefully around the corner to the back of the house. Prince, in the act of entering the kitchen, stopped abruptly, ears pointed. Simon leaned against the house, just out of the dog's sight, and held his breath.

"Now you just get on in here and forget about those squirrels. You hear that? Miss Aletha is callin' for you..." After a quick look around, the dog obeyed. Simon heard the screen door slam. He counted slowly to ten then made his way across the back of the cottage, staying close to the building so that he could peer into each window he passed before moving by, bent double to avoid detection. Clear of the cottage, he bolted for cover. He chided himself as a fool for nearly getting caught and resolved to manage his time better on what he fervently hoped would be his last clandestine visit to Fern Cottage.

*****

194

Rose wasn't sure how it had happened, but in only nine short days, she and Granny Gert had gone from strangers to two of the regulars gathered at the Ludlow home for brunch. *It's amazing how quickly you get to know people when you work together on a focused goal*, Rose thought. She and Amy, the violinist, had made plans to meet for lunch in town later in the week. Mr. Taylor had convinced Rose that only she could recreate the lovely garden his late wife had tended for many years, now fallen into neglect. Pastor Lindeman's wife, Lisa, had invited Rose and Granny Gert to a church-wide ladies event in July. Rose felt a deep sense of contentment. She had only met these people recently but already knew herself to be an accepted and valued member of the Community Church family. Aletha had always been a mainstay of the senior's group, but with Gert as her faithful sidekick, the two had become the life of the party. Rose smiled at the continuous laughter emanating from the dining room.

"Rose, I knew you and your grandmother were going to fit right in the first time I met you," Marilyn had remarked as she greeted the girl earlier with a big hug. She was right. Rose, not so overwhelmed as she had been the first time she had come to the Ludlow's home, now chatted with ease to new friends and fellow laborers in the vineyard. But she was not so comfortable in her new role as to forget her first and best friends. Derek and Abe watched her progress across the room with amusement.

"Our little Rose has bloomed in the sunshine of much favor," remarked Abe.

"Dude, can't you just say 'Looks like Rose is a hit' like a normal person?" Derek chided his friend.

"Ah, but those who rise above the ordinary must speak in the language of the extraordinary."

Derek rolled his eyes and said disparagingly, "I give up."

Tim sat in silence, experiencing a contentment even deeper than Rose's. She *belonged* here. He *knew* it. Did she?

The four enjoyed their meal and fellowship time but broke up the party early because of the barbecue planned for later that day.

"Rose, since you don't know where you're going, I'd be happy to pick you up." Tim offered hopefully. Before she could answer, he added, "Tom said it would be okay if we arrive a little early so I can show you some of the restoration work we did there. In fact, we just finished that job this past week. I thought you might like to see what can be done to renovate an old structure and still maintain its character. The Bennetts don't have a grand Victorian like Aletha but it's an old farmhouse dating back to the early twentieth century. What do you say?"

A little surprised by the added afternoon invitation, Rose said, a little hesitantly, "Oh, well…I guess so. I *would* love to see how everything comes together on a project like that. I just feel a little guilty about leaving Granny Gert and Aletha on the one day I had planned to spend with them…"

"Don't worry about that." Derek jumped in to help his buddy. "Mama's planning to go over there this afternoon and get caught up on the things she hasn't been able to do the past few days. Seems your granny ran you both out of the house so fast yesterday that she had to leave several things unfinished. And since Abe and I will both be at the barbecue, she'd be home alone anyway. Why, you'll be doing everyone a favor. Mama will have somewhere to go and Aletha and your granny will have company." He grinned so convincingly that Rose felt sure she was being hustled.

"Well, I don't know how turning a quiet afternoon by herself into doing chores for my grandmother is doing your mom a favor," Rose answered doubtfully. "But I'll pretend I believe you."

"Rose, I assure you, I am the soul of honor," Derek replied with dignity, his hand over his heart. She feigned ignorance of the barely perceptible wink in Tim's direction. Derek then beat feet to his mother's side to instruct her on her role in the afternoon's plans.

An hour and a half later, Tim was driving out of town on State Street. A mile past the courthouse, the spaces between houses grew larger and the road narrowed. Tree-lined streets turned into open grassland except for the occasional groupings of shade trees around homes. After another mile or so, he turned into a narrow gravel driveway in the middle of an open field with only a mailbox on the main road to herald any signs of habitation beyond the turning. Going over a little rise, the drive was finally granted some shade from the tall narrow poplars lining both sides of the approach, their silvery leaves barely fluttering in the stillness of the hot afternoon. A quarter of a mile further on, the gravel gave way to asphalt as a slight bend in the road afforded the first glimpse of an old-style farmhouse now in pristine condition.

Rose's first impression was of peaks and porches. The roofline of the two-story structure shot out in two steeply pitched gables visible from the front corner of the house with another pointing off the back. She could only guess at a fourth on the far side to complete the building's symmetry. The formerly clapboard-covered exterior now gleamed with fresh vinyl siding in a sunny shade of yellow, accented by dark-green shutters framing the tall narrow windows common to farmhouses of the period. An inviting covered porch wrapped the entire front of the house with a smaller porch off the back entrance. Two porch swings and multiple rocking chairs, padded with checked fabric cushions, vied for decorative prominence over hanging baskets full to overflowing with bright blooms and large potted palms swaying gracefully in the breeze created by whirling ceiling fans. Every detail said welcome. Rose recognized Tom Bennett as he came toward the truck to greet them.

"Rose, we're so glad you could join us. Lucy is around here somewhere, organizing everything. I mostly just try to stay out of her way."

"Coward," said Tim without rancor. "If we run into her, we'll tell her you're looking for something to do."

"You do and I might reconsider letting you squire Rose around so you can show off." Tim lifted an eyebrow and called Tom's bluff. "Ah, heck, you're right. I never get tired of having folks out to look over the place. We're just so proud of it and the fine work that you boys did on it. Well, I won't keep you. You enjoy your tour and don't let him get too technical, Rose. It doesn't take much encouragement for Tim to climb on his hobby horse."

Tom wasn't far off in his estimation of Tim's tour guide skills. But Rose didn't mind. She found the discussion of differences in the simple farmhouse design versus the more elaborate Victorian style fascinating and wondered if any of the interior details of the house, such as deep-pocket doors and not one but two turned staircases with half-landings, could be incorporated into the larger house.

"I'm sorry. I forgot that you haven't actually been inside Aletha's house. It does have all of the above but the craftsmanship is much more detailed. You noticed there wasn't any…what did you call the millwork on Aletha's porch?"

"Wooden lace."

Tim smiled at the description. "I'll have to remember that. But that would not be in keeping with the simple clean lines of this house. This was built to be the home of a working landowner, not a wealthy landowner."

"But it has its own beauty, nonetheless. Can we go upstairs?"

The tour continued from attic to cellar, ending in the big gleaming farmhouse kitchen. They stepped out the side door, onto the smaller porch where Rose discovered that it wrapped around the back of the house in an open deck overlooking a very inviting swimming pool. Here they met their hostess, Lucy, who organized them right onto some deck chairs, insisting they take a dip before eating. "The food'll taste better after you've cooled off."

Tim and Rose were joined by Derek and Abe who introduced her to more as yet unknown church members.

"I hope you've got a good head for names and faces, Rose, because the family of God in Tinkers Well is *loaded* with brothers and sisters." Lucy applauded Rose's efforts to sort everyone out. "You'll get the hang of it after you've been to a few small group meetings. And we host a barbecue here at least once a month during the summer. There's no point in being blessed with a little piece of heaven if you can't share it with others." Her blunt speech reminded Rose of Granny Gert so Rose took to Lucy immediately.

Rose shed her cover-up to reveal an attractive yet modest tankini designed in a nautical theme with boy shorts cut longer over her hips. She jumped in the pool, splashing around in the water heated by the sun, and felt her still-tight muscles begin to relax. A fierce game of water polo, where Rose and Tim were pitted opposite each other, helped the combatants work up an appetite, especially after Rose tried to dunk Tim a few times in a defensive move. He retaliated by scooping her up and neatly tossing her back onto her side of the pool. A delicious meal of smoked pork, brisket, and barbecued chicken with all the trimmings followed, leaving Rose feeling happy, stuffed, and lethargic. Derek nimbly took over the vacated chair next to her when Tim left to discuss a possible reno project for another couple.

"You snooze, you lose, bro. I've got to say, you're pretty competitive in the pool, missy. You go, girl."

Smiling drowsily, Rose replied, her eyes closed, "I just didn't want Tim to think he had the upper hand." She turned her head to look at Derek. "Hey, I don't remember you jumping into the fray. Chicken?"

"*Moi*? For your information, I was entertaining the ladies."

"If you mean Lucy and Lisa Lindeman, they're too old for you and married besides."

"I say equal Derek for everyone. I believe in spreading the charm around."

"Well, that accounts for you but what happened to Abe?"

Derek dropped his usual posturing attitude and answered sincerely, "He's ministering to someone that no one else in the church has been able to help. Look over there, near the shallow end of the pool. You see that kid? That's Brian Jenkins." Rose saw a young redheaded boy of about twelve or thirteen with freckles and a goofy grin. Nothing unique there. Then she noticed the prosthesis on the lower-half of his right leg.

"He had to have his leg amputated in March because of some rare form of malignant tumor in his knee. You met his parents earlier. They had just about run out of ideas to help him deal with the adjustment. His mom started homeschooling him because he couldn't handle going to school and feeling like everyone was laughing at him. They weren't, of course, but he's really self-conscious. He sees an occupational therapist, a physical therapist, and an emotional therapist but he just kept retreating further into his shell. When they were just about at the breaking point, they convinced Brian to come with them to the pool party here last month. That's when Brian met Abe. Finally Brian knew someone he could really relate to. Abe's done wonders for the kid. He gives Brian tips on dealing with the prosthetic leg, including races to see who can get it off and on faster, helps him with weight training to build his upper-body strength, and, probably most importantly, showed him how to laugh again. With all he's been through, Abe is one amazing man."

"I've met a lot of amazing men here. Abe wouldn't even be here to help Brian if it weren't for you." Rose was puzzled by Derek's response.

"What you don't realize is that *I* might not be here if it weren't for Abe." He stood abruptly, excusing himself with a half-hearted smile and left her wondering what on earth he meant. She would ask Tim about it on the ride home.

About half an hour before dusk, Tom drove up on his newly washed but long-used John Deere™ tractor, easily recognizable by its characteristic green exterior. The old tractor was towing an even older hay wagon loaded with bales of hay in the middle, allowing for riders to sit on the edges of the wagon and dangle their feet over the sides.

"Who's ready for a hayride? Bring your towels to sit on so the hay won't scratch your legs. That's it, plenty of room for everyone." Rose couldn't have been more pleased. Tim helped her up to a bale on top where she could see over the tops of the others' heads. She watched Abe encouraging Brian to try and climb onto the wagon without assistance. It wasn't a graceful move but Brian managed it, pride in his accomplishment showing in the big smile on his face. Rose could also see his parents, fighting back tears as they celebrated their son's small victory, trying not to let him see their emotion.

Lucy hopped onto a little side seat mounted perpendicular to the driver, presumably to give her husband orders. They followed a rough track across a recently harvested cornfield, rolling over the broken stubble and stopped by a churning creek, still full from the recent rain, where they were treated to a full-throated bullfrog chorus before moving on. The kids in the party made a game of trying to trap fireflies on the go, and someone started singing old folk songs that Rose hadn't heard since she was a little girl—"I've Been Working on the Railroad," "Oh Susanna," "Sweet Betsy from Pike." Daylight was all but gone when the wagon made its way back to the far side of the house and a roaring bonfire that crackled with heat and produced an almost-blinding light. The Lindemans had sent their kids on the hayride while they stayed behind to get the fire started and lay out all the fixings for s'mores. It was the perfect end to a near-perfect day. But Rose still held a memory of Derek's comment in the back of her mind.

She sat quietly for a while on the drive home, tired, happy, and content. Then concern for Derek surfaced again.

"Tim?"

"Mmm?"

"I…well, I…don't really even know how to say…I mean what to ask…"

Sensing the troubled tone in her voice, Tim asked, "What is it, Rose? Something's bothering you. Didn't you have a good time?"

"Of course I did. This is the best day I've had since coming to Kansas. It's been absolutely wonderful—especially since my sore muscles loosened up a little."

Better than your days spent with Simone Applegate? Now that's encouraging, Tim thought. "But…" he prodded her aloud.

"Well, I was talking to Derek. He told me about Brian Jenkins and how Abe was helping him adjust to life without a leg. Derek obviously respected Abe for his act of service and compassion. He said Abe was an amazing man, and I said I'd met lots of amazing men since I'd been here. Then I said Abe wouldn't be here if it weren't for him, you know, Derek. Then he told me *he* wouldn't be here if not for Abe. Derek didn't explain what he meant. He just got up abruptly and I never saw him the rest of the day. Did I do or say something wrong?"

Tim paused before answering. Then he chose his words carefully. "First of all, you did *nothing* wrong. It is difficult for those who have never experienced combat or similar high-stress situations to understand the baggage that some guys bring home. Derek's personal demon is one of misplaced guilt. It doesn't matter that it's senseless—he has really struggled to let it go."

"I'm sorry, I don't understand…"

"Do you remember Abe's testimony when he explained that Derek was his platoon leader? A military leader, at any level, is responsible for the safety and well-being of his or her people. Up to a point. We can train and plan and prepare for the worst but none of us can control the unknown. Derek blames himself for Abe's injury and for the death of the other soldier in his platoon. He's convinced it's his fault, though he *knows* he couldn't possibly have known those bullets would hit those two men at that precise moment on that particular patrol. Heck, if it hadn't been for his quick thinking, there might have been more casualties. I know it's hard to understand, but in some ways, Derek is more wounded than Abe. He had pretty serious bouts of depression when he first left the army and moved him and his mom here. I don't know if he ever reached the point of actually considering suicide but I *do* know that when he found out about Abe's family situation, Derek changed. He found a focus and purpose in helping someone else. I know it helped me deal with my own father's death. Anyway Abe was so humbled and touched by our offer for him, a relative stranger, to move out here and be a part of the Warner family and our construction business, that he has moved heaven and earth to affirm Derek and help him to see God's hand in the whole process. Which is kind of strange when you consider that Abe is the baby Christian. But maybe the situation helped Abe to see the big picture more clearly. Anyway Derek is doing much better. I think being able to throw himself into hard physical labor has also been kind of cathartic. Plus we're part of a great community here. I think you've discovered that," he added with a smile, glancing at Rose.

"You're right about that. I have met so many awesome people that have made me feel right at home."

"Those awesome people really supported Derek—and Abe—to help them move on with life. It's just that sometimes, a chance remark or situation will trigger that sense of guilt. When it does, we try to remind Derek of the truth and give him some space to work it out. You might wonder why that didn't happen the Sunday Abe gave his testimony."

Now how did he know that's exactly what I was thinking? He and Aletha must *be related,"* Rose mused inwardly.

"That day, the focus was on Abe's salvation and the part Derek played in it. His leg was almost incidental to the overall story. Don't be afraid to talk to Derek. To ask him about his actions or, I should say, reactions. In a sense, you may be a better person to draw him out than Abe or me. You can be a completely objective impartial observer. Don't give up on him."

"I guess what really threw me was the personality change. He's *always* laughing and joking. But he became so *serious* when I made that comment about what he had done for Abe."

"A person can hide a lot of pain behind laughter but I think most of it is pretty genuine now." Glancing at her troubled expression, he added, "Don't worry too much about it. Just be his friend and pray for him. God's listening, even if Derek isn't always."

They had reached the cottage. Tim walked her to the door, carrying her tote bag stuffed with the leftovers Lucy had insisted on sending home with Rose. As she bade him good night, Rose momentarily lost her grip on reason and did something completely unexpected. She stood on tiptoe and kissed Tim's cheek. Appalled at what she had done on a spontaneous whim, she was covered in confusion and barely managed a disjointed "Thank you for a great time" before disappearing through the door. "Well, he probably thinks you're certifiable now, you goof," Rose chided herself. "I can only hope he took that as a sign of friendship..."

Tim thought Rose was completely wonderful and took the kiss as an optimistic sign. He was so lost in a blissful fog, it was a miracle he made it home in one piece.

Rose, snuggled under the covers with Granny Gert snoring softly in the neighboring bed, allowed her mind to wander over the events of a very eventful weekend. Just as she was sinking into a sea of happy oblivion, her tired brain shot straight back up to the surface of consciousness. She hadn't thought about Simon Applegate for two whole days! The man of her dreams had been all but forgotten. What was *wrong* with her? While he had been working hard all weekend in Topeka and Lawrence, probably missing her terribly, she had been playing water polo and roasting marshmallows! Her overdeveloped sense of conscience failed to register the hours of manual labor she had invested in the garden project or the time spent escorting Granny Gert and Aletha to church. Rose only knew herself to be a traitor. She fell asleep planning all the ways she would convince Simon of her undying devotion when next they met.

*****

Sitting in his dingy motel room, Simon focused on ensuring the listening device in his pocket would pick up an adequate recording. He tested it outside where road noise posed a challenge and again inside with the TV on. His spoken words were picked up beautifully, even with the background clamor. He repeatedly rehearsed his conversational gambits, designed to draw out the precise words he needed Aletha to say, confident that he could easily manage the fluffy-headed old woman.

He then checked all the disguise elements necessary to perpetrate his final act of investigation. He hoped it wouldn't come to that but best to be prepared. The sooner he got the recording of Aletha's voice to the agency, the sooner their techno wizards could work their magic with vocal manipulation software. Simon didn't need to know how it worked, he didn't even care. He just knew that this case was proving to be a bigger challenge than he had anticipated—and that Miles Hawthorne was going to pay through the nose for his services. As if by the caprice of a twisted providence, Simon's cell phone rang at that exact moment. It was Hawthorne.

Eyeing his phone with loathing, Simon let it ring a few times before answering it in what he hoped was a nonchalant voice. "Hello, Mr. Hawthorne…Yes, everything is going precisely as planned…"

His mouth set in a hard thin line, Simon stared at the phone for a full minute after ringing off, still idly turning and twisting a pencil with his long thin fingers. He never noticed when it snapped completely in two.

CHAPTER 14

Look, I am sending you out as sheep among wolves.
So be as shrewd as snakes and harmless as doves.

—Matthew 10:16 (NLT)

The morning sun sent speckled patterns of light dancing across the front of Fern Cottage as it made a rapid ascent on the far side of the circling oaks. Aletha savored its warmth as she waited for the arrival of her guest. As soon as she heard a car door slam, she assumed an attitude of vacuous delight.

"Mr. Applegate, I've been *so* looking forward to the pleasure of your company. Won't you join me on the swing for a cup of coffee?" she said, patting the cushion next to her. The swing was the seating option closest to the open window and allowed Aletha the best opportunity to observe her guest. As planned, Gert and Angelica were secreted in the house within hearing range and Prince was poised to perform at the appointed moment.

Accepting the proffered coffee mug, Simon wondered, *Now how could she be sure it was me?*

"Your shoes make such a pleasant sound on the flagstone walk, sort of a *click-tap* rhythm." Simon never imagined that his expensive Italian shoes could give him away. He would have to tread more carefully around the blind woman.

"I wouldn't dream of putting you out by arriving even a minute late for our little chat. I feel quite honored by claiming so much of your time," Simon responded gallantly. Aletha kept a placid smile on her face while mentally labelling him a toadeater.

"Not at all, dear boy. And let me just say at the outset that I must apologize for any reserve I may have shown in my manner when we first met. You know, a woman in my situation has to be careful but I feel quite assured now that I am safe with you. I can just sense that you are trustworthy." Then as if doubting herself, Aletha asked, concern in voice, "I *can* trust you, Mr. Applegate, can't I?"

Simon sat his coffee mug on the little side table and stilled her fidgeting hands with his own, speaking soothingly, "Implicitly. I am both the soul of discretion and one who believes that chivalry will *not* die if I have any say about it." He separated her hands and laid his flatly against hers. "You see, no electronic devices today."

"How kind and *clever* of you to remember," Aletha said as she pulled her hands away. Leaning a little closer to him, she heard some barely perceptible feedback from her hearing aid. *No phone but some sort of recording device, I imagine*, she thought, well-pleased. *How convenient that one can always count on devious persons to follow their baser instincts. Makes dealing with them so much simpler, really.*

"Now that we've established that we are quite alone, why don't you tell me a little about yourself," Aletha continued coyly.

Laughing in a self-deprecating way, Simon said modestly, "Oh, there really is so little to tell. I come from a middle-class family in London, was educated at a relatively obscure but sound public school called Broadmoor—thanks to some timely scholarships—and worked my way to America. I practiced investigative journalism as a freelancer for a number of years until more and more newspapers failed, then decided to try my hand at twenty-first-century freelancing—blogging. It affords me a respectable living, a flexible work schedule, and the privilege of traveling this beautiful country and meeting fascinating people, like you, dear lady."

Aletha had to credit him with a well-rehearsed backstory. For a story was surely all it was. She had met several wealthy industrialists from England when married to her first husband, James. She knew, therefore, that Broadmoor was neither obscure nor merely sound. Many lesser gentry and those in trade educated their children at the prestigious school when they were unable to gain entry to the more elite Eton or Harrow. She and James had even considered sending their son to school there at one time but couldn't bear the idea of him being so far away. Thoughts of her beloved son, so long dead to her, temporarily diverted her attention from the business of the moment.

She was recalled from her abstraction by Simon asking solicitously, "Mrs. Mason? Mrs. Mason, are you quite all right?"

"Oh my. You must forgive the mental aberrations of an old woman. Now where were we?" Aletha asked politely.

I will have to keep her on task if this conversation is to be productive, Simon thought grimly. Aloud he said, "I was merely recounting my less-than-noteworthy past. But I am far more interested in you. If you will permit my impertinence, I would like to, in essence, interview you. I solemnly swear not to use a word of our conversation in my blog without your complete approval. Would it be acceptable to you if I just take a few notes? I'm afraid it's an occupational hazard. I hope you understand."

"Well, it makes one feel rather pompous, but if you like, I shall be happy to be interviewed."

"Wonderful. Now pretend that you are, say, writing your memoirs. How would you begin?"

"Really, this is most unusual," she said, adopting a first-rate dithering manner, "but I will try my best. I suppose I would start out by saying something like, this is Aletha Mason, and these are my memoirs. Something like that. Is that the sort of thing you're looking for?"

"To the letter." Simon smiled inwardly. *This will be a walk in the park if she continues to be so easily led.*

"Now, Mrs. Mason—"

"*Aletha,* dear boy..."

"Aletha, we can say that you reside in a quaint Victorian cottage on the outskirts of Tinkers Well but to where do you enjoy traveling? You might begin with something like, 'When I'm not at home, I enjoy...'"

"Oh yes, I see what you mean. How is this? When I'm not at my *dear* Fern Cottage—" She was interrupted by Simon clearing his throat. "Oh dear. Let me try that again. When I'm not at..." Aletha glanced at Simon who watched her critically, "home..." She saw his expression relax. "I enjoy traveling into Tinkers Well to do a little shopping. And of course, I check in at the bank periodically to see if Mr. Thurston at Midwest Union, Bank that is, needs me to sign anything. You know he takes care of all my business affairs, though I don't suppose your readers would be interested in that?" Aletha asked innocently.

"Well, actually, anything that will afford Tinkers Well an aura of stability with solid dependable services will always be of interest to potential residents. Can you tell me any more about the estimable Mr."—Simon made a pretense of checking his notes—"Thurston and the services his bank offers?"

"Oh, certainly. How's this? He pays all my bills, makes sure I have enough funds in all my accounts, and has access to my safe deposit box. Your readers might find this interesting too. They have such lovely safe deposit boxes—the old-fashioned kind with pretty scrollwork around the box numbers. And absolute privacy for anyone that wants to go through their valuables. They, the nice people at the bank, are also very amenable to allowing other family members to add things to the box—with the proper authorization of course. Should I add that the family member could be a husband or wife or even a son or daughter or say, nephew?"

"No. I think that quite covers the bank. Why don't you talk a little about your social life? I know, from blessed personal experience, that you have two delightful guests staying with you at present. And I must say, I can't wait to see Rose this afternoon. I've missed her terribly the last two days, as you may well imagine. I do hope she hasn't been too lonely without me..." Simon finished on an inquisitive note.

Aletha had to bite back the pithy reply, "Why, I doubt she even noticed you were gone. Her time has been monopolized by her many new friends—Tim Ludlow in particular." But she adopted an empathetic air, saying only, "You have no idea."

Simon, attempting to sound diffident, said, "I don't know whether to feel guilty or glad. Either way, I hope to show Rose an enjoyable afternoon. I *would* like to let her know where we'll be going this afternoon but she must have left her cell phone here while she's working so hard to put your lovely garden in order. I don't suppose—"

"Don't give it a thought. Just leave your message with me and I'll pass it along when she returns. Besides I'm sure she'll be delighted with whatever you have planned," said Aletha graciously, intentionally adding to his already monstrous sense of superiority.

"I'll see to that. I do apologize for allowing myself to be led astray. I'm afraid Rose has quite captivated me. But back to another fascinating woman." Aletha simpered demurely and reached for her mug. "I will only mention your blindness if you permit and as it relates to your canine companion. It may be helpful for people with disabilities to learn of access to helper animals in the area. Can you comment on that?"

"What shall I say? My sweet Prince was a gift from my husband. He's really more of a companion than a helper dog but he is *always* at my side." As an aside, she said, "Except, of course, when I leave him in another room should a guest be leery of his presence. But he really is a pet. Why I can just snap"—in the acting of bringing the fingers of her right hand together, her left hand, holding her coffee mug, jerked and spilled its contents all over Simon's lap "my fingers and he will—is there a problem, Mr. Applegate?"

Simon swore softly but Aletha's sharp ears caught the sound. "Oh dear. Have I spilled my coffee?" She reached out to touch his leg, pants soaked through. "Oh no, and all over your pants too. You must go inside and clean up."

"No, no, dear lady. I assure you, it's nothing." All the while thinking, *Damn! The daft woman has ruined my trousers. I'll have to go and change now. I don't think it penetrated to the recorder in my pocket though.*

"Now really, I insist." Aletha grabbed his arm, pulling him toward the front door while waving her hand wildly behind her in a signal to Gert. On cue, Prince ran to the closed front door where Angelica teased him with a chew toy. He growled and barked as Gert and Angelica threw the toy back and forth. It was a pity that Simon could not see the dog's frantically waving tail.

Simon only heard the sound of a vicious animal. He quickly backed away from the door, offering excuses for his hasty departure. Angelica and Gert could barely contain their laughter as he made a beeline for his car. Aletha added the crowning comical note by waving guilelessly in farewell, adjuring him to not be a stranger. But the car door had slammed before Simon could respond.

With lips pursed and eyes narrowed, Aletha said softly, "Now I wonder what precisely that ne'er-do-well is up to…" Entering the house, she announced to her accomplices, both regarding Aletha with awe after her masterful performance, "I think it's time I paid a call on Mr. Thurston."

*****

The little front loader worked overtime that morning. Abe had volunteered to operate the machine to complete the final preparations for the laying of pavers on the walkways at the main house. Marilyn, Rose, and, later in the morning, Angelica raked and leveled the sand until their backs were aching. By the time they finished, the sun had risen well into the sky, leaving all shade behind.

"It *must* be time for lunch," Abe commented hopefully.

"It will be just as soon as you get that thingummy cleaned up and loaded on the trailer," said Angelica. "And don't you try that starvin' waif look on me, young man. I *know* how much you ate for breakfast."

Acknowledging a hit, Abe grinned and started unwinding the hose.

"I'll help you, Abe." Turning to the two older ladies, Rose said, "You two go on. I don't want you getting overheated and have the wrath of Derek or Tim come down on me."

"As *if* they would even notice," Angelica said with an ironic smile as she and Marilyn walked off toward the cottage.

Rose turned to encounter a full-frontal assault by the garden hose. She paused only a split second to gasp for air after receiving a direct stream of water to the face before running toward the laughing Abe.

"You…jerk!" Rose sputtered as she grabbed the hose from her assaulter and turned it on him. They wrestled for control, both soaking wet and giggling like ten-year-olds. Abe finally cranked the spigot until the stream of water stopped.

"Now don't you feel refreshed?" he asked politely.

"I feel like a drowned rat, you turkey," Rose responded, still laughing. "Is this any way to treat your sister?"

Abe's grin faded to be replaced by a pensive faraway look. "Actually it's precisely how I would treat my brothers and sisters."

Unwittingly Rose had done it again. A seemingly harmless remark had induced a complete change in her companion, just as it had with Derek the evening before. The teasing Abe had become a serious man, carrying a heavy burden. She was slowly beginning to—if not fully understand—at least appreciate, the complexities of these young men who had surrendered themselves to the call of duty and the call of faith.

"I'm sorry, Abe. I didn't mean to bring up painful memories. You're such a part of the community here that I almost forgot about your actual family. You must really miss them."

"There isn't a day goes by that I don't think of each one. But they aren't painful memories, not exactly." He had turned on the water again after attaching it to a pressure washer and began methodically cleaning dirt from the vehicle's tracks.

"Are you able to communicate with them at all?" Rose didn't want to pry but wanted to offer him a sympathetic ear if he felt like talking.

"Oh, sure. My siblings are all adults now—well, if you count my youngest brother an adult at eighteen. Other than Husam, who will be entering university this fall, only my youngest sister, Samia, still lives with my parents while she finishes her studies to become a registered nurse. The other two are both married and one has a baby, a niece that I have never seen before. They are all followers of Islam and were saddened by my conversion to Christianity. And like me, they respect our parents and our traditions. But after the initial shock, despite wanting to honor our parents' wishes, they started responding to my e-mails. I think they avoid commenting on Facepage posts, where I can't help mentioning what Jesus has done in my life, for fear that Aby or Ommy might see them. I have even spoken to Husam a few times. Despite our age difference, we are the most alike in personality and interests, and I think he misses me as much as I miss him."

As Abe worked his way around the little front loader with the hose, Rose used a rough brush to knock off stubborn mud clods loosened by the water.

"You are an inspiration to me, Abe. I'm afraid I take my family too much for granted but I can't imagine how it would feel to be cut off from them almost overnight."

He was silent for a few minutes, as if he was wrestling with his thoughts, then said haltingly, "I…sometimes I…I get so…*angry* with God. I lost a leg. I gave up…all the beliefs I had clung to for a lifetime to follow Him, and on top of all that, I had to give up my family too. It just doesn't seem fair."

"But during your testimony, you said—"

"I said that following Jesus Christ was worth all of the sacrifice? I believe that to be absolutely true but I'm human, just like every other Christ follower. And just like it is with every other Christian, Satan knows the exact buttons to push to try and undermine my faith. To cause me to question my decision." After a short pause, he directed a home question at Rose. "It's none of my business but I'm curious. Haven't you ever felt anger or resentment toward God for things that have happened in your life?"

Wow! Rose thought to herself. *How can I compare my minor setbacks with the enormity of the challenges Abe has faced?* She took her time answering as she scrubbed a particularly stubborn glob of mud. "It's so different for me, Abe. I mean, I've known about Jesus my whole life and made a decision for Him when I was in high school. My whole family celebrated and shared in my baptism. I've never faced any real challenges in my life other than being fired from a couple of less-than-stellar jobs. Nothing like what you've had to deal with. Or Derek who lost his dad when he was young and lives with PTSD, or even Tim who had to start up his own business while helping his friends who had even bigger problems. My parents are both alive and well. I talk to them and my sisters all the time. I've made great new friends," she said, smiling at Abe, "and I'm dating an incredible man who is like someone from a dream. It's *easy* for me to praise God. He just keeps showering me with blessings. But you've really known struggle yet you *still* honor God despite your tests of faith. I think that's why I admire my three brothers so much."

"Then I am happy for you and hope that He will continue to bless you." After a few moments of silence, he added in a lighter tone, "You know, I don't believe that I *have* lost my family completely. I not only think of them daily, I *pray* for them daily. And it is my fervent prayer that they will *all* come to know Jesus someday. What a joyous reunion that will be!" He spoke as if looking into a shrouded yet hopeful future.

"Then I'll pray for them too," Rose said as they finished their mucky task. "And I want you to know that you can count on me to be your sister while I'm here and even when I go back to Kentucky, if you need someone to talk to."

"Now it is I who am richly blessed," Abe replied with simple sincerity. The innocent girl, whose grasp of the scope of human experience had been limited to the somewhat restricted reality of an uneventful life and the fanciful exploits of fiction, was touched by his humility. Her sojourn in Kansas would not leave Rose unchanged.

Her morning with Abe, however, certainly left her preoccupied. As Simon and Rose made their now-routine scouting excursion into Tinkers Well, he had to repeat his question for a third time. He found her distraction irritating. His usually well-modulated tone acquired an edge that finally broke through her sober thoughts.

"I'm sorry, Simon. Did you ask me something?"

"Three times, as a matter of fact," he replied with a glittering smile devoid of warmth.

"Oh, gosh! I am *so* sorry. I guess I was still thinking about something Abe told me this morning. Have I told you about the rift between him and his parents over—"

"Yes, I believe you mentioned that before," said Simon, cutting short a story he had found tedious the first time she had recounted it. He could muster little sympathy for someone who had the good fortune to no longer be saddled with the unwanted baggage of a family. "I was trying to ascertain your preference for tackling city hall and the county seat of government or looking into local banking options."

Neither sounded particularly interesting to Rose but she felt Tinkers Well City Hall might at least shed some light on local customs and holiday celebrations. "Well, if I have a choice, I think I'd like to learn more about the local community and even about other towns nearby. But only if that's all right with you," she added, hoping her deference to his will might make up for her earlier lapse of attentiveness. It worked. Rose's willingness to yield to his superior claims served as a balm to Simon's ego. He graciously bowed to her choice.

Because the courthouse served the entire population of Harrington County, the halls bustled with local citizens renewing car, truck, tractor, and boat registrations while hopeful teenagers paced nervously in a crowded waiting room, anticipating the test for their first driver's permit or, better yet, their first license. Rose was pleased to discover that she and Simon would be escorted through the hallowed halls by the county clerk, Jim Hastings, who just happened to be one of the attendees at the Bennett's pool party. Jim, a good-natured rotund individual with a booming voice that matched his outgoing manner, was pleased to greet Rose but was less thrilled to welcome the slim elegant Simon. When Jim saluted Simon with a neighborly slap on the shoulder, after enveloping Rose in a friendly bear hug, he nearly knocked the smaller man off his feet. Simon recovered with as much dignity as he could and hurried to catch up with the other two, well away on an impromptu tour.

The gleaming corridors of the courthouse were connected by marble floors that led from one imposing carved wooden door to another, and vintage wrought iron chandeliers illuminated the entrance to the moderately sized yet dignified courtroom. Fortunately no cases were being heard that day so they were free to wander up to the elevated judge's bench where sentence had been passed on decades of local offenders of the law. The ever-imaginative Rose felt a shiver of awe in contemplating the decisions made there and how they had effected the lives of those involved. Simon, who made it a practice to *avoid* courtrooms, found this one awash in the archaic. Rich wooden wainscoting was overhung with the images of stern-faced judges in somber black robes. Greek-style Doric columns supported the outside walls between ten recesses containing the windows lining opposing sides of the courtroom—each window a stained glass rendering of one of the Ten Commandments. Rose could have stayed there for hours, studying the artistic details and pumping Jim Hastings for any colorful stories about infamous outlaws of the past, but Simon focused her attention on the other stops on their itinerary, thanked Jim for his services—from a safe distance—and stepped out into the corridor, headed for the door leading to city hall. Catching sight of a familiar figure nearly filling that particular doorway and sporting a silver-blue wig and an enormous swath of bright yellow muumuu, Simon spun Rose around, walking quickly toward the main entrance to the courthouse on State Street. He was in no mood to make nice with the effusive Dottie Patton of The Unique Antique.

"Simon, isn't city hall the other way?"

"I have a confession to make," he improvised quickly. "All that stone and marble made me feel like I was wandering around in a whopping great cave. I'm afraid I'm feeling a bit claustrophobic."

Her ready compassion aroused, Rose was quick to fall in with his wishes to leave the building by an alternate route. "I had no idea. Simon, why didn't you say something earlier?"

"I had no intention of spoiling your fun. You seemed to be having such a jolly time with the estimable Jim." The guilt on her face spurred him to add, "I do *so* want you to enjoy yourself on our little adventures."

"Oh, Simon. You are too good to me. I don't deserve it but I promise to make it up to you."

"Nonsense. You deserve the very best of everything, my darling." Now standing on the covered portico outside the building, Simon turned to Rose, cupped her face with his hands, careful not to jostle the camera gear around her neck, and looked searchingly into her eyes, holding her captive with ardent desire shining from his own. She waited breathlessly for the kiss that must come. He drew nearer, their lips inches apart—then abruptly stepped away. Rose, leaning toward him in anticipation, nearly fell when Simon moved. She was instantly mortified. Had she misread the moment?

"I'm a damned scoundrel!" Simon exclaimed, covering his eyes with a shaking hand. "I should never allow my desire for you get the better of my judgment." Turning to look at Rose, her expression a study in hurt and confusion, he stepped toward her with his hands outstretched as if to take hers, then withdrew them to run his fingers through his hair in a frustrated fashion. "I have sensed on other occasions that you have been somewhat embarrassed by my innocent greetings when in the company of your grandmother and her friends, and here I am, wanting to make love to you on the steps of the most noble structure in town. Folly!" He held his hand up to stop Rose's protestations. "I am a gentleman. You are a lady. It doesn't matter how I feel about you. I *must* respect your sensibilities and reputation. *Please* forgive me, dear Rose." The inexperienced young woman felt as if she had stepped onto an emotional roller coaster and been denied the thrilling plunge and recovery from the highest peak, only to learn that the ride had been closed by an unbelievably conscientious operator.

"Oh, Simon," Rose said with a catch in her throat, "there is *nothing* to forgive. I...I didn't...realize..."

"How I felt about you? Have my emotions been so obscure, my love?" The words were uttered with such longing they pierced her heart.

"I...I wondered...hoped..."

"I will not speak now. But I reserve the right to feel," he said, looking at Rose with such deep intensity that she had to look away, her face flushed. Simon took a deep breath, blowing it out slowly as if to exorcise his demons, then took her hand gently and led her down the steps to a bench in the park facing the courthouse.

"I think you can get a smashing shot of this marvelous old edifice from here." He spoke as if the past five minutes were figments of her imagination. But standing next to him, Rose felt the restraint in his manner, a restraint imposed for her benefit. She adopted the same light attitude and duly snapped away with the camera, holding the memory of that tender interchange in her heart.

Making their way back across State Street to the Tinkers Well City Hall behind, Simon and Rose agreed to an unspoken but implicit understanding. Business as usual. On entering the small office building adjacent to the community center, where Rose had delivered a bingo beatdown to Tim Ludlow on Thursday, they were greeted unexpectedly by another of Rose's new acquaintances. Lucy Bennett welcomed Rose with a warm hug, just as Jim Hastings had, but merely smiled mechanically and nodded to Simon by way of recognition.

How has she made so many new friends in such a short space of time? Simon mused. *It would appear that her self-appointed guardians are legion!*

"I just work here in the afternoons when it's too hot to be outside. It keeps me busy and out of Tom's way for a few hours," Lucy remarked to Rose by way of explanation. She introduced them to the mayor (insisted he speak with them even though he was obviously busy on a project) and tracked down the president of the chamber of commerce at his place of business, ordering him to city hall. Both men welcomed Rose and Simon after darting a glance at Lucy fraught with meaning. Bent on a single-minded purpose, she blithely ignored the unspoken message of indignation and shepherded everyone into the conference room. Apparently Lucy "organized" city hall along the same lines as the Bennett household.

Mayor Teasdale and Freddie Freck, owner of the general store of the same name, both painted glowing pictures of the town's citizenry, history, and opportunities. There were great days ahead for Tinkers Well, they assured the newcomers. Rose was most interested in the community events calendar but was a little saddened by the thought that she would not be in attendance at the Harvest Festival or the Tree Lighting Ceremony at Christmas or Community Sunrise Service at Easter. She didn't know where she would be but surely she would be with Simon.

At their parting on Friday, Rose had promised Simon a surprise on his return after his weekend away. It wasn't much but she hoped its novelty would make up for lack of substance. So after their information gathering was completed for the day, she asked him to drive out to Sunrise Lake, about fifteen miles north of town, instead of going to the Early Bird Bakery for tea.

"What's this? I hadn't counted on anything special today—other than being with you." The blatant sentiment surprised Rose a little after Simon's earlier emotional withdrawal but it was spoken in such an open lighthearted manner that she merely took it in stride.

"I know how you enjoy your afternoon tea and well…"

"I've been a trifle disappointed with the local offerings?"

Laughing, she responded, "I think that's safe to say. So as a treat, I asked Angelica to make a pot of tea and put it in a thermos to stay warm. *And* I convinced her that it would not be a *proper* tea without some of her heavenly pastries. They're not exactly scones but I think you'll be happy with them."

"You've got my mouth watering already. How far away is this lake?"

A few minutes later, they drove into a nearly empty parking lot. Finding another human being would have been more challenging than finding a cozy picnic table for two. A few trucks with boat trailers were the only signs of fellow lake visitors and they were obviously all on the water. A hardworking community had little time to spare for recreation during the week but she imagined the draw of water sports would paint a very different picture on the weekend.

Rose reached for a large tote bag as Simon walked around the car to open her door. He had noticed the oversized bag Rose deposited behind her seat that morning but thought little of it. Rose's vagaries were only of interest to him as they directly affected his mission. Seated on the picnic bench, he watched, enthralled, as she pulled more items out of the carryall than a magician from his hat.

A red-and-white checked tablecloth. Cloth napkins. Real porcelain plates and teacups. A small canister of sugar and bottle of cream stored in an even smaller cooling package. And finally, the promised thermos of tea and biscuits dripping with strawberry jam.

"Rose, you're a genius!" Simon exclaimed with genuine enthusiasm.

Any tension or awkwardness between them was left behind on the courthouse steps. The two enjoyed the delicious repast in the shade of a huge overhanging silver maple tree while watching a solitary ski boat taking a circuitous route back to the dock. The water skiers moved freely across the lake in the late afternoon sun without bothering the local fisherman who all knew that the best time for fishing is at or near daybreak before the sun heats the surface of the water, sending the fish down to the deeper cooler pools of the lake.

As Rose began replacing the now-empty plates and thermos in her bag, she reached a little too far and strained one of her already aching back muscles. She paused in midmotion, letting out a resounding "Oooh"! She tried rubbing the precise spot but found it difficult to administer self-massage on her own back.

Simon, seizing on an unlooked-for opportunity, asked if he could be of assistance.

"I just pulled a muscle in my back. I should be able to stretch it out." The effort elicited an even louder "Oooh!"

"Don't be ridiculous," Simon said briskly as he cleared the remaining items to one end of the tablecloth and insisted Rose sit on the bench and reach her arms across the table. "Now let me do something special for *you*." At that, he began rubbing the muscles in the small of her back in rather expert fashion. Among his many other skills, he had acquired a most effective massage technique from one particularly shapely masseuse he had met in the course of an investigation in San Francisco's Chinatown.

"Oooh!" This time, the single syllable was more indicative of relief than pain. As his magical fingers worked their way up her back, Simon gently pulled Rose to a sitting position and began plying her shoulder and neck tendons until she was putty in his expert hands. She began to feel a sense of well-being that went beyond relaxed muscles. As Simon's touch became lighter, the tingling sensation it left behind became more intense until she felt herself breathing more quickly, all the while aware of his body just behind hers and his breath on her cheek as he leaned over her shoulder.

"Feeling better?" Simon asked. It was almost a whisper in her ear.

"*Yes*," Rose answered on a sigh. Abruptly the magic stopped.

"Good. I'm happy to have been of assistance," Simon said in a matter-of-fact voice. "Now before you tempt me further to go beyond the line of what is pleasing, I think I should get you home."

Her thoughts and feelings in turmoil, Rose felt, yet again, an unwarranted sense of guilt. Simon's words, spoken seemingly in jest, held an underlying element of truth. She had allowed herself to act the fool in responding to his generous offer to alleviate her physical discomfort and blamed herself for any temptation her unguarded reaction to his ministering touch might have caused.

The drive to Fern Cottage was largely a silent one. Rose wanted to discuss all that had transpired that day but would not breach the invisible barrier between them. Just before she opened the door to let herself out of the big Escalade, Simon caught her left hand in a compelling clasp and drew it to his lips, planting kiss after kiss on her fingers and palm.

"Rose, my dearest love, I fear I revealed too much today of my inner struggle when in your company. I sincerely hope you will not think ill of me, for every hour spent with you has truly been my greatest pleasure. I want you to know—I *need* you to know that I regard you with the highest honor, and for that reason and that reason alone, I think it best that I not see you for a few days."

Had her foolish reactions to his restrained expressions of affection given Simon a distaste for her society? His next words wiped away all worry and left her weak with relief and—gratitude? Expectation? Disappointment?

"I need time," he continued, "to train myself to remain more detached in your company, not because I wish to be but because I desire more than anything to pursue you as only a gentleman can. I would have you know that my passion for you still burns and all the brighter because it burns in silence." Kissing her hand once more, Simon released it, saying, "May I call on you Thursday?"

Moved by his earnest speech and rendered incapable of any kind of intelligent response, Rose merely nodded her head as she grabbed her bag and stepped out of the car. For several minutes after Simon drove away, she stood looking after the absent suitor as if his essence still lingered.

In the past week, she had met amazing men who put honor and loyalty above self in ways that she had never fully understood before. Men who lived every day with the scars of war and family tragedy.

But she had never encountered anyone, outside of the fantasy world of her dreams, who cared for, dared she say *loved*, a woman so much that he would deny himself even her presence in order to master his emotions until he could meet her again without fear of indiscretion or impropriety. Rose would definitely not leave Kansas unchanged.

*****

Simon allowed a slow smirk of satisfaction to appear as he drove away from the cottage, leaving the impressionable Rose in his wake. He had realized all too quickly that both he and Rose were becoming a little too recognizable in the tiny hamlet of Tinkers Well. It was as well that she had chosen to explore the halls of government instead of finance that day. Anonymity was crucial to successful reconnaissance of the bank and it now appeared necessary that he accomplish the task in disguise which meant no Rose. It was inspired genius that gave him the spur of the moment idea of almost declaring himself to the gullible girl, then pulling away out of honor. What better excuse for avoiding her, allowing him to operate under deep cover for a few days. Remembering the scene at the courthouse, Simon had to admit that he had enjoyed the impassioned performance for her benefit. The fortuitous need for a massage later had offered him the perfect vehicle to awaken her physical desires without her even realizing what was happening, leaving Rose with an enticing hint of what she could look forward to in a fairy-tale future. To his mind, Simon had done a good day's work. Having set the hook the previous week, he was now positioned to reel her in when it suited his needs. Rose was the puppet and Simon the puppet master, and he had no intention of leaving town without sharing a grand finale with his lovely ingénue.

CHAPTER 15

*Keep on asking, and you will receive what you ask
for. Keep on seeking, and you will find. Keep on
knocking, and the door will be opened to you.*

—Matthew 7:7 (NLT)

Both Aletha and Gert noticed a change in Rose. The normally lively girl, who habitually radiated sunshine and vitality, roamed listlessly through the cottage, her churning thoughts a thousand miles away; her voice, with a hint of laughter always lurking near the surface, preserved relative silence during dinner. Aletha kept up a flow of light conversation to forestall any ill-timed questions by Gert who obviously wanted to know what had wrought such a transformation in her granddaughter. Gert's curiosity was tinged with hopefulness for Rose wasn't exactly glowing with happiness. She was more a contrasting study in uncertainty and tentative anticipation.

The unsettling events of the day followed Rose into sleep. Her restless dreams vacillated between visions of a glowing future unfettered by restraint between Rose and her beloved, where love (the chaste variety of her imagination) could be expressed freely and openly, to images of a tormented Simon separated forever from his darling Rose because of unnecessary scruples brought about by her thoughtless gestures of affection. A beautiful white wedding, ardent kisses, walking hand in hand down quaint streets from Maine to Mexico. A distraught Rose reaching for Simon, her arms longing to hold him, to assure him his love was reciprocated and welcomed. Happiness and distress. Light and darkness. Joy and sorrow. She eventually fell into shallow troubled slumber and finally into the deeper sleep of exhaustion. She woke late the next morning, feeling anything but refreshed.

Granny Gert left Rose to rest as long as need be, having witnessed her tossing and turning during the night. Anticipating the girl's reluctance to do anything but withdraw into a world of physical and mental inertia, Gert was ready to hand Rose her favorite coffee with hazelnut the moment her granddaughter showed signs of life. As Rose slowly sipped the rich brown elixir, Gert opened all the window blinds, letting the warmth and energy of the sun do their own inspiring work on the lethargic figure now sitting up in bed.

"Angelica kept a plate of her famous cinnamon rolls warm for you in the oven before joining Marilyn in the garden. I understand you ladies will be planting today. Best do that before it gets too hot. I know you remember Grandpa Ernie telling us to plant when it's cool and get everything well-watered in so the young plants can withstand the heat of the sun without shocking too much." As she spoke, Gert pulled out shorts, T-shirt, and underthings and placed them at the end of her own neatly made bed, the soft-pink chenille coverlet spread evenly without a wrinkle showing anywhere. "Now you just slip into your work clothes while I make up your bed." As Rose started to protest, Gert coaxed her toward the door. "Go on now. The bathroom is all yours, and you don't want to keep Angelica and Marilyn waiting."

Though Rose's conscience had already taken a beating by her own hands, she couldn't help but respond to her grandmother's urging. As much as she would have preferred staying in bed, contemplating a future so ambiguous as to be almost mythical, Rose knew she had an obligation to finish the work in Aletha's garden. The thrill of the project momentarily eluded her but her recognition of responsibility did not.

She was greeted on the jobsite by Derek who proudly proclaimed himself to be her partner in crime for the day. Even Rose's subdued spirits were no match for that ebullient smile. She was also heartened by his obvious return to an innately buoyant disposition. The stash of plants under the shade of the expansive willow dwindled steadily as the foursome found homes for blooming annuals and shrubs in the ready planting beds prepped the previous weekend. Rose and Derek worked side by side, his endless flow of conversational nonsense keeping her laughing as the work itself began its own miracle of meaningful purpose. Rose found pleasure and a deep sense of accomplishment as she watched the empty earth fill with color and life.

Sun-loving cannas and begonias adorned opposite corners of the main front yard while impatiens, geraniums, and endless varieties of coleus were destined for beds near the old stonewalled sitting area where the willow branches would provide an afternoon respite from the burning Kansas sun. Black-eyed Susans and dianthus contributed a lower-growing splash of yellow and pink hues around the central fountain, allowing room for the Vermillionaire firecracker plants to grow beyond them to attract hummingbirds with their elongated reddish-orange blooms. Lena Thompson, champion gardener and owner of Plants Aplenty (Rose liked to think of her as a long-lost cousin), had done a masterful job of combining familiar favorites with lesser known (to Rose anyway) varieties of hardy annuals like Savannah ruby grass and the flowering succulent Mezoo Trailing Red. It had been an education for Rose to learn the names of unfamiliar bloomers and just how to mix the plants for optimal color and spread, both horizontally and vertically. With many of the plants in the ground, the beds still looked fairly sparse but would fill in nicely as the summer progressed.

Lena had also insisted on a few ornamental and border trees to draw the eyes upward and provide additional shade without detracting from the house itself. Though rather late in the season for planting trees, she had promised to stop by the following week to make sure they were thriving in their newly appointed homes. A blue Chinese wisteria tree would take up residence on the east side of the house while a deep-red Rose of Sharon temporarily took root in a large pot so that it could be moved to add color and elegance anywhere in the garden until a permanent planting in the fall. Two ornamental maples were destined for either corner on the south side of the garden where they could frame the front facade of the house without blocking the view. Spartan junipers were chosen to line the new driveway where it reached the western border of the yard.

Maturing at just fifteen feet, the shrubs would form a natural wall to partially block the side view of the house, enticing visitors to drive to the front parking area in order to see the mansion in its full glory. And finally, another willow would occupy the space in between the junipers and the building, owning the western section of the yard and providing afternoon shade for that side of the veranda.

It was a grand scheme, and even with four sets of hands, the work could hardly be finished in a day, much less a few morning hours. After taking a lunch break at the cottage, Marilyn, Angelica, and Derek expected Rose to excuse herself to prepare for her ritual afternoon with Simon. When she announced instead that she planned to get the shade-tolerant plants in the ground after lunch since she could work in relative cover, everyone, Gert and Aletha included, looked at her in amazement, each burning to ask the obvious question but tacitly agreeing to avoid it.

"How did you know I was going to suggest that, Rose? You're not some kind of mental genius like Abe, are you?" Derek asked with exaggerated comical suspicion. His response was perfect, Rose barely had time to register the elephant in the room before laughing in reply.

"Hardly. I'm just anxious to see it all come together. Just the little bit we accomplished this morning has whet my appetite to get more done."

"Do you hear that? *Little bit?* I don't know if I'm willing to work for an ungrateful drill sergeant…" Derek said in an injured voice, trying to hide the smile at the corner of his mouth.

"Derek Warner," Angelica said sternly, "I thought I taught you to have more manners. Now you just finish eatin' and get yourself out there and help Miss Rose," she admonished her son with a wink hidden from Rose.

"Well, if you feel you're not *strong* enough for the work, Derek…" Rose let the bait dangle, her face the image of innocence.

"Not *strong* enough? Let me tell you, missy, Derek Warner is strong enough for *anything.*" Then mumbling as if to himself but making much of his performance for the benefit of the table at large, "I get no respect. I get no respect from Abe. I get no respect from

Tim. And even my own mama…" He broke off to finish off a plate of potato salad with a wounded air.

Rose walked up behind his chair, put her arms around his shoulders, and kissed him soundly on the cheek, saying, "*I think you're the best.*"

Grinning from ear to ear, Derek turned around and asked, "Which flowers did you say we were planting this afternoon?"

Convincing Angelica and Marilyn to take the afternoon off, Rose and Derek accomplished the planned task and sat on the old stone wall during a water-break, weighing the rival merits of getting the wisteria tree into the ground while it would have a good sixteen hours out of the full sun or waiting until the morning when working conditions would be more favorable.

"Derek, I can't tell you how much I appreciate your help with this project."

"Don't give it a thought. This is a priority for all of us, and since it's tough for Abe to work on the ground, I thought I'd do my part today for your garden project. Besides Abe's got a bunch of admin stuff to do." He laughed shortly before going on. "Tim is a master carpenter and I've gotten pretty good at handling the rough stuff, but you should have seen the mess our records were in when we started our business. It was just Two Brothers then," he said. "We could barely file our tax returns that year! Then Abe's crisis became our salvation. The man really is a genius, but if you tell him I said that, I'll deny every word," he said with raised eyebrows.

Rose laughed then replied as a fellow conspirator, "Your secret is safe with me."

"He organized everything—manages inventory, billing, and tax records with software I've never even heard of. He keeps records of every call that comes in, stays on good terms with the building inspector by playing chess with his grandfather every week, and knows the names of most clients' kids, dogs, and great-aunts. We'd be lost without him."

"And he'd be lost without you." Rose hesitated before continuing, "Derek, I'm not just glad that you're here today, I'm glad that you're back to you today."

Now it was Derek's turn to pause. After looking down at his filthy calloused hands and trying to clean them with an equally filthy towel, he turned to look at Rose. "I'm sorry about Sunday night. Tim told me you asked about my... reaction to what you said." Turning to look out over the peace of the garden, he went on. "I really am trying to see God's hand in...life. And He helps me to see it a little bit more every day. He keeps sending special people into my life— like you...and Granny Gert," he added with a grin. "Whether you realize it or not, you've both pulled me a little more out of myself and back into the world."

Touched by his honest sincerity, Rose impulsively hugged him then pulled back with a grimace. "Ew! You're—"

"Yeah, well you're no prize either, missy." Looking at her sweat-stained clothes and mud-caked skin, Rose reluctantly agreed.

"You may have a point..."

"Hey, what do you say we get that wisteria planted?" Her slow response prompted him to pop her with the towel he was holding then take off running before she could retaliate.

The wisteria got planted, Rose got her revenge—the tree was not the only thing watered and her dreams that night were filled with delicate blossoms and shimmering leaves.

*****

"I don't know what happened. She just told me that Mr. Perfection wouldn't be around for a few days. I would say good riddance but I'm afraid she's still smitten. Made some comment about his gentlemanly honor and chivalrous behavior or some such nonsense. I tell you, Letha, he's up to something."

"I'm inclined to agree with you, Trudy." They were sitting on the porch swing after seeing Rose off to her now-daily chores. The morning breeze had sprung up, lifting the fragrance of gardenia and damp grass still lightly coated with dew. A determined woodpecker could be heard in the distance, intent on finding some insect larvae for breakfast. Nearer at hand, Angelica sang a lilting calypso melody as she cleaned the kitchen. "That's why I've asked Angelica to drive us into town this morning. Well, that's at least *one* of the reasons," she added suggestively.

"What are you up to, Letha? Whatever it is, count me in. We need to be *doing* something," Gert added, slapping her knee for emphasis.

"And so we shall," Aletha said soothingly, reaching to pat her friend's hand. "And Angelica is going to help us. While she is with us, Marilyn will be tutoring Brian Jenkins so that he's ready to go back to school this fall. Do you know, Abraham has done wonders in helping that young boy learn how to live beyond his handicap? Oh, but you probably don't even know who I'm talking about."

"I suppose you mean the freckle-faced redhead I noticed talking to Abe on Sunday."

"That's him. Anyway since both Angelica and Marilyn are busy this morning, guess who will be helping Rose with her project?"

"Why, Letha, you schemer!"

"Oh, don't thank me. It was Derek's idea. He doesn't know anything about Simon's absence either but he suggested it might be a good idea for Tim to be very present today just in case Simon… wasn't. He also mentioned something about digging holes…"

*****

"And I'm not digging anymore holes until my blisters heal!" Derek checked the back of the truck to make sure he had everything he needed for work at Milly's. Then counting off on his fingers, he said, "There are still at least one…two…three……*ten* more trees that need to be planted, and I'm telling you, digging holes with a shovel for every one of them is *not* the answer. So I suggest you use the power auger we got at that auction last month."

"But we've got to pick up and hang all the Sheetrock today," Tim argued, loading two five-gallon buckets of drywall compound into the truck.

"It was delivered thirty minutes ago. I signed for it myself." Abe had been waiting patiently at his desk to contribute his mite on Derek's behalf. "And I have already recorded it in the materials inventory."

"Look, you two. I appreciate what you're trying to do but don't you think it'll look a little obvious if I show up there when Rose knows I'm supposed to be working at Milly's?"

"It will look strange if you don't," Abe countered. "I was there on Monday…"

"And I was there yesterday." Derek held up his bandaged hand by way of proof. Pointing to Tim, he said, "And now it's *your* turn." Tim rolled his eyes in defeat. "Besides you finished all the framing yesterday. I can handle this, and Abe's coming over later to help me with the mudding. Bro, you know you hate mudding."

"Okay, okay, okay! You win. But the walls had better look good when I get there this afternoon." Derek and Abe exchanged glances. No need to mention that Tim might be gardening all day. Tim turned to walk back into the shop and saw Derek's battered white pickup parked there. He spun around as realization dawned.

"Hey, that's *my* truck!" he yelled after Derek who had made good his escape.

"No worries, I've got the keys for Derek's old wreck," said the always accommodating Abe. "And we loaded the auger earlier this morning so you're all set."

Glaring at Abe, who grinned in delight at the success of his and Derek's plan, Tim snatched up the keys and climbed into Derek's truck. It didn't help his temper any that he had to adjust the seat to accommodate his much-longer legs. He screeched off, a black scowl on his face. Tim did not appreciate being managed.

His humor was not much improved by the time he reached the big house. Mentally consigning all meddlers to the deepest pits of purgatory, Tim drove toward the house, catching sight of Rose already at work. She was wheeling a barrow of lantanas up to the porch when she saw Derek's truck approaching and lifted her hand to wave in welcome then turned her attention to laying the plants on top of the soil preparatory to planting, alternating the bloom colors for maximum effect. She heard the door slam and muffled footsteps on the thick sod. Still engrossed in her task, she spoke over her shoulder in a fair imitation of Angelica's voice, "Now don't you sass me, young man. You just get to work."

"I make it a point never to sass young ladies with pointed trowels in their hands," Tim replied calmly, smiling in spite of his determined reserve.

Caught off guard, Rose spun around so fast in her squatting position that she lost her balance. Arms flailing wildly in an effort to regain her balance, she ended up on the ground with feet and hands in the air like a capsized turtle. Her infectious laughter broke down the last of Tim's self-imposed restraint.

"I don't recommend tightrope walking as a career," he said, helping her up, "but you might consider shooing pigeons, though I hear it doesn't pay well."

Still laughing, Rose squeezed the hand that continued to hold hers and said with innocent openness, "I didn't know you'd be here today, Tim. I'm so glad to see you." Leaning in as if to share a secret, she said, nodding knowingly, "Work was too hard for Derek yesterday, was it?"

A spontaneous shout of laughter from Tim affirmed her suspicions. "He's still whining about his blisters."

"Right? I *told* him to wear gloves for the rough shoveling but *no...*"

"And that's why we love him." Tim stood quietly for a few moments looking around the garden, appreciating the change inspired by Rose's determination and hard work. That many others had helped didn't really register. His thoughts were all for Rose.

"So what are your orders, boss?" he asked with a smile.

"Well, I need to get the rest of these bedding plants in the ground then, I suppose, we ought to plant the trees...but...well..."

"What is it?"

Rose turned to look up at Tim, indecision on her face. "I'd really like to get the pavers on the walkways. Yesterday we were trying to step over them to avoid messing up the raked sand, which was a nuisance, and we still had to rerake spots we accidentally stepped on. But moving all those pavers is an all-day job and I don't know how much longer the trees will hold up in their transport pots before they're planted…"

"If there's one thing I've learned in the construction business, it's to lay out a work schedule in the most practical order possible. Sometimes you have to adjust because a subcontractor can't get needed prep work done on time, or a delivery is delayed, but everything we need is already here. Let's go inspect the trees. If they look like they'll hold another day, I say it's paver time."

Rose reached out impulsively to take his hand, "Oh, Tim, that would be wonderful! But can you spare a whole day away from your other work?" she asked anxiously.

Conveniently forgetting his heated argument with Derek thirty minutes earlier, Tim covered her hand with his other one. "I've got all the time you need." His sincerity didn't embarrass Rose as Simon's had. She simply felt reassured. Her friend would be here for her.

She turned, tugging on his hand as she walked toward the holding ground under the willow. Both agreed that the trees would keep so Rose went back to finish the lantanas while Tim loaded the first of the pavers into the old wheelbarrow.

The morning flew buy. Sandy paths became brick walkways, cleverly laid out in a herringbone pattern suggested by Tim. "You have a little waste because you eventually have to cut some of the bricks but the pieces can usually be used somewhere else." Rose was delighted with the results. She felt a little self-conscious about Tim doing all the heavy hauling but he insisted. He wouldn't even let her carry a partial five-gallon bucket of sand for filling in between the bricks. At the first sign of indignation, he assured her, "I know you're a strong capable woman but I insist you let me do this." Grinning, he added, "Derek's not the only one with muscles." Rose couldn't argue there. Tim soon shed his outer T-shirt as the sun began its rapid ascent, raising the temperature exponentially. His singlet undershirt left little to the imagination. Bulging triceps were completely unmasked and sweat molded the soft cotton fabric to a flat stomach rippled with well-defined abs. Rose couldn't help but admire the strength of the man who made lifting and hauling appear almost effortless, using his powerful thighs as leverage instead of his back.

Tim, in his turn, had to give Rose her due. She tried to match him step for step as they filled the wheelbarrow and unloaded it at each new stretch of walkway. She learned the pattern quickly and made a valiant effort to lay the pavers across the width of the surface, but Tim could see the reach was a problem for her so he suggested they work from opposite sides toward the middle to alleviate her back strain. He intentionally worked well past the middle, leaving her to finish the other side while he retrieved another load of bricks. When he noticed her flagging, he announced that *he* needed a water-break.

"Phew! That's a great idea," Rose said, trying to catch her breath after the strenuous task. They rested under the cover of the veranda, leaning against the walls of the house. Rose pulled out a bright-red bandana and mopped her streaming brow.

"No, that's not the way you use it on a crew," Tim said, taking the scarf and folding it into a long, thin stretch of fabric and tying it around her forehead.

"I feel like a pirate." Rose smiled at Tim.

"You need an eye patch…," he said, returning her smile.

"And a beard."

Scrutinizing her face for a few moments, he looked away then shook his head. "Nah. I don't think you'd look good in a beard."

Laughing, she nudged his shoulder with her own and said, "I'm glad you think so!"

"Hey, what do you say we make it to that intersection," said Tim, leaning forward to indicate the spot where the path split—one branch leading to the willow tree and walled seating area and the other leading to the large circular bed containing the water fountain. "Then we'll break for lunch. Up for it?"

"Aye, aye, Cap'n."

"Argh, matey," Tim replied, pulling her to her feet. Milly's Diner was a thousand miles away and Rose was chatting happily beside him. He could have moved a mountain that day. By late afternoon, Rose felt like they had.

But a sound night's sleep and a healthy dose of ibuprofen worked wonders. Aletha had invited Tim for breakfast so he and Rose walked slowly to the big house together, enjoying the morning sights and sounds. "I think this is my favorite time of day," Tim remarked, matching his longer strides to Rose's short ones. Six foot two versus five foot four never works out evenly without some compromise. "It makes me think of what the Garden of Eden must have been like before the fall. Adam and Eve enjoying God's presence, spending their time naming the plants and animals, enjoying the beauty of a perfect day."

"Wow. Who knew you could be so poetic?" Rose teased, looking at his profile. Noting his self-conscious expression, she quickly added, "But as it happens, I couldn't have described it better myself." After a few moments of companionable silence, she said, "Have I thanked you for all your help?"

"About a thousand times," Tim said, a smile in his voice. "I'm here because I want to be." No need to say, *I love spending time with you.* Instead he said, "It's been a nice break for me to be working outside. Other than building decks or hanging siding, we don't get back to nature much."

Then how did you manage that gorgeous tan? Rose wondered.

"The only reason I'm not pasty white is an addiction to swimming and water sports."

Again with the mind reading! she thought.

"There's a fair-sized lake about fifteen miles north of town—"

"Sunrise Lake."

"You've been there already?" Tim asked in surprise.

"Mmm, just a few days ago. Lucy Bennett mentioned the lake to me at the barbecue since I obviously *also* enjoy water sports—"

"When not trying to drown your polo opponents..."

"Exactly." Rose smiled at the memory. "Simon and I"—Rose could almost sense Tim's palpable withdrawal—"had a picnic there on Monday."

But Tim replied naturally enough, "Then you must have noticed skiers on the lake." At her nod, he continued, "I try to get out there as often as possible with whomever I can convince to come with me— Derek or Abe or friends from church. It's a great way to cool off and unwind at the end of a bruising work day." He added hesitantly after a short pause, "Maybe you could join us some afternoon..."

"But I don't know how to water ski," Rose had to admit reluctantly.

"I can teach you. Believe me, after watching you work over the past few days, I don't think there's *anything* you can't do."

She was touched by his faith in her. After a season of humiliating failures, Rose was gaining confidence in herself as she watched the garden take shape and as she built new friendships, even a new life, in Tinkers Well. Bolstered by her growing self-assurance, Rose suggested she have a go at running the auger. Tim had already dug the holes for the willow and one of the junipers. It didn't look all that hard. He knew the weight and torque of the powerful machine would be too much for her but didn't want to shut her down without at least letting her try. He placed the machine on the next marked spot and showed her where to grip while she pulled the starter cord. As the engine roared to life, Rose felt a thrill of excitement until she squeezed the lever to engage the auger. The torque created by the large auger head would have thrown her to the side had Tim not been standing right behind her, ready to grab both Rose and the machine as she let go of it in surprise.

"Whoa!" Tim shouted as he pinned Rose to his chest while struggling to keep the auger upright. He had to release her to reach the power switch then turned to apologize, "I'm sorry. I should have warned you about—"

Rose cut him short. "Don't be silly. I'm the one that insisted on trying it. Thank *you* for giving me the chance, even though I'm pretty sure you knew it would be too much for me to handle," she added sheepishly.

"Well, you never know whether something is possible until you try it."

"And then you have to graciously admit defeat when you can't," Rose countered.

Not willing to let her have the final word, Tim added, "Which is why God created us all with different gifts and strengths and abilities. He gave me physical strength but He gave you the gifts of vision and encouragement. I for one think those are the more valuable."

"That's the nicest way I've ever heard anyone tell me to stick with shoveling dirt."

Tim laughed and finished digging the row of planting holes while Rose shoveled the resulting dirt piles into the wheelbarrow. It was the perfect division of labor shared by a perfectly matched team working in harmony.

The older members of the Fern Cottage household also worked perfectly in tandem—concocting creative plans to keep Tim and Rose in close proximity to each other without benefit of unneeded chaperones. Outside in the gazebo, Angelica had kept Tim's breakfast plate full and Rose's attention engaged while Aletha and Granny Gert prepared and stuffed enough food and water into a small cooler to feed a fleet of gardeners. No need for the two youngsters to spend their lunch break with three widow ladies when they could spend that time getting to know each other better.

The wisdom of age had prevailed. Tim and Rose sat on the veranda, enjoying the spoils of their elders' efforts. Over the course of the morning, between ditch-digging and dirt-hauling, they had talked of everything from stories of childhood folly to family vacations to their respective college years. Tim shared with Rose, as he had with few others, the deep sense of pain and loss he had experienced at the death of his father, Peter Ludlow. Rose spoke of her frustration in finding direction in life and her sense of inferiority around her sisters. As they sat enjoying the enhanced tastiness of ham sandwiches eaten outside, overlooking a beautiful garden, there was a sense of comfort and ease that usually only developed over years of friendship. Each forgot any other responsibilities or cares in the sweet communion of being together.

*****

As suggested at their parting earlier in the week, Simon called at Fern Cottage to invite Rose on an expedition of exploration and renewed dalliance that would take up the greater part of Thursday afternoon, only to be greeted instead by the hostile Granny Gert and the information that Rose had returned to her work at the main house right after lunch.

"I expect you're not used to manual labor, mister, but for folks that know how to work with their hands"—she paused to glance contemptuously at his neatly manicured nails—"early morning is the best time to get started. But if you can't get the job done then, you keep working at it till you do get it done. You ought to try it some time," she added with a grim smile.

Simon ran Rose to earth outside the main house where she was steadily shoveling dirt, her back toward the drive. Parking his shiny Escalade just past the greatly diminished piles of sand and gravel, he struggled to circumvent their dusty residue without damaging his designer shoes and was reduced to shouting and waving his arms to get her attention over the sound of the auger digging the final hole for the other maple. His efforts were rewarded by a look of self-conscious surprise and an upheld pointed finger, signaling him to wait for her to finish her task. Rose pushed the loaded wheelbarrow toward him, a shy smile of welcome on her face, but his evident annoyance made her feel inexplicably guilty again. Wiping the dust off his shoes with what *had* been a spotless handkerchief, his look of barely concealed disgust for her cutoff jeans and stained T-shirt didn't help. Simon had little tolerance for a slovenly appearance in a man. In a woman, he found it insufferable. So despite Rose's engaging smile, he found it difficult to see past the filthy arms and legs where dust had mingled with sweat, or to smile upon a face devoid of makeup and topped with a grimy bandana tied over matted curls.

In response to her tentative hello, he remarked testily, "You've spent so much time as Mrs. Mason's jobbing gardener lately," Simon said, looking with revulsion at Rose's worn work gloves and heavy boots, "that we hardly have time for more civilized pursuits. Surely you haven't forgotten about our planned outing this afternoon..." Rose hadn't thought about it since Tuesday morning.

"Oh my gosh! Is this *Thursday* already?" she exclaimed in dismay. "Oh, Simon, I'm *so* sorry. It's just that I've been so focused on the garden and we've made such incredible progress." Turning to gaze over the promising green space sprung with great effort from the dusty Kansas soil, she said, not looking at him, "Isn't it lovely?"

"Lovely." Grudgingly, he added, "You've obviously been working very hard. In fact, if I didn't know better, love, I'd suspect you of enjoying grubbing in the dirt to fancying my company," he said with a brittle smile. His obvious contempt of Rose's predilection for menial work failed to make an impression on her but she hastened to assure him of her decided preference for Simon's companionship.

"I...I know I caused you to...I mean...you felt badly because..." Rose halted, unable to articulate her bewilderment at their last parting.

"I felt such desire for you that I needed time to master my emotions." Simon was crooning softly now, drawing Rose's attention away from Tim who was trying to work as unobtrusively as possible in the opposite corner of the garden. "I needed that time away but I, at the same time, longed for you." Rose felt the power of his voice wash over her. "That's why I was so disappointed to find you here rather than sitting on the porch swing, waiting for me in your most fetching frock. But I can see that this is important to you so it must be important to me too."

"Simon, you have no idea what that means to me." As she spoke, she instinctively reached out a hand to touch his arm but he recoiled in disgust.

"No. I will not allow myself to be tempted," Simon ad-libbed quickly. "You must finish your work here and then we can be together. Surely by tomorrow..."

Rose hesitated. She knew they still had to mulch the whole garden which could take a full day. "Simon, you know I...want to spend time with you." She had almost said *longed* but the word felt awkward in her mind. "I'm afraid I'll be working most of tomorrow as well," she admitted, feeling guilty. At his expression of resentment, inspiration dawned. "But we could spend this evening together, if you like. We can drop off Granny Gert and Aletha at the community center, have dinner, then pick them up after bingo is over." Rose looked hopefully at her tortured beau who was working feverishly to produce an excuse to forego such a generous offer. He had to get into the cottage that evening—alone.

"No. I won't hear of it. I know you are sacrificing your duty to your grandmother and hostess simply to ease my pain of disappointment. I can't let you do that."

Rose began to experience the same disordered emotions and confusion she had mulled over on Monday. Simon resented time spent on Aletha's behalf in the garden but insisted she honor her responsibility to escort Aletha and Granny Gert to bingo. It didn't make sense but perhaps men in love aren't supposed to make sense, she told herself. The thought reassured her, though Simon had never actually spoken the word 'love' openly. Before she knew it, she had agreed to an intimate movie night at the cottage on Friday (without first clearing the invitation with Aletha) and lunch out on Saturday. Rather than planting a chaste salute on her dirty cheek, Simon merely blew Rose a kiss, made his careful way back around the remaining sand and gravel, and sped off in the Escalade, sending loose gravel flying and a thick cloud of dust hanging in the air. Rose, giggling at the comical figure Simon made in his efforts to avoid any contact with dirt, started coughing as the dust reached her. By the time she had stopped choking from the heavy air and was able to breathe freely again, her eyes were red and wet from irritation and her throat sore from coughing. Feeling a genuine twinge of annoyance at the man she had put on a pedestal, she stood looking after him for several moments, hands on hips, thinking, *Now why did he do that? Surely that was unnecessary.* Then light dawned as she noticed Tim approaching. *He's jealous. Simon is jealous of my friend. He must be in love!*

Rose greeted Tim with a cheery smile, her doubts about Simon put to rest. The two dirt-stained partners worked together to finish the last of the planting. Later, cleaned up and each with their best foot forward, they fought side by side as adversaries in another heated engagement on the field of bingo. Tim emerged the victor in the skirmish but went home without the prize he desired above all else. Rose would have been astonished had she known that it was Tim Ludlow, not Simon Applegate, who was deeply, helplessly in love.

CHAPTER 16

*The one who narrows his eyes is planning deceptions;
the one who compresses his lips brings about evil.*

—Proverbs 16:30 (HCSB)

Simon had made efficient use of the days spent away from Rose. If toiling in the soil tested her strength and resolve, the preparations he made for a fallback plan tested his ingenuity and resourcefulness. He made multiple trips to the Midwest Union Bank on Tuesday, Wednesday, and Thursday, but none of the staff, including the estimable Mr. Thurston, recognized any of them as repeat visits. Simon pulled out all the stops to operate incognito, particularly on his initial reconnaissance.

He waited in a third rental vehicle, a nondescript black compact sedan, stationed in front of Settlers Park, providing himself an excellent vantage point of the bank located in a place of prominence at the intersection of Main and State Streets. He waited patiently. Haste could be one's downfall in this game. When he finally judged enough of the inhabitants of Tinkers Well to have gathered in the town's premier financial institution, Simon made his way across the street and climbed the broad front steps to the heavy double oak doors, the grand title "Midwest Union Bank and Trust" etched in gold lettering across the inset frosted glass.

It was an imposing building. The original wooden structure, erected in 1870, had been replaced fifty years later by the current marble edifice. Having been built and furnished on a pontifical scale, the bank eclipsed even the county courthouse for architectural honors. Corinthian pillars supported the beautifully sculpted frieze climbing up and down the gabled roofline of the main facade, the images depicting the rural agricultural cycle. Ten-foot oak doors with enormous brightly polished brass handles, despite nearly a hundred years of touch by thousands of hands, gave entry to the cavernous lobby, topped by an arched dome ceiling. Directly opposite the main doors, an imposing oak staircase with ornately carved newel posts led to a second-floor gallery, allowing entry to the offices of bank managers and accountants. The entire gallery was lined with double-polished brass railings, their only detractor being the presence of clear plexiglass walls behind the rails to accommodate more modern safety standards. To complete the illusion of a time warp, tellers still worked behind a solid-paneled half-wall, topped with individual teller stalls, complete with sliding windows. Intentionally appearing a bit lost, Simon surreptitiously noted details such as the location of the new accounts desk, the security guard, and the entrance to the vault via a short flight of stairs located under the grand staircase. While still absorbing all the grandeur, Simon was greeted by the great Mr. Thurston himself who routinely walked through the lobby to see that all was running smoothly and to simply serve as a presence. It was his presence that completed the perception of time travel. In a pinstriped suit, complete with vest and gold watch chain, the jovial Mr. Thurston was almost a caricature of his profession. His thick gray hair was actually parted in the middle and plastered in place with hair oil, and his smile of welcome was eclipsed by a precisely trimmed handlebar mustache. Simon half-expected to look down and see the man sporting spats over his shoes.

Not the least bit put out by Simon's open appraisal of both the bank and its president, Mr. Thurston genially offered his services to the newcomer.

"I'll wager you didn't expect to find such a magnificent specimen of the banking world in our little town, Mr...er..."

"P-P-Paulson," Simon stuttered in soft tones that perpetually sounded apologetic. "Floyd P-Paulson. I'm just traveling through the area on my summer vacation and n-needed to cash a check. I had no idea I would find anything this grand on my journey."

Mr. Thurston smiled mechanically, thinking to himself, *Kind of a paltry fellow. I'll have him see Trix. She ought to cheer him up.*

"Well, Mr. Paulson, I believe we can take care of that for you." And duly leading Simon to a window almost filled by a buxom forty-year-old, christened Beatrix Charmaine but answering to the simpler Trix, he left the stranger in the hands of the bank's most gregarious employee.

"What can I do for you, sweetheart?" Trix asked around the gum in her mouth. She pushed a pencil over her ear, sending a strand of her short improbably bleached-blond hair sticking out at an odd angle in the process. If Mr. Thurston thought Floyd Paulson paltry, Trix found him downright pathetic. From his thin hair, combed unsuccessfully to hide a large bald spot, horn-rimmed glasses repaired with tape, and stooped shoulders to his long-sleeved plaid shirt, buttoned to the neck, he was a miserable creature. Trix's motherly instincts were aroused.

"Well, I'd like to cash this check please," the awkward young man said timidly. "I know I hold no account here b-but I hoped I m-might cash it and p-p-pay a small fee. Can that be arranged?" Simon asked with such a pitiable expression that Trix would have paid the fee herself to alleviate his worry.

"I'm sure that can be arranged. Do you have a photo ID?"

"I d-do," "Paulson" said proudly as he carefully produced the card with the correct name and image. The trouble with mastering so many aliases is the danger of producing evidence of the wrong one. But Simon thrived on danger.

The check was drawn on a bank used by all Landrum agents. There were multiple accounts to accommodate whatever cover an operative might need. Though most financial transactions in the twenty-first century were handled through unregistered, untraceable credit cards, the respectability of a bank account sometimes helped to establish a creditable cover.

As Trix processed the check, she asked, "And what brings you way out here from…Terra Haute, Indiana, Mr. Paulson?"

"Well, I'm a librarian and I read about lots of d-d-different places, so when I have a holiday, I try to get out and see something n-new. I read about Tinkers Well on a travel blog last week. It was by a fellow named Simon Ap-p-legate. Have you ever heard of him?"

"Heard of him? Why, honey, he's just about the hottest thing to hit Tinkers Well since indoor plumbing! You know, I think he might still be in town. I actually met him last week at Gayle's boutique when I popped over there during a break to pick up some new span…Well, never mind about that. Anyway you'll know him if you see him. Tall, gorgeous smile, dreamy eyes, and an accent that sends most women's temperatures up about five degrees but I don't suppose you'd care about that."

"*No*, b-but I'd like to thank him for the b-b-beautiful p-p-pictures and wonderfully descriptive account of the town. It almost m-m-makes me want to move here. That's p-partly why I came to the b-bank today. I wanted to see for myself if it would b-be adequate for my needs. I d-don't suppose you have safe deposit b-boxes, do you?"

"Well, of course we do. I'd show them to you but I'm afraid Dragon Lady would catch us."

"D-D-Dragon Lady?"

Trix leaned toward the window, the buttons of her blouse straining under the pressure. "*Mrs*. Simmons. More like *per*simmons. She's in charge of all new accounts and deposit boxes. *Very* persnickety."

"Oh, dear," Mr. Paulson said with consternation. "I d-d-don't think I could d-deal with someone like that." With one finger, he pushed his glasses back into place as they were about to slide off the end of his nose. Looking despairingly at Trix, he added, "You see, I'm a little shy and forceful p-p-people frighten me. Now if someone like you c-could help me…"

Realizing the Dragon Lady would eat him for breakfast, Trix offered, "Well, I don't suppose you'll ever actually move here, but if you did, you could talk to her assistant, Lindsey Morton. She covers for the old bat during her lunch hour, but you'd have to come in around one o'clock to be safe. Lindsey's all right. She's just out of college and thinks she knows everything until somebody questions her, then she sort of dissolves into a mess, but she somehow gets the job done all the same."

You might survive her, you poor lamb, Trix thought. Then in her most encouraging manner, she completed the transaction. "Now here's your money and don't you worry about a fee. I think we can handle that," she said with a broad wink that seemed to incorporate her whole face. Even her gum-laden tongue stuck out.

"Oh, thank you, k-kind lady. You've b-b-been most helpful."

A librarian. Figures, Trix thought. *He's probably better off staying in Terra Haute.*

Promptly at one o'clock on Wednesday afternoon, a burly heavyset man with a round face, almost hidden by bushy sideburns and a six-inch beard of bright-red hair mixed with gray, stood in the center of the Midwest Union Bank, staring fixedly at a slip of a girl in a neat suit with a bun wound tightly at the nape of her neck. The fresh-faced young lady in question was seated at the desk designated "New Accounts." She glanced up from perusal of yet another bank protocol book to see an alarming creature glaring at her. Unlike Mr. Thurston, Lindsey Morton tended to become flustered under close scrutiny. She tried to ignore the man but couldn't help glancing in his direction again. For a split second, she thought two fuzzy caterpillars had somehow affixed themselves to his face then realized that they were actually eyebrows. His long-sleeved flannel shirt and corduroy pants looked particularly out of place in his surroundings, and as he walked purposely toward her, she imagined his feet, clad in heavy boots, shook the marble floor beneath her. She looked around for escape but nothing presented itself.

Lindsey swallowed and summoned what little courage she possessed, forced her quivering lips into a smile, and asked in a voice that sounded like a high-pitched five-year-old's, "May I help—" Clearing her dry throat, she tried again, this time with more success. "May I help you, sir?"

"Oh, for sure," the man answered in a gruff but civil voice. "The name's Halverson. Erik Halverson. I hope you'll forgive me if I don't shake your hand. Mine were injured in a fire a while back so I don't use them unless I must." He raised both hands covered in thick leather gloves.

Taken aback by such a confession, Lindsey wondered if the long sleeves and full beard also signaled an effort to cover charred skin. The thought made her feel a little queasy and she experienced an odd mix of horror and pity. Lindsey indicated a chair opposite the desk and invited him to be seated. She tried to muster an attitude of calm professional aloofness but registered only fearful curiosity.

"How can I help you, Mr. Halverson?"

"I'm not one to mince words. The long and the short of it is, I will be moving myself and my family down here from Minnesota in a few weeks." Lindsey was distracted by his pattern of speech and long O, reminiscent of the lip-rounded vowel she had studied in high school German. "I've got a cousin lives hereabouts who's invited us to take up living on his farm since I can't work mine anymore." He raised his gloved hands again as if to verify his words. Lindsey cringed inwardly.

"Will you be needing a checking account, sir?" The words were barely audible.

"Oh, yah, you betcha. And a savings account too, I suppose, though they don't pay anything these days. All the same, I'm not much for trusting my hard-earned money to some faceless bank on the Internet."

"Well, we can certainly take care of that for you."

Lindsey reached in the desk for a new account package and was startled into nearly dropping it when Mr. Halverson said suddenly, "Uuf-da! You surely don't expect me to give you my money without a look at your vault. What do you take Erik Halverson for? I'm no fool, dontcha know. Also I will need a safe deposit box. You keep them also in the vault, yah?"

"W-w-well, yes, but it's quite unusual to show new account holders the vault until they are…new account holders." Lindsey finished limply.

"It is no problem, young lady. Erik Halverson will find another bank. Good day to you."

"*When potential clients walk through our doors, they should not walk out until they are customers.*" Lindsey could still hear Mrs. Simmons' parting admonition ringing in her head.

As Mr. Halverson stood, Lindsey stood also and hurried into speech. "I'm afraid I may not have been clear. Most people don't ask to see the vault or deposit boxes which is why it's unusual to show them. But I would be happy to do that for you. Won't you follow me?"

"You betcha."

Mr. Halverson, a.k.a. Simon Jones/Atherton/Applegate, studied the safe deposit boxes carefully. Despite the size of the bank, the boxes were all contained in one room and lined the walls on three sides from the floor up to about six feet. In number, there were over three hundred.

"I'll need to know which boxes are available." Seeing the look of surprise on Lindsey's face, he explained, "I'm a bit superstitious, dontcha know. And I won't be having my valuables stored in an unlucky box."

"I can show you a list of boxes at my desk but I don't have that information with me, I'm afraid."

Hesitating, Mr. Halverson asked, "Can you at least tell me if you have any on this side?" He indicated the wall to the left of the doorway. "This is the lucky side, for sure."

"I'm certain we can accommodate you, Mr. Halverson."

Simon left with the key for box 67. It was midway along the wall—a strategic position. Reaching his hotel room in record time, he fairly tore off the facial hair, clothes, and excessive wadding necessary to create the bulk for Erik Halverson. It was miserably uncomfortable, especially during a Kansas summer, but effective.

He donned the trappings of his favorite impersonation for a late-afternoon encounter with the dragon lady.

"Mrs. Agnes Pennyfeather. You may call me Mrs. Pennyfeather." An elderly woman, bent nearly double from spinal stenosis, sat opposite the efficient Mrs. Simmons. Age had taken the old woman's strength, and her speech was weak and hoarse and occasionally slurred, but she obviously possessed a fiery spirit.

"As you wish, Mrs. Pennyfeather," the dragon lady replied politely.

"Well, it isn't at all what I wish, young lady!" No one had addressed Mrs. Simmons as young lady in a *very* long time. She found it disquieting as if she had somehow been robbed of her status.

"I *wish* to stay in Evansville," Mrs. Pennyfeather said vehemently and thumped her cane on the floor, loosening one of the many black lace shawls wrapped around her shoulders. "I *wish* I hadn't outlived all my friends." She thumped the cane again, this time dislodging a small handbag laying on her lap. "I *wish* I had someone—*anyone*—to look after me other than my nephew." The cane thumped a third time. Mrs. Pennyfeather quickly reached up to her mouth, removed her loosened upper plate, and restored it *almost* to its proper place. The slight misalignment caused a sibilant, hissing sound that rattled even the unflappable Mrs. Simmons.

"I am only relocating to thiss hamlet at the express wissh of my nephew, a thoughtless, sselfish sscoundrel living in Kansass City who would have my money tomorrow if I didn't know a ssthing or two." The old woman struggled to raise her head and stare fixedly at Mrs. Simmons. "You don't live to be ninety-four without knowing a ssthing or two." Mrs. Pennyfeather tapped on her head a few times then had to resettle her elaborately coiffed wig. She only succeeded in tilting it to the other side. "Losst my hair yearss ago. Thiss thing is a darned nuisssancce."

Eager to rid herself of the most repellent client she had serviced in many years, Mrs. Simmons suggested the ill-humored nonagenarian tell her exactly what services she required.

"Haven't you been lisstening, you ssilly woman. I want a box. A ssafe depossit box. That'ss where I'll keep my money. I want it now. Brought my money with me," she said, nudging the carpet bag on the floor with her cane. Mrs. Simmons waited in unhappy expectation of something else falling off the old woman. The pince-nez on her nose became the next casualties but were fortunately tethered to a chain around her neck. "Now when can I ssee it? I want one oppossite the door sso no one can ssee what I have in it."

"If you'll just sign here, I'll be happy to take you to the vault where you can deposit whatever you wish in your box."

"I'm not ssigning anything until I can ssee my box and get my money ssafely sstowed away."

A forced smile, barely discernable, covered the grinding of her teeth as Mrs. Simmons stood to escort Mrs. Pennyfeather to the vault. She even offered to carry the older woman's carpet bag but felt the thump of the cane on her hand as she tried to lift it.

"Nicce try but nobody carriess thiss bag but me."

The sorely tried Mrs. Simmons finally satisfied her client by locating an empty box right at eye level—Mrs. Pennyfeather's eye level. But Mrs. Simmons insisted that she must be present to turn the bank's box key in addition to the key now in Mrs. Pennyfeather's possession.

"It's nothing more than a security measure, I assure you. Now I will turn my back while you complete your business. There is a table in the middle of the room where you can move your box for easier access."

As Mrs. Pennyfeather filled her box with wads of blank paper, her creator reviewed the situation. If he could find Aletha's safe deposit box key, Simon could produce enough of a diversion to move the bank's key to her box. All he needed was a box on the third wall so he could easily cover the entire room. Who next might require the services of Midwest Union Bank?

Breakfast on Thursday morning brought inspiration from the informative Sunny of The Early Bird Bakery. Her lopsided bun had disappeared in favor of a limp ponytail hanging over her right ear. Only slightly sunnier at nine o'clock in the morning than at four thirty in the afternoon, she was nonetheless happy, relatively speaking, to again wait on the handsome stranger of the previous week.

"Oh sure, I have an account at Midwest Union. Not that I make enough here to bother about putting anything in it. I just have to take it out again to pay my bills. I wouldn't have bothered except that my little sister is good friends with that new girl, Lindsey Morton. She and Melody, that's my sister, went to high school together. And even though Lindsey went off to college, she's still a good old girl at heart. She tries to act all professional at her little desk in the bank but

I've caught her listening to country Western music when nobody's around—usually during the dragon lady's lunch hour."

"The dragon lady?

"That's her boss, Mrs. Simmons. Lindsey tries to pretend that she's not afraid of the old warhorse but she is. So lunchtime is Lindsey time. She really likes Lyle Branson which I say shows good taste. Lindsey's still a pretty good kid despite all her education. Now can I get you another coffee, maybe a sausage biscuit?"

"No, thank you, Sunny. I think I have all that I require." He left her a big-enough tip that she considered a midweek trip to the bank. Simon beat her to it.

He sat in the black sedan in an unused parking lot north of Settlers Park off of State Street. The locale held little interest other than its bird's-eye view of the backdoor of Midwest Union Bank. At 12:45 p.m. precisely, the door opened as Mrs. Simmons departed punctually for her allotted lunch hour. Waiting until she had disappeared around the corner of Main Street in a white compact sedan, even more ordinary than that which Simon occupied, he emerged from the vehicle and donned a large white cowboy hat, à la every swaggering western film star that ever drew breath, as he slowly sauntered to the front of the building. Tight-fitting blue jeans with a boot cut to accommodate his fashionably well-worn boots emphasized his narrow hips. Two-inch heels and lift inserts furthered the tall lanky look and a casual western-cut shirt in pale pink, worn untucked and partially unbuttoned at the neck and sleeves, gave the impression that he had just stepped off a concert stage. As he entered the bank, he removed his hat, partly because he despised the thing and partly to display a thick thatch of blond hair worn longish and wavy. Making his way to the new accounts desk, he was pleased to find it temporarily unoccupied, allowing him time to set the stage for the next act. He undid another shirt button and partially rolled up his sleeves as he took a seat, slouching slightly with one leg out before him and the other crossed over it. Beating rhythmically on his boot, he started singing under his breath but loud enough to be heard by the primly dressed girl walking toward him.

*Now I'm headin' down the road in my pick-up
truck,
Got my rifle and my rod and my lady luck.
We'll wander through the woods, then we'll float on
the lake,
And if we don't get nothin'—there's always lovin' to
make.*

"Excuse me. Uh, sir…"

As if returning reluctantly to the mundane of everyday life, the young man opened his eyes, stopped singing abruptly, and jumped to his feet, hat in hand. "I'm real sorry, ma'am. I guess I was lost in my own little world. I hope I didn't bother you with my singin'…" he said in a Southern drawl.

"Oh, *gosh* no! Was that…were you singing…a Lyle Branson song…"

The man grinned and pleased her immensely with a reprise. "'*And if we don't get nothin'—there's always lovin' to make*' I can see you know your country music, ma'am."

Lindsey Morton blushed and replied candidly, "It's my favorite."

"Well, I can see we're gonna get along just fine."

Still blushing, she made an effort to assume her formal assistant-manager-of-new-accounts facade but found it almost impossible to concentrate with a blatantly admiring grin and deep sapphire eyes fixed squarely on her. Trying not to grin in return, Lindsey covered her mouth, cleared her throat, and attempted a nonchalant attitude. "What can I help you with today, sir?"

"You already have. I kinda dreaded comin' to the bank because I was sure I'd be facin' a fire-breathin' uptight old lady, and then *you* showed up. Are all the girls in Kansas as nice as you?" he asked with unassuming sincerity.

Lindsey looked down at the papers on her desk to avoid eye contact but couldn't avoid a giggle escaping her tightly compressed lips. Emboldened by the stranger's open friendliness, she countered with, "Are all the men in…"

"Nashville…"

"*Nashville* as bold as you?"

It was the man's turn to laugh. "I knew I was makin' a good decision to move out here to your neck o' the woods. But where are my manners? My name is Pinkerton. Allan Pinkerton but I hope you'll call me Allan." The founder of the famous Pinkerton National Detective Agency might have been amused at the use of his name in such a context. "I'm determined to make it in country music but the competition back home is so fierce, I thought I might try and get some gigs in Kansas City and see where it takes me."

"You're a *country music star*?" Lindsey asked in amazed delight.

"Whoa, now hold on there. I'm not a star *yet* but I hope to be someday."

"Oh, I'm sure you will be. You *look* like a star already," Lindsey commented shyly. Allan Pinkerton was indeed the image of a successful country singer. The combination of blond hair, a charming smile, framed by a neat mustache and goatee, and drop-dead gorgeous blue eyes were enough to ensure that female fans would follow him whether he sang well or not. But Lindsey was certain his long slender fingers were made to play a guitar and the little she had heard of his voice convinced her of certain success.

"If you believe in me, then how can I not believe in myself?"

If Simon Applegate had swept Rose Thompson off her feet, then Allan Pinkerton had completely bowled over the usually pragmatic Lindsey Morton. Almost melting into the floor, she somehow gathered enough information to open a checking account and assign a safe deposit box for her handsome client. Never had Lindsey been so thankful that the critical Mrs. Simmons was nowhere in sight.

"I'm so glad you'll be moving to Tinkers Well, though I can't help wondering why you wouldn't prefer living in Kansas City…if that's where you'll be…you know…working."

"That's because you don't know what happens to these small towns when a nearby city takes off." At her questioning look, he explained, "There's a quaint little town called Franklin, about twenty-five miles south of Nashville, about like Tinkers Well from Kansas City. Anyway until about thirty or forty years ago, it was just a quiet county seat until wealthy people in the Nashville music industry started movin' there to get away from the city and enjoy small-town livin'. Now ordinary folks can hardly afford to live there anymore. So I figured I'd kinda get in on the ground floor in Tinkers Well, you know, sorta like an investment."

"I can't image our little town could ever become trendy, but if it does, I'll be able to say, 'I remember when the famous Allan Pinkerton lived here.'"

"And just for that, I'm gonna send you front-row concert tickets for my first show, little lady. Do you have one o' them business cards?" Lindsey moved as if in a dream. When she handed Allan the card, he held onto her hand and leaned over to plant a chaste salute on her cheek. The softness of his lips and goatee sent tingling shock waves where they touched her skin. She was still standing on the spot where he left her when Mrs. Simmons returned ten minutes later. Even her sharp words of censure were unable to penetrate the cloud of expectant rapture that enveloped Lindsey. Assuming the girl to be ailing, the dragon lady sent her home early. Allan, in parting, had at least granted Lindsey a few hours of blissful freedom

*****

"I won't hear of it, Trudy," Aletha said with finality. "These foolish headaches simply spring up from time to time and there's nothing for them but peace and quiet and rest, and I'll manage that better in an empty house. Besides I'll have Prince with me." At the mention of his name, Prince sat up next to the bed, assuming the mien of a noble watchdog.

"I don't like leaving you, and I don't mind saying it, but I suppose you know best. And just in case Tim shows up, that's where Rose needs to be. We'll be sure and not make a sound when we get home, just in case you're able to sleep." Gert patted her friend on the shoulder, made sure she had a glass of water and a cold compress, and went in search of Rose.

The little Chevy had made its second gear change on the bypass road into Tinkers Well before Simon negotiated the opening in the Mason property fence and walked toward the house, checking again to ensure that the utility knife he always carried was still in his pocket. The black leather jacket he habitually wore for furtive activities was more than a bit warm for a Kansas evening but projected his arms against brambles in the heavy brush and provided ample storage for any finds of significance.

Simon was quite pleased with his efforts over the past three days. He was well-positioned for access to Aletha Mason's safe deposit box, he had plenty of time to go through the library before the bingo-crazed inmates of Fern Cottage returned, and he had a few fallback plans in place if his efforts now should prove fruitless. All was quiet as he approached the kitchen door. He knew the house to be empty but innate caution warned him to move with stealth. He pulled on the screen door, and holding it open with his body, he slowly opened the kitchen door and stepped inside.

Simon heard before he saw the German shepherd. A deep throaty growl stopped the man in his tracks. His eyes rolled slowly in their sockets, scanning the room in terror. Then he locked eyes with the big black dog moving toward him. Prince cocked his head as he summed up the interesting newcomer and opened his mouth in a panting smile of welcome, emitting a low rumble from deep in his throat. The newcomer heard only a menacing growl that grew more pronounced as the animal bared his teeth. Simon was immobilized with fear, just as he had been twenty-five years ago when his father had taken him to an illegal dogfight in a vacant garage. His terrorized mind, playing tricks on him, was forcing him back to a time he had spent his whole life trying to forget. But each horrifying detail was dredged up and made immediate as if he was again a small boy of eight embarking on an evening of sport with his dad. He remembered and remembered and remembered…

The smell of blood and sweat mingled with lingering oil fumes gave Simon an instant aversion to the spectacle in the pit. He tugged on his father's arm, whining to be taken home, but his father merely shrugged off the insistent arm and told his son to be quiet if he knew what was good for him. Bored and determined to have a bit of fun, the boy Simon eventually wandered away from his dad who was focused more intently on placing a likely bet than on his son's welfare. Coming upon a locked door at the back of the garage, Simon was convinced that adventure awaited him beyond if he could just find a way through. He was not only curious but resourceful as well. Spying an opening in the wall near the ceiling, he proceeded to pile old boxes and crates one on another until he could climb up to the hole. He couldn't see much from his vantage point, except another maintenance bay containing an old car chassis which, at least, promised an imaginative way to entertain himself while he waited for his father's luck to turn. Unfortunately it was Simon's luck that was out.

Visibility was limited in this newly discovered land of exploration. The old shop lights dangled from the ceiling in broken pieces with only a little light forcing its way through the crack in the garage door. The windows had been painted over, probably to hide some nefarious activity. Simon had no thought for anything but the adventure of examining his singular find. He went through the hole in the wall feet first so he could hang onto the opening and drop to the floor. The petrol fumes were even stronger there than in the room he had just left. There was also a sickly sweet smell he couldn't identify. In the dim light, Simon saw what looked like chemical equipment on a battered workbench, held upright on one end by a cinder block. Chemistry held little attraction for the boy. He was only interested in the notable features of "his" car.

As he rounded the far side of the old chassis, making a thorough inspection as he went, Simon came face-to-face with an English bull terrier. The boy had never before had occasion to fear dogs. The strays in his neighborhood had, more often than not, become objects of cruelty at the hands of thoughtless boys, posing no real threat. But this was a dog raised to be aggressive, mistreated and malnourished until he would fight anyone or anything. Simon sensed danger but was relieved to see that the animal was tied to a support beam with a tattered cord. As he backed away from the bull terrier, now snarling and pulling at the restraining rope, Simon saw scars all over the dog's body. There were even open wounds still festering from recent encounters in the fighting pit. Frightened as much by the animal's appearance as by its vicious conduct, the boy looked for an alternate exit, feeling a need for haste. He nearly cried with relief when he saw that the locked door was merely barred by a wooden beam on his side. Simon ran to the door and lifted the beam to make good his escape just as the worn cord broke and the dog, growling with malice and fury, charged the quaking boy, knocking him to the ground. The bull terrier ripped at the boy's clothes as Simon screamed in terror, covering his face with his left arm to protect it from the razor-sharp teeth. The dog, eyeing a raised target, tore into Simon's forearm, mauling it badly, and might eventually have killed the boy but for a lull between rounds in the adjacent room when the roar of competition fell to loud verbal abuse between disgruntled owners and dissatisfied gamblers. Simon's screams finally penetrated the din, bringing the whole lot to the rescue. Two men threw a large canvas tarp over the dog and secured him in a cage. Simon's father turned white at the sight of his son covered in blood with his bone fully exposed. Onlookers made plentiful, if unhelpful, comments.

"Coo, the li'l nipper's snuffed it fer shor."

"Nah. Don't you 'ear 'im screamin' the 'awse down?"

"Ned, you need to get 'im to 'ospit'l quick step."

"Don't do it, Ned. We'll 'ave the coppers down on us proper."

"Yeah, take 'im 'ome to yer missus an let 'er 'ave a go."

In the end, it was his mother, showing latent maternal instincts, that insisted Simon be treated by a doctor. His father agreed with the proviso that the attack be attributed to a stray mongrel, the attacking dog's owner having threatened to cut Mr. Jones out of the fight club if police were involved or if the dog exhibited any signs of diminished fighting skill from the encounter.

Simon, confronting Prince in the present, recalled the attack as if it were yesterday. His scarred arm began to throb. He broke out in a cold sweat. As he backed toward the kitchen door opening, Prince advanced toward him. Unfortunately Simon failed to notice the dog's wagging tail. Locked in a nightmare as real as the floor under his feet, he saw only a vicious beast intent on his destruction. *If I can just get past the opening,* Simon thought desperately, *I can pull the door to and get the hell out of here.* But Simon's luck was out again. He made it to the doorway, but with limbs numb from fear, he tripped over the doorjamb and stumbled backward till he rested against the railing leading to the gazebo, his hands—palms out—at shoulder heighth. Recognizing a familiar game shared with Tim, though one he understood never to instigate with his frail mistress, Prince lunged, jumping up so that his front paws rested on Simon's shoulders, pinning him against the walkway railing. The dog never barked. He just continued the low rumble, breathing heavily into Simon's face, inches away. Through a heavy fog of fear-induced paralysis, Simon knew he must break free. He willed his frozen limbs to move, pushing the dog away, and turning to run. He was successful in dislodging the heavy body from his own, but as he turned to the right, Prince grabbed the underside of Simon's left forearm exactly opposite the spot little Simon had been mauled all those years earlier.

The pain was blinding, but it was the panic welling up inside him that drove Simon to a desperate move. He had to make the dog release the iron grip on his arm before the searing pain and blood loss caused him to lose consciousness. Prince, once more on all fours, was not only pulling Simon back but also down. Bent practically double, Simon threw his right leg over the dog's back simply to keep his balance, but in so doing, he was able to squeeze the animal's flanks. In an unthinking moment of sheer base instinct, Simon pulled the utility knife from his pocket, tilted the dog's head back, and struck. Prince fell instantly to the deck, his slackened jaw surrendering Simon's arm in a final act.

Simon gripped his aching arm and crumpled where he stood, joining his assailant in a pool of blood. The horror of what he had just done, coupled with the gruesome aftermath, nearly sent his overwhelmed senses into blackness but he struggled to stay alert. He must think. No sign of the recent struggle could be left behind. No one could suspect that Prince was dead. All the alarms would sound in the Mason household and he could on no account allow that to happen until he had secured either the document or the key to Aletha's box at the bank. After resting for a few minutes to allow his head to clear, Simon removed his blood-drenched jacket, not without severe pain, and made an astonishing discovery that rocked the very foundation of the cool-headed seasoned investigator. Every vestige of cocky brashness and calculated cunning were stripped away by the sight that met his incredulous gaze. It wasn't blood or torn flesh that unsettled him to his very core—it was the total absence of either. He sat staring at his exposed arm in disbelief. There wasn't a scratch on it. The only abnormality evident was a large expanse of disfigured skin covered by a labyrinth of puckered scars. Simon sat there for a full five minutes, taking in the enormity of the impossible revelation. The childhood horror that had haunted his dreams for twenty-five years had finally taken control of his reason, driving him to an act of savagery equal to that which he had suffered. It was uncontrollable shivering that ultimately shook Simon out of his trauma-induced stupor into an attempt at rational thought.

The lingering effects of shock left him weak but he mustered the strength to stand, then once again experienced lightheadedness. He leaned against a deck post until the dizziness cleared and forced himself to think past the abhorrent scene. Simon knew the dog's body must be disposed of but feared he lacked the strength to lift it. Looking around the backyard, he noticed that beyond the bordering trees, the land sloped down into a grassy area interspersed with low-growing brush. If he could just get the carcass to the edge of the slope, perhaps he could start it rolling and hopefully fetch up under some brush. Determined to see the plan through, he grabbed the dog's hind legs with both hands and began dragging it in small stages across the yard. Weak and exhausted, Simon made it some way down the slope through sheer willpower and necessity. He sank to his knees, took a few moments to catch his breath, then pushed the black mass down the hillside with every ounce of his fleeting strength. Thankfully it rolled a long way, disappearing from view in a large clump of undergrowth. So much for the body. Now to the blood.

Approaching the porch again with misgiving, Simon felt a wave of nausea engulf him at the sight of the red congealing pool. A convenient bush provided cover for the reappearance of afternoon tea. As Simon wiped his clammy brow, he noticed a hose conveniently located by the backdoor. The concentrated spray nozzle made short work of the sticky mess and the trail of blood across the grass but relief made him careless. After winding the hose again, he slammed the end of the hose against the side of the cottage, letting out an almost inhuman cry of rage in the process. The action was so cathartic that he repeated it again and again until the plastic spray nozzle cracked, then shattered into pieces.

"Prince. Prince is that you? Where are you? Prince…" Aletha Mason stood behind the screen door, her hand pressed to her head as if in pain. "Oh, where have you gone?" she muttered as she retreated back into the house, leaving the kitchen door ajar behind her.

Of course! That's why the blasted animal was here, Simon chided himself severely. *The blind woman stayed at home. You idiot! You bloody, mindless idiot!* Thankful that she was apparently oblivious to his presence, Simon ran from the scene as quickly as his weakened mental and physical condition allowed, vowing to put this disastrous evening behind him. After procuring a fresh pint of whiskey, he returned to his dingy, nondescript motel room and spent the rest of evening drowning the exploits of the past few hours in an abyss of liquid oblivion.

CHAPTER 17

They're compulsive in sin, seducing every
vulnerable soul they come upon.
Their specialty is greed, and they're experts at it. Dead souls!

—2 Peter 2:14 (MSG)

Rose woke early, well-rested after a day of satisfying labor and an evening of congenial company. She smiled, remembering Tim's triumphant victory cry after the final round of bingo—as if he had single-handedly conquered the city of Troy. The smile was short-lived. She heard Aletha calling plaintively from the living room, "Prince. Prince, where are you, boy?"

Rose shook Granny Gert awake. "I think something has happened to Prince." Gert could move amazingly fast when motivated. She quickly donned the robe laying across the end of her bed and joined the other two in the kitchen where Rose was trying to reassure Aletha. "I'm sure he's fine. Now why don't you sit here while I fix you a nice cup of tea." Gert and Angelica arrived in a dead heat.

Surprised to see everyone up and about so early, Angelica asked, "Is everythin' okay?" Then seeing Aletha's agitated hands working themselves frantically, Angelica knelt beside the old woman's chair and placed her hands over Aletha's, saying calmly, "Please tell me what has happened. Do you not feel well?"

"It's not me. It's my Prince. I've called and I've called and he won't come. I thought I heard a noise outside after Rose and Trudy left yesterday so I got out of bed. Prince wasn't in the room. I just thought he'd gone to investigate the sound too. But the kitchen door was open, and when I called for him through the screen door—

nothing. And I was *sure* I had closed that door, don't you remember, Trudy?" Gert merely grunted in agreement. "My head was hurting so badly, I just had to lie down. I left the door open so I could hear Prince when he returned. I must have fallen asleep because I don't remember anything until I awoke this morning to find him still gone…" Her voice was suspended with tears. Angelica gently cradled the old woman in her arms.

"There, there. His Highness probably just fancied a night out and simply hasn't come back yet," Angelica said soothingly, knowing full well that such behavior was quite out of character for the faithful canine. "Now you just sip this nice cup o' tea that Rose has kindly prepared for you while we go and call him. You'll see, he'll be runnin' home in no time." Angelica asked Gert to stay with Aletha.

"Don't you worry. I'm not going anywhere," Gert replied gruffly, moving to the chair next to Aletha's.

Rose was leaving to change her clothes when the kitchen door opened a second time to admit Tim. Hope flitted across Aletha's countenance as she heard the door open but it dissolved into tears again when she heard Tim's voice in greeting. He took in the room in a glance and was about to inquire about Aletha's obvious distress, but Angelica caught his eye and ushered him into the dining room, Rose following closely behind. She felt no self-consciousness in Tim's presence as she might have in Simon's. The fact that she was still in her pajamas, crowned with a bad case of bedhead, never crossed her mind. She only felt confident that Tim would know exactly what to do. He did not disappoint. As soon as he heard Angelica's succinct explanation of what had happened, he took charge as handily as he might have planned a bridge crossing.

Tim turned to Rose and put his hands on her shoulders. He would have moved heaven and earth to wipe the anxious expression from her face but knew the best way to accomplish that was through action. "I want you to go to the main house and keep an eye out for Prince there. It's one place he has spent a lot of time and he might have wandered off in that direction. I'll call Mom to come and help you. I suggest you keep working on the garden project." Anticipating her protest, he hurried on. "Because it will keep your mind occupied, and if something *has* spooked Prince, he's more apt to come out of hiding if he sees people he trusts working in the area." Rose agreed—reluctantly.

"Angelica, I think you probably ought to stay here today. I know it won't be easy but try to keep Aletha from worrying too much." Having received her marching orders, Angelica agreed and went back into the kitchen.

Before she had passed through the archway, Tim was on the phone to Derek. "Hey. We've got something of an emergency over here." And he filled his friend in on the details. "You'll have to make our excuses to Milly. I'm sure she'll understand. I need you and Abe at the cottage ASAP. Right. Out." Tim glanced at Rose as he hit another speed dial number and almost lost his resolve when he saw the tears in her eyes. Thankfully his mom answered the phone just as he was about to reach out to the distressed girl. "Mom, could you hold on for a second?"

"Go on, Rose. I'll have her meet you at the main house." As she turned to go with a heavy heart, he called after her, "Hey, Thompson, keep your chin up, okay?"

Rose answered with a half-hearted smile. "You too, Ludlow." He watched her padding away through the living room before answering the insistent questions coming from his phone.

"Yes, I'm fine...no, the chin up was for Rose...yes, she's fine too...Mom...Mom...*Mom*!" Tim quickly repeated the news about the absent Prince and gave instructions to his mother with an added admonition to encourage Rose. "She has such a tender heart that I think she's not only upset for Aletha's sake. I believe she really cares about that dog...I agree...just do what you can. Thanks, Mom."

Tim met his friends outside and outlined their respective duties. "Abe, I need you to make up some flyers. I think I remember seeing a framed picture of Prince with Aletha on the library desk. Blow it up and put it on the flyer with my cell number and the number for the landline to the cottage in case anyone has spotted Prince. Then put them up around town. You can probably get Lucy Bennett to help you and maybe the Lindeman kids. After you get that organized, I need you to call every vet in Harrington and surrounding counties, just in case he got hit by someone crossing a road."

"You can count on me, Cap'n."

"Thanks, man. You'll have to take Derek's truck—"

"Take *my* truck? But that's my *baby*, she's one of a kind, she's..." Derek looked at the old white pickup marked with dents and scratches and silently handed the keys to Abe.

"Exactly," Tim said. "I need your help here. We're going to have to beat the bush for about a two to three-mile radius." Lowering his voice, he added, "I don't want anyone else around here to stumble on him if he's been hurt and is...well, you know."

The assembled task force was augmented by Mr. Taylor and Tom Bennett, but even with their numbers, it was virtually impossible to cover all the acreage around the cottage. Rose and Marilyn, duly following orders, walked all the way around the grounds of the main house, then poked through every corner of the garage. No dog. Rose agreed to Marilyn's quiet suggestion that they get to work on the mulching but with a decided lack of enthusiasm. Mulch was the icing on the cake. The dark-brown mixture of wood chips, cedar mulch, and compost provided continuity for the garden and a rich background for the vibrant colors around it. Rose knew it was the final touch that would bring the garden to life, but with her mind consumed with concern for the lost dog, it became an onerous task. She tried, half-heartedly, to focus her attention on filling the old wheelbarrow but her limbs felt heavy and unwilling to lift the heavy shovel loads.

"I think that's enough for this trip. Where do you want to start, Rose?" The girl was staring hopefully into the shadows of the original tree-lined lane. "Rose, honey. Which bed would you like to start with?" Marilyn asked gently.

"Huh? Oh," Rose said apologetically. "I'm sorry. I'm having trouble focusing today. Did you ask me something?"

Marilyn thought it best to take on the onus of decision-making as Rose was clearly, and understandably, preoccupied. "I just wondered if you agreed that working on the beds farthest away might be the thing to do while we're both fresh and rested. Then we can work our way back here so we're not having to wheel the mulch so far as we get tired."

"That's a great idea," Rose said with relief. "I honestly just haven't been able to wrap my head around the work today." She lifted the wooden handles and started pushing her cumbersome load with flagging steps while Marilyn carried shovels and buckets.

The two women worked in relative silence as they spread the mulch around the beds under the old willow tree. Marilyn tried to engage Rose in conversation to distract her troubled thoughts but received only desultory replies. After three trips to the mulch pile, she noticed that Rose had tears in her eyes. The older woman, afraid that Rose might quit altogether and allow herself to surrender to the weight of her anxiety, decided it was time for open communication, even though it might cost herself some pain in the process. "You know, this isn't the first time Prince has run off?"

Rose looked up from her listless efforts to smooth out yet another mound in the blanket of black compost. "Really?" she asked hopefully.

Finally rewarded by Rose's attention, Marilyn began her narrative while keeping her eyes on the fragile bedding plants, careful not to bury any under the ground cover. "About two years after we moved to Tinkers Well, there was a terrible storm. Tornados were cropping up all around us. The sound of howling wind and crash of thunder and lightning was almost deafening. My husband, Peter, and I had come to the cottage for dinner that evening. We decided it would be best to ride out the storm in the Mason's cellar instead of attempting to drive back to our place. Anyway as we were headed down the stairs, we called for Prince but he didn't come. I took Aletha downstairs for safety while Peter and Matthew searched every room for the dog, but he had somehow gotten out. Aletha's blindness was fairly new to her then and she was very dependent on Prince, not so much for guidance but for comfort. Matthew had given Prince to her as a gift to help her through the transition." Marilyn noticed that Rose was working more steadily now, listening for the story to unfold. Just knowing that Prince had been lost and found once before encouraged the young girl's heart. She waited expectantly as the two women transitioned to the Japanese wisteria and shrubs along the east side of the house.

"Now where was I? Prince was a gift. A priceless gift. Aletha loved that dog and Matthew loved Aletha so he was determined to find the dog and insisted on going out in the storm to look for him."

"Oh my gosh! How old was he then?"

"He was eighty-five. Can you imagine? Peter tried to convince him that the dog would instinctively find shelter but Matthew was insistent, and since Peter wouldn't hear of him going out alone, the two set out together."

"Well, they must have found him. Where was he? Maybe we could look there—"

"We don't know where he was. Matthew and Peter never came back." Marilyn's voice had grown quieter, though her hands kept moving with a sort of deliberate intensity. "When we knew the storm was moving away from us, Aletha and I went upstairs. You know how the cellar stairs are next to the backdoor…" Rose nodded her head. "When he got to the top of the stairs, we heard Prince whining on the back deck. Of course, Aletha was overjoyed. But we sat up all night, waiting for Peter and Matthew. The local first responders were spread so thin because of all the storm damage that we didn't get any news until the next morning. They found them under a fallen power pole. Peter had covered Matthew's body with his own. We can only guess that they were checking the roadside culverts when the pole came down." Marilyn paused in her narration to straighten her aching back and to wipe her brow.

"Oh, Marilyn! I'm *so* sorry. I didn't know," Rose said candidly.

"That's why I told you," Marilyn responded gently. "You see, Tim won't talk about it. He foolishly thinks he's somehow responsible because he wasn't here. He was deployed to Iraq at the time. I don't know how he thinks he could have prevented it, but men—good, caring, honorable men—try to shoulder the burdens of everyone around them, even when it's not possible—or rational."

"Is that why he left the army?" Rose asked shyly. "He said he moved here to take care of you after his father died…"

"And I told him I could take care of myself. But he was head of the family, by golly, so he left a job he loved for the people he loved." Her voice broke a little on the last phrase. "And to be fair to him, he didn't move here solely on my account. Aletha has always been a... well, a grandmother to him and he knew she would be devastated."

Rose had also paused at her labor as if in reverence for two men she had never met. "And Prince became Aletha's best friend," Rose said. "No wonder she's so upset about his disappearance. It probably brings back all those memories of loss."

"Which is why we need to finish this project. Aletha can come here and walk the old paths that she once walked with Matthew when they first married, when they dreamed of creating a little paradise for their retirement years. She won't be able to see it now but she can listen to the fountain and smell the flowers and remember."

Rose was struck by the romantic picture Marilyn had drawn and felt an inexplicable kinship with the older woman. She too hoped that this lovely peaceful place would lift Aletha's spirits. Tim had been right when he suggested that adding a final layer of beauty to the garden might lessen her worry. It wasn't so much that she was less concerned over Prince but Marilyn had helped her see their work in the light of a ministry to a wonderful old soul who had known much trouble. She retrieved the next load of mulch, determined to view the toil from a fresh perspective.

Angelica had sent some fruit and granola bars with Rose so the two women worked straight through lunch, breaking only for water and a snack. Gloves had protected their hands from the layer of black grime that covered every other exposed inch of flesh so they could consume the finger food with a modicum of hygiene. With backs and legs aching and brows dripping with sweat, Rose and Marilyn gazed at the garden, exhausted but supremely satisfied.

"I'm so filthy, I've got to get home to clean up but please let me know if you hear anything. I don't know when Tim will be home so I'm counting on you for a report," Marilyn said as she carefully sat on paper bags she had spread over the driver's seat to protect the upholstery.

"I promise." Rose smiled and waved as she walked toward the cottage. But no report came. She had showered and eaten a light supper when the men called it quits for the day.

"I'm sorry, Aletha," Tim said gently as he knelt by her chair. "There's no sign of him yet but you know he came back once before so we'll just give it a few days and hope for the best. There are people on the lookout all over town, so if he's out there, we'll find him."

"Bless you, Tim," Aletha said as she reached out and he guided her hand to his face. "I know you've done your best." She spoke with resignation and gratitude. Tim covered her delicate hand with his strong calloused one then gently withdrew it and lightly kissed her palm before replacing it in her lap. Rose had experienced the thrill of just such a gesture by Simon, but this interchange between the frail old woman and the powerful young man seemed somehow infinitely more tender and caring. Rose still had much to learn about all the nuances of love.

*****

Simon's hangover reached epic proportions. He tried every remedy he knew but to no avail, so he surrendered the pain to sleep once more, waking late in the afternoon, if not refreshed, at least almost human again. With a clearer head came memories of the previous day's fiasco. And with the memories came nightmare images that sent him running for the bathroom to rid himself of the last of the whiskey and the lowering effects of the worst failure he had experienced in his notable career.

Simon Atherton would not be beaten. Not by a dog. Not by a childhood demon. And certainly not by an old woman. A shower, shave, and clean clothes put the finishing touches on his social mask. Now ravenously hungry and not wanting to appear at the cottage until the older members of the household had toddled off to bed, Simon happily realized it was Friday and decided to try the elevated cuisine of Louis' Bistro. Though usually not accessible without a reservation, Simon's reputation had opportunely proceeded him so he was able to get a table after gallantly paying homage to his host and hostess and promising an entire blog post dedicated to their exquisite establishment. Whether his palate had been tainted by The Early Bird Cafe or he was simply too hungry to care, he found the food quite passable and enjoyed a repast of duck tart followed by lamb loin with eggplant and fried brussels sprouts. A light Pavlova completed the meal that was offered free *gratis* by the grateful owners. They also offered a bottle of their finest Cabernet Sauvignon but Simon was taking no chances that night. He would need all his wits about him.

Having lingered as long as he possible at Louis', he reached Fern Cottage just before nine o'clock and was greeted at the door by an obviously surprised Rose.

"Simon! I didn't...that is...were you...what are you doing here?"

Affecting the mien of a wounded cavalier, Simon assumed an expression of deep distress. "Rose, my love, could you...no it can't be," he said, shaking his head, then looking again at the confused girl. "Could you have *forgotten* that we were to spend this evening together? I even brought one of your favorite movies—*Emma*."

Light dawned. Rose slapped the palm of her hand on her forehead and said, "Oh, Simon! I'm so *sorry*! Yes, I completely forgot about our movie night. You see, it's been an *awful* day. Prince has gone missing and Aletha is upset, and I've been moving tons of mulch so I'm—"

"Exhausted. I understand. With so much going on, it's no wonder you forgot about your poor humble Simon..."

"Oh, no, no, no! I could never forget about you." She hadn't thought about him for three days, except in passing.

"Then you've missed me as much as I've missed you. Please say I can stay, darling." He was at his coaxing best. Not too pushy but allowing his disappointment to show. Rose could not refuse him.

"Of *course*, you can stay. Please, come in," she said as she stepped aside for him to enter. He started to walk into the darkened living room but Rose stopped him, saying, "No, the TV is in the library. This way."

"What a cozy room. This is delightful. Darling, do you suppose you could fix us a spot of tea. I know it will be perfect if *you* make it."

After showing him the DVD player and remotes, she complied with his request, all the while trying to muster some enthusiasm for his company. She would have asked for a rain check but she just couldn't bear to disappoint him, especially after his foolish jealousy of Tim. She smiled at the memory as she gathered all the elements for the tea tray.

"Let me get that door for you, love," Simon said gallantly as she struggled with the handle. She could have sworn she had left the door ajar. "I was right. This looks perfect," he said as he took the tray from her and sat it on a side table. Rose was then taken completely off guard when Simon clasped both her hands and pulled them behind his neck, letting his hands slide down her arms until they encircled her waist. Rose could feel the warmth of his body and smell the heady scent of his cologne. His kiss was the ultimate surprise. It was neither chaste nor hesitant but rather purposeful and lingering. When at last he pulled away, Rose felt an unexpected sense of relief which she quickly attributed to her worry and exhaustion. And true to recent form, Simon poured cold water over her confused emotions when he stepped back, drawing her hands down to rest on his chest.

"You *have* alerted your estimable grandmother of my presence, haven't you?" When Rose shook her head in bemused denial, he instantly released her and said, "Off you go then. I won't have anyone saying that I took advantage of you." Rose was on the sensory roller coaster once more. She tried to rationalize her conflicting thoughts as she slipped down the hall to tell Granny Gert of Simon's arrival. Aletha had already gone to bed.

Gert was sitting up in bed, reading. She was none too pleased with the news of Simon's presence in the house but was too tired to put up much of a fuss. Besides she reasoned with herself, how much mischief could he get up to practically under her nose? "You be sure and keep that door open, young lady," she called after Rose as a parting shot.

Simon was sitting in the big overstuffed chair and waved Rose over to join him. She felt a bit self-conscious about sitting so close to him—the chair was not really designed for two people. But as she sat tentatively on the edge of the cushion, Simon put one arm under her

LINDA EDMISTER

legs and the other around her hips pulling her sideways so that her legs overlapped his and her body was nestled into his circling arm. She was suddenly a little breathless so she focused on the captivating opening score of the Miramax version of her favorite Jane Austen novel.

"Now this *is* cozy," Simon said softly as he handed her a cup of tea. He kissed her hair and settled in to watch the movie. Rose began to relax and enjoyed the wedding celebration of "Dear Mrs. Weston" and the arrival of Mr. Knightly. The accents sounded so much richer as her drowsy mind began to superimpose Simon's image over that of the film's hero. She remembered nothing after the introduction of Harriet Smith into the menagerie.

Simon watched Rose out of the corner of his eye, waiting patiently for signs of drowsiness. He encouraged her to finish her tea, then turned her face toward him to drop gentle kisses on her heavy eyelids. When he felt her slump against him, he carefully disengaged himself and got to work. Unearthing a completely unexpected find in the recesses of the library desk, he felt immeasurably cheered until he turned from perusal of an interesting false book with an inset box to see the gorgon staring a hole through him with her piercing eyes over that great beak of a nose. He tried to palm the box while backing down the library stepstool but Gert had been watching him for some time.

"I'll just take that little box from you, mister. I wouldn't want you to be troubled to put back anything that isn't yours."

He'd had to surrender what could potentially hold the coveted safe deposit key. He might have been able to bluff his way past Rose but not her grandmother.

"Dear Rose was so exhausted she just dozed off and I was so drawn by the interesting collection on these shelves—"

"Save it. I'll be getting Rose to bed now so I think it's time for you to leave." She jerked her head toward the door and waited for Simon to precede her, then followed so closely behind him she fairly pushed him out the front door, offering no pleasantries as she slammed it in his face.

268

"Damn! Damn! Damn! I was *so* close," Simon swore as he drove away. "It would appear that Plan B will be necessary after all."

*****

Simon was growing desperate. As he prepared to execute a last-ditch move, he fumed over his wasted efforts during the past two weeks. He'd gone through all those confounded boxes to no avail and searched every conceivable hiding place in the living areas and bedrooms of Fern Cottage during the two occasions the ladies had been absent from the house—the first bingo evening and church on Sunday past. The last bingo night, two days ago, had proven a disastrous wash so he'd had to fall back on his long-range game plan the night before. Then all the painstaking preparation he'd made in gaining welcome admission to the house had failed when that blasted old woman had interrupted him while searching the library. Had he fully appreciated her penchant for keeping such an eagle eye on Rose, he might have put something in her tea too so she would have nodded off to sleep as expected rather than catching him out in the middle of his search. The glib excuse he offered for thumbing through countless dry tomes in the library, when he was supposed to be watching a favorite film with Rose, had sounded flat even to his ears. At least he'd unearthed something that evening before being unceremoniously shown the door. It wasn't the document Hawthorne was so anxious to locate but Simon knew he could use this particular certificate as a bargaining chip. Knowledge really is power, and he now possessed a piece of paper potentially worth tens of thousands to an enterprising negotiator. As much as Hawthorne wanted his land deal to go through, Simon was fairly certain, he would abhor any attachment of scandal to the proceedings, especially any that would expose his underlying ruthlessness in such an unfavorable light.

Simon recounted all these grim details in his mind as he drove. Rose, sitting beside him, would ordinarily have been making naive remarks about the beauty of the sky, the glorious warmth of the sun (which Simon found unbearably hot), or pointing out some quaint farm. But today, Rose was not feeling her best. Having awakened to a splitting headache, she would rather have stayed at the cottage. Her head felt better after a cool shower and some aspirin but she was still worried about Prince and wanted to help with the search. She sensed though that Simon was losing patience with her other pursuits (he must really be in love with her) so she thought it best to keep their date, especially after falling asleep on him the night before. She hardly noticed when he stopped the car.

Simon unloaded a stuffed picnic basket and quilted blanket from the back seat. So lost was he in his own thoughts that he forgot his customary practice of opening and closing the car door for Rose. She had been so unusually silent on the drive from Fern Cottage that he had, in fact, momentarily forgotten her presence altogether. He was recalled to his role of skilled suitor when he heard the car door slam and turned to see her hurrying after him. He forced a smile to his lips and apologized for his lapse in courtesy. "I'm afraid I've been rather preoccupied lately. I've had a few…setbacks in my work and then there's the shame of my failing you in my weakness. Forgive me."

Forgive me. Rose had the oddest feeling of déjà vu. She couldn't recall the previous incident but was sure the words had been spoken to her recently by someone else and with honest contrition. Looking at Simon's rueful expression and winsomely crooked smile, she wondered.

On one of their many drives over the local winding roads that often seemed to be going in two directions at once, Simon had noticed a secluded copse of trees not far off the road and had made a mental note that it's privacy might prove useful for a quiet afternoon rendezvous if necessary. It had proven necessary. What he had not realized, because of the miles covered to get there, was its close proximity to the Mason home and its location on Mason property. The clump of trees conveniently blocked any direct sight line from the road and opened onto a shallow valley, really little more than a depression in the landscape. Beyond the valley, about a hundred yards away was another circle of trees, but not being any great lover of nature, Simon had given little thought to their ordered planting or any civilization they might signal in an otherwise open grassy countryside.

Sensing an almost imperceptible withdrawal by Rose who normally offered open admiration of his charm and instant grace for his failings, Simon tried to introduce a note of romance by taking her hand as they walked toward the trees, singing in a pleasant tenor an ancient English folk song.

Alas, my love, you do me wrong, to cast me off discourteously.
For I have loved you well and long, delighting in your company.
Greensleeves was all my joy, Greensleeves was my delight,
Greensleeves was my heart of gold, and who but my lady Greensleeves.

Your vows you've broken, like my heart, oh, why did you so enrapture me?
Now I remain in a world apart, but my heart remains in captivity.
Greensleeves was all my joy, Greensleeves was my delight,
Greensleeves was my heart of gold, and who but my lady Greensleeves.

Rose's conscience was stricken by the poignant text and Simon's obvious efforts to woo her out of her uncharacteristic reserve. She reluctantly fell into step as he began waltzing with her while he sang. Despite her lowered spirits she even laughed spontaneously as he spun her in a final twirl among the trees. Her concern over the missing Prince was temporarily forgotten, and she chastened herself for doubting Simon's sincerity. She even felt some recurring guilt for her role in causing him inward turmoil about their relationship. Accordingly she set about convincing him of her delight in the idea of a picnic (despite feeling a little inappropriately attired in the dress with the form-fitting bodice and flared skirt) instead of going to a stuffy restaurant for lunch.

They spread the quilt under an evergreen where spongy moss and fallen pine straw provided a natural cushion. Simon leaned against the trunk and patted the ground next to him invitingly.

"I'll try to sit as ladylike as possible," Rose said modestly with a gurgle of laughter in her throat as she sat near him but not quite touching, lest she again arouse unsolicited temptation in her partner.

"You could never be anything *but* ladylike, my darling," crooned Simon. "We'll leave lunch for a little while so we can simply enjoy each other's company. I've missed spending time with you," he added as he moved closer to her, reaching his left arm around her hips to pull her yet closer. Rose, not accustomed to such smooth, practiced tactics, found herself breathing a little faster, unable to think of any cautionary rejoinder yet feeling responsible for his unguarded touch. She watched, mesmerized, as he took her right hand in his and slowly, lingeringly, began kissing the end of each finger before planting a kiss in her palm, then on her wrist. She felt a bit relieved when he gently laid her hand back on her lap. But unlike previous occasions when he withdrew after brief moments of physical intimacy, the reprieve from his amorous advances was to be short-lived. She felt a shiver of delight—fear—run through her as he moved his hand up to stroke her cheek and tuck a stray strand of hair back behind her ear while his lips pulled playfully on her lobe.

"Dear Rose, you are truly a treasure. We have made quite a team, haven't we?" he whispered, his breath warm against her neck. He observed the rapid rise and fall of her bosom and continued in something akin to a purr. "In vain, I have struggled for mastery over my very natural desire for you. We could be so much more, my love. Have so much more. I know it's what you want, what any mature sophisticated woman wants with a man who adores her."

In the tiny corner of her brain that still functioned under Simon's determined attack on her reason through sensual overload, she tried to convince herself that this *was* what she wanted. *Wasn't it?* Rose asked herself. *Besides, Simon has always acted as a gentleman. Surely he wouldn't go beyond the dictates of propriety.*

"We might have enjoyed a more intimate evening yesterday but you fell asleep on me, poor darling." He chuckled softly as his lips explored her neck, setting every inch of her body tingling.

Or would he?

"We might try again tonight." He hinted, sliding the dress strap off her shoulder and nuzzling the vacated spot.

Maybe he would.

Turning her flushed face toward him, he breathed just before his lips covered hers. "Mightn't we?" The kiss, at first a revelation for Rose, became more insistent and decidedly frightening. She gasped for air as he paused to suggest, his lips hovering over her face, her chin, her neck, while his finger lightly traced the top of her bodice, "You could let me into the house without anyone knowing, surely? And as I recall, that great overstuffed chair in the library was quite comfortable. Certainly more comfortable than this blanket. Though I'm willing to overlook that for now if you are…" The insistent kisses resumed as Rose became aware of his hand, at first resting on her knee, slowly slide up her leg under the hem of her dress.

That tiny corner in her brain was now fighting valiantly to bolster her diminishing reason. In those deep recesses, Rose could hear her mother's voice saying, *"Just remember, no touching between the neck and the knees"*—then shouting—*"No touching between the neck and the knees!"*—all the while aware of Simon's hand reaching beyond her hemline. Rose's innocent, idyllic fairy-tale romance had somehow become a dangerous game of seduction, and it was spiraling rapidly out of control. She began to feel a sense of panic, even as her swirling senses threatened to drown in an alarming sea of strange newly awakened sensations. She forced herself to open her oddly heavy eyelids and look beyond the immediacy of the moment. Her swirling senses morphed into a swirling circle of movement in the air over the little valley. Focusing deliberately on that movement as she turned her head away from Simon's demanding mouth, she pushed his hand off of her leg and rolled to her side and onto her feet. As she stood staring at the sky, trying to regain her composure, she felt an undefined feeling of dread forming in the pit of her stomach.

"Rose, what are you *doing*?" Simon asked reproachfully with more than a hint of underlying anger. "Wait! Where on earth are you *going*?" he called after the retreating girl who was quickly running down the hill in the direction of some circling birds. He knew nothing of birds but Rose had recognized them as turkey vultures when her brain was finally capable of rational thought. Grandpa Ernie had taught her about birds to watch out for on the farm. Their presence could only mean that some poor creature must have attracted their attention. Her sandal-clad feet slipped a few times on the long silky grass, and she grazed her leg on a hidden boulder after stumbling over a rotten tree branch, but she hurtled toward her goal as if pulled by a powerful magnet.

Rose and the vultures nearly collided at their mutual point of interest. Why she had felt compelled to rush down the hill in pursuit of who knew what, she couldn't later say—other than gaining a much-needed respite from Simon's forceful lovemaking. When she reached the site where the birds circled, she instinctively shooed them away with a large stick before looking through the thick brush for the object that had drawn girl and prey alike.

At first she thought it must be a young calf that had wandered away from its mother and died from any number of natural causes. It lay on its side, its back toward Rose, the once-shiny black coat now matted and dirty. Ordinarily what she had already seen, coupled with the foul smell of decaying flesh, would have sent her right back up the hill but she had to know more. Covering her nose with a shaking hand, Rose moved around the animal's head and discovered that it wasn't a calf at all. Tears sprang to her eyes as she recognized the once-gentle face of the dog Prince now swollen and contorted with blank eyes staring into nothingness. She made another discovery too—a gaping slash just under his jaw where his throat had been cut. Unable to shift her eyes from the horror, Rose felt a wave of revulsion well up inside her and she began to tremble. She stumbled blindly to a point where the dead animal was out of sight, though her mind's eye kept running the scene over and over in a hideous loop. She opened her mouth to scream but no sound came—at first. Her vocal cords finally remembered how to function as she began to hyperventilate and then she couldn't have stopped the screams if she'd wanted to.

Simon, reluctantly following Rose down the hill, realized too late where they stood in relation to the cottage. How could he have known, when he'd dragged that objectionable beast over the edge of the hill behind the cottage and sent him rolling toward the waning sun into an open hollow of grass and brush, that it would fetch up here within shouting distance of the precise spot he'd chosen for his passionate interlude? Damnable luck! When he finally caught up with the distraught girl, he had to yell to be heard over her hysteria.

"For god's sake, girl, pull yourself together. It's just some bloody cur that's had a bit of a dustup with a coyote. I understand they always go for the throat."

Rose continued to scream uncontrollably.

"I said stop it!" And he swung her around to face him. Senses overwhelmed, eyes flooded with tears, Rose heard nothing or she might have noticed that Simon's polished veneer was cracking—badly. She had already dealt his ego a painful blow by evading his amorous overtures (something he was not at all accustomed to), she'd stumbled on the evidence of a misstep he had found as distasteful as it was unnecessary, and there she stood, crowning all that folly by subjecting him to a fit of vapors. Simon eyed her with a growing sense of loathing.

"You stupid twit," he said and dealt her a resounding smack across the cheek with the back of his hand.

Rose stopped in midsob. She stood perfectly still for a full minute Blinking the tears from her eyes, it was as if she could see clearly for the first time since being bulldozed by Simon's patent charm. A thousand memories came flooding in, each one chipping away at the facade she had been so eager to accept. The charming smile that never quite reached his eyes. His determined pursuit of her despite (honesty compelled her to admit) being decidedly anything but his type. His polished manners that lasted as long as she went along with his every suggestion, giving way to thinly veiled impatience when questioned, and only coming to the fore again when she acquiesced to his more dominant personality. It was as if she was a pawn in some game—a game involving Aletha Mason. She didn't know for what purpose but Rose finally realized in that moment of epiphany that ever since they had met at Fern Cottage on that ill-fated day, Simon had been using her to gain admittance to the house and to ingratiate himself with Aletha whose sweet kind spirit hid a shrewd discerning mind. It was a pity that Rose did not share the latter quality.

I must have been a gift to him when I answered the door that day—a dewy eyed, simpering, spineless gift! Rose cringed inwardly at the thought. All of these revelations flashed through her mind in less time than the telling and, with them, one final realization that goaded her into speech. "It was *you*. It *had* to be you. Just now, you said it was a dog but you can't see him from here, and how could you know about…about his…throat…" Suddenly her legs buckled. Rose landed on her knees at Simon's feet and blindly reached out to steady herself as she fell forward, grabbing one of his legs. She then promptly hung her head and threw up all over his $800-designer shoes.

CHAPTER 18

And now, don't be afraid. I will do for you all you ask.
All the people of my town know that you
are a woman of noble character.

—Ruth 3:11 (NIV)

"Derek! Derek, wake up!"

Abe hauled the unresponsive Derek to a sitting position as Scout jumped up on the bed and started licking Derek's face. "Man, you have got to *wake up!*" Shaking his friend's shoulders, Abe finally saw signs of life. Derek slowly raised a hand to push the dog away and rub eyes that refused to open.

"Brother, what *time* is it? Don't you remember that it's *Saturday* and Tim told us to take the day off? I'm going back to sleep…" And he laid down again. Anticipating Derek's unwillingness to join the land of the living a minute sooner than necessary, Abe opened the blinds, pulled off Derek's blanket, and the pillow out from under his head. Scout barked in full voice, wagging his tail wildly in appreciation of a fun new game.

"Aaaaarrrgh! Scout, pipe down!" The dog sat down obediently, whining a little. Derek rolled over onto one elbow, glaring at his friend. "We spent all day looking for Prince then had to make up lost time at Milly's till after midnight so you had better have a darned good reason for messing with me now, Yousef."

Derek never called Abe by his last name unless he was really ticked off, and Abe knew it, so he opted for the most direct route to Derek's undivided attention. "I think Rose may be in danger." That did it.

Derek managed to sit up and swing his legs over the edge of the bed. Shaking his head while trying to engage his foggy brain, he said, "*What?*" Then he raised a halting hand. "Wait. Don't answer that until you get me some—" Abe placed a hot cup of coffee in his friend's hand, waiting for a signal to continue. After a few moments, Derek made a forward rolling gesture with his free hand then motioned Scout to the bed. As he stroked the dog's head, he murmured, "I'm sorry, buddy. I know you were just trying to help," and cocked an expectant eye at Abe.

"Okay. You remember Tim told me to get the photo of Prince from the library?" He paused as Derek nodded. "Well, it was on the desk all right and there was a business card next to it."

Derek rolled his hand forward more quickly.

"The card was for that guy Tim told us about—Simon Applegate. I don't know why I did it, but on some impulse, I tucked it in my pocket. I didn't even think about it again until we got home last night and I was so beat that I just hit the bed and was out. But when I woke up this morning—*several hours ago*—"

"Hey, we can't all be gifted with a limitless capacity for sleep," Derek interjected proudly.

"I remembered the card and looked up the website on the card. It looked all right but Tim doesn't trust the guy so why should I? I did a search for Simon Applegate and his *On the Move* blog and got *nothing.*"

"So? This blog is his one claim to fame. He's a one-hit wonder. There've got to be thousands of people out there trying to make a name for themselves on the Internet. So this one just happened to end up in Tinkers Well. So what?"

"Drink some more coffee. You're not listening." Derek willingly complied. "I said there is *nothing* on the Internet for a blog by Simon Applegate," Abe said, looking meaningfully at Derek, "but there *should* be." Abe waited while the significance of his statement registered with Derek.

"*Oh*, I get it. There *should* be if he's legit but there isn't any so—"

"So I've spent the last three hours searching for blogs on the same subject and found duplicate articles by *other* authors that are posted on *his* site with *his* byline. Since he is clearly not, as you said, legit, I pulled his portrait and started a search for that face using my facial recognition software. The software is pretty outdated so I only got a few hits—ads for his services from nine or ten years ago as a private eye in the UK. And get this, his name then was Simon *Jones*."

"A British PI working undercover? But what could he possibly be looking for *here*? And what's it got to do with Rose?"

"That I don't know but what I *can* tell you is that he's up to no good. The encryption on the blog site was well-constructed but I was able to trace the IP address back to a real estate company which turned out to be just a front. That was a major red flag so I dug a little deeper and hit a firewall for a proxy server—"

"Man, I cannot handle your techno babble this early in the morning. Just cut to the chase."

"So did I ever tell you about the MP officer I met at Walter Reed while we were both going through rehab?"

Derek shook his head, a baffled look on his face. "How am I supposed to jump from firewall whatevers one minute to MPs at Walter Reed the next? You do realize that my brain is *barely* functioning..." He fixed his friend with an intent look from under lowered eyebrows.

Abe hurried on. "Okay, long story short. I went through rehab with an MP captain, Dave Story, who was really struggling with depression—he was a bilateral amputee. And I know I *should* have been depressed too, but thanks to your witness, I had just received eternal salvation and I couldn't stop telling everyone about it—the docs, the nurses, the physical therapists. I guess he overheard me, and one day, he asked me to tell him my story. He *was* a believer but had gone through a real crisis of faith after his injuries. I shared my conversion experience with him, even the loss of my family because of Christ. He didn't say anything, just listened, but I could tell there was some kind of battle going on inside him. Anyway just before we were due to be discharged, he came looking for me. He wanted to introduce me to his wife and kids and his parents. The dark circles of strain were still under his eyes but there was a new light in them, and I could tell that he had begun the process of healing from the inside out. He told me God had placed me in his path when he needed a word of hope the most—just like He placed you in my path."

Derek grinned. "That's awesome, brother," he said, and gave Abe a high five. "But *what has all this got to do with Rose?*"

"I'm getting there. We exchanged contact information and he told me if I ever needed help to call him. I didn't think much of it at the time but we've e-mailed each other once or twice. Turns out, he went to work for the FBI as an analyst. So just on a whim, I called him this morning—while you were *still* sleeping." Derek rolled his eyes. "Without even hesitating, he told me to send him Jones' picture and anything I knew about him. I just got his response." He handed Derek a copy of the e-mail. "This Jones has about ten aliases and works for some big-time investigative agency in New York City as Simon *Atherton*. I gather by what this says that Atherton operates just this side of the law so, like I said before, he's up to no good."

Quickly scanning the single sheet of paper, Derek looked up with a frown on his face and said, "I think you're right. What would a man like this"—shaking the paper—"want with a sweet girl like Rose? She could really be in danger." Then looking accusingly at the ever-patient Abraham, he added, "Man, why didn't you wake me up sooner?" and jumped to his feet, ready for action. "Now where did I put that new pair of jeans?" Abe unearthed them from under the blanket he had pulled off the bed and thrown over a chair in the corner. As Derek was dancing around, in the process of pulling on the jeans, Scout started barking enthusiastically while Abe pulled out a T-shirt and socks from the pile of clean clothes that had been sitting on a corner of the desk for several days.

"We nee do 'ell 'im," Derek yelled from the bathroom, assuming he would be understood through a mouthful of toothpaste. He was.

Abe yelled back, "I called him but he's still on his way back from that little architectural salvage place northwest of KC. He was about thirty miles out. I told him I'd already called the cottage—before I woke you—but Mrs. Gunn told me Rose was still in bed with a headache and couldn't come to the phone so I figured it wasn't urgent. Surely she won't be going anywhere if she's not feeling well…"

"Maybe not," said Derek, emerging from the bathroom, "but I'd feel better if we can see Rose and know she's okay. She's been going out with this guy just about every day for the past two weeks," he continued while stuffing keys and wallet in his pockets, "and nothing negative has happened but now that we know—"

"We have to do something about it," finished Abe. Locking the front door, he joined Derek, with Scout at their heels, and walked toward Derek's truck. "And I promised Tim we'd go to the house and stay with Rose until he can get there. I just don't know how successful he'll be in convincing her that her Adonis is really a wolf in sheep's clothing."

It was just before noon when they pulled up in front of the cottage and were climbing out of the truck when they turned to see Tim's truck flying down the driveway, screeching to a stop in a cloud of dust. Striding purposely to the door, he yelled over his shoulder, "Is she still here?"

"We just got here ourselves so we don't know..." Tim had disappeared into the house. "Phew! He must have broken some land speed record to get here. He *has* got it bad," Derek remarked to Abe as they followed Tim into the house.

They found him in the dining room where the ladies had just sat down to lunch.

"No. I'm sorry, sonny, but she's not here," said Granny Gert when asked about Rose. "I tried to convince her to stay home and take it easy today but she insisted she felt better. She kept looking at that Applegate fellow like she was afraid to tell him no, though I didn't see anything but that uppity look on his smirking face. Why she's taken up with that supercilious pretty boy when there are clearly much nicer young men"—looking meaningfully at Tim—"in the neighborhood beats me." Derek and Abe looked at each other in silent agreement.

"But do you know where they went?" The anxiety and insistence underlying Tim's question must have registered with Gert, for she looked sharply at his face before replying.

"What are you not saying, young man? Is my Rosie in any trouble?" Angelica and Aletha, also concerned, waited for Tim's answer.

"I'm sorry. I didn't mean to alarm you all. I'm sure she's fine. It's just that Abe," he said, nodding in his friends direction, "discovered some pretty damning evidence against Simon Atherton, and I just think it would be best if Rose stopped spending so much—or *any*—time with him. I don't believe, in fact, I know that he can't be trusted. I'd like to explain all of this to Rose so she can make an informed decision about her...companion."

"Well, why don't you try explaining it to us, sonny, starting with the name...Atherton, was it? I thought he calls himself Applegate." Angelica had gestured for the three young men to be seated, then quietly prepared plates, placing one before each man. Derek and Abe tucked in with eagerness but Tim never even noticed.

"It seems that Mr. Applegate is, in reality, Simon Atherton, a private investigator with the..." He looked at Abe for assistance.

"Landrum Detective Agency based in New York City," Abe managed through a mouthful of scalloped potatoes. If anyone remarked Aletha's sudden heightened attention, they said nothing.

"His blog is a complete fabrication. Abe spent several hours this morning searching the Internet and got final verification from a friend in..."

Swallowing a mouthful of glazed carrots, Abe filled in obligingly, "the FBI," before attacking a piece of roast chicken.

"I know he has been...courting Rose..."

"Wheedling his way in, encroaching on her innocent affection..." grumbled Gert.

"But I can't believe that she is the real object of his attention. I have to think that he has just been using her as a means of gathering information about you, Aletha." He turned to speak directly to her. "And because he's been at it for almost two weeks and clearly not found what he's looking for, I'm afraid he may be forced to use extreme measures. You're the only one here with ties to New York and, as a widow of two wealthy men, may be privy to knowledge you aren't even aware of. Aletha, can you think of *any* reason someone would be investigating you or looking for something here in Fern Cottage?"

At the mention of New York City, Aletha had anticipated the question. "Now it's my turn to be sorry, Tim. I'm afraid I can't help you." The statement was spoken with a firm finality uncharacteristic in the gentle old woman.

Turning to the other ladies present, he asked, "Have either of you noticed any unusual behavior by Atherton when he's been present in the house?"

"I can answer that. I was afraid you would all think me just a fanciful old woman, but after hearing your account of that phony, I don't mind telling you what happened last night" Gert said. "That Simon fellow finagled an invitation to watch a movie with Rose. Why, he didn't even get here till almost nine o'clock! I didn't even know he was here till Rosie came to tell me. I made her promise to leave the library door open—I don't trust that fellow." Tim felt his fists clench and his jaw tighten. "I read for a while but I just couldn't get to sleep, kept thinking about my Rosie alone in the dark with... *him*. So I got up around ten to go check on them. Now I know Rose is a grown woman but I feel responsible for her." She spoke in a defensive voice.

"You don't need to explain yourself to me," Tim answered grimly.

"Anyway what do you think I saw? This no good Applegate-Atherton fellow up on a stool, pulling books off the top shelf and leafing through them. The TV was turned down so low I could barely hear it. I watched him for a few minutes, and then I looked over at that big oversized chair where Rose was sitting. She was fast asleep with a tea cup in her hand! Watching a movie, my eye. I got his attention real quick. I had caught him red-handed and he knew it—nearly fell off the stool when I hollered at him. Then he came up with a cockamamie excuse for what was obviously some sort of tomfoolery so I showed him the door and waited till I saw him drive off."

"Bravo! I wish I could have witnessed such a thorough rout," Tim said, momentarily diverted.

"You might not have been so impressed by what I noticed next. I tried to wake up Rosie but she was so sound asleep I had to shake her awake and practically drag her to bed." She paused and added with deliberation. "I think her tea was drugged."

Derek's capacity for sleep was rivaled only by Abraham's capacity for consuming food. But Gert's statement, spoken so baldly and in such deadly earnest, caused Abe to stop with a spoonful of banana pudding halfway to his mouth and look at Rose's grandmother.

"What makes you say that?" Tim asked quietly.

"I've seen men drunk before, not that my Ernie ever got more than a little tippled, but I know what a hangover looks like. And I'm telling you, that's what Rose had this morning—migraine my foot."

"Then how could you let her go off with that man knowing what you do?" It was more an accusation than a question, though Tim hadn't meant to upset the old woman further.

"Now you wait a cotton-pickin' minute, sonny." Granny Gert was on her feet, still barely eye to eye with the seated Tim. "If you think for one second that you care more about that girl than I do, you've got another thing coming."

"Of course I don't. I just—"

"Or that you can look after her better than I can—"

"No, of course not. I mean, you're her grandmother and I'm just—"

"Precisely. Just. I informed his highness that I expected him to have Rose back safe and sound by two o'clock or I would know who to call. I thought that would keep him on his toes, though I don't know how much trouble she can get into if he's just taking her to that fancy restaurant in town for lunch." Tired from her emotional speech, Gert sat down abruptly and dabbed at the tears of worry and doubt that threatened to fill her eyes.

"But, Gertie, they're not goin' to a restaurant." All eyes turned to Angelica who had been sitting quietly during the tense dialogue. "He told me that they were goin' to have a picnic. He seemed right proud o' himself. Called it dinin' alfresco or some such nonsense."

"Did he happen to mention where they were going on this picnic? It's important, Angelica." Tim didn't need to add the last statement. The strain in his voice was evident.

"Well, first I asked him if Rose knew, about the picnic I mean, because I had ironed her pretty pink frock this mornin', and surely, she would need to change into somethin' more fittin' for eatin' outside. He just gave me that look, you know, like he was oglin' a servant and said she would 'better adorn the landscape in her dress.' I've got to say, I'm glad you boys don't talk in such a way—fairly made me blush!"

"Yes, Angelica," said Tim, barely containing his impatience, "but did he mention where they were *going*?"

"I'm coming to that. He kept talkin', boastful like, and said he'd found the perfect spot for a romantic picnic"—Tim audibly ground his teeth—"just off the road about five miles out o' town."

"Oh god, that could be anywhere," Tim said in desperation.

"Oh no, not anywhere. He said it was in a clump o' trees on Old Rogers Road, and every teenager around here knows that there's only one clump o' trees on Old Rogers Road because that's where they go to—"

Planting a kiss soundly on her cheek, Tim said, "You're the goods, Angelica, no matter what Derek says."

"Hey, wait a minute." To his mother Derek said, "Mama I never said anything bad about you." And to his friend who was almost light-hearted with relief—"Bro, I came here to help you and—"

"So you shall, my friend. I'm pretty sure where they've gone, but just in case, will you and Abe head out of town on Coopers Creek Road? That's the only other local trysting spot I can think of. Call me if you find them."

Turning to Gert, Tim took both her hands in his, gave them a reassuring squeeze, and said, "Don't you worry, Mrs. Gunn. I'll have Rose back in one beautiful unbroken piece before you can finish your coffee."

He had barely completed his promise before they heard the front door close behind him.

*****

Simon stood rooted to the spot, quaking with rage. "You wretched mewling cow! Look what you've done!"

Rose, lost in a pit of humiliation deeper than any she had ever known, struggled to lift her tear-filled eyes to see Simon's right foot drawn back. But the vicious kick, aimed directly at her face, never hit its target. It disappeared from her blurred vision as Simon was hit broadside by a human freight train at full steam.

Tim, finding the picnic site deserted, had observed Rose at a distance looking at something in the brush, and Simon moving toward her, so he had started after them. When Tim heard Rose's repeated screams, he began running. He had been near enough to witness Simon strike Rose across the face. Tim had covered the rest of the distance in a bounding hurtle, unnoticed by the pair locked in heated confrontation. When he saw Simon draw his foot back, he hurled himself at the unsuspecting man, knocking the wind out of him as they fell. Tim scrambled to his feet, dragging Simon up with him and, before the other could clear his wits enough to counter the attack, delivered a powerful right hook to the PI's jaw, sending him back to the ground.

Never taking his eye off of his adversary, Tim backed toward Rose, calling over his shoulder, "Rose, are you all right?"

He had to strain to hear her weak answer, "Yes."

Simon, now filled with rage and indignation, struggled to his feet, considerably addled from the punishing blow. He dabbed at his bloody lip with a handkerchief while eyeing his opponent with open hatred. Tim's gallant rescue had been the final straw. If any man was ripe for murder, it was Simon Atherton in that moment. But as much as he craved revenge for all the pain, failure, and disgrace he had suffered at the hands of the loathsome Mason entourage, he was no fool. He knew he was no match for a brawny man half again his own size, and one moreover, who was clearly ready to battle to the death on behalf of that revolting girl. Summoning his last shred of dignity, Simon raised his hand in surrender.

Through clenched teeth, Tim addressed him in a steely level tone that left no doubt as to the veracity of his words. "Atherton, you get in your car and leave Tinkers Well. Now. And if I hear of you operating *anywhere* within a hundred-mile radius, I will personally see you across the state line in no condition to cross over it again. Ever. Do I make myself clear?"

"A bit dramatically perhaps, but yes, I am fully aware of your meaning. And may I say, I wish you joy of our *dear* Rose"—Simon's flippant demeanor gave way to chilling distain—"the most *pathetic* excuse for a woman it has ever been my misfortune to meet." As Tim started forward, fists clenched, Simon turned quickly—too quickly. He lurched sideways as the dizziness in his head threatened to overpower his movements but he somehow managed to right himself and start somewhat haphazardly up the hill.

Rose, still kneeling where she had fallen and reeling from Simon's final verbal blow, barely registered Tim helping her to her feet. With his arm around her waist, she tried taking a few steps but her wobbly knees gave way. Tim tightened his hold on her, bending to pick her up and hold her tenderly in his arms. Rose laid her head on his shoulder without thinking and without constraint, saying nothing. She finally responded to the feeling of movement and stopped him, raising her head to speak.

"Wait. Tim…I need to tell you…"

"What is it, Rose? What do you need to tell me?" he asked softly.

Rose looked at him and said haltingly, "I f-found…him. I found…Prince." Tim followed her distressed glance at a pile of brush twenty feet away. She started crying again, this time in simple sorrow for a lost friend.

"I'm so sorry, honey." The endearment was lost on her. "Let me get you to the truck," Tim said gently, "and I'll come back for him. Okay?" Rose nodded weakly and let her head rest again on his shoulder. He added grimly, "I won't leave him for those filthy buzzards."

Tim carried Rose up the hill as if the 120-pound weight was nothing. After buckling her in the front seat and assuring himself that she would be all right during his absence, he grabbed an old tarp out of the bed of his truck, returning some ten minutes later carrying the body of Prince. If Rose hadn't been so consumed with remorse for the degradation she had foolishly allowed by placing her trust in a lying scoundrel, she might have been moved by the tears in

Tim's eyes. They drove the few miles to the cottage in silence, each burdened by their own grief but unable to share it.

*****

Rose sat on the porch swing, her eyes closed to the rising sun while reveling in its warmth as it bathed her bruised spirit with the promise of another day and a new beginning. But even as its rays suffused the world with their vital intensity, the mortifying events of the previous day cast a veil of darkness between her and the healing touch of God's creation. Rose knew the grief and shame of that shattering hour would cloud countless tomorrows unless she could rid herself of their hold over her mind and heart.

She barely remembered how she'd gotten back to the cottage, to Granny Gert, to safety. After the horror of discovering Prince's decaying corpse and the devastation of Simon's betrayal, all of her senses had gone numb. Rose vaguely recalled Granny Gert rubbing her frozen hands and feet as her body succumbed to the shivering aftermath of shock. Her teeth had only stopped chattering after Angelica had surrounded her with heating pads and practically buried her in blankets. Eventually she had found her voice and, with it, all the sordid details had come tumbling out, as if she needed to purge herself of their memories so that they might be banished. They weren't. They became a recurring nightmare that persisted throughout the afternoon and evening; and with every wave of recollection came gut-wrenching sobs of shame and remorse. But with every bout of tears, Granny Gert had been there by her side, cradling Rose in her arms and rocking her just as she had when a younger Rose needed comfort and unconditional love.

Sleep had finally come, borne of mental and physical exhaustion, leaving Rose wan and drained. She had balked at Granny Gert's suggestion that she join the two elderly ladies for church, unable to face the idea of ever seeing anyone again, forgetting that Gert and Aletha depended on her for transportation. And if she'd given any thought to anyone else's suffering, she might have wondered at Aletha's willingness to endure company after her loss. But Aletha had

had two days to accept the inevitable and knew that the surest way to weather sadness is through the comfort and society of compassionate friends. So she and Gert had driven off with the thoughtful Angelica, leaving Rose to the solace of solitude.

At Granny Gert's insistence, Rose had showered and dressed and felt marginally more herself. She sat on the porch, trying to empty her mind of everything but beauty and light despite the lurking gloom of recent events. A long-forgotten verse came to her from a vault of verses memorized during a high school Bible study.

> *And now, dear brothers and sisters, one final thing.*
> *Fix your thoughts on what is true, and honorable,*
> *and right, and pure, and lovely, and admirable.*
> *Think about things that are excellent and worthy of*
> *praise. (Philippians 4:8 NLT)*

Her mind drifted to images of home—her father's workshop, her mother's quiet grace, the prospect of becoming an aunt. But as her thoughts turned to contemplation of her new friends and their generosity and kindness, she heard the sound of a vehicle coming up the long drive and bolted like a hare for the cover and shelter of the library. Rose heard doors slam—two, three—and the sound of footsteps as they made their way past the front porch to the gazebo. She waited in silence, afraid to see who had come, even more afraid that they might try to talk to her. But no knock came. No door was opened. She tentatively stepped out into the hall and walked slowly toward the kitchen until she was stopped by the unexpected. She heard a guitar being tuned, the blurred pitches gaining clarity with each turn of the tuning knobs. Then a consonant chord, followed by a pattern of chords, plucked into being, one string at a time. And finally voices singing, a baritone and a tenor, first in unison then in harmony. The voices may not have been polished but they were rich with the resonance of honesty, and they sang a beloved old hymn whose words washed over Rose like warm rain, bringing nourishment and life.

Just as I am, without one plea but that Thy blood was shed for me
And that Thou bidst me come to Thee, O Lamb of God, I come, I come

Just as I am, and waiting not to rid my soul of one dark blot
To Thee whose blood can cleanse each spot, O Lamb of God, I come, I come

Rose felt a lump rise in her throat and familiar tears stinging her already swollen eyes. But unlike the previous day, they were tears of surrender and cleansing. When the singers incorporated a new tune with words she had never heard before, the tears flowed freely, providing balm to her wounded soul.

I come broken to be mended, I come wounded to be healed
I come desperate to be rescued, I come empty to be filled
I come guilty to be pardoned, by the blood of Christ the Lamb
And I'm welcomed with open arms, praise God, just as I am[4]

Rose walked without hesitation to join three brothers as they shared in the simple blessed act of worship. Tim and Derek kept singing while Abe played the guitar, recognizing her presence by simply making room for her and handing her a song sheet.

Just as I am, thou wilt receive, wilt welcome, pardon, cleanse, relieve;
Because thy promise I believe, O Lamb of God I come, I come[5]

The four sang as one until the repeat of the chorus when Rose closed her eyes and let the lyrics speak what her lips could not. A simple Communion service followed the music. Tim read elements of the liturgy then began a prayer of confession—a very personal prayer of confession.

"Father, God, please forgive me when I think and act like I know what's best for everyone as if my arrogant, selfish plans could

---

4. Travis Cottrell, Sue C. Smith, and David Moffitt, "Just As I Am" (Nashville: Universal Music, Brentwood Benson, CCTB Music, Revelation Music [administered at CapitolCMGPublishing.com], 2012). Used by permission.
5. Charlotte Elliot, "Just as I Am" (1835).

ever be better or richer or more perfectly timed than your sovereign plan. Please strengthen my faith and trust in your divine will."

After a brief silence, Derek began, "Blessed Lord, please forgive my cowardice in the face of personal trial, my stupid pride that has held me back from asking for help from the trained angels you've offered through the VA." Then in a voice thick with emotion, he added, "And I thank you for my brothers that have supported and inspired me through it all. Help me to trust in your divine healing."

Then it was Abe's turn. "Jesus, my Lord. I humbly ask that you will forgive my anger and my doubt. I *know* that you are not only Lord over *my* life but you are Lord over the lives of my family. How could I possibly think that I love them more than you do? And I know that you desire their salvation even more than I do. Please use me as you will for your divine purpose."

Rose had never known a burden as heavy as the one she bore at that moment. She had never known such guilt and shame. But in the midst of acute pain, she was reminded, through the purest form of worship—honest confession—of the privilege of laying her burdens at the foot of the cross.

"Heavenly Father." She began, her throat constricted by almost overwhelming heartache. "I have been *such* a fool. I am *so* ashamed of my behavior, and I know I can't face the world again or begin to live again until I know I am forgiven by you. That's the only way I can ever begin to forgive myself. So even though I don't deserve it, I ask for your divine forgiveness."

Rose raised her head when she felt Tim take her hand and lay a communion wafer in it. She placed it in her mouth then took the tiny cup of grape juice he held out to her. She then served the elements to Abe and so on until all had been served the precious symbols—the bread and wine representing the price paid to purchase God's mercy and their eternal pardon. They read a closing corporate prayer.

> *We do not presume to come to this your table, O merciful LORD, trusting in our own righteousness, but in your manifold and great mercies. We are not worthy so much as to gather up the crumbs under*

your table. But you are the same LORD, whose property is always to have mercy. Grant us therefore, gracious LORD, so to partake of this Sacrament of your Son Jesus Christ, that we may walk in newness of life, may grow into his likeness, and may evermore dwell in him, and he in us. Amen.[6]

Without another word spoken, the three men prepared to leave, each brother hugging Rose in turn, sharing smiles of encouragement. Tim held her longer and tighter than the others, resting his head against the softness of her silken hair. Rose made no move to pull away but clung to him as if drawing courage and reassurance from the strength of his circling arms. As Tim reluctantly loosened his hold, Rose placed her hands on either side of his face, looked into his eyes, and whispered with every ounce of sincerity she possessed, "Thank you." It was enough. The thick fog that had hidden the light of hope from one and obscured the truth from the other had begun to lift.

[6.] Adapted from *The Common Book of Prayer* (1549).

INTERSECTING DREAMS

*Through wisdom a house is built, and by understanding
it is established; By knowledge the rooms are filled
with all precious and pleasant riches.*

—Proverbs 24: 3-4, NKJV

It took several minutes before the sound of a power saw, humming away somewhere inside the house, managed to penetrate Rose's thoughts. It was the silence that followed that finally caught her attention. She hadn't seen Tim or Derek's trucks anywhere around the front or side of the house so she walked around towards the garage where she found the big white pick-up parked inside. Tim had spent so much time helping her finish the garden the previous week that Rose had forgotten he still had to complete work on a second operational restroom for the upcoming church picnic. She knew from personal experience that a functional toilet was in place in the tiny powder room just inside the back door, but she had never penetrated further into the house. Her curiosity aroused, she stood on the small covered back porch and peered inside through the screen door. Not so much as a fleeting second of hesitation impeded her eager expectation of meeting Tim. Without even realizing it had happened, in the past two weeks he had gone from being an awkward, surly acquaintance, to brother in Christ, to the dearest of friends. Whether consciously or not, Rose knew herself to be safe with him.

"Hello! Anybody home?" No answer. Rose waited a few minutes, knocked loudly on the doorframe and tried her hail again. "Hello! Tim, are you in there?" Still no answer. Welcoming an excuse to explore the house, Rose let herself into the kitchen. In the dim light that filtered into the room through tattered window blinds, she noticed again the regrettably worn condition of the space. Some of the cabinets either had doors missing or hanging at odd angles from broken hinges. Dingy linoleum, peeling in the corners revealed solid wood underneath. The old farmhouse sink was scratched and stained with decades of mineral deposits, and a single hanging light fixture emitted a pitiful lack of illumination. As she finished her inspection, Rose heard steps approaching from the front of the house and ducked just in time to avoid being cold-cocked by a load of freshly sawn 2x4s. Perusal of the butler's pantry would have to wait.

"Tim!" she called. She had to repeat herself twice, before her voice registered. Tim swung around so quickly he nearly knocked down the hood mounted over the ancient gas stove.

"Rose!" he said in surprise, quickly dropping his load and removing his hearing protectors and the earbuds attached to his cell phone. "I am so sorry. I didn't know you were here. Please tell me I didn't hit you."

"No. You missed," she said, smiling. "My radar was fully engaged." She couldn't resist adding, "Though it doesn't look like that stove hood faired quite as well."

"The good news is that its days were numbered anyway," he responded with a laugh. Then diffidently, "What brings you over here today?" As soon as the words left his lips he thought, *"Ludlow, you idiot! Why would you even ask? Just be thankful she's here."*

Rose noticed nothing untoward in the question and merely responded that she had walked over to check on the garden, had heard sounds from the house and noticed the truck in the garage. "To be honest, I was kind of hoping you might give me a tour of the interior. I've been so intent on bringing beauty to the outside of the house lately that I've never actually seen any of the beauty *inside*."

"It'll be a long time before *this* room looks even *passable*, but sure, I'd be happy to show you around."

All plans for project completions were immediately pre-empted by Rose's request. Tim removed his work gloves, dusted off his arms and legs and ran his fingers through his hair to dislodge most of the sawdust nesting there. Rose couldn't help laughing. "You really get into your work!"

Tim grinned. "You have no idea." He looked around, blew out his cheeks and said, "Phew! Where to begin?" After a short pause he pointedly addressed his eager companion saying, "You have a pretty good imagination, right?" Her simple affirmative nod qualified for understatement of the year.

"Good. You'll need it." And the tour into another world began. He was again on his hobby horse just as he had been when he took Rose over Tom and Lucy Bennett's renovated farmhouse, but this time it was personal. He took pride in any job, especially for friends like the Bennetts, but this house was almost a calling for him. Not only was it home to people who had practically been grandparents to him all his life, it represented the epitome of the Queen Anne period of Victorian Architecture. It was the ultimate challenge for a craftsman who believed in maintaining the beauty of the past while incorporating modern safety and energy measures. He was committed to reusing or repurposing as much of the original structural material as possible, and had spent countless hours sketching ideas for opening up living areas and adding more functional space such as bathrooms and closets. He had never been able to share his ideas with Aletha because the house layout was only a distant memory for her by the time he had left active duty and moved to Tinkers Well.

Now Tim had the pleasure of sharing his dreams with someone who appreciated the old place as much as he did. He longed to share so much more with her, but he was trying to put his trust in God's plan for his life, with or without Rose. For now he would learn to be content with her friendship and comradery. He would leave the rest to time.

Rose was enchanted by every room, viewing all through the eyes of wishful thinking and with commendable appreciation for the astounding craftsmanship exhibited from floor to high, soaring ceilings. She marveled at hand carved fireplace surrounds depicting the four seasons—summer in the glass-enclosed conservatory, autumn in the dining room, winter in the library, and spring in the front parlor. She was amazed at the effortless movement of massive double pocket doors that opened up the main living areas—dining room and parlor—with another pair of doors allowing access to the expansive foyer. Rose was delighted to see more of the 'wooden lace' millwork she had noticed on the exterior of the house crowning the entry to the main hallway, and stood in awe of the grand staircase rising in flights from the foyer. Tim's descriptions of the artistic details were filled with intriguing terms such as *spiral turned baluster, beaded spindle, scroll-sawn cutouts, newel caps, and face string*—and that was just for the stairs! The rich wooden framed doors and trim work included *incised cornices, rosettes, paneled stiles, and ornate bevels and pendant drops.*

Now in his stride, Tim guided Rose from room to room, commenting as he pointed out one accent element after another, "These homes weren't built by contractors, or even carpenters, they were crafted by *artisans*. And *that's* what I want to preserve here," he added with conviction. He was surprised, and a little embarrassed when Rose laughed unexpectedly. "I apologize. I probably got carried away because…"

"…because you're describing something that you're passionate about," she said with an understanding smile. "Because you can look at a hundred and fifty-year-old building that a thousand other people would call a rundown dump and see its intrinsic beauty, and what it *can* be instead of what it *is*. Now I *get* it!" Tim went from pleased and gratified to confused and clueless in less than a nanosecond.

"Get what?"

"Now I know how my family and friends feel when I try to convince them that I'm not just following a daydream or…or imagining…an improbable possibility. Oh, I'm not making any sense…"

"No! I mean, yes! You are. That's *exactly* how I feel." He guided Rose slowly down the hall to the library where wood-paneled walls and empty bookcases provided the faintest echoes of a by-gone era. "Can you see it, Rose? A well-worn, leather winged-back chair pulled up before a warm coal fire on a dark winter evening…"

"…with heavy draperies drawn to keep out cold drafts and… a…a…" Rose paused, but before she could think up another layer to add to the picture, Tim took up the tale.

"…and a desk lamp, turned down low, casting eerie shadows over the rows of book spines lined up neatly upon the shelves."

Thoroughly enjoying their foray into the realms of fancy, Rose looked appreciatively at Tim and added with mock seriousness, "The book lover sitting there would be wearing a richly brocade dressing gown, *of course.*"

"Of course. With a glass of…malt whiskey…"

"…warm milk…"

Tim made a face and shuddered before concluding, "…on the inlaid occasional table next to him."

Without thinking, Rose leaned her head against Tim's arm as she conjured up the vision before her. "I *can* see it," she said softly. Then she abruptly broke the enchantment of a shared daydream when she stepped in front of him and said firmly, "I want to help."

How does she shift gears so fast? Tim wondered, not sure what she meant. "You want to help…?"

"With this," she said, looking up and down the wide corridor from the grand front entry to the French doors leading into the conservatory. With all of this," Rose added, her arms spread from end to end. "I want to help in any way I can to bring that scene to life in the library. To see a dining room table set for fourteen, loaded with a rich harvest. To hear carols played on a piano in the parlor while a family trims a Christmas tree in front of the bay window." Then she added simply, "I want to help you realize your vision."

"*Oh, my darling Rose,*" Tim wanted to say, "*If only you could see my vision.*" While she had been floating along in the false dream of Simon's feigned affection, Tim had been falling head over heels in love with her. Tim knew she only regarded him as a trusted friend, but he could dream too, and his dreams regarding Rose were wholly honorable. Whether they would ever enjoy a shared future, God only knew, but her desire to support his calling touched him. Deeply. It also blind-sided him. He had obligations to clients. He would be gone for two weeks later in July for Annual Training. He had already made commitments to start new projects when he returned. It was futile to think of undertaking any large scale projects at the big house anywhere in the near future. Impossible to even consider it. Unthinkable to disappoint Rose.

Misunderstanding Tim's hesitation, Rose offered humbly, "I know I don't have any real skills, but there must be plenty of tasks for unskilled labor that I could assist with. I help my dad with things like sanding and painting and stripping the finish off of old furniture. There must be miles of wood trim here that need to be polished or refinished. Or maybe I could learn to run a floor stripper…"

"Rose…"

"…surely it's not as hard to operate as the power auger we used on the garden project. And then there's the demo part…"

"Rose…"

"I can haul out old cabinets or remove busted blinds or…"

"Rose!" Seeing her injured expression, Tim placed his hands on her shoulders and spoke quickly. "I can't tell you how much it means to me that you're willing to give up so much of your time to be a part of…," mirroring her gesture, he spread his arms out, "…all this. And I know you could do any of those jobs and probably a whole lot more, but this is an enormous undertaking. Why, the time alone would be…"

"Time is the *one* thing I have in abundance," Rose said, cutting in eagerly. "And I want to fill it doing something…worthwhile." She paused then said, almost pleadingly, "I *need* to fill it."

That was Tim's undoing. He didn't know how he would make it all work, but he knew he had to. "Then I'll find the time, and we'll do something worthwhile…together."

ABOUT THE AUTHOR

Linda Edmister is a self-proclaimed lifelong vagabond. She was born of military parents in Germany, has lived on four continents, made a home for her army husband and their two children in thirteen different houses in over forty years of globe-trotting. She is a former army major, State Department community liaison officer and church music director. Linda holds a BA degree from the University of Kentucky in music and business administration and a master of music from Middle Tennessee State University. Her favorite authors and literary influences are Agatha Christie, Mary Stewart, Georgette Heyer, and Jane Austen. When not teaching piano lessons or volunteering in her church library, she enjoys gardening, traveling, and Bible study.